He leaned toward her

Suddenly breathless, she stared at Chay, afraid he was going to take her in his arms and kiss her, and more afraid that he wouldn't.

"Dana."

"What?"

"Nothing, I just wanted to say your name."

"Oh." the thought pleased her more than it should have.

"It suits you," he murmured. And then he drew her into his arms.

"I don't think this is a good idea," she said, her voice little more than a whisper.

"You're probably right," he agreed. And then, slowly lowering his head, he kissed her. His kiss was like riding the teacups at Disneyland, watching fireworks on the Fourth of July and sitting in front of a blazing fire on a cold winter night, all rolled into one.

Dear Reader,

Saying goodbye is never easy, and when "goodbye" means leaving a line I've come to love, farewell is even harder. I hope you have enjoyed Silhouette Romance under my leadership and continue to cherish this terrific line under the direction of Ann Leslie Tuttle, Silhouette Romance's new associate senior editor.

And if you're looking for a handsome hero, look no further than Silhouette Romance! From bosses to princes to cowboys to oilmen, you'll find a man for every woman's taste this month.

He's a prince disguised as a sexy American executive; she's a princess disguised as his hotel manager. Don't miss Princess Meredith's last matchmaking attempt—for herself!—in *Twice a Princess* (SR #1758) by Susan Meier, the conclusion to the miniseries IN A FAIRY TALE WORLD....

Trading Places with the Boss (SR #1759) was supposed to be a learning experience. But what this secretary finds is an alarming attraction to her employer—and he seems to feel it, too! Raye Morgan brings us an office romance to remember in the latest book in her BOARDROOM BRIDES miniseries.

When this city girl escaped to the country to mend her broken heart, she finds herself face-to-face with temptation: an ex-rodeo rider working on the neighboring ranch. Will she give in? Find out in Madeline Baker's *Every Inch a Cowboy* (SR #1760).

Two star-crossed soul mates get some heavenly help with their love lives in Debrah Morris's *A Little Night Matchmaking* (SR #1761). This West Texas oilman is always all-business, until he meets his match in a feisty single mom.

May this month's heroes lead you into a world of true love and happily-ever-after.

Sincerely,

Mavis C. Allen
Associate Senior Editor

Please address questions and book requests to:
Silhouette Reader Service
U.S.: 3010 Walden Ave., P.O. Box 1325, Buffalo, NY 14269
Canadian: P.O. Box 609, Fort Erie, Ont. L2A 5X3

Every Inch
a Cowboy

MADELINE
BAKER

SILHOUETTE *Romance*®

Published by Silhouette Books

America's Publisher of Contemporary Romance

SILHOUETTE BOOKS

ISBN 0-373-19760-8

EVERY INCH A COWBOY

Copyright © 2005 by Madeline Baker

This edition published by arrangement with Harlequin Books S.A.

Visit Silhouette Books at www.eHarlequin.com

Printed in U.S.A.

Books by Madeline Baker

Silhouette Romance

Dude Ranch Bride #1642
West Texas Bride #1697
Callie's Cowboy #1728
Every Inch a Cowboy #1760

MADELINE BAKER

has written over twenty historical novels, half a dozen short stories under her own name and over seventeen paranormal novels under the name Amanda Ashley as well as Madeline Baker. Born and raised in California, she admits balancing her love for historical romance and vampires isn't easy—but she wouldn't like to choose between them. The award-winning author has now found another outlet for her writing—with Silhouette Romance! Readers can send a SASE to P.O. Box 1703, Whittier, CA 90609-1703 or visit her at her Web site www.madelinebaker.net.

To the Real
Ashley and Brandon
With hope and love

Chapter One

Dana woke with a groan after a long and restless night. Rising, she took a quick shower, then pulled on a bright yellow flowered sundress, hoping the cheerful color would brighten her mood. It didn't.

Feeling sleep deprived and listless, she fixed breakfast out of habit, though she had no appetite for anything but a glass of orange juice and a piece of buttered toast.

Sitting there, she knew she couldn't go to work. She couldn't face her boss and her co-workers, all of whom had been invited to the wedding. Many of her clients were people she knew, people she saw on a regular basis. By now, she was certain they had all heard that her fiancé, Rick, who was vice president of one of her company's best accounts, had run off to Las Vegas with his secretary.

Her mind in turmoil, she drank the last of the orange juice, took a bite of toast and threw the rest in the garbage. It had been a year since she'd had any time off. Her vacation was overdue and now seemed like the perfect opportunity to take some time off from work. She knew her father would call it cowardly of her to run away at a time like this. He would tell her to stay and face the music, chin up and all that, but she couldn't do it. She just couldn't, at least not now. She needed some time alone, time to sort out her thoughts. Time to come to grips with the fact that she was never going to trust another man and that she was probably never going to get married, never be swept off her feet by a handsome knight on a white horse. Because you couldn't trust knights, either. Even Lancelot had been a tarnished cavalier.

Certain that she was doing the right thing, she called work and told Mr. Goodman that an emergency had come up and that she needed to take two weeks off before the wedding in addition to the week she was already taking for her honeymoon. Since she was a valued employee and she hadn't had a vacation in over a year, her boss reluctantly agreed. Next, she called her mother and told her what had happened. Hearing the sympathy and understanding in her mother's voice brought quick tears to Dana's eyes.

"I'll take care of everything," Marge Westlake said. "Where are you going?"

"I thought I'd go up to the mountains." Dana had a small house in the foothills that her grandmother had left her. Though the house was only a few hours away, it had been years since Dana had gone there. Now it beckoned like a haven of safety, a place where she could hide and lick her wounds.

"That's a wonderful idea, dear," her mother said. "You just go and relax and don't worry about a thing."

"Thanks, Mom. I love you."

"I love you, too."

"Tell Dad I'm sorry…"

"Pish posh," her mother said airily. "Don't give it another thought. Call me when you get there."

"All right, Mom. Thanks again."

After hanging up, Dana packed her bags, dumped them in the back seat of her Toyota and left town. It was a beautiful day for a long drive. The sky was blue, the air warm but not hot. Rolling down the window, she turned on the radio, then settled back in her seat and focused all her attention on the road, determined not to think of the reason why she was going up to the Hollow....

Gradually, the city fell behind. Neat houses and strip malls gave way to scattered ranches and stands of timber. Tall pines lined both sides of the road.

Some time later, she turned off the freeway and onto the winding road that led to Wardman's Hollow, Montana. As she drove down the main street, she was glad to see that the old part of town hadn't changed much since she had been there three and a half years ago. Old Town looked just as she remembered it. Long low buildings built of wood and native stone lined both sides of the street. Hitching posts still stood in front of some of the older buildings, like the Shotgun Saloon and Maud's General Store, both of which dated back more than a hundred years. The newer part of town was as modern as any city in the country, with a Wal-Mart and a Target, and the ubiquitous McDonald's, of course. There were a number of gift shops and restaurants, some dress shops and a movie theater. Wright's Ranch Market marked the end of the older section of town and the beginning of the new. The market had been handed down from one Wright to another for generations.

She passed the Bar W cattle ranch. Like Wright's Market, the Bar W dated back several generations. Cattle marked with the Bar W brand grazed on both sides of the road. A few of the cows looked up as she drove past. The town had been named for Cleve Wardman, who had first settled the place in the late 1800s. The southern edge of the Wardman property bordered a section of Dana's land.

She felt a sense of freedom when she pulled into the

front yard. The house looked just as she remembered it. A weathered single-story dwelling with a redbrick fireplace and forest-green shutters, it sat in a small clearing surrounded by towering pines, wildflowers and blackberry bushes gone wild. A covered wooden porch spanned the front of the house. Her grandmother's rocker still sat in one corner.

Switching off the engine, Dana grabbed her handbag and suitcase and hurried up the three steps to the front door. Slipping the key into the lock, she gave the door a shove, then stepped inside.

A fine layer of dust covered everything. Lacy gray cobwebs hung from the corners of the ceiling. She knew the place would have been in much worse condition except that her parents had spent a week here last winter and two weeks the summer before that.

Still, she was glad there was work to do. It gave her a sense of purpose. Then, too, staying busy would keep her mind off her reason for being here in the first place.

It wasn't a large house, but it was solid. Her grandfather had built it for her grandmother when they were first married. The interior was rustic. The living room was painted off-white. Colorful rugs covered the hardwood floors. The windows on either side of the front door faced the east. A rack of antlers hung above the brick fireplace. A bear rug took up most of the floor space in front of the hearth. As a little girl, Dana had listened countless times to the story of how her grandfather had killed that bear.

The kitchen was painted a cheery shade of yellow. White lace curtains hung from the big double window that offered a view of the garage, the backyard and the winding stream where Dana had learned to fish when she was a little girl. Four scarred chairs surrounded an equally scarred round oak table that held many memories for Dana. She had drawn pictures on that table and written letters to her mom and dad when she got older. It was at that table that her grandmother had taught her how to make apple pies and sugar cookies and gingerbread men. There was a laundry room off the kitchen. The appliances in both the kitchen and the laundry room had all been upgraded through the years, though the house still lacked air-conditioning. Two bedrooms, one painted a robin's-egg blue, the other a pale green, took up the back part of the house. A large bathroom with a tub and a shower was located between the bedrooms.

Dana dropped her suitcase and handbag on the floor inside the door, then spent the next two hours cleaning the house. She swept the floors and dusted the furniture. She uncovered the dark brown leather sofa and the matching easy chair. She wiped the dust from the kitchen sink and the counter, polished the stove, plugged in the ancient refrigerator, glad that she had thought to call ahead and ask the utility companies to turn on the gas and electricity before she arrived.

She put clean sheets on the big old four-poster bed, pulled some clean towels out of the linen closet and hung them from the rack in the bathroom. She let the water run in the sink for several minutes. When the rusty water turned clear, she washed the sink, then scrubbed the small, claw-footed bathtub.

When she finished up in the bathroom, she grabbed her suitcase and went into the bigger of the two bedrooms and put her clothes away.

That done, she took a long hot bubble bath, then donned a pair of comfortable old sweats and a pair of Reeboks that had seen better days. She brushed her hair until it snapped and crackled, then tied it back in a ponytail.

Returning to the kitchen, she pulled a pad of paper and a stubby pencil out of one of the drawers, and then sat down at the round oak table that had been made by her grandfather. Blowing a lock of hair from her forehead, she began writing out a grocery list.

She felt almost cheerful as she drove to the store. For the next three weeks, she would hide out in her house in the woods and lick her wounds. She wouldn't think about work, she wouldn't think about her poor mother returning all those wedding gifts, she wouldn't think about Rick and his new love. She would simply relax and enjoy the beauty of the mountains. She didn't need a man in her life. Lots of single women lived perfectly happy, productive lives. If they could do it, so could she. She just hoped she didn't end up a bitter old lady with a house full of cats.

Chayton Lone Elk rested one shoulder against the side of the barbershop, a cigarette dangling from the corner of his mouth as he waited for Ashley and her friends to come out of the Sunset Boutique across the street.

Shifting from one foot to the other, he glanced at his watch, wondering what the devil they could be doing in there that was taking so long. Ashley was the boss's daughter and if she wanted to spend all day in town, there wasn't a thing Chay could do about it. Lord save him from giggly teenage girls, he thought sourly. To Chay's dismay, Big John had decided Chay should act as chaperon for as long as Ashley's friends decided to stay. As near as Chay could tell, they didn't plan to leave any time soon. They had already been at the ranch for three weeks and it had been the longest three weeks of Chay's life. Sometimes he thought if he had to endure what they called music for one more day or listen to one more minute of their silly chatter, he would go stark raving mad. Boys and clothes, clothes and boys, it was all they talked about. The only thing keeping him sane was the fact that school started in another couple of weeks.

Chay shook his head as he glanced at his watch again.

He figured it was a safe bet that his charges would be in the boutique at least another twenty or thirty minutes, plenty of time for him to run over to Wright's and pick up a carton of cigarettes and then go grab a beer at the Shotgun Saloon.

Tossing his cigarette away, he crossed the street and went into the market.

Betty Wright smiled at him as she rang him up. She was a pretty woman in her mid-thirties with short, curly auburn hair, twinkling brown eyes and a pixie grin.

She shook her head as she bagged the carton. "Chay, don't you know these things will kill you?"

"We all gotta die sometime."

"You really should quit smoking."

"I know. And I will, too, just not this week."

Betty looked at him and laughed. It was the same conversation they had every time he came in to buy a box of Marlboros.

Chay was coming out of Wright's a few minutes later when he heard a muffled crash followed by a soft oath. Glancing over his shoulder, he saw a pretty, young woman in the parking lot. The handle on one of her plastic grocery bags had broken and a dozen or so boxes and cans were rolling around at her feet.

"Here," Chay said, hurrying toward her. "Let me give you a hand."

"I can manage." Stooping, she picked up three of the cans and tossed them in the trunk.

"I'm sure you can," Chay remarked. Reaching under her car, he scooped up five cans of assorted vegetables and deposited them in the trunk with the others.

Dana studied the stranger out of the corner of her eye as he picked up the last couple of cans. He was tall, well over six feet. He had broad shoulders beneath his dark blue shirt, the sleeves of which had been cut off, exposing muscular arms browned by the sun. Fine lines fanned out from the corners of his eyes. A pair of faded blue jeans hugged unbelievably long muscular legs. His thick black hair fell past the collar of his denim shirt. He was, without doubt, the most blatantly handsome man she had ever seen. Next to him, Rick Matheson looked like a washed-out, ninety-eight-pound weakling.

"Thank you, Mr...." She couldn't stop staring at him. Lean and rugged, he looked every inch a cowboy, from the crown of his black Stetson to the soles of his scuffed leather boots. But it didn't matter if he was Mr. America and Brad Pitt all rolled into one. She had sworn off men forever.

"Chay. Chayton Lone Elk."

"Thank you for your help, Mr. Elk," she said stiffly.

Chay watched as she slid behind the wheel and drove out of the parking lot. Who was she? he wondered. He had never seen her before, he would bet his best horse on that. Of course, she might just be passing through, but if that was the case, why was she stocking up on groceries? More likely she was new in town. Maybe she was the new owner of the old Longworth place over off Three Mile Road.

With a shrug, he walked back to the barbershop, the beer he had intended to have forgotten. There were too many pretty girls in the world to worry about one little golden-haired female he didn't even know and would likely never see again.

Taking up his place outside the barbershop, he pulled a pack of cigarettes from the carton and lit up.

She'd had the prettiest blue eyes he had ever seen. The prettiest, and the saddest.

He tried to put her out of his mind, but he was still thinking about her when he drove Ashley and her friends back to the ranch later that afternoon.

* * *

Dana stared out the front window as lightning zigzagged across the skies, followed by a long rolling boom of thunder that sounded as if it was going to come right down through the roof. Rain fell in icy sheets. A fierce wind rattled the windows and flattened the grass. The trees bowed before its power.

Turning away from the window, she added more wood to the fire crackling in the hearth. The electricity was out and the only light in the house came from the fireplace and a few candles.

She was glad the stove was gas and not electric as she filled a saucepan with milk and put it on the stove to heat.

Going to the kitchen window, she pulled the curtains aside, though there was little to see but darkness. She had always been afraid of storms, yet she was drawn to them just the same, fascinated by the power of the wind and the rain. She loved the thunder, but she had been afraid of the lightning that scorched the heavens for as long as she could remember.

She gasped as a jagged bolt rent the skies. In the distance, a tree went up in flames. She leaned forward. Was she imagining things, or had she seen a man out there in the rain? With a shake of her head, she drew back and let the curtain fall into place. She had to be seeing things. People didn't go horseback riding in the middle of a storm.

Frowning, she stirred the milk in the pan, then pulled her favorite mug and a box of hot-cocoa mix from the cupboard. She added a couple of teaspoons to the cup and then, as though drawn by an invisible hand, she went to the window, pulled back the curtains and peered outside again.

Another bolt of lightning revealed that there was indeed a man outside. He was slumped over the withers of his horse. Good Lord, what man in his right mind would be out on a horrible night like this? And what was he doing in the middle of her backyard?

Closing the curtains, she moved away from the window, one hand at her throat.

What should she do? Suddenly aware that the milk was overheating, she went to the stove and turned off the fire and then, moving cautiously, she looked out the window once again.

She could barely make out the shape of the horse. It was standing in the same place as before, its head down. There was no sign of the man. Where had he gone? Was he trying to get into her house, even now?

What should she do?

There was a gun on the top shelf of the kitchen cupboard. It was a reproduction of a Colt .45 that belonged to her father. Dana's mother hated guns and refused to let her husband keep it at home. She had refused to let Dana's father teach Dana how to handle the weapon. In spite of that, Dana's father had taken her into the woods and taught her how to load and fire the Colt. She was glad now that he had done so. Of course, she had never fired at anything except targets.

Her hand was shaking as she picked up the Colt. After checking to see if the gun was loaded, Dana went to the window again. The horse hadn't moved. It stood with its head down, its back to the wind. And then, in a flash of almost blinding light, she saw the man. He was lying facedown in the mud. Was he hurt? Dead? Drowning in the rain?

Dana watched him for several moments, and when he didn't move, she ran out the back door, her slippers squishing in the mud. Slipping the gun into the oversize pocket of her bathrobe, she turned him over.

Another flash of lightning revealed a jagged gash on the right side of his head, just above his ear.

"Mister?" She shook his shoulder. "Mister?"

He groaned softly as his eyes opened.

"Can you hear me?" she asked anxiously.

A soft grunt was her only answer.

"You'll have to stand up," she said. "I can't carry you."

He muttered something she didn't understand.

Assuming he was agreeing with her, she took hold of his arm and pulled. He sat up, then rolled onto his knees. Using her hand for support, he managed to get to his feet.

Wondering if she was doing the right thing, Dana put her arm around his waist and headed for the back door. It was like trying to move a tree. He towered over her. His arm, resting on her shoulder, felt like a lead weight.

Her slippers were ruined, the hem of her robe covered in mud, by the time she got him into the kitchen. She left her slippers outside, kicked the door shut with her heel. One-handed, she pulled a chair out from the table and he dropped into it.

Now that the rain was no longer washing it away, blood oozed from the cut in his head and dripped down onto the collar of his sheepskin jacket. He was soaked to the skin. Grabbing a dish towel, she pressed it against the wound.

"Can you hold that there for a moment?" she asked.

He nodded, his hand replacing hers on the towel. She frowned, thinking he looked vaguely familiar. She was tempted to ask him who he was and what he was doing riding around on a night like this, but decided her questions could wait. The man was bleeding, after all.

She eased him out of his jacket and hung it on a hook beside the back door, unmindful of the puddle that quickly formed beneath it. She helped him out of his shirt and T-shirt, pulled off his boots and socks, and tossed them aside. Going into the living room, she grabbed a blanket from the back of the sofa. Returning to the kitchen, she draped it over his shoulders, then went into the bathroom to see what kind of first-aid supplies she could find.

The medicine cabinet was woefully inadequate. A box

of gauze pads, a roll of adhesive tape, a tube of first-aid cream, a bottle of aspirin. She hoped it would be enough.

She stopped in the bedroom long enough to pull on a pair of thick socks and change out of her wet bathrobe and nightgown and into a pair of sweats.

Returning to the kitchen, she dropped the items she had collected on the table, then removed the dish towel from his head. The cut was about three inches long and looked very deep. She was afraid he needed more care than she could give him.

"Just sit tight," she said, replacing the towel. "I'll get my purse and keys and drive you to the hospital. I think you might need some stitches."

"Doesn't matter what I need," he said. "We're not going anywhere. The bridge is out."

"Are you sure? Well, it doesn't matter. There must be another road."

"No."

"Are you saying we're stuck here?"

"'Fraid so."

She bit down on the inside of her cheek. She was sorely afraid that the first-aid instruction she had received when she was a Girl Scout wouldn't do her much good now.

He looked up at her, his dark brown eyes dulled with pain. "You got any whiskey?"

She shook her head. "Sorry, I don't drink." Going to the sink, she filled a glass with water, shook three aspirin out of the bottle and handed them to him.

"Whiskey would be better," he muttered wryly.

He swallowed the tablets and drained the glass, then set it on the table. Closing his eyes, he swore softly, and removed the towel from his head. He explored the wound with his fingers, then pressed the towel against his head once more.

"Do you think you can stitch it up?"

Dana stared at him. "Who, me?" She shook her head. "I don't think so."

"You know how to sew, don't you?"

"Yes, but you're not asking me to make you a shirt."

He started to smile, then grimaced. "If you can't do it, I can. Just thread a needle for me."

"You?" she exclaimed, horrified by what he was suggesting. Stitch his own wound? That was the stuff of movies.

"I've done it before."

In the end, she agreed to stitch up the wound rather than have him think she was too chicken, though why she cared what he thought about her was beyond her comprehension. She didn't even know the man. And didn't want to. She'd had enough of men to last a lifetime.

She found a needle and thread and since she didn't have any disinfectant, she turned on one of the burners and passed the needle through the flame, although she wasn't sure what good that would do, since there were probably germs on the thread. She gathered up a dozen candles and placed them around the room for light, setting the biggest one in the middle of the table.

"Sure wish you had some whiskey," he muttered as she sat down beside him.

"Me, too." Even though she didn't drink, she was certain a shot of straight whiskey would help to steady her hand and calm her nerves. "Okay, hold still. I'm sure this is going to hurt you a lot more than it does me."

"I'm sure it will," he muttered, and closed his eyes.

Taking a deep breath, Dana closed her mind to the fact that she was sewing human flesh. She was always reading news stories about people who had done things far beyond what they thought impossible because there was no one else to do it. She was about to find out if she was one of them.

Murmuring a silent prayer for strength and a steady hand, she bent her head to her task.

After what seemed like hours, but was more like twenty minutes, she took one last stitch and tied off the thread. Not too bad, she thought. Still, it was a nasty wound. What if he had a concussion?

She taped a gauze pad over the stitches, then went to the sink and washed her hands. She pulled a clean towel from the drawer, dried her hands, then glanced at her patient to find him watching her.

"You should get out of those wet…ah, trousers," she suggested.

He made a soft sound of agreement and rose to his feet.

Her eyes widened when he began to unfasten his jeans.

"Wait! I didn't mean here. You can undress in the spare room. There's a bed in there, too." She studied him a moment, noticing how pale he looked. "Do you think you can make it on your own?"

"Sure." He took a step forward, staggered, and caught hold of the back of a chair.

"Oh, yeah," she said dryly, "you don't need any help at all."

Slipping her arm around his waist, she helped him down the hall to the back bedroom. She was practically carrying him by the time they got there. Sweat dripped from his forehead. His chest was sheened with perspiration. Had she been interested in such things, she would have said that it was a very nice chest.

"Hold still," she said. Then, trying to ignore what she was doing, she unfastened his jeans and dragged the wet denim down over his long, long legs.

She glanced at his briefs. They were wet, too, but if he wanted them off, he was on his own. She helped him into bed and drew the covers over him.

He was asleep as soon as his head touched the pillow.

She stared down at him for several moments, thinking

how handsome he was. And then she realized why he looked so familiar. He was the cowboy who had come to her aid in town that afternoon.

Chapter Two

Muttering a mild oath, Chay kept his eyes closed in an effort to ignore the naggingly insistent voice that was demanding he open his eyes.

"Mr. Elk? Mr. Elk! You've got to wake up."

With a low groan, he opened his eyes. Squinting against the flickering light of the candle on the bedside table, he stared at the woman kneeling beside the bed. "Dammit, woman, go away and let me sleep!"

"Do you know who you are?"

"What?" He looked at her as if she was one flake short of a bale. "Is that why you woke me up? To ask me who I am?"

"Yes. What's your name?"

"Go away."

"Do you know where you are?"

He glanced around the room. The walls were sea green; green-and-white flowered curtains hung at the window. "Your bed?" he asked hopefully.

Her cheeks turned a pretty shade of pink. "In your dreams!"

"A man can hope."

"You're not helping! What's your name?"

"Chay."

"Does your head hurt?"

He snorted softly. "What do you think?"

"Do you feel sick to your stomach?"

"No. Listen, I'm fine. Just a little tired." He stared at her. He recognized her now, the uptight woman from town. Amazing how different she looked with her hair down. It fell over her shoulders in riotous waves of honey-gold silk. Her eyes, those eyes he hadn't been able to forget, were bluer than a robin's egg and still the prettiest eyes he had ever seen, even now, when she was regarding him with what could only be described as resentment. In spite of the fact that she had taken him in and stitched him up, it was obvious she didn't want him there.

"Thank you, ma'am, for looking after me," he said, easing into a sitting position. "If you'll bring me my clothes, I'll get the hell out of your way."

"What? You can't go out in this storm."

"I can, and I will."

"But…"

Chay swung his legs over the edge of the mattress, grimacing as pain lanced through the side of his head. "I make it a point never to stay where I'm not wanted, ma'am."

"Stop calling me that," she said waspishly.

"I don't know what else to call you."

"My name is Dana Westlake."

"Sorry to be such a bother, Miss Westlake. If you'll just tell me where my clothes are, I'll get out of your hair." He stood up, then made a grab for the bedpost as the room began to sway around him.

Lunging forward, Dana grabbed his arm to steady him. "You're not going anywhere except back to bed."

"Yes, ma'am," he said, and fell back on the mattress. "Sorry," he said with a lopsided grin. "It just slipped out."

Fighting back the urge to smile, Dana pulled the blankets up to his chin. She was turning away from the bed when his hand snaked out and caught hers. His palm was calloused, his fingers long and strong. The touch of his hand sizzled through her like a bolt of lightning.

"What do you think you're doing?" she asked sharply.

"Thanking you for stitching me up," he replied, bemused by the electricity that had arced between them the moment his fingers closed around hers.

Dana stared at the hand holding hers lightly but firmly. It was big and brown, the back crisscrossed with tiny white scars. She was startled by the wave of heat that ran from her palm to her heart as his grip tightened. "Let me go."

"Sorry, Miss Westlake, I didn't mean to frighten you."

"You didn't. I…I just don't like being touched."

"By me? Or by men in general?"

She glared at him, wondering why she found him so attractive. Hadn't Rick taught her anything? With a sigh of self-disgust, she jerked her hand out of his, then turned on her heel and left the room.

Chay stared after her, wondering what he had done to upset her. Wondering why he cared. Women didn't usually treat him as if he was dirt. Even though he didn't consider himself to be particularly good-looking, he had never had any trouble attracting the opposite sex. Girls and women alike had come on to him since he turned fourteen. And being a man who liked women, he did what he could to make them happy. He'd had his pick of girls, first in school and later on the rodeo circuit, and now in town.

But this woman looked at him as if he were some kind of vermin.

He laughed softly. There was always one stray in the herd. Still, her standoffish attitude brought out the hunter in him. For some reason he didn't understand, he wanted to make pretty Miss Dana Westlake smile, wanted to hear her laugh. He wanted to run his hands through the honey-gold wealth of her hair, feel her body pressed close to his.

He followed that thought to sleep.

Dana sat at the kitchen table, a cup of hot coffee cradled in her hands. A glance at the clock showed it was a few minutes after nine. Her mind felt like mush. Fearing that her patient might have a concussion, she had set her alarm to wake her every hour through the night so she could check on him. It was a toss-up as to which of them had been more irritable the last time. She didn't know the man and didn't want him here, but here he was and, right or wrong, she felt a sense of responsibility for his welfare.

Earlier that morning, she had tossed his clothing and her robe and nightgown into the washing machine. She had returned the Colt to the top shelf of the cupboard.

Drinking the last of her coffee, she carried the cup to the sink and rinsed it. A glance out the window showed the horse was still standing in the yard. Reins dragging, it was nibbling on a patch of grass, apparently oblivious to the wind and rain. Chay's hat made a splash of black in the gooey brown mud. She felt a twinge of guilt for leaving the animal outside the night before and then shook her head. The horse didn't look any the worse for spending the night in the open. His wild cousins had managed to survive in similar weather. Surely one night in the rain wouldn't hurt this one.

Her heart fluttered in her chest when she heard footsteps behind her. It could only be her houseguest. Turning, she saw him standing in the doorway. He had wrapped one of the blankets around his lean waist. Knowing he wore nothing underneath but a pair of briefs made her mouth go dry.

He jerked his chin toward the stove. "Think I could have a cup of that coffee?"

With a nod, she waved a hand toward the table. "Sit down and I'll pour you a cup."

She took a clean mug from the shelf, filled it and then refilled her own. When she handed him his cup, she was careful to make sure their hands didn't touch.

"Thanks. Is my horse still here?"

"Yes. Outside," she said, and then felt herself blush. Where else would his horse be?

"I need my clothes."

The memory of helping him undress the night before made her cheeks grow hotter. "They're in the dryer. I'll get them."

Hurrying into the laundry room, she pulled his clothing and her gown and robe from the drier. Seeing his jeans tangled up with her robe caused a funny feeling in the pit of her stomach. She shook out his shirt and jeans, folded his socks and T-shirt, her nightgown and robe, and then, taking a deep breath, she returned to the kitchen.

"Here." She handed him his clothing.

"Obliged." Rising, he left the room.

Dana stared after him, bemused by her feelings for a man she didn't even know. And then she shrugged. It was probably just a case of old-fashioned lust combined with her concern for his welfare. After all, she had taken care of him last night, which explained her concern. And even though she had sworn off men forever, that didn't mean she couldn't appreciate a good-looking man when she saw one. And this man was far too good-looking for her peace of mind! She assured herself that any woman looking at him clad in only a blanket would have felt the same rush of feminine appreciation for his wide shoulders and broad chest.

She was still standing there when he returned a few minutes later. Picking up his cup, he finished his coffee, then turned toward the back door.

"Where are you going?"

"To look after my horse."

"It's still raining. I don't think you should go out. I'll take care of it."

He looked skeptical. "What do you know about horses?"

"Not a thing," she said, though that wasn't entirely true. She knew how to ride.

"That's what I thought. I'll take care of her." Moving slowly, he plucked his jacket from the hook. "Thanks again for stitching me up."

"You're welcome."

He studied her a moment before he shrugged into his jacket and went outside.

She stared after him, wondering if he was coming back. With a shrug she opened the refrigerator and pulled out a couple of eggs and a package of sausage, wondering if Chay liked French toast, and then wondering what difference it made. She wasn't cooking for him. She looked at the two eggs in her hand and put them in the sink. After a moment she picked up four more.

She was surprised when, twenty minutes later, the back door opened and he came in.

He took off his jacket and hung it on the hook, along with his hat. They both dripped water onto the floor. To her surprise, she didn't even mind.

Wordlessly she handed him a towel so he could dry off. A corner of his mouth turned up in a half smile as he took it from her hand.

"Looks like it's gonna rain all day." He tossed the towel over the back of a chair, then sniffed the air. "Something sure smells good."

"French toast, scrambled eggs and sausage," she said, uncovering a platter. "Sit down. What do you want to drink? I've got coffee, milk or orange juice."

"Coffee's fine."

She refilled his cup, poured herself a glass of orange juice and sat down at the table across from him. He helped himself to three slices of French toast and six pieces of sausage.

She wondered if she should have made more.

Silence stretched between them, taut as an electric fence, so strong it was almost tangible. She couldn't seem to stop looking at his hands, wondering what they would feel like on her skin. The thought brought a rush of heat to her cheeks.

"So, what brings you to the Hollow?" he asked after a while. "You on vacation?"

"Yes."

"For how long?"

"A few weeks."

"They're having a barn dance in town next week. Would you like to go?"

"No, thank you."

He grunted softly. "Is it just me, or do you dislike everyone?"

"I don't dislike you, Mr. Elk. I came up here to spend some time alone."

"Guess I put a crimp in that, didn't I?"

"It wasn't your fault."

"As soon as I finish up here, I'll be on my way."

"Don't go. It's still raining, and—" she gestured at his head "—you're hurt."

"Don't worry about me—I've had worse. Besides, the home place will be wondering what happened to me."

For the first time, she wondered if he had a wife, a family, waiting for him. "What were you doing out in the storm last night, anyway?"

"One of the pasture fences was down and a couple of our horses got out. I was trying to find them when the storm broke. This is mighty fine French toast."

"It's the cinnamon. Did you find the horses?"

"No. I'll pick up the search on the way back to the ranch." He took another bite of French toast. "Cinnamon, you say?"

She nodded. "How did you hurt your head?"

"I was on my way back to the Bar W when lightning hit a tree alongside the trail. One of the branches broke and knocked me off my horse. Guess I hit a rock." Swallowing the last bite of French toast, he pushed his plate aside and stood up. "I'm obliged to you for looking after me."

Dana gazed up at him, stunned by an almost overpowering urge to beg him to stay. "Goodbye, Mr. Elk."

He regarded her for several seconds, then he crossed the room and plucked his jacket and hat from the peg. Opening the door, he stepped out into the rain. The closing of the door seemed unusually loud.

She stayed where she was, her hands curled in her lap as she imagined him climbing onto the back of his horse and riding out of the yard, and out of her life.

"Rubbish," she muttered. "You're just feeling maudlin, that's all. You don't even know the man. How can you be missing him already?"

Missing Chay? It was beyond ridiculous!

She shook the thought from her mind. How could she be lonely for a man she had just met? How could she be missing any man after what Rick had done?

Reminding herself that she was through with men forever, even a drop-dead gorgeous one in tight jeans and a cowboy hat, she threw herself into scrubbing the mud from the kitchen floor.

Chapter Three

Chay found himself thinking about Dana Westlake on the long ride home. He wasn't sure why he couldn't shake her image from his mind. Sure, she was pretty, with her honey-colored hair and those big blue eyes, but he had met a lot of pretty women in his time. Some of them came on to him shamelessly because he was an Indian, some liked him because he was a genuine cowboy. But he wasn't looking for a woman, pretty or otherwise, at least not the kind of woman who wanted to settle down and raise a herd of kids. Not just yet anyway.

He found three of the four missing horses grazing along the side of the road about a quarter of a mile from the ranch. After rounding them up, he herded them down the road until he reached a gate in the pasture fence. He opened the gate and the horses trotted on through, as docile as sheep. When he got back to the ranch, he would send one of the men out to look for the fourth horse.

Chay felt the same sense of homecoming and bitterness

he felt every time he rode into the yard of the Bar W. Big John Wardman was standing on the front porch, a cigar clenched between his teeth, when Chay rode up. Big John lived up to his name. He stood a good six feet four inches tall and had shoulders as wide as a barn door. He was in his mid-sixties, his thick brown hair just now going gray at the temples. His eyes were as green and sharp as ground glass. As always, tension crackled between Chay and the boss.

"I was just about to send someone out looking for you," Big John said, speaking around the cigar.

"Yeah?"

Big John nodded. Taking the stogie from his mouth, he tossed it into the brass spittoon that had been on the porch for as long as Chay could remember. "I should have known you could take care of yourself."

"That's right," Chay said. "I always have."

Big John's eyes narrowed. He opened his mouth to speak and then, apparently thinking better of it, he turned away and stalked into the house, letting the screen door slam behind him.

Chay stared after him, one hand clenched on the saddle horn. He took several deep breaths, then turned his horse toward the barn.

"Someday, old man," he muttered. "Someday we're gonna have it out."

But not today.

A couple of the cowhands waved to him as he approached the barn and he waved back.

In spite of the trouble between himself and Big John, Chay loved the ranch. It was a part of him, like the color of his skin, deeply ingrained and unchangeable.

Dismounting, Chay tossed the reins over a fence post, and unsaddled the mare. He gave her a good brushing, cleaned her hooves, then led her into the barn. He put the mare in one of the stalls, gave her a bucket of oats and a forkful of hay, made sure she had water, and finally made his way to the bunkhouse.

Some of the cowhands were clustered around the scarred wooden table in the center of the room, playing poker. Chay tossed his hat on one of the hooks beside the door, then nodded to the card players, noting that Vern Kingston was winning, as always.

"You know you're wasting your time working here," Chay told him. "You ought to be in Vegas or Reno raking in the dough."

Kingston laughed. "Yeah, and I'd go in a heartbeat if cowboying wasn't in my blood."

The men at the table laughed at that. Kingston was the laziest cowboy on the place. The only reason he still had a job was because he was a top hand with the wild string.

Miller gestured at the bandage on Chay's head. "What happened to you?"

"I ran into a tree," Chay replied. "Or, more to the point, a tree ran into me during that storm last night. Speaking of which, I found three of those missing broomtails over near Oak Creek." Chay glanced at a lanky cowboy standing on the other side of the table. "Randall, I want you to ride out and see if you can find the other one."

"Sure thing," Randall replied, and headed for the door.

"So," Kingston said, "who bandaged you up?"

"No one you know."

The men at the table exchanged knowing looks.

"You could introduce me," Joe Coffey said, wiggling his eyebrows.

"Not a chance, Coffey Man. She's too good for a brush popper like you."

The men laughed, then turned back to their game.

Chay bummed a cigarette from Kingston, lit up and took a deep drag. He watched the game while he smoked, then tossed the butt in a trash can and headed for his bunk.

Stretching out, he closed his eyes. Dana Westlake was too good for the likes of him, too, he admitted ruefully. She was a classy lady who deserved all the good things in life; he was just a cowhand with little or nothing to offer her. But that didn't stop him from thinking about her.

It didn't take Dana long to realize that once her things were put away, the house aired out, the floors scrubbed, the windows washed, the groceries put away and clean sheets on the bed, there wasn't a lot left to do except take long walks in the woods or sit on the front porch and listen to the radio. She had brought a couple of new paperback books with her, but for the first time in her life, reading held little appeal. Television was out of the question, since no one had ever replaced the one that broke.

She spent Wednesday morning baking chocolate-chip cookies. Later that afternoon she sorted through the drawers and cupboards in the kitchen; Thursday, she rearranged the furniture in the living room.

By Friday she was weary of her own company. Grabbing her purse and keys, she drove into town to buy a small television with a built-in DVD player.

She was standing beside her car while her new television was being loaded into the trunk when she saw Chayton Lone Elk walking down the street in her direction. Her heart did a funny little leap when she saw him and then she noticed the woman walking beside Chay, a pretty, young woman with a little boy in her arms. A little boy with straight black hair and dusky skin.

Chay slowed almost imperceptibly as he approached her. His gaze met hers. He nodded and then he passed by, his attention again focused on the woman at his side.

Dana stared after him for several moments and then, realizing what she was doing, she jerked her gaze away. She thanked the young man who had put the television in her car, closed the trunk and slid behind the wheel.

So, he had a wife and a child. Why was that so surprising? He was as handsome as the devil, with his coppery skin, long black hair and those sexy eyes that were so dark a brown they were almost black. And it didn't matter one bit. She didn't want a man, any man.

She told herself that all the way home.

She was sitting out on the front porch later that night, sipping from a glass of iced tea while she enjoyed the quiet of the night, when she heard hoofbeats approaching. She knew somehow that it was Chay, though she couldn't imagine what he was doing there.

Her first instinct was to run into the house, turn off all the lights and pretend she wasn't home. But that seemed cowardly and besides, her car was parked beside the house, and her living-room lights could probably be seen for a good distance.

Gathering her courage around her, she continued rocking.

He rode up a short time later, giving her a chance to notice how well he sat his horse, the spread of his shoulders, his clean profile beneath the brim of his hat. "Mind if I light a spell?"

She made a vague gesture. "Suit yourself."

He swung out of the saddle. Tossing the reins over the hitch rack, he climbed the stairs. Standing, he towered over her.

"Sit down," she invited, gesturing at the chair beside the rocker.

Chay folded his length into the ladder-back chair, his long legs stretched out before him. "Nice night," he remarked. Reaching into his shirt pocket, he pulled out a pack of cigarettes.

"I'd rather you didn't smoke," she said.

With a grunt, Chay tucked the pack back into his pocket. He had a feeling he'd just given up smoking for good.

"How's your head?"

"Healing pretty well, thanks to you."

"Would you care for a glass of iced tea?"

"Sure. Thanks."

Rising, she went into the kitchen and poured him a glass, dismayed to see that her hand was shaking. What was he doing here, anyway? Why wasn't he home with his wife? She added a few ice cubes, then returned to the porch.

She handed him the glass, shivered when his fingers brushed against hers. "So," she said, resuming her seat, "what brings you out here?"

"I just wanted to thank you again for looking after me."

"That really wasn't necessary. I would have done the same for anyone."

He grunted softly. She was as prickly as a cactus. "Well, you didn't do it for anyone, you did it for me and I'm obliged."

She shrugged, as if it was of no consequence.

"Tomorrow's my day off," he said, wondering why he was pursuing her so hard when she was only going to be here for a few weeks. "How'd you like to go riding with me in the morning? Maybe have a picnic in the afternoon, do a little swimming at the old water hole?"

"I don't think so."

"I know you came up here to be alone, but I'd really enjoy the company."

"I'm sure your wife would love to ride with you, Mr. Elk."

He stared at her blankly for a moment, and then he grinned. "You mean Kimi? She's not my wife. Just an old friend."

He had known Kimimela since middle school. They had dated some in high school and a few times after that and then she had left town. When she came home a year later, she had a three-month-old baby. Kimi had tried to pass the boy off as Chay's and when that failed, she broke down and cried. She didn't know who the father was, she was all alone and afraid. He had tried to comfort her and one thing had led to another. In the end, Chay had agreed to help support her and her son in exchange for a home-cooked meal and a few hours of companionship on Sunday nights.

It galled Dana that she felt such an overwhelming wave of relief. Married or single, it made no difference. She wasn't looking for any entanglements.

Chay took a long drink and let out an appreciative sigh. "You know, I've been spending a lot of time with a bunch of teenage girls the last few weeks. I sure could use some grown-up company." Seeing the question in Dana's eyes, he added, "The boss has me playing chaperon for his daughter and her friends. He's taking them into the city tomorrow, so I've got the day off."

Dana smiled in spite of herself as she imagined the big cowboy herding a group of giggling teenagers.

"Come on," he said, "have pity on me."

It was tempting. He was tempting. But, remembering Rick, she was about to say no. And then Chay smiled at her and all thought of refusing went right out of her head.

"Pick you up around ten?"

"All right."

"Bring your bathing suit." Rising, he drained the glass. "Unless you want to go skinny-dipping."

He was riding away before she could come up with a suitable reply. Once he was gone, a dozen reasons why she should have refused to go with him popped into her head, but by then it was too late.

She woke early on Saturday morning, filled with a sense of nervous anticipation. She had vowed never to get involved with a man again and now, barely a week later, she had accepted a date with someone she scarcely knew. If she was smart, she would pack up her things and go spend the rest of her vacation with her mom and dad.

But, as she had proved in the recent past, sometimes she wasn't very smart.

She heard hoofbeats outside the door on the stroke of ten. Grabbing the bag that held her swimsuit, towel and a few other necessities, she went out to meet him. Clad in a pair of faded jeans, a dark red shirt, scuffed boots and a black hat, Chayton Lone Elk was a feast for feminine eyes.

Chay smiled as she stepped out onto the porch. "I didn't think to ask yesterday," he said, dismounting. "Do you know how to ride?"

"Yes, though it's been a few years." Shutting the door behind her, she descended the steps.

"I thought you said you didn't know anything about horses?"

She shrugged. "I don't, really."

"Well, once you know how to ride, you never forget. It'll come back to you in no time," he promised. "Just like riding a bike." Taking her bag, he tied it onto the pommel of the second horse, a pretty little chestnut with a white face and one white stocking. "This is Daisy Blue," he said.

"I hope she's gentle."

"As a lamb," Chay assured her. "Come on, I'll give you a leg up."

He adjusted the stirrups, then looked up at her. "You okay?"

"Fine."

A little thrill of awareness rippled through her as their gazes met, only to be magnified when his fingers brushed hers as he handed her the reins.

Chay smiled at her, his expression making it clear that he was aware of what she was feeling.

Dana watched him swing effortlessly onto the back of his own horse. "How far is the water hole?"

"Not far. Maybe forty minutes or so. Why? Are you in a hurry?"

"No, but it's been a long time since I've been riding."

He nodded. "Don't worry, Dana. Is it all right if I call you Dana?"

"Of course."

"Okay, Dana, we'll take it slow and easy."

She felt an unexpected rush of pleasure at hearing her name on his lips. "Why did you ask me to go with you today?"

"I thought I made that clear yesterday. You haven't changed your mind, have you?"

"No."

"Good. Are you ready?"

With a nod, she lifted the reins and the chestnut moved out alongside Chay's horse.

It was a beautiful day for a ride. The sky was a bright bold blue, a cool breeze moved through the pines, keeping the heat at bay. Birds flitted from branch to branch, their songs a cheerful serenade.

Chay had been right. In no time at all, she found the rhythm of her mount, and everything she had ever learned about riding came back to her. She had forgotten how relaxing horseback riding could be. The chestnut had a soft mouth and a smooth easy gait. They had been riding about twenty minutes when they came to a long flat stretch of ground. She nodded when Chay asked if she was ready to let the horses run. Chay urged his horse into a lope and the chestnut lined out behind him.

Dana leaned forward, loving the touch of the wind in her face, the sense of freedom that engulfed her as her horse ran through the tall grass. A deer darted across her path and Dana laughed out loud. Why had she ever given up riding? How could she have forgotten how much fun it was?

Chay let his horse run until it slowed of its own accord. Pulling up, he waited for Dana to catch up with him. Looking at her, it was hard to believe this was the same pinchfaced woman he had met in Wright's parking lot. Her cheeks were flushed, her eyes shining with pleasure.

"This was a wonderful idea," she said as she drew up alongside him. "How much farther to the water hole?"

"Just around the bend."

It wasn't a water hole at all, but a man-made lake. Set in a verdant meadow, it was surrounded by tall pines and wildflowers. A large wooden raft with an umbrella was anchored in the middle of the water.

Chay dismounted, then turned to help Dana from the back of her horse. She felt a thrill of pleasure as his hands closed around her waist. He lifted her as though she weighed nothing at all. She fought back the urge to run her hands over his biceps.

She looked up at him when he set her on her feet, totally confused by her reaction to him.

Rick had never set her heart to pounding like this, never made her feel warm all over just by looking at her.

"Did you bring a suit?" Chay asked.

She nodded, wishing she dared go skinny-dipping with him.

"Another hope crushed," he said.

"Didn't you? Bring a pair of trunks, I mean."

"Yeah, but I'm willing to swim in the buff if you are."

She wanted to, she really did, but she just didn't have the nerve. In spite of her attraction to Chay, he was a stranger and she was going home in two weeks.

"Not this time," she said, and wondered if there would be a next time.

"Okay. Men to the left, women to the right."

"Gotcha." Untying her bag from the pommel, she ducked behind a tree to change into her suit, a simple black one-piece. Pulling it on, she wished she had lost that ten pounds she had been meaning to lose, then chided herself for worrying about it. She was what she was and if he didn't like it, what difference did it make? She wasn't interested in winning either his admiration or his affection.

Draping her towel over her shoulder, she took a deep breath and stepped out from behind the tree.

Chay was looking at the water, his back toward her. He wore a pair of navy trunks. Her gaze moved over him in frank feminine appreciation. His skin was a deep copper color all over. His hair fell past his shoulders. He had a tight tush and long, long legs.

He turned as she took another step forward. She felt her cheeks grow warm as his gaze moved over her.

"Nice," he said with a wink.

Her cheeks grew hotter. "Thank you."

He held out his hand. "Ready?"

"Is it very cold?"

"No."

Dropping her towel on the grass, she put her hand in his, felt a rush of electricity flow from his hand to hers as they ran toward the lake and plunged in.

In spite of what he had said, she had expected the water to be cold, but it was perfect. He let go of her hand and she struck out for the far bank, her strokes long and strong, thanks to lessons at the Y. He came up behind her, matching her stroke for stroke.

She was a little breathless when she reached the opposite shore. Climbing out, she sat on the grass while he reversed direction and crossed the lake again.

He swam with ease, drops of water glistening on his broad shoulders, the sunlight casting gilt highlights in his long black hair. She wondered if he did everything as well.

He reached the opposite shore, turned, and swam toward her. She looked up at him as he climbed out of the lake shaking water from his hair, then dropped down beside her.

"It's lovely here," she remarked.

"Yeah. It's always been one of my favorite places."

"Did you grow up around here?"

"Yes."

"On the ranch?"

"Yeah."

"Oh?" There was a wealth of curiosity in that single word.

"My mother used to work for Big John," Chay explained. "She kept his books, stuff like that. She got married ten years ago and moved to Arizona, just outside of Mesa."

Dana remembered Big John. She had seen him one year when she came to stay with her grandparents. She recalled a big, stern-faced man. He had looked at her and scared her half to death. "Why didn't you go with her?"

"No reason to. She didn't need me looking after her anymore, plus I've got a few acres of my own nearby." He didn't mention that his land adjoined Big John's south pasture.

"How long have you worked for Big John?"

"Seems like my whole life." He smiled at her. "How about you? Do you work?"

"Yes, I work for a company that appraises antiques back in Ashton Falls."

"Antiques, huh? I wouldn't think there'd be much call for that kind of work in Ashton Falls."

"You'd be surprised," Dana said with a grin.

"You're pretty far from home," Chay remarked. "What brought you way up here?"

"My grandmother left me her house when she passed away. Talk about antiques! The house, not my grandmother," she clarified.

Chay laughed, and she laughed with him.

"I haven't been up here for several years," Dana said. Leaning back, she braced herself on her hands. "I forgot how pretty it is, how much I've always loved it. I used to come up for vacations when I was a little girl. My grandfather taught me to ride, and my grandmother taught me how to crochet and bake pies."

"What kind of pies?"

"All kinds. Peach, apple, berry, lemon."

"Maybe you could bake me one sometime."

"Maybe."

Their gazes met and locked. Heat flowed through her, as warm and sweet as sun-kissed honey. She swallowed hard. "So, what's your favorite kind of pie?"

His gaze swept over her mouth. "Apple."

He leaned toward her. Suddenly breathless, she stared at him, afraid he was going to take her in his arms and kiss her, and more afraid that he wouldn't.

"Dana."

"What?"

"Nothing, I just wanted to say your name."

"Oh." The thought pleased her more than it should have.

"It suits you," he murmured. And then he drew her into his arms.

"I really don't think this is a good idea," she said, her voice little more than a whisper.

"You're probably right," he agreed. And then, slowly lowering his head, he kissed her. His kiss was like riding the teacups at Disneyland, watching fireworks on the Fourth of July and sitting in front of a blazing fire on a cold winter night all rolled into one.

Closing her eyes, she kissed him back, her arms sliding up around his neck, her body seeking to be closer to his. His skin was warm and still damp and she pressed herself against him, thinking she had never felt anything as wonderful as being in his arms. Never tasted anything as potent as his kisses. Every cell, every nerve ending, sprang to life as his tongue met hers. She wished she had the audacity to take off her bathing suit, to feel the hard length of his body pressed to hers with nothing between them. No man had ever made her feel like this, not even Rick....

Memories of her former fiancé exploded through her mind—Rick holding her in his arms, telling her that he would love her forever, that he would never look at another woman as long as he lived. Ha! Thinking of him cooled her desire as quickly and effectively as a bucket of cold water poured on a campfire.

Turning her head to the side, she broke the kiss.

"Whoa, girl," Chay muttered.

Heat flooded her cheeks. Muttering, "I'm sorry." She tried to wriggle out of his arms, but he refused to let her go.

"Hey, I wasn't complaining." He brushed a lock of wet hair from her cheek.

She looked away, embarrassed by the way she had responded to his kisses. What must he think of her? Another minute and she would have gone up in flames.

Cupping her chin in his palm, he forced her to look at him. "There's nothing to be embarrassed about," he said. "I felt it, too."

"It shouldn't have happened. I'm not looking for...for anything."

"Neither am I." He smiled at her as he released her. "Lighten up, Dana. It was just a kiss."

Just a kiss? Was that all it had been to him? She should have felt relieved. Why didn't she?

"Are you ready to swim back?" he asked. "I had Anna Mae, our cook, pack us a lunch."

With a nod, she got to her feet and plunged into the lake. The water felt cool against her heated flesh.

She had regained her composure by the time they reached the other side. Chay found a shady place to spread the blanket. Reaching into the basket, he pulled out roast-beef sandwiches, potato salad, barbecued beans and a thermos of lemonade.

Dana ate self-consciously, unable to forget the way Chay's kisses had affected her.

"So have you ever been married, Dana?"

"No," she said, startled by the question. "Have you?"

He shook his head. "I came close once."

"Were you in love with her?"

"I thought so at the time. Of course, I was mighty young back then, too young to know the difference between love and lust." He looked at her speculatively. "I'm surprised you aren't married. Pretty girl like you, I'd have thought someone would have snapped you up a long time ago."

She thought of Rick. "Just lucky, I guess." At least he had cheated on her *before* they were married. Her friend, Josey, hadn't been so lucky. Well, *lucky* probably wasn't the right word. Ted had cheated on Josey while she was in the hospital having his baby. Men! You couldn't trust any of them.

Chay regarded her thoughtfully for a long moment. "Somebody hurt you, didn't they?"

It was a wild guess, a shot in the dark, but as soon as he spoke the words, he knew it was true. She had been hurt, he thought, and not too long ago if he was any judge. Although he hardly knew her, the thought of some dumb jackass causing her pain filled him with regret. He wasn't sure how he felt about her, but he knew one thing—she was hurting deep down inside and he didn't like it one damn bit.

"I'm sure I don't know what you mean."

"I'm sure you do."

"I don't want to talk about it," she said curtly.

"Whatever you say." He hadn't meant to upset her. He

looked out over the lake, giving her time to regain her composure. "I'm supposed to bring Ashley and her friends out here tomorrow," he said after a time.

"I'm sure they'll love it."

"Wanna come along and keep me company?"

"I don't think so." The less time she spent with him, the better. She already liked him far too much. She wasn't getting caught up in that trap again, that wonderful glow of infatuation, the excitement and the anticipation, only to have it all come crashing down around her. No, thank you. She had learned her lesson the hard way. She wasn't making the same mistake again, no matter how attractive she found Chay Lone Elk.

"Come on," he coaxed. "You'll have four of the best chaperons in the world."

She shook her head.

"Are you sure I can't change your mind?"

"Quite sure."

They finished the rest of the meal in silence.

Earlier, Chay had loosened the saddle cinches on their horses. Now, while Dana gathered up their used plates and cups and stowed everything back in the basket, he tightened the saddle cinch on her horse and then his own. Taking the basket, he tied it behind his saddle, and then helped her mount. She felt a familiar warmth slide up her arm at the touch of his hand.

It was late afternoon when they reached her place. Dismounting, Chay lifted her from the back of her horse, his hands lingering at her waist.

Butterflies took wing in her stomach as he leaned forward and brushed a quick kiss across her lips. "Thanks for today," he said. "I had a good time."

"Yes," she said, trying to avoid meeting his eyes. "Me, too."

His gaze found hers and held it for a long moment, then

he swung into the saddle and rode out of the yard. He didn't look back.

Standing on the porch, Dana watched him until he was out of sight. In spite of everything, she couldn't help feeling sorry that she would never see him again.

Chapter Four

Too restless to sit down and read, refusing to let herself think about Chay Lone Elk and the time they had spent together the day before, Dana went into the kitchen and pulled out the ingredients for making an apple pie. As she rolled out the crust, she told herself she was making apple because she didn't have the fixings for any other kind. She told herself it was stupid to make a pie when she was going to end up eating it all herself, and that if she wanted to lose that ten pounds, she should be snacking on rice cakes and yogurt. Nevertheless, the fragrant aroma of a pie baking in the oven soon filled the house.

Which again left her with nothing to do. She was tired of watching TV. The bed was made, the breakfast dishes washed and put away, the floor swept and mopped to within an inch of its life, the furniture dusted. Earlier, she had watered the lawn, fed the squirrels, filled the old bird feeder in the backyard. She had done all those things and made a pie, and it was barely two o'clock. She knew now why she liked living in the city, and why she worked six days a week. What on earth did people in the country do with themselves?

The two weeks she had left suddenly seemed like two months.

The pie was cooling and she was thinking about driving into town for lunch when she heard the muffled sound of hoofbeats in the yard. Anticipation fluttered in her stomach. Could it be?

A moment later, she heard the sound of girlish voices and giggles, and then Chay's voice.

"Hey, Dana! Get on out here!"

At the sound of his voice, her heart began beating double time. Still, she forced herself to walk slowly to the front door. She paused with her hand on the latch, took a deep calming breath and stepped out onto the front porch.

Chay was leaning forward in the saddle, his arms crossed on the horn. The horse she had ridden yesterday was on a lead line. Four teenagers were strung out behind him.

"Hey, girl," Chay said, "we came by to see if you'd changed your mind."

Dana shook her head. "I don't think so."

"Daisy Blue misses you something awful," he said with a roguish grin.

Dana's lips twitched in a smile as she glanced at the mare. "She does? How can you tell?"

"She told me so this morning. She said you probably missed her, too, and she begged me to bring her along, just in case you changed your mind. You wouldn't want to disappoint Daisy Blue, now, would you? Not after she came all this way."

As if to add credence to Chay's words, Daisy Blue nodded her head up and down, then whinnied softly.

"You see?" Chay smiled up at Dana, his dark eyes glinting with humor.

Dana laughed out loud, charmed by his words and his

smile. What could it hurt to spend another day with him? At least it would get her out of the house.

Chay lifted his head and sniffed the air like a wolf on the scent of fresh game. "Is that apple pie I smell?"

She lifted one shoulder and let it fall in a negligent shrug. "Could be."

"Did you bake it for me?"

"Of course not."

He looked crestfallen. "Well, how about bringing it along?"

"I didn't say I was going."

"Sure you are," he said, and smiled at her again.

Ten minutes later the pie was packed in a basket and tied behind Daisy Blue's saddle, along with a blanket and a beach towel. Dana had taken the time to put her bathing suit on under her clothes and she was ready to go.

Chay introduced Dana to Ashley and her friends, Megan, Brittany and LuAnn. The girls all greeted Dana with cheerful waves and hellos and then they were on their way to the lake.

Ashley was a pretty girl with wavy brown hair and mischievous green eyes. In spite of the difference in their coloring, Dana thought Ashley bore a striking resemblance to Chay.

Chay and Dana rode ahead a few paces. Dana couldn't help smiling as she listened to the girls' chatter. They talked about boys, the latest fashions, boys, which movie stars they thought were really tight, boys, which rock star was in and which was out, whether LuAnn should get a nose ring and what her father, a judge, was likely to do if she did, and boys. It was obvious the girls had been close friends for years, that they were all from wealthy families and accustomed to having the best of everything.

Chay looked over at Dana with a pained expression.

"See what I've been putting up with for the last three weeks?" He groaned softly. "Almost four weeks now."

"You poor thing."

He nodded, his expression woebegone. "Four teenage girls! No grown man should have to put up with such torture."

"Yes, I can see how you're suffering. How much longer are they going to be here?"

He let out a long aggrieved sigh. "Until the end of summer vacation." He shook his head. "I'm never going to get any work done on my own place at this rate."

"What kind of work are you doing?"

"I'm building a house in my spare time." He grunted. "What little I have."

"You're building it? Yourself? Or having it built?"

"I'm doing it—most of it, anyway."

"Wow, I'm impressed."

"Good. Maybe you'd like to see it sometime?"

"Yes, I would. Are you building it for yourself, or for someone else?"

"It's for me. Of course, at the rate I'm going, I'll be an old man by the time it's finished."

"Well, at least you'll have a nice place to live," she said with a grin. "What kind of work do you do for Big John?"

"Cowboy stuff," Chay replied, grinning. "You know, ropin', ridin', brandin', that kind of thing."

"Just like Roy Rogers?"

He snorted softly. "Hardly. Rogers never got his hands dirty. Or his clothes, either."

Dana laughed. "He sure dressed pretty, though—all those fancy clothes. And those boots! I can't imagine any real cowboy wearing red-and-white boots. Of course, the Lone Ranger never got dirty, either. His clothes were always clean and neatly pressed, even after he'd been rolling around in the dirt punching out the bad guy. I always wondered about that."

"You a big fan of the Lone Ranger?"

"Well, to tell you the truth, I always liked Tonto the best."

"Is that right?"

"Uh-huh." She looked at Chay a moment. "You're Indian, aren't you?"

"It shows, huh?"

She nodded.

"My mother is Cheyenne. She was born on the rez."

"How did she happen to go to work for Big John?"

"She left the rez and went to college. She met Big John in a bar one night soon after she graduated. As fate would have it, he had just fired his accountant. He happened to mention he was in the market for a new one during the course of the evening and…" He shrugged. "One thing led to another, and the next day she had a job."

"That's quite a story. All it needs is a happy-ever-after ending."

A muscle clenched in Chay's jaw. "Yeah."

"Is your father Indian, too?"

"No." The tone of his voice told her it wasn't something he wanted to discuss.

They reached the lake a few minutes later. The girls were off their horses and in the water in nothing flat, leaving Chay to look after their mounts. He unsaddled the horses, hobbled them in the shade, then removed their bridles, leaving them to graze on a patch of grass.

Dana stripped down to her bathing suit, and spread her blanket on the grass next to Chay's. Each of the girls had a picnic basket tied behind her saddle. Dana lined the baskets up along the edge of the blankets, then sat down, thinking how pretty and peaceful it was with the lake and the trees. The air was fragrant with the scent of wildflowers and grass. A squirrel darted up a nearby pine. Birds flitted from branch to branch.

"You look like you're ready for a swim," Chay remarked.

His gaze moved over her, making Dana wish once again that she had lost that extra ten pounds. He looked ready, too, she thought. His black trunks were the perfect foil for his dusky skin and long black hair. He had never looked more Indian than he did now. All he needed was an eagle feather in his hair and a streak of black paint on his cheek.

Dana glanced at the lake. The girls were playing in the water, splashing and dunking each other and generally having a good time. "Maybe later."

Chay nodded. He sat down on the blanket across from her, his long legs stretched out in front of him, a blade of grass tucked into the corner of his lips.

Dana watched the girls. At twenty-three, she was only a few years older than they were, but she felt years older, certainly wiser. If only she could be that young and innocent again, she thought, worried about nothing more earthshaking than going back to school when summer vacation was over.

"Hey." Chay took hold of her foot and shook it. "It's too pretty a day to be looking so serious."

"Sorry, I was just envying them."

Chay glanced at the girls. "I can't imagine why."

She shrugged. "They're so young and carefree. Nothing to worry about except clothes and homework. I wish I hadn't been so anxious to grow up, that I'd enjoyed being a teenager more."

"Does anyone enjoy it?" Chay asked with a grin. "Voices changing. Hormones raging. Trying to find the nerve to ask a girl out. Being scared she'll say no and more afraid she'll say yes. Wondering what to do with her once you've got her alone."

Dana laughed. "It wasn't any easier being a girl, you know. Hoping the right guy would ask you to the movies. Wondering if you should let him kiss you good-night, wondering how you'd feel if he didn't!" She shook her head. "Maybe I don't want to do it all again."

"Yeah, and it's worse for kids today," Chay remarked. "Drugs on every campus. AIDS. Gangs." Chay looked at the girls thoughtfully, his attention settling on Ashley. She seemed like a bright kid. She would be sixteen soon, a dangerous age for teenagers. He didn't know what he'd do if she got into trouble. He knew Big John didn't pay her much attention. Oh, he made sure she had everything she needed, everything except his affection. Ashley wouldn't be the first girl to go looking for the love she wasn't getting at home in the arms of some smooth-talking young stud who would take her innocence and then dump her. He thought about the promise he had made to Big John. With each passing day, it was getting harder and harder to keep.

"Hey." Dana tapped her finger on Chay's big toe. "Who's looking pensive now?"

He smiled at her, and Dana forgot everything else. The man's smile was more tempting than chocolate, warmer than a wool blanket.

"Sorry," he said.

"It's all right. Tell me about your Cheyenne heritage."

He shrugged. "What's there to say?"

"I don't know. You're the first Native American I've ever met." She frowned. "Do you like being called Native American or Indian?"

"Indian works for me. As for never saying anything outright, I've never felt the need. Anybody looking at me knows who and what I am. If they don't like it, that's their problem, not mine. So, what do you want to know?"

"I'm not sure. All I really know about Indians is what I see on TV and in the movies."

"Yeah, well, most of that is wrong. Indian history was recorded by the whites, not the tribes, so anything you see or hear is likely to be totally inaccurate, either portraying Indians as cold-blooded, godless barbarians or highly romanticized as noble savages."

"What's it like on the reservation? I saw a special on TV a while back. Are reservations as bad as they made it sound?"

"Most of them are pretty grim. Lots of unemployment, teenage suicide, alcoholism."

Dana grimaced. It was not a pretty picture. "Do you go there often?"

"I haven't been back for a couple of years. Since my uncle died, I don't have any family left there and—" he shrugged "—I miss it sometimes. I've got some good memories of the place, and some bad ones, too."

"I used to love movies about the Old West. All those handsome cowboys. Of course, it was the Indians I liked best."

"I'm glad to hear that," he said, grinning.

"In the movies it always seemed like such a romantic part of history," Dana mused.

"I'm sure it was a good way to live," Chay said, "until the white eyes showed up and ruined everything." He smiled at her. "Present company excepted, of course."

As hard as it was to believe in this day and age, there was still some animosity between the whites and the Indians. Chay hadn't experienced much prejudice in Wardman's Hollow, but he'd been subjected to some nasty looks and snide remarks in other parts of the country. He'd taken offense when he was younger; these days he mostly let it slide.

"Of course. I read somewhere that the Cheyenne were considered the most handsome people of all the tribes."

Chay grinned broadly. "Is that right?"

She nodded. "I don't know, though…" She tilted her head to one side, her eyes narrowing as she studied him from head to foot. "Not bad. Of course, I've never met any other Indians, so I'm really not a good judge."

"Not bad?" he asked in mock indignation. "Not bad! Is that all you've got to say?"

Dana burst out laughing. "All right, all right, whoever

said it was right. At least where you're concerned. Feeling better now? Masculinity still intact? Ego stroked enough?"

He laughed with her, then leaned back, his weight braced on his elbows. "Sometimes when I'm riding across the ranch, I wish I'd been born back then, when the land still belonged to the Sioux and the Cheyenne and the Arapaho. A man knew who he was, and what was expected of him."

Dana shuddered at the mere idea. "I'm glad I live now. Life was too unpredictable back then. Too hard, especially for women. I can't imagine how difficult it must have been just to survive. Doing laundry in a washtub or in a river, cooking on a wood-burning stove, making everything from scratch. No hospitals. Giving birth out in the wild." She shook her head. "No, thank you."

"Life might have been harder, but in some ways I think it was more meaningful."

"Maybe, I don't know."

Chay glanced at the girls. "I suppose kids have always gotten into trouble, but it seems to me they had less time for mischief back in the old days. Kids today have too much time on their hands and not enough responsibility."

"Well, you can't go back," Dana said, "so you might as well enjoy it here."

Chay sat up, his gaze moving over her face, then settling on her mouth. "Oh, I like it here just fine," he said with a roguish grin.

"Do you?"

"Uh-huh. You're here."

She felt her cheeks grow warm at his words, felt a flutter of excitement at the look in his eyes, the husky timbre of his voice. Inching forward, he ran a finger along the inside of her calf. His touch sent a shiver of delight racing through her. Heat flared in his eyes.

Dana glanced over at Ashley and her friends, wishing

the girls were somewhere else, wishing that she and Chay were alone so that he could take her in his arms and… She took a deep breath and quickly changed the subject. "You said something about a swim…."

Chay's expression told her he was well aware of what she was doing. She was about to ask him if he had changed his mind about a swim when one of the girls screamed.

Chay sprang to his feet. His first thought was for Ashley, but she was fine. She was shouting at him, something about Megan. And then he realized he could see only three of the girls. There was no sign of Megan. Ashley and the other two girls were diving underwater and then coming back up.

Damn! Racing toward the lake, Chay plunged in and swam out toward the wooden raft located in the center of the lake.

He didn't waste time asking what happened. Diving down, he searched for the girl.

He saw her near the bottom, her hair waving in the water like strands of black seaweed. Grabbing her under one arm, he jackknifed to the surface.

"Is she all right?" Ashley asked anxiously.

He didn't waste time talking but struck out for the shore.

Dana was waiting for him. "What can I do?"

"Nothing right now." He laid Megan on the blanket and began giving her artificial respiration. By then, Ashley and the other two girls had reached the blanket, their expressions worried as they hovered over Chay. When Megan coughed up some water, the girls all sighed with relief.

Dana wrapped a blanket around Megan to keep her warm while Chay examined the bump on the side of her head. There was little swelling and no blood.

Turning to Ashley, he asked, "What happened?"

"I dunno," she said with a shrug. "We were just foolin' around. Megan fell off the raft. I think she must have hit her head on the edge. Is she gonna be okay?"

"Yeah, I think so." Chay looked at Megan. "You let me know if you feel dizzy or your vision blurs, or you feel sick to your stomach, okay?"

"I feel all right," she said. "Really."

"You girls need to be careful out there."

"We were being careful," Ashley said, somewhat defensively.

"Well," Chay said, sitting back on his heels, "I think Megan better take it easy the rest of the day. No more swimming."

"All right," Ashley said, obviously concerned for her friend. "Come on, LuAnn, Brittany, let's take our towels over there. Megan, I've got yours. Come on."

The girls spread their towels in the sun, then stretched out on their stomachs, facing each other, their conversation subdued.

"That was a close call," Dana remarked, resuming her seat on the blanket.

"Yeah. Could have been a lot more serious, I guess."

"She doesn't seem any the worse for wear, other than that bump on her head."

Chay sat across from Dana, one leg drawn up, his arm resting on his knee. "I'll be glad when they all go home."

"You'd rather herd cows than kids?"

"You got that right!" He looked at her and grinned.

Dana felt her heart skip a beat as their eyes met. Lordy, but he was a handsome man! His skin was brown all over. Drops of water glistened in his long black hair, dripped down his broad chest. She looked away, sternly reminding herself that Rick had been a good-looking man, too, and that there was more to a man than his appearance. *Handsome is as handsome does,* her mother always said.

Later, after lunch, Megan declared she felt fine and begged to go swimming again.

Chay shook his head. "I don't think so."

Ashley looked at Dana. "Can't you make him change his mind?"

Dana raised her hands. "Oh, no, you're not getting me involved in this."

"You're a woman," Ashley said. "I thought for sure you'd be on our side."

"Why don't you girls take a walk around the lake instead," Dana suggested.

"We might as well," Ashley said with a decided lack of enthusiasm. "Come on, girls, let's get out of here."

Sullen-faced, Ashley turned away, followed by the others.

"She'll get over it," Chay said, noting Dana's expression.

"I guess. It's just that I was hoping we'd be friends, although I'm not sure why. I won't be here long enough for it to matter one way or the other."

Chay leaned forward, his hand covering hers. "Is there any chance you can stay a little longer than planned?"

"I don't know. Maybe. Why?"

"I'd like to spend more time with you. It'll give us a chance to get to know each other better."

"I don't think so."

"I know you've been hurt," he said quietly, "but…"

With a shake of her head, she pulled her hand from his. "Don't."

Chay glanced over at Ashley and her friends. The girls hadn't gone for a walk. Instead, they were sitting with their heads together, whispering and giggling while they cut the pie Dana had brought. Didn't look as if he was going to get any, Chay thought, though that was the least of his worries.

"Dammit," he muttered, "we can't talk here."

"There's nothing to talk about."

Oh, yes, there is, he thought. But it would have to wait.

* * *

Dana stood on the front porch, waving, as Chay and the girls rode away. It was getting to be a habit, she thought, standing there watching Chayton Lone Elk ride out of sight.

The girls had cheered up later, especially when Chay told them Megan could go swimming as long as she stayed close to the shore. Chay and Dana had swum across the lake and back, and then they had packed up and headed for home.

And now it was dusk. When Chay and the girls were out of sight, Dana went inside and got a bowl of grapes, then went back outside and sat down on the rocker, her feet propped up on the porch rail. Two days of horseback riding had left her aching in places she didn't know she had. But she had to admit, they were the best two days she'd had in a long time, and Chay was the reason. Like it or not, she was drawn to him. And she didn't like it. Even if she wanted to get involved with another man—and she didn't!—it was too soon. The hurt of Rick's betrayal was too fresh in her heart and her mind.

"Does the word *rebound* ring a bell?" she muttered. Maybe that was all it was, just a normal urge to find another man as quickly as possible, someone to stroke her ego and make her feel desirable.

Why did she have to meet Chayton Lone Elk now, when she was lonely and vulnerable and unsure of herself? Why did he have to be so tall and so doggone handsome? Why did he have to have a smile that could melt ice on a winter day, and a voice that made her insides quiver like melted Jell-O? Why did he have to look so darn sexy in a cowboy hat and tight jeans?

She blew out a sigh. Sexy, she thought. Had she ever seen anything sexier than Chay in those black trunks? It just wasn't fair that she had to meet him now, when he seemed so right and the timing was so wrong.

She was about to go back into the house when a movement in the shadows drew her attention. Leaning forward, she saw three does picking their way through the underbrush across from the house.

Reaching into the bowl, she tossed a few grapes toward the deer. They looked at her for a long moment, then, ears twitching nervously back and forth, they emerged from the brush to eat the grapes.

They were so beautiful, with their large delicate ears and big brown eyes. She tossed them more grapes, and still more. Rising, she moved quietly down the stairs. The deer backed away. Dana plucked a handful of grapes from the bowl and held her hand out toward them. They watched her warily for several moments, then the smaller of the three took a step forward.

Dana kept very still as the doe moved toward her, held her breath as the doe gently nibbled the grapes from her hand while the other two looked on.

Reaching into the bowl again, Dana tossed a handful of grapes to the other two deer. The movement spooked all three. With a flick of their tails, they disappeared into the darkness.

Setting the bowl on the porch, Dana took a stroll around the house. The yard needed work. Tomorrow she would have a go at the weeds in the front yard and along the driveway. And then she would take a whack at the dead tree in the back of the house, although she doubted she would be able to cut it down herself.

She paused at the foot of the stairs and gazed up at the sky. At home, she'd rarely taken the time to look at the stars. Now, she noticed the beauty of the Milky Way. She found the North Star and the Big Dipper and the Little Dipper. Dana frowned, trying to remember where the other constellations were located.

She took a deep breath, her nostrils filling with the fresh

clean scent of earth and pine. She really did love it here, the trees and the deer and the squirrels. The sky seemed bigger, the stars more plentiful.

Yawning, she went into the house and fixed a light dinner, then, muscles aching, she took a long hot bath. When the water grew cool, she stepped out of the tub, pulled on her nightgown, then grabbed a book and crawled into bed.

She stared at the words on the page, but it was Chayton Lone Elk's face she saw, Chay's image that followed her to sleep.

Chapter Five

"Why the hell weren't you more careful? Dammit, the girl could have drowned."

Chay stood in front of Big John's desk, his hands tightly clenched at his sides as the old man continued the rant that had been going on for the last twenty minutes.

"Well?" Big John spread his hands on his desk and leaned forward. "What do you have to say for yourself?"

"Not a damn thing."

Big John reared back, his eyes narrowing, his face mottled with rage. "Get the hell out of my office."

Turning on his heel, Chay stalked out of the room. He was almost at the front door when Ashley stepped into his path.

"I'm sorry, Chay," she said quietly.

"It's not your fault."

"I know how you hate looking after us. I don't know why Daddy thinks we need a chaperon."

Chay grunted softly. "Today's a perfect example of why

you need a keeper," he said, but there was no anger in his voice, only affection.

Ashley threw her arms around him and gave him a bear hug. "I love you."

"I love you, too, kitten."

"I don't know why Daddy's making such a big fuss. Megan's fine."

"We were lucky," Chay said, ruffling her hair. "It could have been a lot worse. Go along now."

"All right." She started down the hallway, then stopped and glanced over her shoulder. "Are you gonna see Dana again?"

"I don't know, why?"

Ashley shrugged. "No reason. She's pretty, isn't she?"

"She is that," Chay agreed.

"Prettier than me?"

"No one's prettier than you."

With a smile, Ashley ran up the stairs.

Needing some fresh air, Chay left the house and headed for the corral. He whistled softly and his horse trotted up, snuffling softly.

"Hey, girl." Propping one foot on the bottom rail, Chay scratched the mare between her ears. "Damn that old man," he muttered. "If I had any sense, I'd pack up and leave this place." But even as he said the words, he knew he wouldn't go. Not only because he didn't want to, but because it would make Big John's life so much easier if he didn't have to see his illegitimate son every day.

Of course, leaving would make Chay's life easier, too. His mother had tried to persuade him to go with her when she married Frank Heston, but Chay had stubbornly refused to go. Big John was his father and Chay intended to stay on at the ranch until the old man acknowledged that fact to the whole damn world. He had spent most of his life trying to make his old man proud of him. He worked harder than any hired hand on the place, and he was damn good at what he did. He could outrope and outride any cowboy within a thousand miles. He understood horses and cattle as well as, if not better than, Big John himself. And then there was Ashley. She was his half sister and she didn't even know it.

Chay gave the mare a final pat. "See ya later, girl."

Turning away from the corral, he headed for the bunkhouse. He waved to the other cowhands, paused a moment to watch a poker game. As usual, Vern Kingston was winning big. Chay knew some of the other men thought Kingston cheated at cards, but Chay had played enough poker with Vern to know better. Kingston wasn't just good, he had the devil's own luck at the game.

Moving on, Chay dropped down on his bunk, one arm thrown across his eyes. He wasn't surprised when Dana's image immediately popped to the forefront of his mind. She tempted him and intrigued him more than any woman he had ever met, and he had met quite a few. But none of them appealed to him the way she did. She brought out his protective instincts, made him want to shield her from life's heartaches, heal the hurt he sometimes saw in her eyes.

"Damn," he muttered irritably, "you've got it bad."

Yet even as he chided himself for being a fool, he was trying to find a plausible reason to go by her place again tomorrow.

Dana sat back on her heels and stretched the kinks out of her back and shoulders. It had been years since she had pulled weeds, especially this many of the sticky little things. She wouldn't have minded so much if scrabbling in the dirt had accomplished its purpose and kept her from thinking of Chay, but it didn't. She was worse than a teenager with her first crush. She thought about Chay and her insides turned to mush. When she was with him, all she wanted to do was touch him, hear his voice, see him smile. When they were apart, she daydreamed about him. She dreamed of him at night, too.

She shook her head. Last night, she had dreamed of Chay. He had ridden up on his horse, swept her off her feet and carried her away to a house located in a green meadow. There had been cattle on the hillsides. He had carried her into the house and shut the door, and shut out the rest of the world....

She pushed the memory aside. It was only a dream, and dreams were for fools. She was a grown woman with a responsible job, not some silly little girl who had just been dumped for the first time.

Only it *was* the first time. And it hurt. And she never wanted to feel this way again.

With a shake of her head, she started tossing the weeds into a plastic bag. As soon as she finished up here, it would be time to fix lunch. She licked her lips, anticipating an ice-cold glass of lemonade.

Half an hour later, the weeds in the front of the house were gone. Rising, one hand pressed against the small of her aching back, she debated going into town and buying some flowers to line the driveway. It seemed like a foolish gesture when she was only going to be there another two weeks. Still, there was something very satisfying about working in the yard and getting her hands dirty. And flowers didn't cost that much.

Another half hour or so, and she would go inside, get cleaned up and drive to the nursery in town.

It had taken some doing, but Chay had finally found an excuse to ride up near Dana's house again. Of course, having the girls with him wouldn't allow for much courting.... Good Lord, where had *that* word come from?

Chay frowned as he urged his horse up the slope. Courting! Was that what he was doing? There didn't seem much point in it, since Dana would be going back to Ashton Falls in a couple of weeks, but courting or not, he had to see her again.

He glanced over his shoulder to make sure the girls were all behind him. Megan was fully recovered from her incident of the day before, with nothing to show for her mishap but a small bruise on the side of her head. Chay wished he could say that. He was still seething from the tongue-lashing he had received from Big John.

He waved a hand at Ashley when she looked up. The girls rode two abreast, whispering and giggling. He wondered what teenagers talked about these days when there were no adults to overhear their conversations, and then decided he really didn't want to know.

He felt a quickening inside when they turned up the road to Dana's house. Bemused by his feelings, at first he didn't see her kneeling beside the driveway.

She looked up, apparently as surprised as he was. "What are you doing here?" she asked, waving to the girls.

"They wanted to go berry picking," Chay replied. It was only partly a lie. Berry picking had been his idea, but they had been agreeable.

"Isn't it kind of late in the year for berry picking?"

"This high up there're probably a few left. Why don't you come with us?"

She glanced down. Her jeans were dirty and so were her hands. And she still had flowers to plant.

"You're fine the way you are," Chay said, reading her thoughts. "Berry picking can be dirty work."

"I don't have a horse."

His gaze met hers, his dark eyes twinkling with mischief. "It's not far. We can ride double."

The look in his eyes, and the thought of riding behind him, her arms wrapped snugly around his waist, sent a thrill of excitement fluttering through her stomach.

"Well, what do you say?" he asked.

The rest of the flowers could wait. "Just let me wash my hands."

At his nod, she hurried into the house, washed her hands, ran a brush through her hair and tied it back in a ponytail. She debated putting on lipstick and decided against it, but then vanity won out. She checked herself in the mirror one last time, then practically ran out the front door.

Chay rode up beside the porch. Offering her his hand, he swung her up behind him.

"Hang on tight," he said. "I don't want to lose you."

His words filled her heart with warmth. Murmuring, "Yes, sir," she slid her arms around his waist, resisting the temptation to rest her cheek against his back.

They rode around the side of the house and up a long narrow trail that opened onto a flat stretch of prairie. Shrubs and tall trees dotted the landscape, as well as a long tangle of wild huckleberry bushes that still held some of the small blue-black fruit. Montana was known for its huckleberry jams and jellies. You could even buy huckleberry-scented candles. Of course, there were some who said that they weren't true huckleberries at all, but blueberries.

Chay pulled his horse to a stop. He offered Dana his hand again and she swung down from the horse's back. Dismounting, Chay gathered the reins of all the horses and tethered them to a couple of trees. The girls each had a straw basket tied behind their saddles. Retrieving them, they moved among the berry bushes, each boasting they would be the first to fill their basket.

"I'll bet they eat more than they collect," Chay remarked, watching them. "Come on, let's go pick a few before they're all gone."

"Sounds good to me."

And they were good. Chay ate a handful but mostly he watched Dana. She looked as young and carefree as one of the teenagers as she laughed with them. His gaze settled on a drop of berry juice caught in the corner of her mouth. What would she do if he pulled her into his arms and licked that tempting drop away? Deciding it was well worth a kiss or a slap, he drew her into his arms and licked the juice from her lips.

Startled, she jerked back, her eyes widening. "Why did you do that?"

"You had juice," he said, touching his finger to her lips, "just there." He smiled at her. "But it's gone now."

"Really?" Lifting her hand to her mouth, she ate another couple of berries. "Do you see any more?"

"Here," he said, kissing the opposite corner of her mouth. "And here." He nibbled on her lower lip. "And here." This was a full-blown kiss that rocked him down to his boot heels.

"Hey, you guys!" Megan called. "We're supposed to be picking berries!"

"Yeah," Ashley agreed. "What kind of example are you setting for us impressionable teenagers anyway?"

With a groan, Chay released Dana and took a step backward. "Maybe this wasn't such a good idea," he muttered.

Dana made a face at him. "Well, gee, thanks a lot."

"No, honey, I didn't mean kissing you. I meant bringing the girls."

"I thought you said this was their idea?"

"Did I say that?"

"Unless you were lying."

"Well, it wasn't a lie, exactly."

"What was it then, exactly?"

"All right, you caught me. It was my idea. I wanted to see you again, and this was the only reason I could think of for coming up this way."

It was hard to be mad at a man who had lied because he wanted to see her again. But it was still a lie. And even though it was just a tiny little white lie, it still bothered her.

Chay lifted one eyebrow. "What?"

"What do you mean?"

"You're upset about something."

"I don't like lies, even little ones."

"Is that what he did?" Chay asked softly. "Lie to you?"

"Among other things," she replied coolly, and turned away from him.

"Hey, hold on a minute." His long fingers curled around her wrist, drawing her toward him again. "Talk to me, Dana."

She glanced pointedly at the girls, all of whom were watching them avidly.

Chay muttered an oath under his breath. "You're right. This isn't the time or the place." His gaze bored into hers. "But we're gonna talk about this later."

The rest of the afternoon passed pleasantly enough. Dana enjoyed being with the girls, listening while they chatted about which singers they liked best, Ashlee Simpson or Norah Jones, and who had the cutest smile, Orlando Bloom or Johnny Depp. They complained about school and home-work and how unreasonable and demanding parents could be.

By four o'clock, the girls were ready to go home. Chay rounded up the horses and gathered up the baskets and in no time at all, they were riding back down the hill.

Dana again rode behind Chay, her senses filling with his nearness. Not only was he the most handsome man she had ever seen, but he was also the tallest and the most rugged. She knew instinctively that no matter what happened, he could protect her. He was also the sexiest man she had ever met, with his dusky skin and long black hair, not to men-tion his megawatt grin and whiskey-smooth voice.

No doubt about it, she had it bad! And you were through with men, she reminded herself. Ha!

But she couldn't forget he had lied to her. A silly, harm-less lie, to be sure, but then, Rick's lies had seemed harm-less at first, too, and look how that had turned out.

When they reached her place, Chay dismounted. Lifting her from the back of the horse, he walked her to her door. "Thanks for coming with us."

"Thanks for asking me."

"I've got to get these girls back. Remember that barn dance I told you about? Well, it's tonight and they want to go." He shook his head ruefully. "Naturally, I've been assigned to be their driver and chaperon." He cocked his head to one side. "You said no the last time I asked you, but how about going with me?"

"I don't know…"

He ran his knuckles over her cheek. For a touch that was as light as thistledown, it went through her like heat lightning. "Say you'll go with me."

"I'll go with you."

He gave her a quick kiss on the cheek. "We'll pick you up at seven."

"All right. See you then."

"Good. Hang on a minute."

Descending the stairs, he went to Ashley's horse and removed one of the baskets from the saddle.

"Here," he said, handing the basket to Dana.

"Thanks. I suppose you want another pie, since you didn't get any of the last one?"

"That's the idea," Chay admitted with a grin.

"I thought apple was your favorite."

"I like huckleberry, too. See you at seven."

Chapter Six

Wrapped in a fluffy pink towel, Dana stood in front of the closet trying to decide what to wear. She really hadn't brought anything fancy, but then, she hadn't planned on meeting anyone like Chay or being invited to a dance. In the end, she chose a long navy blue and white flowered skirt that was drawn up on one side, exposing a froth of white lace, and a white blouse. She brushed her hair and twisted it into a knot on top of her head, then shook it down again. She pulled on a pair of high-heeled blue sandals, applied some lipstick, splashed on a little perfume and she was ready to go.

Her heartbeat skyrocketed when she heard his knock. Taking a deep breath, she went to answer the door.

Dana sucked in a deep breath when she saw Chay standing on the porch. He was gorgeous. A pair of new black jeans hugged his long legs. He wore a black leather vest over a white western-style shirt. Both complemented his dusky skin and dark eyes.

He touched a forefinger to the brim of his black hat. "Are you ready to go, ma'am?" he asked in his best cowboy twang.

She batted her eyelashes at him. "Why, yes, I am, kind sir."

He offered her his arm. "Your carriage awaits."

Carriage indeed. Dana's eyes widened when she stepped out onto the front porch and saw a long black limousine waiting for her.

Descending the stairs, Chay opened the passenger door for her.

From the back seat, a chorus of female voices called, "Hi, Dana," as she slid onto the butter-soft leather seat.

Smiling, Dana glanced over her shoulder. "Hi, girls."

Ashley lifted a champagne glass filled with soda. "Isn't this great?"

It was better than great. The windows were tinted, the carpets a plush gray to match the seats. There was a small television in the back, as well as a refrigerator.

"Pretty swanky," Dana said as Chay put the car in gear. "Is it a rental?"

"Of course not. It belongs to Big John," Chay said, his reply pitched low for her ears alone. "Like just about everything else in this town."

Dana stared at him, somewhat taken aback by his brusque tone. The bitterness in his voice was unmistakable. "You don't seem to like Big John very much," she remarked. "Why do you work for him?"

"He pays well."

"And that's reason enough to work for someone you don't like?"

He shrugged. "I told you, I've got a few acres here. I run some cattle on it and in another six months or so, the house will be done. It's too much to walk away from."

"You're right, of course. I forgot about the house. I guess it's just hard for me to imagine working for someone I don't like."

"Well, if you've never had to do it, you're lucky."

"Yes," she said wistfully. "Lucky."

Chay pulled up in front of the high school a few minutes later. The girls exploded out of the back of the limo like a covey of quail spooked by a fox.

It was the first time Dana had seen them in anything but jeans. Heads together, they hurried through the door to the gym.

Chay came around to help Dana out of the car. "I hope you like loud music," he said, taking her by the hand.

It had been years since Dana had been to a dance held in a high-school gym. Colorful streamers hung from the ceiling. A long table held bottles of water and cans of Coke. Another table held cakes and pies and cookies. Several adults roamed around the edge of the room, keeping an eye on the kids. Music was provided by a live band. Huge speakers were located at either side of the bandstand. Dana decided loud was an understatement as the singer belted out the latest hit by Alan Jackson.

Chay, Dana and the girls made small talk for a moment, then a tall, good-looking boy sauntered over and asked Ashley to dance.

"That's Brandon DeHaven," Chay said, watching the teenagers melt into the crowd. "His old man owns the spread next to Big John's."

"They look good together," Dana said.

"Yeah. So, how about it?" Chay gestured at the dance floor. "You game?"

"Sure."

The music changed to something sad and slow as he led her out into the middle of the floor and took her in his arms.

"I've never been a country-music fan," Dana said. "Seems like every other song is about broken hearts and starting over."

"Did he break your heart?" Chay asked quietly.

"Are we back to that again?"

"Talk to me, Dana. Tell me what he did to you."

She glanced around. "This isn't the time or the place to discuss it, you know, so why don't you just forget it?"

"I'd like to," he said. "But it's like an itch I can't scratch." Holding her close, he guided her around the floor, his body brushing intimately against her own. "You can trust me, Dana. I won't betray your trust."

"That's what Rick said, in the beginning. He told me that he loved me and he promised that he would never, ever hurt me, or leave me. Only it was all a lie. Everything he ever told me was nothing but a damn lie!"

"I'm sorry, Dana." His voice, soft and low, wrapped around her like a warm cotton quilt. "I'm sorry he hurt you."

"It doesn't matter now. It's over."

"Is it?"

"Yes, and I don't intend to let anyone hurt me again."

"That's no way to live."

"Have you ever been hurt by someone you loved?" she asked. "Someone you trusted? Did you plan a wedding and buy a dress that cost a month's pay and send out the invitations, only to have the man you loved call you the week before the big day and tell you he was marrying someone else?"

Chay swore. "Is that what happened?"

"Yes." Twisting out of his arms, Dana ducked out the side door and into the darkness beyond before she broke into tears and made a complete fool of herself.

She should have known Chay would follow her.

"Dana, wait!"

She would have kept going, but his hand on her arm stayed her. She blinked back the tears that threatened to fall. "Chay, just let it go."

"I would if I could. I know we just met a few days ago, but you're under my skin."

"Like an itch you can't scratch?" she asked, sniffling.

He laughed softly. "I guess you could say that." He pulled a handkerchief out of his pocket and gently wiped her eyes. "Admit it, there's something between us. At least give us a chance to find out if it's worth pursuing."

"What's the point? I'm only going to be here another two weeks."

"Then give me those two weeks."

"You're very persistent."

"You ain't seen nothing yet."

She stared up at him. If she was smart, she would pack up and go home tomorrow, before things got any more complicated than they already were. She liked Chay. She was attracted to him, and that fact scared her half to death. She had been attracted to Rick, too, although what she had felt for Rick was like comparing a summer breeze to a hurricane. There was just no comparison. Her attraction to Rick had never been as strong as what she felt for Chay.

His hand slid up her arm to rest on her shoulder. Heat flowed in the wake of his touch. "Come back inside and let's finish our dance, all right?"

With a nod, she let him lead her back into the gym. He took her in his arms again, their bodies moving together as if they had danced this way for years. His nearness did funny things in the pit of her stomach, made her wish that they were alone somewhere. Made her wish for things she had convinced herself she no longer believed in. The touch of his hand at her waist burned through her blouse, spreading heat up and down her spine. She had danced with lots of men, but it had never been like this. Being in Chay's arms was more than mere dancing.

She was sorry when the song ended. Leaving the dance floor, they moved toward the refreshment tables. She chose a slice of cherry pie; he picked apple. Carrying their plates and cups of hot apple cider, they found a vacant table and sat down. While they ate, he entertained her with humorous stories about the local townspeople, all the while keeping a watchful eye on Brandon DeHaven, who seemed glued to Ashley's side.

Dana was struck again by the uncanny resemblance between Ashley and Chay, though she couldn't pinpoint exactly what it was. Their coloring was different, but there was something about their eyes, the shape of their mouths, even the way they carried themselves.

"Hey, girl, where are you?"

"What? Oh, I was just watching Ashley. She's such a pretty girl."

"Yeah, she sure is. She'd most likely be causing her old man a lot of sleepless nights if he gave a damn about her."

"He must care," Dana said. "If he didn't, why would you be chaperoning her everywhere she goes?"

"It's only for the summer. When it's over, she'll go back to school, and I'll go back to being a cowboy."

"So she doesn't live at the ranch all year?"

"No, just summers and during Christmas vacation."

"That's too bad." Dana took a sip of her drink. "Where's Ashley's mother? You've never mentioned her."

"She hightailed it out of here a couple of years ago."

"Why didn't she take Ashley with her?"

"Big John wouldn't let her."

"But if he doesn't really care…"

"Big John keeps what he wants to keep, one way or another." Big John had given Chay a thousand acres of prime grassland, figuring that the land and the promise of having his own ranch one day would be the one thing Chay couldn't walk away from. Big John had been wrong about that, he just didn't know it. The one thing Chay didn't understand was why the old man wanted to keep him around. They hadn't exchanged two congenial words in the last fifteen years. It didn't make sense, but then, Big John did a lot of things that didn't make sense. Chay had stopped trying to figure the old man out years ago.

Chay watched Ashley laugh at something Brandon said. Ashley was the only reason he stayed on at the ranch. He could have walked away from the old man. He could have left the thousand acres he owned without a backward glance. But he couldn't walk out on Ashley. She needed somebody on her side, and Chay was all she had. He had loved Ashley from the moment Jillian brought her home from the hospital, had been her slave ever since the day her dimpled fingers first curled around his fourteen years ago. Once she learned to walk, she had followed him around the ranch, wanting to be wherever he was, wanting to do everything he did. He was still living in the main house back then and she was always sneaking into his bed at night. Years later, it had been Chay she had turned to for comfort when her mother packed up and left the ranch, Chay she talked to in the middle of the night whenever something was bothering her. Sometimes he felt more like her father than her half brother.

He glanced at Dana when she tugged at his arm.

"So," she asked, "where were *you?*"

"Just remembering when she used to follow me around like a puppy, copying everything I did. Treating me like I'm her big brother."

"I always wanted an older brother or even a sister, but my mom couldn't have any more kids after I was born. Do you have brothers or sisters?"

Chay hesitated a moment, and then shook his head. As much as he wanted to tell Dana the truth, he couldn't do it. Years ago, Big John had made Chay promise that he would never tell anyone that Ashley was his half sister. Even now, Chay wasn't sure why. He doubted Big John gave a damn what his neighbors or anyone else thought of him. Big John had had a brief affair with Chay's mother.

Since then, he had been married four times. None of his wives since Jillian had stayed around more than two or three years. The old man had sworn off marriage after the last one left. The last Chay had heard, Big John was keeping company with Georgia Cookson. Georgia owned a boutique in town. She was a voluptuous blonde, at least fifteen years younger than the old man.

"Sad, to be all alone in the world," Dana murmured.

"Yeah. Looks like the party's breaking up. I'll go round up the girls."

"Okay."

She watched Chay move through the crowd. It was easy to follow his progress across the room; he stood head and shoulders above just about everyone else. Though she couldn't hear what was being said, it was obvious that Ashley and Chay were having an argument. Judging from the sullen expression on Ashley's face as she followed Chay across the floor, Dana guessed Ashley wanted to spend more time with Brandon. Dana couldn't blame her. Brandon was a good-looking, clean-cut kid and seemed very nice.

Once they were all in the limo, Ashley's mood brightened up. The girls laughed and giggled on the drive back to Dana's house, comparing notes on the boys they had danced with, occasionally making catty remarks about some of the other girls.

Chay pulled up in front of Dana's house. Getting out of the car, he walked around the front and opened Dana's door for her.

There were good-natured hoots and catcalls as he walked Dana up the steps to her door.

"Thank you," she said. "I had a nice time."

"Me, too."

"Hurry up and kiss her," Megan hollered.

"Yeah," LuAnn said. "Get it over with so we can go home!"

Chay laughed softly. "What do you say?"

"We shouldn't disappoint them," Dana murmured.

"No," Chay agreed. "We wouldn't want to do that."

Dana looked up at him, her heart beating triple time as he lowered his head. She closed her eyes as his lips claimed hers. Since there were four teenage girls in the car looking on, Dana had expected a quick kiss good-night, but Chay was in no hurry. His lips moved slowly over hers, his tongue lightly stroking her lower lip as his arms drew her body up against his.

Dana leaned into him, grateful for his support as her legs turned to jelly. Her every sense was aware of the man holding her in his arms. She ran her hands up and down his broad back, a shiver skittering down her spine as she felt his arousal. She was grateful she was a woman. She might be every bit as hot and bothered as he was, but at least it didn't show!

She moaned softly, wondering how it was possible for one kiss to affect her so quickly.

She stared up at him, mutinous, when he took his lips from hers.

"I know, sweetheart," he said, his voice low. "We'll continue this some other time when we don't have an audience."

Only then did she remember Ashley and her friends were watching avidly from the windows of the limo.

Chay kissed her again, then, whistling softly, he descended the steps to the car and slid behind the wheel.

Grateful for the shadows that hid her blush, Dana waved at the girls, then stood on the top step, watching the taillights of the limo grow fainter and fainter until they were out of sight.

Chapter Seven

The next morning after breakfast, Dana put on a pair of well-worn jeans, a T-shirt and a pair of boots and headed for the garage. Inside, she found a handsaw and an old pair of work gloves. She glanced around the garage, thinking it could use a good cleaning. There were old tools and boxes piled in one corner along with bits of old tack and coils of rope. But cleaning out the garage was a project for another day.

Pulling on the gloves, she went out to tackle the big old dead tree in the backyard. It was really a foolish endeavor. There was no way she could cut down the trunk or remove the stump unless she called a professional, no way she could cut off the highest limbs, since she didn't have a ladder that was tall enough to reach them. On top of all that, she was only going to be here for less than two weeks, so what did it matter? In spite of all the obstacles, it was something to do.

It took her two hours to saw off four of the lower limbs. She had never been much for hard physical labor, but she found the task oddly satisfying. And since the wood was so dry, it would make great firewood. Of course, she wouldn't have much need for firewood anytime soon, since she would be back home long before winter set in.

Deciding it was time for a break, she removed her gloves and went into the house for an apple and a glass of lemonade.

Sitting at the kitchen table, her thoughts turned to Chay. Nothing unusual about that, she thought dryly, since it seemed that hardly an hour went by when she wasn't thinking of him. Or dreaming of him, like last night. Oh, my, what a dream that had been!

She smiled just thinking about it. They had been at the lake, just the two of them. In her dream, she had found the courage to overcome her self-consciousness and her modesty and go skinny-dipping with Chay. It had been glorious, exhilarating, though she couldn't say why. She was naked when she took a bath, but swimming in the nude was completely different. Maybe it was the feel of the water moving over her nakedness. Maybe it was the touch of Chay's gaze on her bare skin....

She felt herself blush as she recalled how they had made love on a blanket under the bold blue sky. Of course, since she had never gone all the way, parts of her dream had been a little sketchy, but the buildup had been explosive.

Pressing the cool glass to her forehead, she closed her eyes. If a dream could get her that worked up, what would the real thing be like?

She drank the last of the lemonade, put the glass in the sink and went out the back door, pulling on her gloves as she walked toward the old tree.

With the lower branches gone, it looked even more pathetic than it had before. It looked taller, too, she thought, gazing up. There was a stepladder in the garage that would allow her to reach the next three or four branches.

"No point in stopping now," she muttered, and set off toward the garage.

She was coming out of the garage, carrying the ladder, when Chay drove up.

Her heart seemed to skip a beat the moment she saw him.

With a wave of his hand, he parked in front of the porch and got out of the truck. "Hey, what's the ladder for?"

"I'm cutting down a tree in the backyard."

"I don't believe it."

"Well, it's true!"

"Here, let me carry that," he said, relieving her of her burden.

"Thanks. I could have carried it, you know. I'm not helpless."

"I never said you were," Chay replied.

In spite of her words to the contrary, she was glad she didn't have to tote the heavy ladder. Made of wood, it was as tall as she was, and weighed almost as much.

Chay grunted softly when he saw the tree. "Were you planning to cut down the whole thing?" he asked, glancing at her over his shoulder.

"Hardly. I was just…" She shrugged. "Pruning it."

Laughing out loud, he put the ladder down next to the tree, then pulled a pair of leather gloves from his back pocket. Grabbing the saw, he climbed to the top of the ladder and began sawing the nearest branch.

Dana watched the play of muscles beneath his chambray shirt. Being a modern woman, she should have been offended that he had so high-handedly assumed that he could do the job better than she could. Of course, it was hard to be offended when he was right. Then, too, letting him take over gave her a chance to watch him work, something that was extremely enjoyable.

Standing in the shade, she admired the way his jeans molded his tight buns and hugged the length of his long, long legs. She admired the width of his powerful shoulders, the ease with which he cut through a branch as thick as her thigh, the way his muscles bunched and relaxed as he tackled the next branch, and then all the ones within reach in the time it had taken her to saw through one.

She laughed softly. Sometimes it just took a man to do a man's job, and my oh my, but Chay was all man.

"What are you laughing at?" Chay asked, glancing down at her.

"Oh, nothing."

"Uh-huh. We need a taller ladder. I can climb up a little higher and get the next few branches, but—"

"Oh, I don't think that's a good idea!"

"Worried about me?" he asked with a wicked gleam in his eye.

"What if I am?"

"Just checking." Climbing down from the ladder, he studied the tree for a few moments. "I think maybe it would be easier to just cut the tree down and then chop it up for firewood."

"Why didn't you think of that sooner?"

His gaze moved over her, long and slow and hot. "I had other things on my mind," he said. "The way you were watching me nearly singed my back pockets."

"I wasn't watching you!"

"No?" he asked, a challenge in his eyes.

"Well, maybe a little," she admitted.

He lifted one eyebrow. "Just a little?"

"Oh, for goodness' sake, just cut down the tree."

"All in good time. We need to discuss my payment first."

"Payment! What kind of payment?"

"I'll think of something." His gaze lingered on her lips. "Let's see…" He counted the branches he had already cut.

"Nine branches." He looked thoughtful for a moment. "How about a kiss for each branch? That sounds about right to me."

"You're kidding!" she exclaimed, but her stomach was already turning somersaults at the thought of his mouth on hers.

"Too much?" he asked, smothering a grin.

"Well, perhaps not."

"Okay," he said in a brisk, businesslike tone. "Nine kisses and one glass of lemonade."

She was laughing now.

The sound wrapped around Chay's heart. It was good to see her smile and hear her laughter. "So," he said, "do you want to pay up now?"

"Do you want to collect your pay all at once?"

He nodded. "I think so." He pulled her into his arms. "Remember, we still have to discuss the payment for cutting down the tree and chopping it into firewood."

"I'm not sure I can afford that."

"I'll go easy on you," he murmured as he drew her closer.

She swallowed hard. "Will you?" she asked breathlessly.

"Trust me," he said, and kissed her.

Liquid heat flowed through her veins as his mouth settled over hers in a long, drawn-out kiss.

He drew back, a mischievous look in his eyes. "That's one."

She blinked up at him. "I'm not sure I'll survive two."

"Sure you will, darlin'," he said. "Just hang on tight."

To her amazement, each kiss was a little different from the last. Where the first was long and slow, the second was as quick as a flash of lightning and charged with electricity. The third was a delicious dueling of tongues, the fourth, fifth and sixth were a series of quick butterfly kisses on the tip of her nose and her eyelids. After the seventh, she lost the ability to think. She was drowning in an ocean of sensation, her whole body aching and alive and yearning for more than kisses. Much more.

When he withdrew his lips from hers, it took her a moment to realize that he was no longer kissing her.

"Nine," he said.

She nodded.

"I think I should have asked for more."

Dana shook her head. One more kiss, and she would have been pulling him down on the grass and begging him to make love to her. And she didn't want that, wasn't ready for that. Was she?

"Hey." He chucked her under the chin. "You still owe me a glass of lemonade."

"What? Oh, yes, of course." Turning on her heel, she hurried toward the house. Space, that was what she needed.

But it wasn't to be. Chay followed her through the back door and into the kitchen, stood with his hip braced against the corner of the counter while she filled two glasses with ice and lemonade, then handed him one. She took a long drink, hoping to put out the fire that was still roaring through her. If his kisses could make her feel like this, what would making love to him be like?

Chapter Eight

The memory of Chay's kisses stayed with Dana long after Chay had gone home. Because he had work to do at the ranch, he had told her he would be back tomorrow to finish cutting down the tree, payment to be determined later.

The thought of what that payment might be kept her awake into the wee small hours of the morning and followed her into her dreams when she finally fell asleep, dreams that featured a tall, dusky-skinned man riding across the prairie on a big black horse. In her dream, he rescued her from a horrible fate—on waking, she couldn't remember what it was—then carried her away with him to a hide tepee pitched beside a bubbling brook where he took her into his arms and made love to her for hours and hours.

She woke to the touch of the sun on her face, expecting to find him lying there beside her.

She shook off her disappointment at waking in bed, alone.

"Geez, get a grip, Dana Elizabeth Westlake!" she muttered. "Have you already forgotten about Rick? No matter how sexy Chay Lone Elk might be, he's not for you, remember? You've sworn off men for life!"

But she couldn't stop thinking about him. Not through breakfast or while she was washing the dishes or in the shower or while she was throwing her dirty jeans into the washer. The worst part was, even though she kept telling herself to forget him, she didn't really want to.

He hadn't said what time he would be there today so, of course, no matter where she was or what she was doing, she kept going to the front window or the door, hoping for a sign of him.

It was just after lunchtime when he drove up.

As usual, butterflies erupted in her stomach at the mere sight of him. Today, he wore a pair of faded blue jeans and a plaid shirt with the sleeves rolled up to his elbows. She watched him slide out of the cab of the truck, her gaze drawn to him like the proverbial moth to a flame. And, like the moth, her fate would be sealed if she let him get too close. Reaching into the back of the truck, he pulled out a saw, not an old rusty handsaw like the one she had been using the day before, but a nice shiny new chain saw with a wicked-looking blade.

He held it up and grinned at her. "It's important to have the right tool for the right job."

"Looks dangerous."

He shrugged. "It can be." He drew on a pair of heavy work gloves. "That's why I'm going to be very, very careful."

She nodded. "Anything I can do?"

"Just stay out of the way," he said, putting on a pair of safety glasses.

"I can do that."

With a wink, he walked over to the tree and set to work. Soon the air was filled with the whine of the saw. Wood chips exploded through the air. A bird hopped from branch to branch and finally, with an angry screech, flew off in search of quieter lodgings.

It was while she was watching Chay cut through the trunk that she remembered they hadn't discussed what his payment would be.

Would he ask for more kisses? The mere thought made her heart race. Or would he ask for something else? Something more intimate than kisses? That thought sent a rush of heat to her cheeks. But of course he wouldn't ask for *that!* She told herself she was relieved and tried to make herself believe it.

Noting the way he was sweating while he worked, she went into the house to make a pitcher of fresh lemonade. She had made another apple pie the night before—because she happened to have a lot of apples, of course. She cut a large slice for Chay, a smaller one for herself, put the plates, two glasses filled with ice and the pitcher on a tray, and carried them outside, only then noticing the quiet. Was he finished already?

Rounding the corner of the house, she saw that he had stopped working and that he was no longer alone. Ashley had arrived and the two of them were so deep in conversation that neither of them noticed Dana's presence.

"…and talk to him!" Ashley was saying. "He won't listen to me."

"You're only fifteen," Chay said.

Ashley straightened her shoulders and stuck out her chest, displaying an impressive amount of cleavage. "I'm almost sixteen!"

"A vast age, to be sure."

"Oh! I can't believe it! You're siding with him! I thought you'd be on *my* side." Ashley turned her back on Chay. Noticing Dana for the first time, she said, "You'd let me go on a double date, wouldn't you?"

"At fifteen? I don't think so.'

"Why is it grown-ups always stick together?" Ashley exclaimed. She turned to face Chay again. "In the old days, women were having babies at my age. And I'll be sixteen next month!"

"They're still having babies at your age," Chay remarked dryly, "which is probably why your old man won't let you go out on a date."

Ashley sent a look at Chay that could have peeled paint off a wall, then, with a huff that clearly said she was fed up with the entire adult population, she jumped on the back of her horse and rode out of the yard.

Muttering something under his breath, Chay stared after her.

Dana set the tray on a crate, then handed Chay one of the glasses. "Here, you look like you need something to help you cool off."

"Thanks." He shook his head. "Kids. Why do they all want to grow up so fast?"

Dana picked up the other glass. "Didn't you, when you were that age?"

"Yeah, I guess so. The thing is, Ashley and her old man don't get along and they can't talk to each other. They never could. A girl that age needs a mother, or at least a woman to look after her. All Ashley's got is the old man's housekeeper and she's so old, I'm sure she's forgotten what it was like to be young."

"It's never easy, is it?"

"No."

"Are you hungry?" she asked, gesturing at the tray.

Chay picked up one of the plates. "My favorite."

She shrugged. "It's no big deal. I had a lot of apples and I didn't want them to go to waste."

"Uh-huh." He wolfed down the pie, then smacked his lips appreciatively. "You know what they say, don't you? About the way to a man's heart?"

"Yeah, right."

"So," he asked, "what happened to all those huckleberries?"

She shrugged. "I decided to make jam out of them."

He grinned a knowing grin. "You made this apple pie because you know it's my favorite. Admit it."

"Maybe I did," she said, stifling a grin. "And maybe I didn't."

"You did," he said confidently. "You can't fool me."

Lifting the glass, he drained it in three long swallows. Setting it aside, he wrapped one long muscular arm around Dana's waist and drew her close.

"What are you doing?" she exclaimed.

"What do you think?" Lowering his head, he kissed her, long and deep. "I'm collecting part of my payment in advance."

"Oh."

He winked at her. "We'll talk about the balance later," he said with a roguish grin.

Replacing his safety glasses, he grabbed up the chain saw and went back to work.

Too nervous to sit still, Dana carried the tray back into the house. Standing at the sink, she washed the plates, her gaze constantly straying toward Chay. She had known him for less than two weeks. How had he become so important in such a short time? And how was she to know what she really felt for him? She knew very little about the man, yet he occupied practically every waking moment, and most of her sleeping ones!

Maybe it was just a case of good old-fashioned lust. After all, he was tall, dark and handsome and blessed with enough charisma for a dozen movie stars. It didn't hurt that he looked good sitting a horse or wearing a cowboy hat, or that he had a hard lean muscular body that beckoned her touch. She reminded herself that there was more to love than just physical attraction, that it took time to get to really know and care about someone, and that the only way to do that was to spend a lot of time together. And she didn't have a lot of time. In less than two weeks, she would be back at work in Ashton Falls, with no hope of any more time off until her vacation next year.

She washed the forks and glasses, then picked up a towel and began to dry the dishes. In a year, Chay Lone Elk would be nothing but a pleasant memory. But until then, she couldn't seem to stop watching him!

She watched appreciatively as he approached the back door. He rapped his knuckles on the wood, then stepped into the kitchen.

"All done?" she asked.

He pulled off his gloves and shoved them into the back pocket of his jeans. "Yep. Got any of that lemonade left?"

"Sure." She poured him a glass, watched with something akin to fascination as he gulped it down, then dragged the back of his hand across his mouth.

"So," he said, "I'm thinking dinner and a movie on Friday night might just take care of the balance due."

"Is that right?"

"I'd like to make it sooner, but I'll be busy running the girls around until then. So, how does Friday night sound?" His gaze moved over her ever so slowly. "Of course, if that doesn't suit you, I could probably think of something else. Something a little more intimate." His gaze lingered on her lips. "You wouldn't even have to leave home."

"Pick me up at seven."

"Another hope crushed!" He grinned good-naturedly. "Seven it is." He handed her his empty glass. "See you then."

Thursday morning after breakfast, Dana went into town. As she walked down the street, window-shopping and pausing now and then to say hello to people she hadn't seen in years, she was surprised to find herself wondering what it would be like to live there. True, it wasn't a big city like Ashton Falls, but there was something to be said for living in a town where everyone knew you and you knew everyone. Even though she hadn't been in Wardman's Hollow for several years, people remembered her. Back home, she didn't even know her neighbors, and she had lived next to them for over three years. Walking down the streets at home, she never saw anyone she knew. At night, she made sure all the doors and windows in the house were locked.

She ate lunch at the café, then went to Wright's and picked up a few groceries. She took the long way home, admiring the beauty of the countryside. Back in Ashton Falls, there was little to see but look-alike houses and tall buildings with mirrored windows. Out here, cows and horses grazed in pastures on both sides of the road. There were trees and mountains, hay fields and haystacks, vacant lots dotted with wildflowers, men riding tractors, kids riding horses. The sky was a gorgeous blue, the air clean and filled with the scents of hay and grass instead of gray and smoggy. Once, she pulled off the road and spent ten minutes watching an eagle soar overhead.

She spent the rest of the day considering the pros and cons of moving to Wardman's Hollow. Of course, it all boiled down to Chay Lone Elk. Did she want to give up her job and her life in Ashton Falls for a man she had met less than two weeks ago? Did she want to risk her heart again so soon? And what if nothing came of her attraction to him? Would she still want to live here?

She shook her head. Her life sounded like a soap opera. Will John come home? Will Mary find love again? Tune in next week, same time, same station.

Friday morning bloomed bright and clear. Dana's first thought on rising was that she had a date with Chay. He was in her thoughts constantly, whether she was changing the sheets on the bed or washing the breakfast dishes. She wondered what he was doing and if she was in his thoughts the way he was forever in hers.

She was thumbing through a fashion magazine she had picked up at the store when the phone rang.

"Hello?"

"Seven o'clock," said a deep male voice. "Don't forget."

Dana smiled. "I'll be ready."

"Can you be ready at six?" he asked. "I don't think I can wait until seven."

She smiled. "I can't wait, either, but what about the girls?"

"Big John's home. The girls decided to stay in tonight. They're going to roast marshmallows in the fireplace and watch some DVDs. So, what have you been doing all day?"

"Thinking about you, mostly," she admitted.

"Really?" She heard the smile in his voice. "Well, darlin', I've been thinking about you, too." She heard voices in the background, then he said, "Listen, I've got to go."

"All right."

"See you soon."

"Bye." Smiling, she hung up the phone.

She was on pins and needles the rest of the day. At four, she took a long bubble bath, then washed and blow-dried her hair. By five-thirty, she had tried on every outfit she had brought with her at least twice. At five forty-five, she decided on a pink-and-white-print sundress and a pair of sandals. She ran a brush through her hair, applied a fresh coat of lipstick and managed to look calm and cool when he knocked on the door ten minutes later, even though her heart was beating a mile a minute.

As always, her breath caught in her throat at the sight of him. Tonight, he wore black jeans and a long-sleeved black shirt over a white T-shirt.

He whistled under his breath when he saw her. "Honey, you look good enough to eat."

"Thank you." She knew she was blushing but she couldn't help it. She knew the pink-and-white sundress she had chosen flattered both her figure and her complexion, but nobody had ever looked at her quite the way Chay was looking at her.

Taking her by the hand, he led her out of the house and down the stairs. He held the truck door open for her, then slid behind the wheel and gunned the engine to life.

"Where are we going?" she asked.

"I thought we'd go to the steak house, if that's okay with you."

She nodded. She wasn't much for red meat, but the steak house served a great Cobb salad and had some of the best sourdough bread she had ever eaten.

"How's Ashley doing?" she asked.

"I don't know. She and the old man got into it again just before I left. Seems like all they do is argue lately. Ashley locked herself in her room and wouldn't come out. The Three Musketeers are hiding out in the family room watching a movie. I tried to talk to Ashley, but she wasn't having any. And Big John…" Chay shook his head in disgust. "He doesn't give a rat's…sorry. I just wish he'd…"

Chay's voice trailed off when he saw the curiosity in Dana's eyes. His hand tightened on the wheel. He should tell her the truth, he thought, tell her the whole ugly thing, but why go into it? Dana would only be here for another week or so. What was the point in airing the old man's dirty laundry?

"Chay? Hey, where'd you go? One minute you're here, and the next you're a million miles away."

"What? Oh, sorry. Do you want me to come by tomorrow and cut that tree up for firewood?"

"Did I miss something?"

"What do you mean?"

"We were talking about Ashley and the trouble she's having with her father."

"Yeah, well, why don't we talk about something a little more cheerful?"

"Like what?"

"Practically anything. What do you like to do when you're not appraising antiques?"

"Oh, lots of things. Read. Jog. Go to the movies. What are we going to see tonight?"

"Whatever's playing," he said with a grin. "With only one theater in town, there's not a whole heck of a lot of choice."

"Right. I forgot."

Chay pulled into the restaurant parking lot a few minutes later. Inside, they were seated immediately.

Dana glanced around. "The place hasn't changed much since I was here last," she remarked. "Same tablecloths, same paper on the walls. Is the food still as good?"

"Best in town."

He looked up and smiled as the waitress came to take their order. In true manly fashion, he ordered a steak, rare, with all the trimmings, and a cup of coffee, black. She ordered the Cobb salad and a glass of iced tea.

They made small talk for a few minutes and then Chay started telling her about the ranch house he was building, describing it so beautifully that she could see it clearly in her mind, the big country kitchen, a living room with a big stone fireplace, a bedroom that faced the east, a front porch that faced the west so he could sit there in the evening and watch the sun set. "Of course, there's not much to see now," he said. "Just the foundation and a frame, but one of these days…"

"It sounds wonderful," she remarked. "I can't wait to see it…" Her voice trailed off. She would be long gone before his house was completed.

During dinner, she told him about some of the rare antique vases and furniture she had appraised. "I love the look and feel of old oak," she said. "It's so beautiful. In the old days, men took pride in their work, you know? You can almost see the love they put into each piece. You're laughing at me," she said when he grinned.

"No, not at all. It just seems, I don't know, odd to hear a pretty, young woman carrying on about antiques." He grinned at her. "I always thought appraisers were a bunch of old men who were almost as ancient as the pieces they appraised."

"Very funny."

He gestured at her plate. "You about done there? The show starts in fifteen minutes."

She nodded. "I'm through. And I'm stuffed."

"Good. I won't have to buy you any popcorn."

"No popcorn? Then I'm not going."

Grinning, he paid the check and they left the restaurant. They reached the theater with five minutes to spare.

"Where do you like to sit?" Chay asked. "Front or back?"

"Either one."

"I like the back," he said. "Here's two together."

The theater lights went off just as they sat down. Chay reached for her hand, his fingers threading through hers. The touch sent little frissons of pleasure moving through her.

The previews were still rolling when Chay's fingers tightened on her hand. "Is something wrong?" she whispered.

He swore softly. "Ashley's here."

"What? Where?" Dana peered into the darkness.

"Over there, on the aisle."

Leaning forward a little, Dana saw Ashley sitting beside a tall young man with long blond hair. "I thought you said she'd locked herself in her room?"

"Yeah. Dammit! What was she thinking?" He ran a hand through his hair. "If the old man finds out…"

"Relax," Dana whispered. "You can't do anything about it now."

"Yeah. Yeah, you're right." He settled back in his seat. A moment later, the movie began.

She didn't think Chay saw much of the movie. He spent most of the time watching Ashley. And Dana spent most of her time watching him and wondering why he was so concerned about his employer's teenage daughter. Not that that was a bad thing. She was glad he took his responsibility seriously. It was just that his worry seemed out of proportion, almost obsessive, somehow. He worried about Ashley as if she were a part of his family…but that was ridiculous. If Ashley were related to Chay, he would have told her so. Besides, they didn't act as if they were even remotely related.

With a shake of her head, Dana turned her attention back to the screen.

When the movie was over, Chay stood but didn't leave the theater. When Ashley and her boyfriend approached, Chay stepped out into the aisle, blocking their path.

"Chay!" Ashley's eyes grew wide. "What are *you* doing here?"

"I might ask you the same thing. Come on, let's get out of here."

"I'm going home with Nick."

Dana got her first good look at the boy beside Ashley. Blond and blue-eyed, he wore a cutoff sweatshirt and a pair of jeans with a hole in the knee. He had a gold hoop in one ear, and a tattoo of a spider spinning a web on his left shoulder. Dana thought he looked as if he was in his early twenties, far too old to be dating a girl on the shy side of sixteen.

She glanced at Ashley. She wore a bright pink tube top, a pair of skintight red jeans, lavender eye shadow and purple lipstick. Dana was shocked by the girl's appearance.

Had she seen her on the street, she wasn't sure she would have recognized her. Always before, Ashley had been clean-scrubbed and well dressed.

"You're going home with me," Chay said. "Right now." He fixed the boy with a hard stare. "I don't want to see you around my…" Chay cleared his throat. "I don't want to see you with Ashley again, you got that?"

Nick nodded sullenly.

Taking Ashley by the hand, Chay turned and headed for the door, practically dragging her along behind him. Dana hurried after them.

Once they reached the parking lot, Chay rounded on Ashley. "What the hell were you thinking, going out dressed like that?" he demanded angrily. "Don't you care what people think?"

"How could you humiliate me like that?" Ashley replied heatedly.

"You should be humiliated, to be seen in public with that scumbag. What would your father say? Where'd you meet that loser, anyway?"

Ashley glared at him. "I met him at a party, if you must know. As for my dad, he doesn't even know I'm alive! I don't care what he thinks."

"Well, you'd damn well better care unless you want to spend the rest of your life locked in your room."

"You had no right to interfere like that," Ashley said hotly. "You're not my keeper!"

"No, but you sure need one."

"Everyone treats me like a child!"

"When we get back to the ranch, I'll tell the old man that Dana and I took you to the movies."

"Tell him the truth. I don't care!"

Chay blew out a breath of exasperation. "Listen, Ashley, I'm just trying to keep you out of trouble."

"Oh! You're just like my dad, always trying to keep me

from having any fun," she muttered, and lapsed into a sullen silence.

"Dana, do you mind if I take you home first?"

"No, of course not."

They reached her place a short time later. Chay parked the truck, opened the door for her and walked her to the porch.

"I'm sorry," he said. "This isn't exactly the way I thought the evening would end."

"It's all right."

He drew her into his arms. "What are you doing tomorrow?"

Tomorrow! If Rick hadn't deserted her, it would have been her wedding day. "I…I think I'm just going to stay home."

He drew back a little. "I see."

"No," she said. "You don't."

"Then tell me."

How could she say it out loud?

"Come on, Dana, you can tell me anything. I don't want any secrets between us." He felt a little guilty as he said the last, since he was keeping several secrets from her.

"Tomorrow was supposed to be my wedding day."

He drew her back into his arms. "I'm sorry, honey. I guess there isn't much I can say to make things better."

She hid her face against his shoulder so he couldn't see her tears. He was right, there were no words to ease her pain, but it felt good to be in his arms, to hear his voice murmuring soft words of comfort. Did she dare trust her feelings for this man? Or was she just asking for another heartache? She had vowed never to love again, but she had been drawn to Chay from the first. Maybe it was fate. Maybe she was just on the rebound.

"Don't stay home alone tomorrow," he said, dropping a kiss on the crown of her head. "It's the old man's birthday tomorrow and he's giving himself a big party. Barbecue, rodeo, dancing, the whole nine yards. Say you'll come and cheer me on when I ride."

She had to admit it sounded a lot better than staying home alone, feeling sorry for herself. "You're going to ride in the rodeo?"

"You bet."

"Okay, I'll go," she said. "What time?"

He tapped her chin with his forefinger. "That's my girl. I'll pick you up around noon. The rodeo starts at one."

"What should I wear?"

"Jeans and a T-shirt are fine, but you might want to bring a dress along for later."

"All right."

He hugged her and then, no doubt mindful of Ashley watching them from inside the truck, he kissed her quickly. "Sweet dreams."

She murmured, "Good night," and then, as she had so often in the last few days, she stood on the porch and watched him drive away until he was out of sight.

Chapter Nine

Chay glanced at Ashley. She had moved as far away from him as she could get. She was staring out the passenger window, her arms folded across her chest.

"Is this the first time you've snuck out to meet that loser?" he asked.

"What difference does it make? It's none of your business, anyway."

"Did you look at yourself in the mirror before you left the house?"

"So you really don't like my outfit?"

"Not much. What look were you going for? Teenage hooker of the month?"

"Very funny. Don't you think I look sexy? Nick does."

"I think you look ridiculous."

She glared at him. "I do not."

"You don't see Dana parading around like that. What happened to Brandon? I thought you were stuck on him?"

She shrugged. "I like him okay, but Nick's…" She lifted a hand and let it fall.

"Exciting?" Chay supplied dryly. "Forbidden?" He grunted softly, knowing he was on the right track by the look on her face. "You'd better hope we can sneak you into the house before Big John gets a look at the way you're dressed. If he says anything about your being gone, I'll tell him Dana and I took you to the movies with us."

"What makes you think he'll believe you? And what excuse will you give for not taking Megan and LuAnn and Brittany?"

"I don't know. I'll think of something."

"Even if he believes you, I'll still be in trouble," she said. "He'll yell at me for not telling him that I was going and then yell at me for going off with you when I had company."

"Like I said, I'll tell him it was just a misunderstanding, that I thought you'd told him, and that you thought I did. I'll tell him I asked the other girls and they didn't want to go. When we get home, you hightail it up to your room and wash that crap off your face, then get into bed. I'll talk to your old man."

"All right."

"Just promise me you won't pull a stunt like this again."

"I love Nick."

"Love! You don't even know what the word means. Besides, he's too old for you. Didn't you ever ask yourself why he isn't dating girls closer to his own age?"

"He loves me."

Chay swore under his breath. "How long have you known him?"

"Not very long," she admitted sullenly.

Chay took a deep breath. Anger and recriminations weren't the answer. "Listen, honey, you're gonna meet a lot of guys before you find the right one. But right now you need to be careful. There are a lot of guys out there who'll take advantage of you if they can. I don't want you to get hurt. Or to wind up pregnant."

"Is that all you're worried about? That I'll get pregnant?"

"I don't want you to get hurt, Ashley. I don't want to see you make a mistake that will ruin the rest of your life."

"Is that what you think babies do, ruin your life?"

"They do when you're fifteen and unmarried. Whether you keep it or give it away, you'll never be the same. Enjoy being young, Ashley. Don't get caught up in things you're not old enough to handle."

He pulled up alongside the house and cut the engine. "Get going."

He watched her shimmy up the tree that grew alongside the house and made a quick mental note to have one of the men cut off the big branch outside her window first thing in the morning.

Exiting the truck, he went into the house. He found Big John in the kitchen.

"Have you seen Ashley?" Big John asked. "She's been missing all night. Those silly girls said they didn't know where she was."

"She's fine. I took her to the movies."

"The movies! Why the hell didn't you tell me?"

"I thought she did."

"Well, she damn well didn't! I was just about to call the police. Where is she now?"

"Calm down. She's upstairs getting ready for bed."

"I'll be glad when she goes back to school."

"I'll miss you, too, Daddy."

Big John whirled around at the sound of his daughter's voice. Ashley stood in the doorway wearing a bathrobe over a pair of pajamas, her face scrubbed clean. Tears glistened in her eyes. Before Big John could say anything, she turned and ran down the hall.

Chay heard her footsteps running up the stairs, the slam of a door.

Big John muttered something under his breath, then stalked out of the room.

Chay let out a heavy sigh, wondering if Ashley and the old man would ever find a way to get along. As far back as Chay could remember, the two of them had been at loggerheads. Big John had no patience for her, no time to spend with his only daughter.

Leaving the house, Chay determined that, in the future, he would keep a closer eye on Ashley's comings and goings whether she liked it or not.

Chapter Ten

It would have been her wedding day.

It was Dana's first thought when she woke on Saturday morning. Feeling thoroughly depressed, she stared up at the ceiling, overcome with a sense of lethargy. She never should have agreed to go to the barbecue with Chay today. She wasn't going to be good company for herself or anyone else. She hated feeling this way. She wasn't the first woman this had happened to and she wouldn't be the last. Why couldn't she just shake it off and get on with her life? It wasn't the end of the world.

She needed to call home. She had called her mother when she arrived at the Hollow, but that had been weeks ago. She had put off calling again because she didn't want to talk about Rick. Surprisingly, she had rarely thought of him at all, thanks to her infatuation with Chay.

She glanced out the window. It was a beautiful day. The words *happy is the bride the sun shines on* drifted through her mind. She wondered if it had been sunny on the day

Rick married his new love. Rather uncharitably, she hoped there had been a cloudburst!

With a sigh, she grabbed a book and went into the bathroom where she took a long hot bubble bath. She didn't get out until the water was almost cold.

After dressing, she went downstairs and drank a glass of orange juice, then fixed herself a cup of strong black coffee.

She was stalling, but no matter how long she put it off, sooner or later she had to call her mother.

She felt a little better when she hung up thirty minutes later. Her mother, bless her heart, had taken care of everything, just as she'd said she would. She had called the guests, canceled the church and the flowers and the caterer, returned all the gifts. Friends and family had been sympathetic, her mother said, expressing their love and their regrets that things hadn't worked out.

Dana stared at the phone, thinking that she should just call Chay and tell him she couldn't make it. She was reaching for the phone when it rang. She knew, somehow, that it was him.

Lifting the receiver, she murmured a quiet hello.

"Good morning."

A familiar warmth filled her at the sound of his voice. "Good morning. I was just about to call you."

"I hope that means you were missing me as much as I was missing you," he said, and she heard the smile in his voice. "Any chance I could pick you up at eleven instead of noon?"

She opened her mouth, intending to tell him that she had changed her mind and that she wouldn't be going, but her heart had other ideas. "I'll be ready."

"Good. See you soon."

She hung up the receiver and glanced at the clock. Ten-fifteen! If she was going to be ready by eleven, she had to hurry!

* * *

Chay arrived at eleven on the dot. He was clad in a pair of faded blue jeans, a slipover buckskin shirt with fringe dangling from the sleeves and snakeskin boots. There was no mistaking his Indian heritage today.

"Hi, cowboy," she said, opening the door for him.

"Hey, gorgeous." He kissed her on the cheek. "Are you ready?"

"Yes, just let me grab my bag." It was amazing, but just the thought of spending the day with him chased all the dark clouds from her mind. Who needed Rick when Chay was here?

She picked up her bag, which held a sweater in case it got cool, a dress and shoes for later, a brush, comb and her makeup.

Chay opened the truck door for her, winked at her, then went around to the driver's side and slid behind the wheel.

"Ready for a good time?" he asked.

She smiled at him. "More than ready. Thanks for asking me."

"Hey, I usually go to these things alone. Today I'll have the prettiest girl in town on my arm."

She blushed at the compliment. It wasn't true by any means, but she could have kissed him for saying it. Today, of all days, she needed to feel good about herself.

"So, you said Big John does this every year?"

"Yep. Guess he figures no one else could give him a party as big as the one he can throw for himself. It's something just about everybody in town turns out for."

"Amazing."

"Yeah, it is that."

"Do I sense a note of bitterness in your voice?"

"Probably."

She waited, but he didn't elaborate. "So," she said, "are you still baby-sitting?"

"No. Yesterday was the last day. Their folks are picking them up today. You don't know how relieved I am that they're going."

"Don't you like kids? They seemed like pretty nice girls to me."

"I love kids but four teenage girls are more than I can handle." He grinned at her. "I won't have to worry about them again until next summer. Who knows, the way girls grow up these days, they might all be married by then."

Dana nodded, her good mood momentarily shattered. Married. Today was to have been her wedding day.

"Hey," Chay said, taking her by the hand. "I'm sorry."

"It's okay."

He gave her hand a squeeze. "I was supposed to make you forget what day it is, not remind you."

"It's okay, really." She forced a smile, and changed the subject. "Will your mother be at the party? I'd like to meet her."

"I'd like for her to meet you, too. But it won't be today. I can't think of anything that would bring her back here."

"What about your father?" she asked.

A muscle worked in Chay's jaw, reminding her that his father was a topic that he had refused to discuss once before.

"I'm sorry," she said quickly. "Forget I asked." But she couldn't help wondering at Chay's reticence in talking about his father. Was it because his father wasn't Indian? Or, horrible thought, maybe he didn't know who his father was.

They pulled into the driveway of Big John's ranch a few minutes later. Chay parked alongside the house, switched off the ignition and stepped out of the truck. Walking around to the passenger side, he opened the door for Dana and handed her out of the cab.

She glanced around, awed by what she saw. A huge two-story white house sat on a small rise. A wide veranda stretched across the front. Dark green shutters hung at the windows upstairs and down. Tall trees grew along both

sides of the house. Colorful flowers bordered a well-man-
icured lawn. There were cars and trucks parked everywhere. She guessed there were already close to fifty. Music
filled the air, growing louder as Chay took her by the hand
and led her around to the rear of the house.

Dana blinked at what she saw. There were men, women
and children everywhere, most decked out in jeans, cowboy shirts, big hats and boots. There were four bounce
houses for the kids, as well as a snow-cone machine and a
cotton-candy machine. A man wandered around making
balloon animals for the youngsters. A clown was entertaining old and young alike with a magic show. A couple of
fiddlers stood off to one side playing country music.

A ways off in the distance, a group of men were throwing horseshoes. There was also a baseball game in
progress. What looked like a whole side of beef was slowly
turning over an open pit. Colorful canopies shaded two
dozen long tables and another dozen round ones, all of
which were laden with food. Galvanized tubs were filled
with ice and every brand of beer and soft drink known to
man. A large arena had been set up on one side, complete
with bleachers.

Dana shook her head. "Wow."

Chay grinned at her. "Pretty impressive, huh?"

"I'll say. How many people is he expecting?"

"Oh, about two hundred, I guess, not counting kids. Do
you want to get something to eat or drink?"

"Sure."

She had never seen such a spread in all her life. There
were bowls of fresh fruits and vegetables, a variety of dips
and sauces, trays of bread and rolls, cheeses, pickles and
chips, salsa, barbecued chicken, Swedish meatballs and
cocktail wieners, as well as hamburgers, hot dogs, shrimp
cocktail and every kind of salad you could imagine, as
well as carrot and celery sticks.

It all looked so good, Dana took a little of everything. "You gonna eat all that?" Chay asked incredulously.

"Just watch me," she replied, grinning.

He laughed out loud. "I like a girl with a healthy appetite. Come on, I see an empty table over there."

Sitting down, Dana took a good look at her plate and wondered if maybe she'd taken a bit more than she needed.

Chay put his plate on the table. "Best save some room," he warned. "This is just a snack."

"A snack?" she said in disbelief. "You mean there's going to be more?"

"Sure. Dinner will be served after the rodeo."

The food was excellent and she ate way too much, considering there was more to come. She was looking forward to sitting in the shade, relaxing, when Chay stood and took her hand.

"Come on," he urged. "It's rodeo time."

"Already?"

"Yep."

He led her to the arena and found her a seat in front. "How about a kiss for luck?" He didn't wait for an answer, but swooped down and kissed her.

"Be careful," she admonished.

"Always," he said, winking at her.

Before long, the bleachers were full. Dana was feeling a little out of place until Ashley and her friends dropped down beside her.

"Hi."

"Hi, yourself," Dana replied, glad for the company. "Nice to see you again, girls."

LuAnn, Megan and Brittany grinned at her as they sat down.

"I love to watch Chay ride," Ashley said, munching on a hot dog. "He's the best."

"I've never been to a rodeo before," Dana said.

"Never?" Ashley looked at her as if she had just admitted she had never seen a horse before.

"I'm a city girl, remember?"

"You'll love it," LuAnn said.

Ashley grinned. "Chay wins every year, you know."

"'Cause he's the best." The words were spoken simultaneously by Megan, Brittany and LuAnn. The way they said it led Dana to believe that the girls had heard the same thing from Ashley many times before.

"Well, he is!" Ashley said.

Just then the loudspeaker rumbled to life. "Afternoon, ladies and gents, kids of all ages. Welcome to Big John's birthday bash and rodeo. I sure hope you're ready for some excitement 'cause we've got some top broncs this year and they promise to give our cowboys a run for their money. The rider who scores the most points this year will win a cash prize of two thousand dollars and one of Big John's prize heifers. First up is saddle bronc riding…"

What followed was unlike anything Dana had ever seen before as one cowboy after another exploded out of the chute on the back of a thousand pounds of bucking horseflesh. It was the most amazing thing to watch and she was caught up in it until she heard the announcer call Chay's name. Suddenly, what had been fun and exciting took on a whole new dimension. It had been one thing to watch strangers get thrown, but she knew Chay Lone Elk personally and that made all the difference in the world.

She leaned forward, hardly daring to breathe, as the chute opened and a big black horse came out bucking for all it was worth.

Ashley stood up, screaming, "Go, Chay! Yeah, Chay!" She looked down at Dana. "Isn't he great?"

"Great," she murmured, unable to take her gaze from Chay. He stuck to the saddle like glue, one arm raised over his head, his body rocking back and forth as the horse bucked and pitched. After what seemed like eight years but was only eight seconds, the whistle blew and the pickup man rode up alongside Chay.

Dana blew out a deep breath, relieved that it was over. Only it wasn't. Next came bareback bronc riding, then calf roping, then steer wrestling and then bull riding. Dana thought each event was worse than the last. Riding a bucking horse was bad enough, but then Chay came out on a bull that looked madder than hell and must have weighed two thousand pounds. And he won every event but steer wrestling, where he came in second.

Ashley yelled and screamed when they announced Chay had won the top prize of the day and Dana stood beside her, yelling until her throat hurt. For all that she had been scared to death the whole time, watching Chay ride had been the most exciting thing she had ever seen.

Moments later, he was taking a victory ride around the arena. Dana felt her heart turn over in her chest as she watched him wave to the crowd and then he was riding toward her.

Dismounting, he ducked under the bars of the corral and scooped her into his arms. The shouts and cheers of the crowd faded into the distance as he lowered his head and kissed her.

Dana felt her cheeks grow hot when the announcer said, "You can come up for air now, cowboy. Eight seconds has come and gone."

The crowd roared with laughter.

Chay kissed her again, then left to get cleaned up and change clothes for the barbecue.

Ashley linked her arm with Dana's. "Come on, let's go find a table." She glanced at her friends. "You coming?"

"No," LuAnn said. "We'll catch up with you later. Megan has to go eat with her parents and I told Brittany I'd help her watch her little sister while her mom nurses the baby."

"All right," Ashley said. "See ya."

The air was redolent with the scent of barbecued beef. The tables had been cleared of leftovers and now groaned under the weight of sliced beef, platters of corn on the cob and bowls of potato and macaroni salads, baked beans and baked potatoes, an assortment of rolls and bread and green salads.

Chay joined them a short time later. Taking her by one hand and Ashley by the other, he led the way to the front of the food line. "Winners always eat first," he told Dana with a wink.

Dinner was a lively, noisy affair. The air was filled with conversation and laughter. Dana laughed along with the other women at the table as Chay exchanged stories with the cowboys sitting on either side of him. They talked about bad broncs and rank bulls, about hauling hay in the middle of winter and breaking through ice to get water. They made jokes about being stomped and gored and snake-bit, about stampedes and breech births and why any man with any brains would work with cattle, surely the dumbest creatures on God's green earth.

"I don't know who's dumber," one of the women said, grinning, "the cows or the women who love the cowboys."

At that, one of the men started singing "Mama, Don't Let Your Babies Grow Up to Be Cowboys," then yelled "Ouch!" when his wife punched him on the arm.

After most everyone had gone back for seconds, or thirds, things quieted down a bit.

And then, as a man picked up a microphone and climbed up on a chair, the crowd broke into a round of applause.

Dana looked at Chay.

"That's Big John," Chay said. "He's about to make his yearly speech."

Dana studied the man. Big was an apt description, she thought. He was well over six feet tall, with a shock of dark brown hair, bushy brown eyebrows, a nose that had been broken at least once and a strong, determined jaw. Like most everyone else, he wore jeans, a plaid cowboy shirt, boots that probably cost more than her apartment and a Stetson.

"Welcome, friends and neighbors."

His voice was big, too, she thought.

"I hope you're all having a good time, and that you got enough to eat!"

Whistles, applause and shouts of affirmation rang out from the crowd.

"I'm glad to hear it!" Big John exclaimed. "'Cause if you're still hungry, it sure as hell isn't my fault!"

Someone called, "Forget the sweet talk, you old horse thief, and tell us how old you are."

"It's a running joke," Chay told Dana. "Every year, people try to find out Big John's age."

"What's the big secret?" she asked.

Chay shrugged. "Beats the heck out of me."

"Do you know?"

"I've got a pretty good idea," Chay replied with a shrug.

A pretty, blond woman wearing a bright red, low-cut sundress sashayed up beside Big John and took the microphone from his hand. She nodded to the band and they broke into a rousing rendition of "Happy Birthday." The crowd began singing as two men came forward carrying the biggest cake Dana had ever seen.

Wearing a grin as wide as the Grand Canyon, Big John blew out the candles.

"Hey, John," called a man in a big black hat, "what did you wish for?"

"None of your business!" Big John hollered back, and then he looked at the lady in the red dress and waggled his eyebrows.

"That's a mighty young heifer you've got there," Black Hat said. "You sure you can handle her?"

"Damn right!" Big John said and, sweeping the blonde into his arms, he kissed her soundly.

The men in the crowd hooted and hollered.

Big John came up grinning. "I've had my dessert," he said. "You all help yourselves to yours. The dancing will start in about thirty minutes. Ladies, feel free to change into your dancin' duds up at the house." He slipped his arm around the blonde's waist. "You all have a good time now, hear? Oh, we've got plenty of guest rooms if any of you get so soused you don't want to drive home."

This announcement was met with more applause.

"I'm gonna go get some cake," Ashley said. "Do you guys want some?"

"Yes, thanks," Dana said.

Chay shook his head. "Bring me a beer, will you?"

"Okay." Rising, Ashley headed for the cake table.

A moment later, Big John made his way toward their table with the blonde hanging on his arm. "Evenin', Chay."

"John."

"Who's this pretty little filly?"

"Big John, this is Dana Westlake. Dana, this is Big John."

"Happy birthday," Dana said.

Big John smiled at her. "Westlake? You're not related to Elsa, are you?"

"She was my grandmother."

"Wonderful woman. We were sorry to lose her."

"Thank you."

"How are your parents? I haven't seen them since they were up here, oh, when was it? Last year, I think."

"They're doing well, thank you."

Big John nodded. "Enjoy yourselves."

"Thank you."

She watched Big John walk away, then glanced at Chay. "You really don't like him, do you?"

"Not much."

"I think I'd quit if I were you. Why work for someone you don't like if you don't have to?"

He shrugged. "I don't know. Guess I'm just a sucker for punishment."

Dana stared at him a moment, then frowned. Chay didn't look anything like Big John and yet there was something…before she could put her finger on it, Ashley returned carrying two enormous pieces of cake and a bottle of beer.

She set the plates on the table, handed the bottle to Chay, then plopped into her chair.

"What's wrong?" Dana asked.

"Everything."

Chay took a swig of beer. "What's bothering you now?"

"I'm bored." She glared at him. "If it wasn't for you, Nick would be here tonight."

"I don't want to go into that again," Chay said.

"Of course you don't. My life is ruined, but why should you care?"

Chay glanced past Ashley. "Cheer up. Here comes Brandon."

Ashley rolled her eyes. "Brandon! He's about as exciting as vanilla ice cream."

"Hey, Ashley," Brandon said, coming up behind her. "Are you going to the dance? Hi, Chay."

Ashley blew out a sigh. "Of course I'm going."

Chay glared at Ashley, warning her to mind her manners before saying, "Dana, this is Brandon DeHaven. Brandon, this is Miss Westlake."

"Pleased to meet you, Miss Westlake."

"Thank you, Brandon."

"Come on, Bran," Ashley said, rising. "Let's go find the girls."

Dana stared after the young couple as they disappeared into the crowd. "I thought she liked him."

"I thought so, too, but that was before she met Nick."

"Ah, yes," Dana said. "Nick, the bad boy. Why is it young girls are always attracted to boys like that?"

Chay shook his head. "You tell me."

"I was asking you."

"Beats the hell out of me. All I know is that Nick is trouble and she's chasing after it with both hands."

Dana had been inside nice homes before but Big John's house was unlike anything she had ever seen. The rooms were huge, the furniture comfortable and obviously expensive, as were the paintings on the walls and the sculptures on the shelves.

A maid escorted Dana to a guest room. "Just ring if you need anything," she said before closing the door.

Decorated in shades of hunter green and mauve, the room was quite lovely, with a king-size bed, a full-length mirror and a bathroom with a sunken tub.

Dana washed her hands and face, applied fresh makeup, then changed into the dress she had brought with her. Slipping on her sandals, she studied her reflection in the mirror. The dress complemented the color of her hair and skin, but she knew it was the prospect of dancing with Chay that had put the glow in her eyes and the flush in her cheeks. How had he become so important to her so fast? She was perilously close to losing her heart to a man she had met less than three weeks ago, a man she was afraid was keeping a secret from her. Though he had told her about his mother, she was certain that he was keeping something from her, but what? She hoped she was wrong.

She ran a brush through her hair, then left the room.

Chay was waiting for her at the foot of the stairs. He had changed clothes, too, and now he wore a pair of black jeans, a long-sleeved white shirt, a black leather vest and black boots. He looked good enough to eat.

The dance was held outside under a huge canopy. A six-piece band was playing a slow country tune when they arrived. The long tables had been taken down and a bar had been set up. Four bartenders handed out drinks and jokes. Colored lights ringed the dance floor. Several dozen couples were dancing while other guests conversed in small groups or stood at the bar, talking and laughing.

Chay nodded at the dance floor. "Shall we?"

She nodded and he led her onto the floor, then drew her into his arms. She nestled against him, her head resting on his shoulder. It felt wonderful to be in his arms, to feel his body brushing against hers, his breath warm upon her cheek. She felt cherished, protected, in a way she never had been before. It was a good feeling.

Sensing his gaze, she looked up, her eyes meeting his. Neither spoke. For a moment, her breath caught in her throat and then he was lowering his head toward hers. She closed her eyes, a sigh escaping her lips, her stomach fluttering in anticipation of his kiss, a kiss that was pure and sweet and achingly sensual all at the same time. A kiss that made her pulse race and her knees weak. His arm tightened around her waist and she grinned inwardly, wondering if it was passion that caused him to hold her closer or if he knew the effect his kiss was having on her and he was trying to keep her on her feet.

Gradually, she became aware that the music had stopped. Opening her eyes, she blinked up at Chay. He was grinning at her. At first, she didn't know why, and then she realized they were surrounded by couples, all of whom were watching them with varied expressions of amusement.

She felt a rush of heat climb up her neck into her cheeks when she noticed that Big John and the blonde in the red dress were standing nearby.

"You two better find a room or set a date," Big John suggested, his voice booming in the sudden stillness.

Dana felt her blush deepen.

Chay glowered at the older man. Taking Dana by the hand, he led her off the dance floor and into the shadows beyond.

"He's a fine one to talk," Chay muttered.

"What do you mean?"

"Nothing."

"You're doing it again," Dana said.

"Doing what?"

"You're muttering under your breath about Big John. Honestly, I don't know why you work for the man. You're a top hand. I'm sure you could find another job."

"Yeah, I'm sure I could."

"So, why do you stay?"

"Maybe I'll tell you someday."

"But not tonight?"

"Not tonight." He blew out a deep breath, then drew her purposefully into his arms. "I can think of a lot of things I'd rather do than talk about that bullheaded old man," he said, and kissed her.

There was nothing remotely gentle about this kiss. It was bold and possessive and it drove every thought from her mind but her need to be held in his arms, to feel his lips on hers.

When he drew away, she knew she was lost. In spite of everything, she was falling in love with Chay Lone Elk.

Chapter Eleven

A loud pounding on the front door woke Dana from a sound sleep. Reaching for the lamp beside her bed, she turned on the light, grabbed her robe and hurried through the dark house to the door.

She peeked through the curtain that covered the front window, then quickly unlocked the door.

"Chay! It's after three o'clock. What are you doing here? Is something wrong?" A silly question, she thought. He wouldn't be there at such an hour unless something was wrong.

"Have you seen Ashley?"

"Not since the party. Why?"

"She's gone."

"Gone?" She stepped back. "Come in."

He followed her into the living room. Removing his hat, he ran a hand through his hair. "It looks like she's run away. I didn't think she'd come here, but I had to make sure."

"Why do you think she's run away?"

"Her bed hasn't been slept in. The old man called the

girls. None of them has heard from her since they left the ranch last night."

"But why would she run away?"

"She had another fight with Big John. Apparently he caught her making out with Nick behind one of the barns." Muttering an oath, Chay removed his hat and ran a hand through his hair. "Dammit, I didn't even know Nick was at the party. I should have kept a better eye on her."

"Are you supposed to chaperon her all the time?" Dana asked. "I thought you only had to do that when she was away from the ranch."

"I'm responsible for her."

"Why?"

"Because the old man doesn't give a damn what she does most of the time." He jammed his hat back on his head. "I've got to go. I'm not going to find her hanging around here."

"Do you think she ran away with Nick?"

"If she did, I'll kill the little weasel. I told him to stay away from her."

Dana nodded. Looking at Chay, she felt a sudden fear for Nick. "Do you want me to go with you?" she asked, thinking she might be able to calm Chay down if they found Ashley and the young man together.

"Sure, if you want."

"Just give me a minute to get dressed." Going into her bedroom, she pulled on a pair of jeans and a long-sleeved sweater.

Chay was pacing the floor when she returned to the living room. Moments later, they were in the truck heading toward town.

"Do you know where Nick lives?" Dana asked.

"Yeah. He's got a room over one of the bars on Main Street."

"You seem to know a lot about him."

"Everybody knows about him. He's the town bad boy."

"What if she's not with him?"

"I hope to hell she isn't, but it's the only place I can think of that she might go."

"Does she stay in touch with her mother?"

"Sure. Jillian writes to her once a month or so. Jillian remarried a couple of years ago, some guy who sells RVs in Salt Lake."

"Would Ashley go there?"

"I don't know. She might."

A short time later Chay pulled over and parked in front of a rather seedy-looking saloon called the Dirty Shame.

Chay opened the door for her; then, hand in hand, they walked around the corner of the building to a flight of rickety wooden stairs. When they reached the top, Chay knocked on the door. If Nick was home, he would know, from that knock, that it wasn't a friend coming to call.

A couple of minutes passed before Nick opened the door. A cigarette dangled from a corner of his mouth, his hair was uncombed, he was shirtless and barefoot.

Looking over Nick's shoulder, Dana saw a girl sitting on a sofa. It was easy to see that they had recently made love.

Nick braced a shoulder against the doorjamb. "Yeah, what do *you* want?"

"I'm looking for Ashley."

"She ain't here."

"I can see that," Chay said brusquely. "Do you know where she is?"

"She called a few hours ago. Sounded like she was cryin'. She asked me to drive her to the airport. Said she was gonna go see her old lady."

"And you took her?"

"Hey, she wanted to go. What was I supposed to do?"

"Do you know what time her flight was leaving?"

Nick shrugged. "I don't know. Six, six-thirty."

"And you left her at the airport, alone?"

Nick took a step backward, obviously threatened by the menacing tone in Chay's voice.

"She said she was gonna get a room at the hotel across the street."

Chay clenched his hands into fists. For a moment Dana thought he was going to give Nick a much-needed punch in the nose. Instead, he turned away from the door. Dana followed him down the stairs.

"Looks like you called it," Chay said when they were back inside the truck.

"Lucky guess. Now what?"

"I'm going after her." He started the engine and pulled away from the curb. "Do you want to go along?"

"Sure."

"If we don't get there in time to stop her, I'll be going on to Salt Lake."

Dana smiled. "Sounds like this might turn into quite an adventure."

"Yeah," he said dryly. "An adventure."

They drove in silence for a time. Dana looked out the window, her mind on Ashley. It amazed her that the girl had the nerve to run away in the middle of the night and ask Nick to take her to the airport.

She slid a glance at Chay. He was watching the road, both hands clenched on the wheel. She wondered again at his devotion to Ashley Wardman, especially in view of his obvious dislike for Ashley's father. While she found it odd, she also found it strangely appealing that Chay was so concerned for Ashley's welfare. It boded well for the kind of father he would be when he had children of his own…beautiful children, no doubt, with dusky skin and black hair.

She couldn't help but envy the woman who would give him those children…. She shook the thought aside, annoyed by the surge of jealousy that rushed through her at the thought of Chay holding another woman, kissing her, making love to her. Again, she wondered how she had come to care so much in such a short time, and what she would do when it was time to go back home.

"I would never have had the nerve to run away like this when I was Ashley's age," Dana remarked.

"She's not afraid of much," Chay replied. "She goes to see her mother a couple times a year, so she's used to flying and she knows how to make reservations."

"Where did she get the money?"

Chay grunted softly. "She's got more money in the bank than a lot of men I know, including me. The old man's always giving her cash. He gives her money when she gets good grades and money when he misses a school event, which is most of them. He gives her money for her birthday and Christmas and whenever his conscience starts to bother him. The sad thing is, she'd rather have his attention than the money."

Dana nodded. All girls wanted and needed their father's attention and approval.

Bright lights signaled they were approaching the airport. Chay parked the truck. Minutes later, they were checking departure flights to Salt Lake City. There was a flight at 6:05. The next flight was at one o'clock in the afternoon.

Dana checked her watch. It was a quarter after five.

"Let's go," Chay said. "If we hurry, we should be able to catch her."

As luck would have it, the passengers hadn't boarded yet.

Chay spotted Ashley immediately and struck out in her direction.

The girl didn't look at all happy, Dana thought as she hurried after Chay. Ashley was sitting in a corner by herself, her arms crossed over her chest, looking as lost and alone as only a teenage girl can.

Ashley looked up, obviously startled to see Chay standing in front of her.

In the next instant, the little-girl-lost evaporated, to be replaced by a look of bored indifference. "What are you doing here?"

"Taking you back home where you belong."

Ashley shook her head. "I'm going to see my mom."

"If you wanted to worry the old man, you've done it. He had some kind of attack when he found out you were missing."

Ashley made a sound of mingled disgust and disbelief.

"It's true," Chay insisted. "The doc was at the ranch when I left or I'd have been here sooner."

Dana looked at Chay in surprise. Why hadn't he told her that? What other secrets was he keeping from her? Of course, it wasn't really a secret, but why hadn't he told her? Why was he so reluctant to share things with her?

"Why didn't you tell me?" Dana asked.

He shrugged. "I was worried about finding Ashley. Nothing else seemed important."

"Is he going to be all right?" Ashley asked anxiously.

"Sure. He's too mean to die." Chay held out his hand. "Come on, let's go."

Ashley hesitated a moment, then put her hand in Chay's and let him pull her to her feet.

"Do you have any luggage?"

"Just my carry-on."

He picked up her bag and they headed for the exit, the silence between them thick enough to cut with a knife.

When they reached the truck, Chay tossed Ashley's bag into the back, then unlocked the doors. Dana got in first and Ashley climbed in after her. Chay shut the door behind them; a little harder than Dana thought was necessary.

Sliding behind the wheel, he put the key in the ignition and pulled out of the parking lot.

Dana sat between the two of them. The tension in the cab was so thick, it fairly crackled. Ashley stared out the window, her whole body rigid, anger radiating off her like heat from a forest fire. Chay had a stranglehold on the wheel.

"Why'd you run away?" he asked at length.

Ashley didn't answer, only continued to stare out the window. Just when Dana was sure she wasn't going to reply, Ashley said, "I wanted to be with someone who has time for me. Someone who'll listen to me. Someone who loves me."

"I love you," Chay said quietly.

Ashley turned away from the window and looked at him. "Do you, Chay?" she asked, and Dana heard the hopeful note in the girl's voice.

"Of course I do," Chay said. "Like a brother."

"You've always been there for me, just like a big brother, and I love you for it, but…I wanted to be with my mom, with family that loves me."

"The old man's your family and he loves you," Chay said.

"No, he doesn't!" Ashley retorted, her eyes flashing. "He's not worried about me. All he cares about is what people think. He wants everyone to believe he's the perfect father. Well, he's not! He's mean and—"

"Don't say something you'll regret later," Chay warned.

The fire went out of Ashley. Shoulders hunched, she stared out the window again.

After a time, the silence got to Dana and she turned on the radio, flipping through the stations until she found one playing country music.

They were nearing town when Chay said, "Do you mind if I drop Ashley off before I take you home? It might do the old man some good to know she's all right."

"I don't mind."

A short time later, Chay pulled up in front of the Wardman ranch house. Ashley got out of the truck and ran up the stairs and into the house.

Chay let out a sigh. "I'm tired and I'm hungry," he said. "Do you want to come in and have some breakfast before I take you home?"

He looked tired, she thought. There were dark shadows under his eyes and he looked just plain beat. She was pretty sure most of it came from worrying about Ashley. "Sounds good."

She followed him up the porch steps and into the house, which was eerily silent.

Chay removed his hat and hung it on the rack inside the front door. He glanced up at the second floor, wondering how Big John was doing. Wondering why he cared.

"Come on," he said, and she followed him down a long narrow hallway into a spacious kitchen.

There was a woman standing at the stove. She was short and plump with a knot of gray hair. She turned when they entered the room. A broad smile lit her face when she saw Chay.

"'Mornin', Mr. Chay. Can I fix you and your friend some breakfast?"

"Sounds good, Anna Mae," he said. "Dana, this is Anna Mae Waters, the best cook this side of the Mississippi. Anna Mae, this is Dana Westlake."

"Pleased to meet you, Anna Mae," Dana said.

"Why, it's right nice to meet you, too, Miss Westlake. What can I fix for you?"

Dana lifted her hand and let it fall. "Oh, I don't know. Anything is fine with me, really."

"I'll have pancakes and bacon," Chay said. "And a cup of black coffee."

"I'll bet you want that coffee now," Anna Mae said.

"You're an angel."

She beamed at him. "Coming right up. Pancakes and bacon all right with you, Miss Westlake?"

"Sure."

"All right, skedaddle," Anna Mae said, making a shooing motion with her hands. "You know I don't like anybody in my kitchen when I'm cooking."

With a grin, Chay held the door open for Dana, then followed her into the dining room.

He gestured at a chair covered in a deep wine-colored velvet. "Make yourself at home."

They had no sooner sat down than Anna Mae came in carrying a coffeepot and two large mugs. She poured them each a cup, then looked at Dana. "Do you take cream and sugar?"

"No, black is fine."

With a nod, Anna Mae returned to the kitchen.

Dana picked up her mug and took a sip. It was, she thought, the best coffee she had ever tasted.

She studied Chay over the rim of her cup. She noticed again how tired he looked, but what she saw was more than just weariness. Worry took a heavy toll on a man, she thought as she glanced around the room. Like the rest of the house, it was lavishly appointed. The table at which she sat probably cost more than her whole house and everything in it. Twelve chairs ringed the table. There was a matching breakfront filled with crystal and silver. A painting of a buffalo stampede hung on one wall.

She wondered if all of Big John's hired hands were welcome in the house and if Anna Mae cooked breakfast for them, too. Sometimes it seemed like Chay was almost part of the family.

She stared at Chay. She had been wondering for days who Chay reminded her of and now she knew. It was Big John. There was nothing as obvious as the two of them having the same color hair or build, but they had the same eyes, the same strong stubborn chin, the same way of walking, as though they owned the world and everything in it.

The thought had no sooner crossed her mind than she remembered thinking that Ashley bore a strong resemblance to Chay....

"Why are you looking at me like that?" Chay asked, frowning.

She shook her head. "No reason."

Before he could question her further, Anna Mae entered the room carrying a large covered tray. In moments, a feast was spread before them: golden-brown pancakes dripping butter, strips of lean perfectly cooked bacon, fluffy scrambled eggs, bran muffins warm from the oven and a pitcher of fresh-squeezed orange juice.

Dana shook her head. "Is this just for the two of us?" she asked Chay when Anna Mae left the room, "or are you expecting company like, say, the whole town?"

Chay forked three pancakes onto his plate. "Anna Mae believes breakfast is the most important meal of the day."

"It looks to me like she thinks it's the *only* meal of the day."

Chay grinned at her, then filled his plate with bacon and eggs. "Best dig in before it's gone."

Dana helped herself to a couple of pancakes, a strip of bacon and a spoonful of eggs.

"Is that all you're gonna eat?" Chay asked. "You'll hurt Anna Mae's feelings."

"Well, I wouldn't want to do that." Dana picked up a bran muffin and cut it in half. She slathered it with butter and took a bite. It was so light, it practically melted in her mouth. The rest of the food was just as good, everything cooked and seasoned to perfection.

"No wonder you don't want to leave here," Dana remarked.

She glanced upward, her attention drawn by the sound of Ashley's voice.

"…see him anytime I want and if you don't like it, well, I just don't care!" The girl's voice rose with every word. A door slammed and then Dana heard the sound of feet running down the stairs.

A moment later, Ashley burst into the room, her eyes

red and swollen. She looked at Dana, then threw herself in Chay's arms. "He's so mean! Why won't he let me go to Mom's? He won't even know I'm gone!"

Chay stroked Ashley's back. "You're his daughter," he said quietly. "He may not know how to show you that he loves you, but he does."

"Oh, stop defending him. You don't like him and everybody knows it!"

"No, I don't, but that doesn't matter. He's your father, and you should respect him."

"That's easy for you to say. He's not your father."

A muscle worked in Chay's jaw.

"I wish *you* were my father!" Ashley said. "At least you listen to me. You don't treat me like I'm six years old. Well, you do sometimes, but you never—"

"Your father!" Chay exclaimed, cutting her off. "Hell, it's hard enough being your brother…."

Chay closed his mouth with a snap, and silence fell over the room.

Ashley jumped to her feet. "What did you say?"

Chay looked up at her, his hands clenched in his lap. "Nothing."

"Brother." Ashley drew the word out, as if she had never heard it before. "You're my brother?"

Chay blew out a heavy sigh that seemed to come from the soles of his feet. "Yeah."

"I don't believe you. Why didn't you tell me before? Why didn't anyone tell me?"

"Big John made me swear not to tell anyone."

"But why?" Ashley asked, her eyes wide with disbelief.

"Why? Because he didn't want anyone to know he had a half-breed bastard for a son, that's why."

"I don't believe you."

"It's true whether you believe it or not."

"All this time, and you never told me." She shook her

head. "How could you keep a secret like that? How could he?" She stared at Chay. "I've got a brother. I don't know whether to laugh or cry."

Chay pushed his chair away from the table. Rising, he drew Ashley into his arms. "I wanted to tell you," he said quietly. "You don't know how many times I started to tell you."

She rested her head on his shoulder. "I wish you had. It sure explains a lot," she said wryly.

Chay grinned. "Yeah, I guess it does."

"Do we have any other brothers or sisters that I don't know about?"

"I hope not."

Ashley looked up at Chay. "Can't you talk to him for me, please? I want to go stay with my mom. I need to be with her for a while, you know? Sometimes a girl needs her mother."

"I know, but I don't think the old man will listen to anything I've got to say. He never has. And this really isn't a good time to upset him."

Ashley sighed dramatically. "Yeah, I guess you're right. But you'll talk to him, won't you? As soon as he's better?"

"Sure."

"Thanks, big brother." She kissed him on the cheek, then left the room.

Chay watched her out of sight, then sat down at the table again. He frowned when he saw the expression on Dana's face.

"Are you hiding any other secrets?" she asked, her tone icy. "You don't have a wife and six kids somewhere, do you?"

A muscle worked in Chay's jaw. "Of course not. You heard what I told Ashley. I promised Big John I wouldn't tell anyone. *Anyone*," he repeated. "That includes you." He took a deep breath. "I wanted to tell you, just like I wanted to tell Ashley, but a promise is a promise."

"Yes," Dana said slowly. "I suppose so."

"But you think I should have told you anyway?"

"Yes. No. I don't know." She pushed away from the table and stood up. "It's been a long night. I'd like to go home."

With a nod, Chay rose from the table.

She couldn't think of anything to say on the ride home. Apparently, neither could Chay. Dana stared out the window, annoyed with herself for being angry with him. He was right, a promise was a promise and yet, right or wrong, she felt as though he had lied to her. Maybe it didn't matter that Big John was his father and Ashley was his sister. Maybe she was making a mountain out of a molehill, but it hadn't been that long ago that another man had lied to her. She didn't believe for a minute that Rick had fallen head over heels in love with the blond bombshell in a matter of days. Looking back, Dana was certain he had been dating his secretary while he was engaged to her. Now that she thought of it, there had been too many times when he had canceled a date at the last minute, or made some flimsy excuse to take her home early. Once she had caught the scent of perfume on him that wasn't hers. When questioned, Rick had said a saleslady spritzed him with perfume by mistake. How could she have been so blind!

Lost in thought, she didn't realize they had reached her house until Chay pulled up in front of the porch.

"Thanks for bringing me home." She reached for the door handle, hoping he would say something, anything, to stop her.

But he just looked at her, his dark eyes giving nothing away.

Fighting back her tears, she got out of the truck and closed the door.

He didn't say anything, just looked at her for a long moment, then put the truck in gear and drove away.

She stood in the yard until he was out of sight, then burst into tears.

Chapter Twelve

She cried until she was empty inside, and then she went to bed and cried herself to sleep. When she woke, her cheeks were still damp with tears. Had she been crying while she slept, too? It wouldn't have surprised her.

She looked at the clock. It was almost four. She should get up, take a shower, change her clothes. Instead, she stared up at the ceiling.

Why had she behaved as if Chay had lied to her? A silly question, she thought, because she felt as if he had lied to her. But it wasn't really a lie. He had made a promise and honored it. Why had she overreacted? Why had she made such a big deal out of it when it was really nothing? Maybe she had just been in shock to discover that she had been right all along. Instead of being upset, she should be glad that he kept his promises, that he was an honorable man, a man of his word.

Trust, she thought, it all boiled down to trust. Rick had betrayed her and now she was afraid to trust Chay. But who could blame her? Chay was tall, dark and handsome. She

was, at best, ordinary. He could probably have his pick of
women, so why did he want her? She wasn't beautiful. She
didn't have any special talents. She wasn't even a very
good cook.

And there was the real problem, she thought. She lacked
self-esteem. But then, she always had. Deep down, she had
always known Rick would leave her for someone else,
someone better, someone prettier. And that was exactly
what he had done. Was that why she had pushed Chay
away? Why she had made such a fuss over nothing? So she
could leave him before he left her?

"Pathetic," she muttered. "You're pathetic."

Tossing the covers aside, she got out of bed. She was
heading for the shower when the phone rang.

Her heart skipped a beat as she ran to answer it. "Hello?"

"Hi, Dana. Is everything all right?"

"Oh. Hi, Mom."

"Are you all right, dear?"

"Oh, sure, I'm fine. How's everything at home? You and
Dad okay?"

"What's wrong, Dana?"

She sat down heavily. There was no use trying to fool
her mother. Marge Westlake had always known when her
daughter was in trouble or in pain. "Oh, Mom, I've made
such a mess of things."

"Is this about Rick? He was never right for you. I know
this sounds cruel, but I think what happened was for the
best. He would never have made you happy."

"It's not about Rick. It's, well, I met a man up here…"

There was a barely noticeable pause on the other end of
the phone. "Go on."

In a rush, Dana told her mother everything that had happened. All her doubts and fears poured out in a flood of
words and tears. "And now," she said, "I don't know what
to do."

"I remember Chay," her mother said. "You say he's Big John's son? I met Chay and his mother one summer. He was a good-looking young man, very quiet, as I recall. Very polite. Chay was only, oh, I don't know, fifteen or sixteen I guess. His mother was lovely." Marge paused a moment before asking, "Are you in love with him, Dana?"

"I think so."

"I see."

"You don't approve?"

"I didn't say that. But you've only known the man for a short time. Less than a month. I don't want to see you get hurt again, and I think maybe you're rushing into something you're not quite ready for."

The words flitted through Dana's mind. It wasn't the first time she had wondered if she was making a mistake. But being with Chay didn't feel like a mistake. He made her feel beautiful, desirable. Likable. Rick had said he loved her, but he had always made her feel inadequate, as if she wasn't quite good enough or smart enough or pretty enough. He had made her feel as if anything she thought or wanted wasn't as important as what he thought or wanted. Chay had never made her feel like that. Rick had declared she was beautiful, but she had frequently caught him looking at other women. When she was with Chay, she always had his full attention. When she was with him, she felt as if she was the only woman in the world. And that day at the lake, he had made her feel beautiful.

Why had she acted so foolishly? She knew why, though she was loath to admit it. She had started a fight and left him before he could leave her. Well, not exactly a fight, she amended, but she had withdrawn from him mentally and physically, and he had known it.

"Dana?"

"What? Oh, sorry, Mom. Listen, I've got to go. Thanks for calling. Give my love to Dad, will you?"

"All right, dear. We'll see you when you get home."

"All right. Bye, Mom."

Dana hung up the phone, then ran to her room and changed her clothes. She had to go see Chay. She had to apologize for her foolish behavior and hope that he would forgive her for acting like a total idiot. She was only going to be up here for a short time, and she wanted to spend as much of the time she had left with Chay.

She only hoped she hadn't shattered the tenuous bond between them.

Chapter Thirteen

Chay stood just inside the door of Big John's bedroom, one shoulder braced against the wall. Sometime in the last few hours the old man had taken a turn for the worse. Chay had summoned the doctor, who had examined Big John, then shook his head. Chay couldn't believe there was no hope left. He had assured Ashley that her father was going to be fine, had believed it himself. Big John had always seemed indestructible. But years of over-indulgence had taken their toll on the old man's heart and now it was just a matter of time.

Ashley sat at her father's bedside, her hand tightly grasping his, her gaze never leaving his face.

"I'm sorry, Daddy. I didn't mean to upset you. Please forgive me. Please don't leave me. I love you."

She had repeated the same words over and over again during the last two hours, convinced that she had somehow caused her father's relapse. Her eyes were red and swollen, her cheeks damp with tears that seemed to have no end. Chay had tried to comfort her, tried to get her to go lie down for a little while, to try to get some sleep, but she refused to leave Big John's side. Looking at the old man, Chay couldn't blame her.

Big John lay unmoving, his eyes closed, his breathing shallow. There was an unhealthy pallor to the man's skin. His cheeks looked sunken. Chay shook his head. Though there had never been any love lost between the two of them, he knew he would miss Big John when he was gone.

The doctor hovered on the far side of the bed, coming forward every fifteen minutes or so to take Big John's blood pressure and listen to his heart. Chay could tell, from the doctor's expression, that there was little hope his patient would recover.

Chay had left the room only once since Big John had lost consciousness, and that had been to put in a call to his mother. She had listened quietly to what he'd had to say, then asked him to send Big John's plane to pick her up.

Chay checked the clock on Big John's nightstand. It was just after five. His mother should be at the ranch within the hour.

Anna Mae tiptoed into the room, bringing a pot of fresh coffee for Chay and the doctor and a cup of hot chocolate for Ashley. She knelt beside Ashley and gave the girl a hug.

"Young Mr. DeHaven called," Anna Mae said. "He's on his way over."

Ashley nodded, but didn't reply.

Rising, Anna Mae looked at Chay, her eyes filled with sorrow. "Is there anything I can do?"

"Just let me know when my mother gets here."

With a nod, Anna Mae left the room.

Chay blew out a sigh. If Big John died, he knew he was going to spend the rest of his life wishing he had tried harder to win his father's acceptance. Muttering an oath, he walked over to the window and stared into the distance.

He was twenty-nine years old, and still trying to win his old man's love and approval.

His gaze wandered over the ranch, wondering what would happen to it when Big John died. He had no doubt that Big John had left it all to Ashley, but she was too young to look after the place. One thing was for certain, he couldn't leave here now, not when Ashley would need him more than ever. She would be able to live here year-round now, if she wanted, or she could go and live with her mother. Chay grunted softly. Either way, Chay would have to stay on at the ranch and look out for her best interests until she was old enough, and wise enough, to do it on her own.

He glanced over his shoulder at Ashley. He knew her better than she knew herself, knew she wouldn't leave the ranch now. He wondered if Jillian would move back to the ranch to look after her daughter, wondered if Big John had bequeathed anything to the two women who had borne his children. And Georgia Cookson. No doubt the old man had made provisions for his latest paramour, as well.

Chay blew out a sigh. Deep down in a dark corner of his soul where he didn't look too often, jealousy reared its ugly head. Though he didn't really begrudge the ranch to Ashley, he couldn't help feeling it should rightfully be his—or at least partly his. Whether Big John liked it or not, Chay was his firstborn. No one loved the place the way Chay did. No one else had put in the long hours he had to make sure things ran smoothly. Sure, Ashley loved the place because it was home, but the ranch was in Chay's blood, as much a part of him as the color of his hair or the dusky hue of his skin. Working on the ranch was more than just a job to Chay. His heart and soul had been poured into every inch of ground.

Chay muttered an oath under his breath, hating the feelings coming to the fore. He had told Dana he stayed because of that thousand acres, but the truth was he would have stayed because he loved the land itself. Dana…the rift between them had left an ache in his heart. He knew she was angry with him for no good reason. She acted as if he had lied to her when all he had done was keep a promise he had made. Was that any reason for her to act as if he had betrayed her trust? He thought about it and decided she was just running scared, afraid to get involved with another man so soon after she had been hurt. He could understand that, and maybe he didn't blame her, but he wasn't going to let her go without a fight. She was overreacting, and when she'd had time to think about it, he was sure she would realize it, too. He wasn't so sure he could convince her that her place was here, with him. She was a city girl, after all, and as much as she seemed to be enjoying her vacation, he didn't know if she would want to live in this part of the country all year long. So, he thought with a wry grin, he would just have to persuade her.

A heart-wrenching sob from Ashley drew Chay's attention. A cold certainty welled in his heart as he turned slowly from the window. Ashley sat at her father's side, shaking her head, murmuring, "No, no, no," while the doctor bent over Big John.

Chay closed the distance between them in two long strides, drew Ashley into his arms and led her out of the room.

"No!" She looked up at him through red-rimmed eyes. "He can't be dead, Chay! Not now. I have to tell him I'm sorry. I have to tell him that I loved him!" She twisted out of his arms, intent on returning to her father's room.

Chay caught her by the hand and drew her into his arms once more. "Ashley, honey, you need to get some sleep."

"I can't! I have to tell him…don't you understand? The last thing I told him was that I hated him…and…"

"He knows you didn't mean it, honey. There's a lot that will need doing in the next few days. You need some rest."

She stared up at him, mute. "It isn't fair. So much has changed so quickly."

"I know." He hugged her close, his heart aching for her loss, for the pain etched in her face. "I'll be here for you, you know that. Your mother is on her way, and so is mine. Everything will be all right." Putting his arm around her shoulders, he led her down the hallway to her bedroom. She sat down on the edge of the bed and he pulled off her shoes and socks, then tucked her into bed. "Go to sleep, honey."

She clung to his hand. "Stay with me."

"All right."

Chay pulled her old rocker up next to the bed and sat down, her hand clasped in his. "He knows you loved him," he said quietly. "He knows you didn't mean any of the things you said, just like you know he loved you, no matter what."

She nodded. "Did you love him, Chay?"

"No, but I respected him."

"He didn't love you, either, did he?"

"No."

"Why not?"

"Maybe because we were so much alike in some ways and so different in others."

"I love you," she said with a yawn. "I've always loved you."

"I know." He brushed a lock of hair from her forehead. "Go to sleep now."

With a sniff, she closed her eyes. Moments later, she was asleep.

Chay stayed by her side for a long while, watching her sleep. How different their lives had been. Ashley had been treated like a princess her whole life, pampered and spoiled by everyone who knew her, including him, while he'd been forced to pretend he was nothing more to Big John than just another hired hand. Well, as far as he was concerned, people could go on thinking that.

Rising, he brushed a kiss across her forehead. She was likely one of the richest girls in the state now. In a few years, she would be swamped by men, young and old alike, who would be eager to marry her for the ranch alone. Well, he thought as he left her room and closed the door behind him, they would have to come through him first!

Anna Mae was waiting for him at the bottom of the stairs. "We have company," she said, nodding toward the front parlor. "Your mother is here."

Chapter Fourteen

Chay felt himself smiling at the thought of seeing his mother again. He hadn't seen her in over a year and he had missed her.

After thanking Anna Mae, he hurried into the parlor.

At fifty-three, his mother was as beautiful and vibrant as she had been at twenty-three. Her thick black hair fell to her waist. Her skin, a shade darker than his own, was smooth and unlined.

A smile lit her face when he entered the room. *"Na-eha,"* she murmured. My son. She opened her arms and he went to her.

"Na-hkoe," he said, embracing her. "How was your flight?"

"A little bumpy," she said with a grimace. "You know how I hate planes."

Chay led her to the sofa and sat down beside her.

"I'm too late, aren't I?" she asked softly.

Chay nodded. "He died about an hour ago."

With a sigh, she reached for his hand. "I'll miss him,"

she said, and he heard the surprise in her voice. "I loved him and I hated him." Tears welled in her eyes. "But I never thought I'd miss him." She wiped away her tears. "Did you two ever make peace?"

"No. He would never let me in." Chay shook his head. "Why did he hate me so much?"

"Because you were everything he wanted to be. He had money, but you had integrity. He had power, but you had courage. He could command people to do his bidding, he could earn their respect, but never their devotion. And I suspect part of his hatred for you was because of me, because I turned my back on everything he could give me and walked away. He never forgave me for that." Her fingertips slid down his cheek. "You were a constant reminder to him of what I'd done. How's Ashley taking it?"

"Not very well. They had a fight just before his attack. She's feeling guilty, blaming herself for what happened."

"Have you called her mother?"

"Yes, she's on her way."

"Is there anything I can do?"

"I don't know. I haven't thought that far ahead."

"Why don't you let me take care of the funeral arrangements."

"Are you sure?"

"Of course. I'll talk to Anna Mae and get a list of people who need to be told."

"Thanks, *Na-hkoe*."

"I'd like to go freshen up a little if it's all right."

"Sure." Rising, he offered her his hand. "I had Anna Mae make up your old room for you," he said, then frowned. "Maybe you'd rather not stay there."

"No, it will be fine." She smiled up at him. "Not all my memories are bad. Is dinner still at eight?"

Chay nodded.

"I'll see you then."

"Right. Let Anna Mae know if you need anything."

He walked her to the staircase, then, in need of some space and fresh air, he left the house.

Feeling restless, he went down to the barn and saddled his favorite horse. He had a good three hours until dinner. There was nothing to be done this afternoon. The doctor had made arrangements to have Big John's body taken into town. His mother would take care of all of the funeral arrangements. The foreman would make sure the ranch work got done.

Swinging into the saddle, Chay rode out of the yard. He told himself he was just going for a short ride even as he turned his mount toward the path that led to Dana's place. He just hoped she was still there.

Dana got out of the car and stared at the rear right tire. Of all times to get a flat, why did it have to be now? Muttering under her breath, she kicked the tire, wincing as pain lanced through her big toe.

Grimacing, she limped over to the porch and sat on the bottom step. She could call Chay, but she really needed to see him, to apologize face-to-face, although doing it over the phone would undoubtedly be easier, especially if he wouldn't forgive her.

She stared into the distance, wondering if she was making a mistake. Maybe her mother was right and she was just setting herself up to be hurt again. Maybe she should just pack up and go back to Ashton Falls where she belonged. She couldn't hide up here forever. Sooner or later she had to go home and face her friends and family, endure their sympathy and their snickers and get on with living.

She looked over her shoulder, thinking that she would miss this house, this place, but most of all, she would miss Chay, the crinkle around his eyes, the touch of his hand in her hair, the way he sometimes whispered her name, the sound of his laughter, his kisses that were more potent than the oncoming storm.

She glanced up as lightning flashed across the skies followed by a low rumble of thunder. Dark clouds scudded across the sky. Another bolt of lightning sizzled through the heavens, unleashing a sudden downpour.

Jumping to her feet, Dana ran up the porch steps, then stood in the doorway, watching the rain come down.

She was about to go into the house when she saw something move just beyond the trees.

Peering through the downpour, she saw a horse and rider emerge from the woods, felt her heart skip a beat as she recognized the rider.

It was Chay.

He dismounted in a single lithe motion and ground-tied his mount, then ascended the steps two at a time. He stood on the porch, hat in hand. Raindrops rolled off the brim and splattered on the porch at his feet.

Dana gazed at him, speechless, her hands itching to reach for him, yet something held her immobile.

"I would have told you if I could," he said. "I'm sorry."

"It was silly of me to expect you to go back on your word. I'm sorry."

They spoke simultaneously, the tension between them evaporating as soon as the words were said.

"Come on in," Dana said. "Let me get you something hot to drink." Taking his hat, she hung it on the hook inside the door. Feeling as if a load had been removed from her shoulders, she led the way into the kitchen.

Chay followed her, then stopped in the doorway. "Dana."

She turned at the sound of her name, knew what he was going to say even before he spoke.

"He's gone," Chay said, his voice heavy with regret.

"Oh, Chay, I'm so sorry." Taking him by the hand, she went into the living room. Sitting on the sofa, she drew him down beside her and put her arms around him.

He rested his forehead against hers. "It's so hard to believe he's gone. He seemed so strong. Indomitable." He swallowed hard, his hand reaching for hers. "I waited all my life to hear him call me his son, to tell me that he loved me. It'll never happen now."

She didn't know what to say. Except for her grandparents, she had never lost anyone close to her. A sob racked his body. She held him close as his pain washed over her. For all that Chay had said he didn't love Big John, the tears in his eyes proved otherwise.

He was quiet for several minutes and then he drew away. "I'm sorry," he said somewhat sheepishly. "I haven't cried since I was six."

"You don't have to apologize or be embarrassed. No matter how you felt about him or how he felt about you, he was still your father."

"Yeah." He blew out a soul-deep sigh. "I'm going to be pretty busy for the next couple of days, and then we need to talk."

"All right."

His gaze searched her face. "You'll still be here? You're not leaving?"

"No," she said. "I'm not leaving." And she knew, in that moment, that if he asked her, she would stay here, with him, for as long as he wanted her.

"I've got to get back," he said. "My mother's at the ranch. I'd like for you to meet her."

His words warmed her heart. "I'd like that."

He kissed her lightly, then gained his feet. Moving toward the front door, he picked up his hat, ran his fingers around the brim.

"What is it?" she asked.

"I'd...would you come to the funeral? I'd like for you to be there."

"Of course."

"I'll call you and let you know when it is."

She nodded, then rose on tiptoe and kissed him. "I think I love the rain," she said. "It always seems to bring us together."

He smiled faintly, then left the house.

As always, she stood on the porch and watched him until he was out of sight.

Chapter Fifteen

The funeral was held at eleven o'clock on Wednesday morning. Dana hadn't seen Chay since he came to her house the Sunday before. She regretted each day without him.

The memorial service for Big John was, as expected, the biggest one the town had ever seen. The pretty, old-fashioned church on Sycamore Street was filled to capacity. In addition to family and friends, it looked as if practically every man, woman and child in Wardman's Hollow had turned out to pay their respects to the town's leading citizen. Newspaper reporters hovered outside like vultures, hoping to get a word with a member of the family.

The immediate family sat in the front pew. Dana sat on Chay's right. Ashley sat on his left. Ashley's mother sat beside her daughter, and Chay's mother sat beside Dana.

Dana couldn't help thinking that Big John's taste in women varied greatly. Ashley's mother, Jillian, looked like a fashion model. She was tall, willowy and blond, with clear blue eyes and a flawless complexion. Chay's mother, Claudia, whom Dana had met only briefly, was not quite so tall or willowy but she was equally beautiful, with large dark eyes and smooth dusky skin. Dana felt overshadowed by both women.

Big John's mistress sat across the aisle and several rows back. She wore a demure black dress and a large black hat with a veil. Dana couldn't help wondering how many of the other black-clad women scattered throughout the church had had affairs with Chay's father.

Glancing around, Dana spotted LuAnn, Megan and Brittany a few rows back. Brandon DeHaven was also there.

During the service, several people got up to speak, relating the details of Big John's life, telling how he had inherited the Bar W from his widowed mother at a young age, how the ranch had prospered under his hand. They spoke of his shrewd business sense, his larger-than-life sense of humor that was matched only by his temper, his generosity.

Dana tried to pay attention to what was being said, but she was distracted by Chay's nearness, by the way he held himself, stiff and unmoving, as if he was afraid that any show of emotion would be his undoing. Ashley leaned against him, weeping softly into a handkerchief. Jillian wept along with her daughter. Claudia listened intently to what was said, her face impassive, her hands clasped tightly in her lap.

There was a short service at the graveside, and then the family and those who had been invited drove out to the ranch for lunch.

While standing near the long buffet tables that practically groaned beneath the weight of food and drink, Dana couldn't help overhearing bits and pieces of stories and anecdotes about Big John. He had, indeed, been bigger than life. Whether people loved him or hated him, they had all respected him.

She was feeling rather out of place as the afternoon wore on. Sitting in the living room, surrounded by friends of the family, none of whom she knew, she wondered why she had let Chay talk her into coming. Except for Chay and Ashley and Ashley's friends, she didn't know a soul. The couple nearest her were speculating about just how much money Ashley stood to inherit, and who would run the ranch now that Big John was gone. Both agreed that Ashley was far too young to run the place. The woman wondered if Jillian would move back to the ranch and stay with Ashley. The man wondered if Big John had left anything to his assorted mistresses.

With a sigh, Dana glanced into the other room. She could see Chay there, talking with several people. He nodded at something one of them said, accepted a hug from another. She wished she had brought her own car so she could go home.

Rising, she made her way through the kitchen and out to the backyard. No matter what happened after today, it was sure to make a big change in Chay's life. Knowing him as she did, she knew that he would feel obligated to look after his sister and the ranch. No doubt he would be extremely busy for the next few months. Then, too, he had his own place to look after.

She was standing by one of the corrals, petting a pretty, little brown-and-white pony, when she heard footsteps behind her. She turned, hoping it was Chay seeking her out. Instead, she saw his mother walking toward her.

"I saw you leave and thought this might be a good time for us to get acquainted," Claudia said, coming up beside Dana.

Dana nodded.

"Chay seems rather smitten with you, though I understand you've only known each other for a couple of weeks."

"I'm rather smitten with him, as well," Dana confessed.

"He's a good man, my son."

"Yes, he is."

"He's had a difficult life," Claudia said, then shook her head. "I'm not saying this well. I don't mean that he's been neglected or abused, only that he was never able to have the one thing he wanted the most."

"His father's love," Dana said.

"He told you that?"

"Yes. I asked him once, before I knew that Big John was his father, why he stayed on at the ranch. He said it was a good job. I know now that it was so much more."

Claudia nodded. "He loves the land. He loves Ashley. And even though he'll never admit it, even to himself, he loved his father. When Chay was a little boy, I tried to make it up to him but there comes a time when a boy needs his father, when he needs a man's example to guide him. But Big John didn't have time for a son who was not only half-Indian, but who had been born on the wrong side of the blanket. Oh, he provided for us. Big John's pride wouldn't let his son do without, but Chay didn't want clothes or a pony, he wanted his father's attention, and that was something he never had. To tell you the truth, sometimes I'm surprised that Chay turned out so well."

"Did you want to marry Big John?" Dana asked.

"No." She smiled. "And a good thing it was, too, because he never would have married me. He was angry when I left, but I couldn't stay any longer. Chay was grown by then and he didn't need me anymore."

Dana smiled, remembering how Chay had said he hadn't gone to Arizona with his mother because she hadn't needed him anymore.

"So, how serious is it between you and my son?"

"It isn't. Not at all. I mean, I hardly know him." She knew she was babbling, felt her cheeks grow hot under Claudia's pointed stare. "Perhaps if we had more time… I… It's just…"

"You're in love with him, aren't you?"

Dana nodded. "But it doesn't matter. I'm leaving on Friday."

"So soon?"

"I have to be at work next Monday." She smiled wistfully. "Anyway, I don't belong here. I don't think I was cut out to be a country wife."

"I see." Claudia glanced over Dana's shoulder. "Here comes Chay now. It was a pleasure meeting you, Dana. I hope everything works out for you."

"Thank you."

Claudia squeezed Dana's hand then turned and walked toward the house.

Butterflies danced in Dana's stomach as she watched Chay stop to speak briefly with his mother, then continue toward her. She loved watching him, loved the way he moved, like some large jungle cat on the prowl, always so self-assured, so confident.

"Here you are," he said. "I've been looking everywhere for you."

She shrugged. "I, well, I felt out of place, you know?"

"I'm sorry. I shouldn't have left you alone."

"No, it's all right, really. You needed to be there. How's Ashley doing?"

"She's still pretty shaken up, but she'll be okay. She's Big John's daughter, after all."

"Yes."

His gaze moved over her. "When are you leaving?"

"Friday morning."

"Any chance you could stay a little longer?"

"No, I'm afraid not."

He muttered an oath, his expression turbulent. "I had a feeling you'd say that. Knowing how stubborn you can be, I was going to follow you home."

"You were?"

"Yeah."

"But you've changed your mind?" Disappointment sat like a lead weight on her heart. She would have loved to spend more time with him, to show him around Ashton Falls, to introduce him to her friends.

He folded his arms over the top rail of the corral. "The lawyer came to the house last night and read the will."

"Oh? I suppose Big John left everything to Ashley."

"Not exactly. He left half of the place to me on the provision that I stay here and look after her until she marries or until she turns twenty-one."

"That's wonderful!" Dana exclaimed. "I'm happy for you, Chay, really I am." It was something he would have done anyway, she thought.

He nodded. The terms of the old man's will had been so unexpected, he wasn't sure how he felt. He had been tempted to give his share to Ashley and walk away. Even if he'd had to leave the ranch, he would have been close enough to look after her anyway. Damn the old man! Was this Big John's way of trying to make up for a lifetime of neglect? Well, it was too damn late! The old man didn't have to leave him a damn thing. Chay had always looked after Ashley. Big John didn't have to bribe him to stay and do what he'd done most of his life. He had told Ashley as much later that night, but, bless her heart, she had said it was only right, after all, and that he deserved more than half the ranch, that it should all have been his in the first place. After all was said and done, Chay knew he couldn't turn his back on the land or on his sister. He loved them both and, except for his mother, Ashley was the only family he had.

"Anyway," he said, "I can't leave the ranch now. I've got a lot of paperwork to take care of, and I need to go over the ranch accounts."

Dana nodded.

"Jillian's going to stay for a week or two, but then she'll

be heading back to Salt Lake. Anyway, you can see why I can't take off."

"Of course," Dana said. She forced a smile, hoping he couldn't see how her heart was breaking. "Ashley will need you more than ever after her mother goes home."

But, oh, she thought, *I need you, too.*

Turning away from the fence, Chay drew her into his arms. "I'll miss you."

"I'll miss you, too."

"Will you write me when you get home?" he asked.

"Sure."

"Maybe we could go out to dinner tomorrow night…no, I forgot, I'm supposed to be taking Ashley and Jillian and my mother out to dinner. Why don't you come with us?"

"No, I don't think so. Anyway, I need to pack and close up the house."

He nodded. "Come on. I'll take you home."

She sat close to him in the truck on the way home, thinking how much she would miss him. He had said he would miss her, too, and perhaps he would, though she wondered when he'd have the time. Between settling the estate, running the ranch and looking after Ashley, he wasn't going to have a lot of spare time on his hands.

Chay walked her to her door, then drew her into his arms. She nestled against him and he thought how right it felt for her to be there. His nostrils filled with her scent— cologne and shampoo and woman. He had never felt this way about any of the women he had dated, but then, he had been careful in his choice of dates, making sure the relationship stayed casual, never letting things get serious. But Dana was different. He had known that from the first.

"Listen," he said, "once things quiet down around here and Ashley's feeling better, I should be able to take some time off. What would you say if I came to Ashton Falls for a couple of days?"

"I'd like that."

"This isn't goodbye, Dana. I won't let it be goodbye. I'll be there as soon as I can get away."

She nodded.

"Don't forget about me."

"No, I won't."

He kissed her then, a slow deep kiss that he hoped conveyed what he felt deep inside but seemed unable to put into words.

There were tears in her eyes when he broke the kiss.

He hoped that was a good sign.

Chapter Sixteen

Dana stood in the middle of her apartment. It seemed smaller somehow. Though she had only been gone for three weeks, it seemed like years since she had been home. The place hadn't changed, she realized, but she had.

Chay might never call. She might never see him again. But he had given her a sense of self-worth, made her feel beautiful, worthwhile.

Blinking back tears, she unpacked, took a long hot shower, then pulled on her nightgown and sat down to write him a letter. She had known, as soon as she walked in the front door, that she had made a mistake. Jobs came and went, but a man like Chayton Lone Elk was one of a kind. He had never said he loved her. She had never said she loved him. But there was definitely something between them, something wonderful and rare and worth pursuing.

Going to the front window, she looked out into the night. Neon lights shone on the blacktop. Houses, like boxes, lined the far side of the street. A few palm trees grew along the sidewalk. A few stars twinkled in the sky. There were no deer grazing along the edge of her property. She couldn't see the Milky Way. There were no pine trees. There would be no birds singing in the morning, no squirrels darting from tree to tree, no eagles soaring in the sky. Chay wouldn't come knocking at her door.

Sitting at the kitchen table, she found a sheet of paper and a pen and began to write, telling him how much she had enjoyed their time together, how much she was looking forward to seeing him again if he found the time to come to Ashton Falls.

Sitting back, she relived all the good times they had had, the way he made her feel, his concern for Ashley, the pain he had tried to hide when his father died.

"I love him," she murmured. "I love everything about him."

And it was time to tell him so. But not on paper. She tore up the letter and tossed it in the trash. She went to the phone and picked up the receiver, but a phone call didn't seem right, either.

Smiling, her heart soaring, she danced around the apartment, laughing out loud. Tomorrow, she was going to quit her job and move to Wardman's Hollow. It might be the biggest mistake she ever made…no, Rick was the biggest mistake she had ever made, she thought, grinning. But, right or wrong, she was going to follow her heart back to Wardman's Hollow.

Before she met Chay, she would never have had the nerve to do such a thing, to open herself up to rejection, but Chay was worth it. And if it turned out he didn't love her, well, he had given her the courage to overcome that, too.

Her boss couldn't believe it when she told him she was handing in her two weeks' notice. He ranted and raved and then begged her to stay. In the end, he wished her well, wrote her a reference so flattering it sounded as if she had

written it herself, and gave her an extra two weeks' sever-
ance pay "because she deserved it." Her mother and father
couldn't believe it when she told them she was moving to
Wardman's Hollow, permanently. They both tried to talk
her out of it. Her father told her she was being too impet-
uous—something she had never been before. Her mother
told her to wait a few weeks, to let Chay make the first
move, to think of what she was doing, what she was giving up. But Dana couldn't wait. Deep in her heart, she
knew it was the right thing to do.

She spent the next two weeks sorting through her be-
longings, putting them into two piles—things she was taking, things she was leaving behind. She called the utility
companies and told them she was moving, canceled the
newspaper, and did the hundred and one other things that
had to be taken care of.

Her last morning at home, she packed up everything she
was taking with her, hauled the rest of it to the Goodwill,
told her parents she would see them at Christmas, then
jumped in her car and headed back to Wardman's Hollow.

It was late Sunday night when she reached the house
nestled in the hills. For a moment, she sat in the car, looking up at the house. Home, she thought, this was home now.

Bags in hand, she paused on the top step of the front
porch to look at the sky. The night was breathtakingly
clear. The Milky Way stretched overhead like a pathway
through the heavens. Millions of stars winked at her. A
bright yellow moon hung low in the sky.

Going inside, her first thought was to call Chay and tell
him she was back, but then she decided to wait. This wasn't
something that should be said in a telephone call. She
wanted to see his face when she told him she loved him,
wanted to see his eyes.

Unable to sit still, she went through the house, removing the dustcovers from the furniture. Going into the bed-

room, she put her clothes away, then stowed her suitcases in the back of the closet. Whatever happened, she wouldn't be needing them again right away.

Later, she wandered through the house, deciding where to put her unicorn collection, the painting she had bought from an art gallery last year. It was her favorite piece, and now she knew why. It depicted a warrior astride a big black horse, a warrior who looked remarkably like Chay. She hung the picture over the fireplace, found herself looking at it over and over again as she moved through the house.

It was only later, lying in bed, that doubts assailed her. What if she was wrong?

What if he didn't love her the way she loved him?

Monday morning Chay sat in the kitchen, a mug of coffee cupped in his hands as he watched Anna Mae teach Ashley how to make a pumpkin pie. Ashley should have been at school, but she'd caught the sniffles over the weekend and he'd decided to let her stay home one more day. It touched a chord deep within him to hear his sister laugh at something Anna Mae said. He had let Ashley stay home from school the week following the funeral and then, hoping to cheer her up, he had invited the Three Musketeers over for the weekend. It had done Ashley a world of good to spend time with her friends and her mother.

Ashley had asked her mother to stay on at the ranch, but Jillian had refused. Her life was in Salt Lake with her husband, she'd said, but Ashley was more than welcome to come and stay with her. Chay had been a little surprised when Ashley decided to stay on at the ranch. But then, maybe it wasn't such a surprise. Ashley had never cared for Jillian's husband.

Chay blew out a sigh. It wasn't easy, running the ranch, taking care of the books, making sure the cowhands were doing their jobs, keeping an eye on his sister... He grinned inwardly. His sister. Word of his relationship to Ashley and Big John had spread through Wardman's Hollow like wildfire. Jillian and his mother had ordered Big John's headstone and now it was carved in white marble for all the world to see:

John Matthew Wardman, beloved father of Ashley Marie and Chayton Lone Elk.

The people in town and at the ranch looked at him differently now. He wasn't just one of Big John's hired hands. He was half owner of one of the biggest cattle ranches in this part of the country. Yes, people looked at him differently, and he wasn't sure he liked it. He was still the same, yet even as the thought crossed his mind, he knew he wasn't. He had responsibilities now. Sometimes he felt as if he was carrying the weight of the world on his shoulders, felt as if everyone was watching him, waiting for him to fail. He had been a cowhand all his life. Now, suddenly, he was responsible for the success or failure of a ranch that had prospered for generations.

He stared into the mug cradled in his hands as if he could see the ranch's future in the coffee cooling inside.

Muttering an oath, he set the cup on the table. He wasn't really worried about the ranch. He wasn't worried about Ashley. And he didn't give a hoot in hell about what the cowhands or the people in town thought of him. The only thing he was worried about was Dana and whether they had a future together. Well, he had waited long enough to find out. Next week he was driving down to Ashton Falls to see Dana. He was going to tell her how he felt, ask her to give them a chance. If he had to, he'd go down on his knees and beg, though he hoped it wouldn't come to that.

He shook his head. He hadn't been this infatuated with a woman since he fell head over heels for his sixth-grade teacher and even that didn't compare to this. He had never known a woman like Dana, couldn't forget the awareness that sizzled between them whenever they touched. Though he had only known her a few short weeks, she had carved a place for herself in his life and in his heart that he knew no other woman would ever be able to fill. He couldn't stop thinking about her, couldn't stop wanting her. It was more than mere desire, more than just physical hunger. He knew what that felt like, and what he felt for Dana was as far from lust as the sun from the moon.

He swore under his breath. He couldn't explain his attraction for her any more than he could ignore it. He only knew he felt incomplete without her.

Pushing away from the table, he grabbed his hat off the rack and left the house.

Ten minutes later, he was riding toward her house in the hills, drawn by a sudden need to walk the land where she had walked.

Dana glanced at the clock, willing the hands to move. She had been up for hours, unable to sleep, unable to think of anything but seeing Chay again. She glanced at the clock for what must have been the tenth time in as many minutes. Eleven-fifteen. She had been about to leave the house when she realized that Chay would be at work by now, probably out on the range somewhere, branding cattle or whatever cowboys did during the day. Why hadn't she thought of that sooner? She frowned. Maybe he didn't do cowboy work now that he owned half the ranch.

Whatever he was doing, she wouldn't be able to see him until tonight.

She stamped her foot in frustration. How was she supposed to wait until then? What if she lost her nerve?

Feeling as though the walls were closing in on her, she pulled on a heavy jacket and a pair of gloves and went out onto the front porch. She paced back and forth for several minutes, then dropped into the porch rocker. She couldn't just sit here all day. Maybe she would drive into town and pick up some groceries or take in a movie. Or buy a new dress. Yes, a new dress to wear for Chay, something that would knock his boots off!

She was about to go into the house when Chay emerged from the trees.

She stopped, frozen in place at the sight of him. He sat tall and straight in the saddle, his black hat pulled low over his eyes, his broad shoulders filling out the heavy sheepskin jacket he wore. Her heart quickened as she drank in the sight of him. He was here, she thought, and then wondered what he was doing there. Had someone told him she had returned? But that was impossible. No one knew she was here except her parents and they certainly wouldn't have called to tell him.

Excitement fluttered in her stomach as he reined his horse to a halt in front of the porch. He pushed his hat back on his head, then sat there, looking up at her. It was hard to think, hard to breathe, with his dark gaze fixed on her face, and then he dismounted in a single fluid movement.

He was here. Every fiber of her being, every cell in her body, yearned for him. She hardly knew the man, and yet, in some ways, she felt as if she had known him all her life. She had been attracted to him from the first, drawn to him in ways she had never been drawn to any other man she had ever met.

He ground-reined his horse, swung out of the saddle, vaulted the porch rail, lifted her from the rocker and kissed her.

Her eyelids fluttered down, her senses reeling with his nearness, the heat of his kiss, the shelter of his arms around her. How had she ever thought she could live without him? He was as necessary as the very air that she breathed.

She whimpered in protest when he took his mouth from hers.

"Be quiet," he admonished, and then he was kissing her again, stealing the strength from her legs so that she leaned against him, her arms tight around his waist, her body seeking to be closer to his, though she was certain that was impossible.

She gazed up at him when he broke the kiss.

His gaze trapped hers, his eyes dark and intense upon her face. He was holding her so tight, she could almost feel the beat of his heart. "We belong together, Dana. I know it. I can feel it."

She started to say she agreed, but Chay put his hand over her mouth, stilling her words. Was he perhaps afraid that she might disagree?

"Search your heart," he went on. "You know it's true."

Joy filled her heart, soared through her soul. She removed his hand from her mouth. "Of course I know it's true," she said, laughing. "Why do you think I came back?"

"I don't know. Why did you come back?"

"To tell you that I love you."

He blinked at her. "You do?"

She nodded.

"You're sure? We hardly know each other."

She frowned at him. "Wait a minute. Didn't you just say we belonged together?"

"Yeah, but I thought you'd argue with me. I was prepared to drag you back to the Bar W and lock you in my bedroom until you agreed that I was right." He laughed sheepishly. "Guess I wasn't prepared for you to give in so quickly."

"I wasn't, either, but the minute I got back to Ashton Falls, I knew leaving here had been a mistake. I started to write you a letter, but I threw it away. Then I thought I'd call, but..." She shrugged. "I wanted to see your face when

I told you. And if it turned out that you felt the same way, I wanted to see your face when you told me you loved me. Do you love me, Chay?"

"With all my heart."

"Say it."

"I love you, Dana. I'll love you as long as I live. I can't promise that I'll never hurt you or that I won't let you down once in a while, but I'll never betray you and I'll never leave you. I swear it on all I hold dear."

"I believe you."

"Then you'll marry me?"

"Yes, any day you say, anywhere you say."

He let out a war whoop that would have sent shivers down a settler's spine. It sent shivers down her spine, too, shivers of delight. And then he swept her into his arms again, his mouth claiming hers, branding her as his for all time.

Chapter Seventeen

Between planning the wedding and spending as much time as she could with Chay, the next few weeks passed quickly. Dana's parents were less than thrilled to learn that their daughter was going to marry a man she had known such a short time. Even the fact that he owned half of the biggest cattle ranch in Montana couldn't mollify her father. Her mother tried, in a nice way, to convince Dana to wait a year, six months at the least, "just to make sure, dear."

Dana agreed that she had only known Chay a short time but as someone had once said, hearts weren't concerned with clocks or calendars. Besides, she knew couples who had dated for two years or more who ended up divorced. A long courtship didn't ensure a lasting marriage. And she knew in her heart of hearts that she was doing the right thing. For the first time in her life, she had no doubts, no second thoughts, and though she listened politely and patiently to her parents' well-meant advice, she was too much in love to be swayed by their disapproval. They had agreed to be there, and that was all that mattered.

Chay wanted to be married before Christmas so that they could spend it together as man and wife, and Dana had agreed. They set the date for the week before Christmas. Her mother, still hoping to change Dana's mind, had taken the opportunity to suggest that they might want to wait until spring, reminding Dana that Chay had just buried his father and some might consider it unseemly, maybe even disrespectful, for Chay to marry so soon, but Chay had brushed her mother's concerns aside. He didn't want to wait, and neither did Dana, but they both agreed that a small wedding, with just family and a few close friends, would be appropriate, considering the circumstances.

One Saturday afternoon, Dana picked Ashley up at the ranch and they went shopping for Dana's wedding dress. Ashley had been rather subdued on the ride to town, but once Dana started trying on dresses, Ashley got into the spirit of it. She started bringing in the most outrageous dresses for Dana to try on and before long, they were both laughing hysterically.

A short time later, the saleslady brought in a dress with a square neck and a fitted bodice. It had a slim skirt that was longer in the back than in the front. They both knew it was the right one when Dana tried it on.

"Wait until Chay sees it," Ashley said. "You'll knock his socks off."

Dana smiled. "That's what I had in mind."

"You love him, don't you?"

"Well, I hope so. I'm marrying the man."

"Do you think Chay's right about Nick?"

"Yes, I do. Why don't you give Brandon a chance?"

Ashley shrugged. "We've known each other for years. Do you think it's possible to know someone too well?"

"No. Anyway, I'm sure you'll fall in love a thousand times before you meet Mr. Right."

Ashley rolled her eyes. "That's what Chay says, too."

"Well, if two people tell you you're sick, lie down."

"What?"

"Never mind. Help me out of this dress and I'll buy you lunch."

A short time later they were seated in a small café sipping iced tea. It was a cozy place. Red-and-white checked cloths covered the tables. Matching curtains hung at the windows. There were framed pictures of country singers on the wall, along with old-fashioned signs and posters.

"I still can't believe that no one ever told me Chay was my brother," Ashley remarked.

"It must have been hard for you, finding out the way you did."

"Yeah. I'm glad, though. I've been pretending that he was my brother ever since I was a little girl."

Dana smiled. "He told me how you were always following him around. I always wished I'd had a big brother. It's lonesome, being an only child. I didn't mind so much when I was little. It was kind of fun, getting all the attention and all the presents. My folks always made a big fuss over me, but now I really wish I had some brothers and sisters."

"I'm glad you're marrying Chay. You don't think he'll send me away to school after you get married, do you?"

"Why would he do that?"

"I don't know." Ashley bit down on her lower lip. "With you here, he might not want me around anymore."

"Don't be silly! He loves you very much."

"You won't mind having me there, will you?"

"Of course not! Didn't I just tell you I wished I had a sister?"

Ashley looked relieved. "Are you nervous about getting married?"

"A little."

"Is Chay…never mind."

"Is Chay what?" Dana asked, then gasped. "Ashley!"

"Well, is he?"

"I don't know."

"You've never slept with him?"

Dana shook her head, unable to believe she was having this conversation with a sixteen-year-old girl. A girl who probably knew more about the matter than she did. It was embarrassing.

"What about that other guy? The one you were engaged to before?"

"No, never. And aren't I glad now?"

"Are you still—" Ashley leaned forward and lowered her voice "—a virgin?"

Dana nodded, wondering why she suddenly felt as if she was confessing to something unnatural.

Ashley shook her head. "I don't believe it."

"Does that mean…you and Nick haven't…have you?" Dana asked, dreading the answer.

"No. He wanted to, but…well, I just wasn't ready."

Dana breathed a sigh of relief.

"I guess that's why I like Brandon so much," Ashley said. "He doesn't pressure me. Of course, he wants to do it, too, so he's not that much different than Nick."

"They all want to," Dana said with a grin. "But smart girls, especially teenage girls, wait. It's a precious gift, you know, and shouldn't be given away. Once it's gone, you can't get it back, so you need to be sure, Ashley, really sure."

Dana blew out a sigh, then reached for her drink. She was glad beyond measure that she hadn't given in to Rick. What a huge mistake that would have been!

"I guess you're right," Ashley said. "I never really thought of it that way. It seems like most of the girls in my class have gone all the way at least once. Most of them weren't that impressed, and I know a lot of them were sorry, afterward."

"It doesn't mean anything if there's no love between the man and the woman," Dana said. "My mom told me that when I was about your age. It's something I never forgot."

Ashley nodded. "My friend Jenny did it with some guy she knew and she got pregnant. She didn't even love Jeff, she just wanted to see what all the fuss was about. She just had the baby a couple of months ago. A little girl. Her parents wanted her to give the baby away, but she wouldn't. She had to quit school so she could take care of it."

Dana nodded. "It happens all the time. On a happier note," she said, smiling, "I need a maid of honor. Would you like to stand up with me?"

"Me? You want me?"

"Very much."

"Oh, wow! That would be great."

"Wonderful."

"What kind of dress do I get to wear? Something long and pretty?"

"If you want. I was thinking of midnight blue. What do you think?"

"Sounds perfect." Ashley quickly drank the rest of her iced tea. "Can we look today?"

Later that night, wrapped in Chay's arms in front of a toasty fire, Dana told him about her trip to town with Ashley.

He chuckled softly on hearing the note of embarrassment she couldn't keep out of her voice as she related the rather startling conversation that she'd had with Ashley.

"Well," he said, "she won't listen to anything I say. Maybe she'll listen to you."

"I hope so." She stared at the flames, thinking how quickly one's life could change. Not long ago, she had been certain she would never fall in love again.

"Just think, this time next week, you'll be Mrs. Chayton Lone Elk."

Excitement bubbled within her. "It sounds wonderful, doesn't it?"

"I think so."

She looked up at him, admiring the strong lines of his face, the love she saw in his eyes. "I don't think I've ever been this happy," she remarked, "not even the day I won the spelling bee in sixth grade."

"Gee, thanks."

"Hey, that was a big day for me."

Chay grunted. "At least I'm in the top two."

He looked so crestfallen, Dana burst out laughing. "I'm kidding, silly. I've never been this happy in my whole life. Never!"

"That's better," he said, and crushed her close, his mouth seeking hers in what she had come to think of as his caveman kiss. It was long and hard and totally uncivilized, and it always made her toes curl.

Chay released her with a sigh. "I'd better get going. I've got an early day tomorrow."

He kissed the tip of her nose. "Unlike some people I know, I can't sleep until noon."

She punched him on the arm. "I wish! I have a ton of last-minute errands to run."

"Okay, okay." Chay rubbed his arm. "Is this the kind of abuse I have to look forward to?"

Looking property contrite, Dana kissed his arm. "There. Does that make it better?"

"No, but this will." He kissed her until she couldn't breathe, then rose to his feet, drawing her with him. "Behave yourself, woman."

"Yes, master," she said, and stuck her tongue out at him.

Laughing softly, Chay left the house.

Chapter Eighteen

And suddenly it was her wedding day. Dana woke with a smile on her face. She lay in bed for several minutes, contemplating the day ahead, silently thanking Rick for leaving her. If he hadn't been such a jerk, she might be married to him now instead of engaged to the most wonderful man she had ever known.

She glanced at the clock, gasped when she saw the time. Bill Jenkins, one of the ranch hands, would be there in less than three hours to drive her to the church. Throwing back the covers, she hurried into the bathroom. So much to do, and so little time to do it!

Dana was putting the finishing touches on her makeup when Jenkins arrived.

She took a last look in the mirror, grabbed her suitcase and overnight bag, and hurried out the door.

Chay looked out the window of the limo, glanced at his watch, drummed his fingers on the armrest. It was his wedding day. Somehow, he hadn't expected to be this nervous about something he had been anticipating for weeks.

Derek, his best man, chuckled softly. "Wedding jitters getting to you?"

"Of course not!" Chay snapped.

Derek laughed. "It's normal. I've never known any man who didn't have a few second thoughts right before the ceremony. Of course, I've known a few men who never made it to the ceremony, too."

Chay grunted. He supposed he was having second thoughts, but not about marrying Dana. He was suddenly afraid that he wouldn't measure up to what she expected, that she might be disappointed or that, in time, she'd be like Ashley's mother and take off, declaring she didn't want to be a ranch wife anymore. Maybe Dana's mother was right. Maybe they should have waited a while, given Dana a little more time to see what it was like, living on the ranch. Dana had said it herself. She was a city girl, and even though the ranch had all the modern conveniences anyone could ask for and they lived near a good-size town, the big city was a good distance away and he didn't get there often in the dead of winter.

Chay swallowed hard. Maybe he was just kidding himself. Maybe he wasn't ready. Or maybe Derek was right, and it was just a case of wedding day jitters. Whatever it was, he didn't like it.

Where was he?

Trying to appear calm, Dana stood in front of the mirror and made a minor adjustment to her veil. Where was he? He should have been there twenty-five minutes ago. The guests were getting restless. The organist had started repeating her repertoire.

Where was he?

Dana looked at her mother and Ashley. Marge's expression was sympathetic. Ashley shrugged and glanced away.

"He'll be here," Dana said. "I know he will. Something must have delayed him."

"He could have called," her mother remarked.

Dana bit down on her lower lip. She wouldn't let doubts eat away at her. She believed in Chay, believed in their love. He could have been detained at the ranch, his best man could have been late, he could have…

Changed his mind. The words whispered through the back of her mind. She shook them off resolutely. Chay wasn't like Rick. Chay loved her.

She clung to that knowledge, refusing to give in to her doubts.

Ten minutes later, there was a knock at the door and the wedding coordinator entered the room. "The groom's here at last," she said, smiling. "And I must say, he's worth waiting for. Are you ready?"

"Yes," Dana replied with a smile. She sent a look that clearly said *I told you so* to her mother, then took up her bouquet and followed the wedding planner toward the chapel.

Chay ran a comb through his hair, blew out a sigh of relief. He had been half-afraid that by the time he made it to the church, Dana would have written him off as a lost cause, packed up and gone back to Ashton Falls once and for all.

He glanced in the mirror, straightened his tie, dusted off his jacket.

"You look fine," Derek said. "You ready?"

"More than ready," Chay said, and opened the door that led into the chapel.

A hush fell over the crowd as Chay and Derek took their places at the altar.

Chay took a deep breath. The organist started playing and Ashley walked down the aisle. She carried a bouquet of pink and white roses. She looked lovely and all grown up in a modest dress of midnight blue. He winked at her and then, as the music heralded the approach of the bride, Chay forgot everything else as Dana appeared in the doorway. Sheathed in a whisper of white satin, one hand on her father's arm, she moved gracefully toward him, her face radiant behind a gossamer veil, so beautiful she took his breath away.

"Who giveth this woman to be married to this man?"

"Her mother and I do," Mr. Westlake said, and placed Dana's hand in Chay's.

His fingers curled around hers.

Caught up in her beauty, Chay scarcely heard what the minister had to say until he came to the part where he asked if Chay would have Dana as his wife.

Chay nodded. "Yes." He cleared his throat. "Yes," he repeated.

"And do you, Dana Elizabeth Westlake, take Chayton Lone Elk to be your lawfully wedded husband?"

Dana squeezed Chay's hand. "Yes."

"Then by the power vested in me, and in the presence of this company, I now pronounce you man and wife. Chay, you may kiss your bride."

Dana's heart was pounding like a war drum as Chay lifted her veil.

"I love you, Mrs. Lone Elk," he murmured for her ears alone, and then he kissed her.

She had warned him about this kiss. It was to be short, just a shadow of a kiss, nothing outrageous. Apparently Chay hadn't listened. He took her in his arms and kissed her until her toes curled inside her shoes. Kissed her until muted laughter rolled through the church. Only then did he draw away.

Dana tried to glare at him but all she could do was smile.

The minister cleared his throat. "May I present Mr. and Mrs. Lone Elk, the newest couple in our fair city."

Chay took her by the hand and they walked down the aisle and out of the church. Once outside, Chay pulled her into his arms and kissed her again, and then, with a grin, he swung her into his arms and carried her down the stairs and into the waiting limo.

The driver shut the door and then Chay was drawing her into his arms once again.

"Just a quick kiss," Dana scolded. "You promised."

"I know," he said, nibbling on her earlobe, "but you didn't tell me you were going to look so beautifully irresistible."

"You were late," she said.

"I know, I'm sorry. Derek decided to take a shortcut and we had a flat. His spare wasn't in much better shape but we got as far as the gas station before it gave out. They didn't have a new tire that was the right size and it took some time to get the old one patched." He shook his head. "I was afraid you'd be long gone by the time I got to the church."

"Never. I knew you'd come. I never doubted it for a minute."

Chay caressed her cheek. "That's my girl."

The reception was everything Dana had ever dreamed of. Though the guests were few, they hadn't skimped on anything. The tables were set with crystal and fine china, there was food and champagne in abundance, soft drinks for the youth. When the meal was over and the tables moved to the edge of the floor, there was dancing.

Naturally, the bride and groom shared the first dance.

Dana moved into her husband's arms feeling more confident, more beautiful, than she ever had in her whole life. Chay looked stunning in his tux. That wasn't surprising, since a tux did amazing things for even the most ordinary men, and Chay was far from ordinary. Just looking at him made her heart skip a beat. She could hardly wait until it was time for them to slip away. Just thinking of being alone with Chay brought a flush to her cheeks.

Later, Dana saw Ashley and Brandon dancing together. Dana smiled as Brandon twirled Ashley around the floor. It was good to see Chay's sister laughing and having a good time. Dana had always wanted a sister and she was glad that Ashley was staying at the ranch. It would give them a chance to get to know each other better.

She watched as Megan, LuAnn and Brittany clustered around Ashley and Brandon when the music ended. Dana smiled inwardly, thinking of the fun they would all have next summer, and how relieved Chay would be that he wouldn't have to act as chaperon.

The rest of the evening passed in a blur. They cut the cake. Her father made a toast to their happiness. Chay's mother also said a few words, her smile warm as she welcomed Dana into the family. Dana danced with her father while Chay danced with his mother.

And then, at last, it was time for them to go. Dana kissed her mom and dad goodbye, hugged Ashley and Claudia, and then she and Chay slipped out a side door to where the limo was waiting.

As soon as they were alone, Chay pulled her into his arms and kissed her, his hands moving over her back, across her breasts.

"Chay!" She glanced at the driver, wondering if he was watching them or the road.

"It's one-way glass," Chay said. "He can't see us."

"Are you sure?"

"I'm sure, darlin'," he said, his voice low and seductive. "Come here."

She lifted one eyebrow. "What do you want?"

"What do you think I want?"

"I truly don't know, sir," she said with mock innocence. "I've never been married before." She paused. "I've never been intimate with a man before."

But that was about to change. The thought sent a rush of heat spiraling to the deepest core of her being. She only hoped she wouldn't disappoint him. "Have you been with a lot of women?"

"A few," he admitted, "but they weren't you."

"Have you ever been in love before?" she asked, and wondered what perverse demon had made her ask such a question at such a time.

"I've been in serious lust a few times." He brushed his lips over the tip of her nose. "But I've never been in love. I know now I was waiting for you."

Sweet words that warmed her inside and out.

"We're here," he said as the limo pulled over to the curb in front of the Wardman Arms Hotel.

Like everything that carried the Wardman name, the hotel was first class all the way, from the etching on the glass doors to the expensive carpet in the lobby.

The driver opened the door for them. He winked at Chay, smiled at Dana, then opened the trunk and carried their bags inside.

Taking Dana by the hand, Chay led her into the hotel lobby and signed the register.

"Mr. and Mrs. Lone Elk," the clerk said, handing Chay a key. "I trust your stay will be a pleasant one. Your bags will be sent up to your room immediately."

Chay nodded his thanks. Dana gasped when Chay swung her into his arms and carried her across the lobby toward the elevator.

"I can walk."

"I know you can," he said amiably, "but I like this better."

Since it was useless to argue, she settled into his arms,

her head resting on his shoulder. It was rather enjoyable, being held in the arms of a strong, handsome man.

Inside the elevator, he nuzzled her neck, sending shivers of anticipation racing down her spine.

He carried her down the hallway to their room, slipped the key card into the slot and carried her over the threshold.

"Here we are, Mrs. Lone Elk."

She nodded, feeling suddenly shy.

A knock at the door announced the arrival of their bags. Reluctantly Chay put her down and opened the door.

The bellboy put their bags in the bedroom, then pointed out the features of the room.

Chay tipped the young man and walked him to the door.

"Enjoy your stay," the young man said. "If you need anything, just let me know."

Chay glanced at Dana. "I've got everything I need right here."

"Yes, sir!" the young man said, grinning, and closed the door.

"Now," Chay said, "where were we?"

"I believe you were about to kiss me."

"I believe you're right."

She smiled as he drew her into his arms.

"Did I tell you how beautiful you are, and how happy I am that you're my wife?"

"Not yet."

He chuckled softly. "You're beautiful, darlin', and I'm the luckiest man in the world."

"I think you're beautiful, too," she murmured.

"Handsome," he corrected.

"All right, handsome, if you insist."

"Enough talk," he said. And then he kissed her with all the love in his heart, and each kiss was a promise of forever.

"I need to get out of this dress," she said when he broke the kiss.

"Let me help you." He turned her around and began unfastening the back of her gown.

His fingertips were warm against her skin. He slipped the dress over her shoulders, let it fall to the floor, then turned her to face him again. "Beautiful!"

She flushed with pleasure and a hint of embarrassment at standing there clad in nothing but her underwear and high heels. "I'll be right back."

He nodded and she hurried into the bedroom to slip into her nightgown. It was long, white and sleeveless, and so sheer it was like wearing nothing at all.

When she returned to the other room, the look on Chay's face told her the gown had been worth the exorbitant price she had paid for it.

He whistled softly, his whole body coming alive at the sight of the vision standing before him. She looked like a naughty angel, innocent yet provocative, Eve before she bit the apple, Pandora before she opened the box.

"Well?" She tilted her head to one side.

"I'm speechless."

She smiled as she glided toward him, then tugged on his jacket. "Are you going to wear this to bed?"

Chay laughed as he shrugged out of his jacket and tossed it over a chair. His tie and shirt followed, then his shoes, socks and belt. Clad only in his trousers, he swung her into his arms and carried her into the bedroom.

Putting her on the bed, he began unfastening his trousers.

Dana's eyes widened. "Aren't you going to turn out the lights?"

"Do you want me to?"

She thought about it for the space of a heartbeat. "No." Wide-eyed, she watched him take off his pants. If she'd had any doubts about whether he wanted her or not, they were soon put to rest.

Still wearing his shorts, he slid into bed beside her and

drew her into his arms. He showered her with warm, sweet kisses, murmuring that he loved her, adored her. Ah, the wonder of his kisses. Somehow, her nightgown disappeared and she reveled in the touch of his bare skin against hers.

Her fingertips glided across his broad chest, feathered over his strong, flat belly, as she marveled at the sheer beauty of the man. His skin was like copper, warm and smooth. His muscles rippled as she caressed him, making her stomach flutter. He let her explore his body to her heart's content, her hands moving a little lower each time until he obligingly removed his shorts. She found that part of him that made him a man as impressive as the rest.

He grinned, obviously pleased. And then he was touching her, his hands patient and gentle as he taught her that there was far more to intimacy than the act itself, that true love between a man and a woman was far more than the joining of passion-heated flesh. It was a uniting of hearts and souls and spirits, a coming together that was stronger than yearning, more enduring than desire.

She felt a soul-deep sense of rightness as their bodies merged and became one. She cried his name, her heart overflowing with wonder and delight as he took her to heights and depths she had never known existed. His clever hands aroused her until she writhed beneath him, yearning, reaching for something that remained just out of her reach until, at last, he carried her over the edge, and the world as she knew it shattered and became something new, something bright and more beautiful than anything she had ever imagined. She was floating on air, riding on a warm sea of sensual pleasure that crested and broke and crested again.

Breathless, unable to express what she was feeling in words, she held him close, her heart swelling with love and gratitude for this man, this moment.

She had never really believed in happy-ever-after, but now, curled in Chay's warm embrace, the ending she had once dreamed of became a reality.

Epilogue

Ashley shook her head when she entered the living room and found Dana and Chay sitting on the sofa, kissing. "Hello. Hello!"

Chay looked at her over the top of Dana's head. "Hello yourself."

"Do you two ever do anything but kiss?"

Chay glanced pointedly at the cradle beside the sofa where his seven-month-old daughter slept. "We make beautiful babies."

Ashley rolled her eyes. "That's what comes from all that kissing. Honestly, you'd think you two were still newlyweds."

Dana smiled. Though she and Chay had been married almost two years, she still felt like a new bride. Her pulse still raced when Chay entered the room. Her heart still swelled with love whenever she saw his smile or heard his voice. Each night in his arms was as wonderful and as exciting as the first time.

She loved being Chay's wife. She loved being a mother. She loved living on the ranch.

And she loved having Ashley and the girls underfoot for the summer. LuAnn, Megan and Brittany had arrived the week before and the house seemed to be in a constant state of activity, the air perpetually filled with the sound of feminine giggles and whispers. The girls all adored the baby and fought over whose turn it was to hold her. One good thing about a houseful of teenagers was that there was always a baby-sitter handy when she needed one. Dana had thought Ashley would want to spend her summers with her mother but Ashley didn't want to be away from the ranch that long. Instead, she went to see Jillian during Easter vacation and for a week at Christmas.

"I hate to bother you," Ashley said, "I just came to remind you that we're going to town with Brandon and some friends."

"Right," Chay said. "Don't be too late."

"Have a good time," Dana said. It was hard to believe that Ashley was almost eighteen, or that she was still seeing Brandon. Ashley dated other young men and Brandon dated other girls, but Dana had a feeling that the two of them were meant to be together. It would, she thought, be a good match.

And life was good, Dana mused as her husband kissed her again. So good, and it only promised to get better.

"Well, don't let me disturb you," Ashley said. "I'm sure Debra Ann would love to have a little brother."

Chay looked down at his wife and smiled. "Sounds like a good idea to me. What do you think?"

"I like it," she said, winking at him. "Let's talk about it later."

Chay nodded. "It's a date."

And later that night, they went upstairs to their room and locked the door.

So they could talk.

* * * * *

If you enjoyed what you just read,
then we've got an offer you can't resist!

Take 2 bestselling love stories FREE!

Plus get a FREE surprise gift!

Clip this page and mail it to Silhouette Reader Service™

IN U.S.A.
3010 Walden Ave.
P.O. Box 1867
Buffalo, N.Y. 14240-1867

IN CANADA
P.O. Box 609
Fort Erie, Ontario
L2A 5X3

YES! Please send me 2 free Silhouette Romance® novels and my free surprise gift. After receiving them, if I don't wish to receive anymore, I can return the shipping statement marked cancel. If I don't cancel, I will receive 4 brand-new novels every month, before they're available in stores! In the U.S.A., bill me at the bargain price of $3.57 plus 25¢ shipping and handling per book and applicable sales tax, if any*. In Canada, bill me at the bargain price of $4.05 plus 25¢ shipping and handling per book and applicable taxes**. That's the complete price and a savings of at least 10% off the cover prices—what a great deal! I understand that accepting the 2 free books and gift places me under no obligation ever to buy any books. I can always return a shipment and cancel at any time. Even if I never buy another book from Silhouette, the 2 free books and gift are mine to keep forever.

210 SDN DZ7L
310 SDN DZ7M

Name	(PLEASE PRINT)	
Address	Apt.#	
City	State/Prov.	Zip/Postal Code

Not valid to current Silhouette Romance® subscribers.

Want to try two free books from another series?
Call 1-800-873-8635 or visit www.morefreebooks.com.

* Terms and prices subject to change without notice. Sales tax applicable in N.Y.
** Canadian residents will be charged applicable provincial taxes and GST.
All orders subject to approval. Offer limited to one per household.
® are registered trademarks owned and used by the trademark owner and or its licensee.

SROM04R   ©2004 Harlequin Enterprises Limited

Books by Holly Chamberlin

LIVING SINGLE

THE SUMMER OF US

BABYLAND

BACK IN THE GAME

THE FRIENDS WE KEEP

TUSCAN HOLIDAY

ONE WEEK IN DECEMBER

THE FAMILY BEACH HOUSE

SUMMER FRIENDS

LAST SUMMER

THE SUMMER EVERYTHING CHANGED

THE BEACH QUILT

SUMMER WITH MY SISTERS

Published by Kensington Publishing Corporation

The Family
Beach House

Holly Chamberlin

KENSINGTON BOOKS
http://www.kensingtonbooks.com

As always, for Stephen
And this time, also for Joseph C. Donner

Acknowledgments

My sincere thanks to John Scognamiglio for his support, creativity, and good humor.

Welcome to our home, Cyrus Smith. Thanks to Dr. Jeffrey Robbins for his care of our kitties. And welcome to the family, Newman and Mr. Bean.

Thanks to all of our good friends in Ogunquit, Cape Neddick, and Portland, Maine.

Special thanks to Kit and Carrie for valuable insights, deviled eggs, good advice, and happy times.

This book is in memory of Callie Ryan-Boyd. She was quite a gal.

Prologue

The Present

Craig McQueen breathed deeply. It was a mid-morning in July and the air was warm but fresh, not humid or close. He had been walking Ogunquit Beach for over an hour, back and forth, stopping to pick up stones and bits of sea glass that caught his attention (only green; he had never found blue), stopping to watch seagulls whirling over the gentle waves. He loved seagulls. He liked their audacity. The tide was going out, leaving seashells on the damp sand—snails' shells, some occupied, some abandoned; broken razor clam shells; and the shells of surf clams, some as long as eight inches, the clams locals collected for chowder.

The beach was busy and would continue to teem with people—families, young people, leathery skinned sun addicts, day-trippers, and those on weeklong vacations—until around five o'clock, when cool showers and fruity cocktails and dinner and ice cream beckoned. Craig didn't mind the crowds. No one in particular owned Nature. And he wasn't a possessive person in any sense.

Craig's eyes scanned the gentle curve of the beach. The

Abenaki Native Americans had it right when they named this place Ogunquit, or "beautiful place by the sea." Supposedly they had summered here in pre-colonial times. Now, hundreds of years later, Ogunquit Beach was considered one of the top ten most beautiful beaches in the United States. Some things never changed, and in this case, Craig thought, it was a good thing.

In the ten years that Craig had lived in Ogunquit year round certain things had, of course, changed—gift and trinket shops had come and gone, as had several restaurants—but, like the beach, other institutions such as Barnacle Billy's remained, their lush, perfectly tended gardens one of the main attractions in Perkins Cove. Reliably, Lex Romane and Joe Riillo were still playing jazz and blues in restaurants and at birthdays and weddings. And down in York Beach, kids were still enjoying the Wild Kingdom Zoo and Amusement Park and the carousel and arcade. Ogunquit's annual Patriots' Day celebration was still alive and well, as was Christmas by the Sea, the mid-December event that marked the official start of the holiday season for residents.

Weeks, months, years. Ten of them. It was hard to believe it had been that long since his family had gathered at Larchmere for the memorial of Charlotte McQueen's death. Charlotte—matriarch, wife of Bill and mother to Adam, Tilda, Hannah, and Craig.

What a strange time that had been! Within two weeks a full-scale drama—could it be called a melodrama?—had unfolded. It was complete with arch villain—that would be his older brother, Adam—and damsel in distress, who would be his sister Tilda, or maybe, thinking more about it, his sister Hannah, Craig supposed.

The thing that had started it all was the stunning news of his father's new romance. Then had followed the panic over the future of Larchmere, the beloved family beach house. Added to this were the private conflicts that, by the weeks' end, had resolved for better or worse, depending on whose opinion you asked.

If you asked Craig, he would say that things had worked out just fine. At least they had for him. He knew he had never been in serious contention for ownership of the family house, for Larchmere, and that had in some way made him a spectator to the main events, though he had had his own existential crisis to handle. Existential crisis—was that what it had been? Yes, he thought that it had. He had confronted his place in the world and had grappled with the question of how to live his life meaningfully. It was a big question deserving, but rarely getting, a lot of thought.

A childish scream of glee erupted to his right and Craig sidestepped a toddler tumbling toward the water, his harried mother right behind him. Craig smiled. He looked at his watch, the one his father had left him when he died the year before, the one Bill had received from his own father so many years ago. The face was round and the band, replaced many times over the years, was brown leather. It was the first watch Craig had ever worn. He liked the way it felt on his wrist. He liked that it once had belonged to his father and grandfather. It made him feel connected to something good, something stable and continuous.

The watch told him that it was eleven o'clock, almost time for lunch. Craig, realizing that he was starved, turned back toward Larchmere, toward home, where Nigel and the other beloved members of his family would be waiting.

1

Tilda McQueen O'Connell had gotten to Ogunquit, and to the house, Larchmere, well before noon. She had left South Portland around ten-thirty, hoping to avoid commuter traffic (which was never very bad going south, anyway), made a stop at a farm stand for blueberries, and gotten to the house just as her father was leaving for a golf game with his old friend and personal lawyer, Teddy Vickes.

Tilda had noted that her father, Bill McQueen, looked hale and hardy, wearing his favorite blue Oxford shirt and that goofy hat he loved. And he had seemed in a particularly good humor. He had even laughed about the inevitability of his losing to Teddy. Not that Bill was, by nature, a grim or dour man. It was just that Tilda had not seen him quite so upbeat in a long time. It was a bit interesting, given the fact that the family was gathering at Larchmere in the next few days to mark the tenth anniversary of Charlotte McQueen's passing. Well, she would take her father's good mood as a positive sign. He had been widowed for ten years. There was no point in prolonged and unnecessary mourning.

If only she could convince herself of that. Frank, her husband, had been gone for a little over two years now, but the fact, the shock, of his loss still seemed so fresh.

Tilda put her travel bags in her room, the one she had always shared with Frank, and did what she always did upon arriving at Larchmere. She went for a stroll around the house and grounds, noting the familiar and the new, and remembering.

Tilda McQueen O'Connell was built like her mother, Charlotte. She was tall—five feet, nine inches when she wasn't slouching, which she lately had a tendency to do— and thin. Also like her mother, and like her older brother, Adam, her hair was dark brown and her eyes hazel or green, depending on the light and what color blouse she was wearing. She wore her hair in a short, stylish cut that softened her longish face. She used very little makeup and her taste in jewelry was simple and classic. Most of it had come from Frank, including the little emerald studs that made her eyes look very, very green.

That day she was wearing a cream-colored linen blouse she had gotten on sale at Marshalls years ago, and olive-colored chinos that were at least six years old. Tilda couldn't remember the last time she had shopped anywhere but at discount stores and outlets. It wasn't that she was overly penny-pinching or seriously in lack of funds. It was just that she saw no reason to pay full price when there was an option not to. For that matter, she also could hardly remember the last time she had shopped just for fun. Retail therapy had lost its appeal about the time of Frank's diagnosis.

Poor Frank. He had never understood why Tilda had stopped wearing skirts a few years back. If you had long, slim legs, he would say, why would you want to cover them? Tilda had no good answer to that. But wearing only pants eliminated one little daily decision, so expediency had won out over vanity. Maybe it was an age thing. Tilda was forty-seven—some would say "only" forty-seven—but sometimes she felt much, much older. Even before Frank had gotten sick she had started to feel—redundant.

Tilda walked down the steps of the front porch and viewed the large, well-kept lawn. The air was warm but fresh. A vibrantly yellow butterfly fluttered past and darted into the stand of tall, graceful, ornamental grasses her mother had loved so much. Tilda breathed deeply. She was happy to be "home." Now, more than ever, Larchmere felt like her refuge, her safe haven. She wished she could spend the entire summer there, and as a high school English teacher she might have been able to but her sister, Hannah, had helped Tilda to get a part-time job as a freelance proofreader at the ad agency where she worked. The summer job would help make ends meet and it would also, maybe more importantly, keep her from feeling too lonely. Frank was gone and the kids, now college-aged, spent more and more time out of the house, as was to be expected. In fact, for the first time ever both Jon and Jane were spending the summer at home in South Portland where each had a job. In past summers they had lived at Larchmere with their mother, grandfather, grandmother, and aunt, waiting tables at local restaurants when they were old enough and spending free time with friends. This summer, Tilda was experiencing her own, unique version of empty nest syndrome.

Tilda walked in the direction of the gazebo. She remembered a particular hot summer night, not long after her wedding, when she and Frank had taken refuge there while a passing thunderstorm drenched and cooled the air. The storm was magnificent. Frank's arms were strong and loving, his kisses warm. She had wished the rain would go on forever.

But rain wasn't always welcome. The summer before, Tilda remembered as she walked on past the gazebo, had been abysmally rainy, the wettest southern Maine had experienced in many years. Farmers had lost entire crops, business owners had suffered, tourists had grumbled, and locals had gone mad—figuratively and literally. But this summer, Tilda thought, at least so far, was truly perfect in comparison. There had been lots of sunny days, a normal amount of rain to nourish the crops and flowers, and a romantic amount of morning fog over the water on more humid days.

Because it was July, Ogunquit and the surrounding areas were decorated with masses of orange day lilies (also called tiger lilies) and vibrant red day lilies. Wild daisies, clover, Queen Anne's lace, and buttercups filled the fields and lined the roadsides. Cattails were wildly growing at the edge of marshes and valerian, with its powerful scent, was invading any empty space it could find a hold.

Nature was certainly prolific, not only in its flora but in its fauna, too. Tilda remembered a spring afternoon, a long time ago, when the entire front lawn of Larchmere had been covered with robins, some busily searching for food, others standing immobile, seeming to stare into space. There had to have been a hundred of them. It was as if someone—the Robin King?—had called a meeting or a convention. Where had they all come from? Why had they gathered that particular afternoon? And why on Larchmere's lawn? It was weird and disturbing, all those feathered creatures, a flock of robins, not seen before or since.

Tilda now approached the enormous pine on which she once had seen perched a great blue heron, a massive blue gray bird swaying in the wind at the very top of the tree. The bird had a cry like a harsh croak, not pleasant to humans, and built its bulky stick nests in trees or bushes. Not far from Larchmere she had once seen a rookery of twenty-three nests. It was an impressive sight. How did birds make such strong, beautiful nests, with no hands and fingers and opposable thumbs? Tilda shook her head. And humans thought they were so special.

Stepping carefully, Tilda made her way into the woods that edged the back of the lawn behind Larchmere. She was about to pay her first visit in years to the fairy house. She wasn't sure why she wanted to see it. For a moment she felt lost, unsure of where the house stood. It was the only fairy house she knew of on this bit of land. On Mackworth Island and Monhegan Island and at the Coastal Maine Botanical Gardens in Booth Bay there were colonies of fairy houses, magical places that compelled you to speak in a hush and watch carefully for signs of fairy dust.

The first fairy house Tilda had ever seen was on the grounds of her aunt's friends Kit Ryan and Carrie Boyd, just over the town line of Cape Neddick. She had been a child, maybe about six or seven, and had been immediately enchanted. She had totally believed that fairies—who were, of course, real—made their homes in the little fantastical constructions of twigs and moss and stones.

When Jane was about five, Tilda had helped her to build her own fairy house with twigs and moss and interesting little rocks and shells they had collected on the beach. Each evening, when Jane had gone to bed, Frank would sneak out and leave little plastic fairies, tinier plastic animals, and even notes from the fairies, written in green ink, on minuscule pieces of paper, in and around the house for Jane to find in the morning. When was it that Jane had finally stopped believing that fairies, the kind in her storybooks, the kind with tiny translucent wings and curly toed booties, weren't real? Tilda thought it had been around the time that puberty reared its ugly head and life lost a certain sort of magic and became all too prosaic.

Larchmere's fairy house had been neglected since Frank

got too ill to maintain it. Why he had continued to care for it after Jane had lost interest was anyone's guess. Tilda thought that maybe it was his way of holding on to his little girl. But maybe she was wrong. She had never asked him why he still cared about the fairy house. She wished that she had.

There it was, or, what remained of it. She looked down at the house in ruins. The roof, a large piece of bark, was on the ground, in pieces. A curious animal had long since carried off the last little plastic figurine. The bright white shells were now only broken, dirty bits. Tilda felt ineffably sad. She turned and walked quickly back to the open and sunny front lawn.

The fairy house was gone. Frank was gone, too, though thoughts of her husband were never far from Tilda's mind. Frank O'Connell had been the physical opposite of his wife, only about five feet, eight inches and always struggling with an extra ten or fifteen pounds. He had been an economics major in college and had gone on to become the small business specialist at Portland's main branch of a large bank. It was a job he loved, helping people with a dream and a passion get started and eventually achieve results.

At work Frank had liked to dress nattily in classic cut suits and vibrant ties and shiny Oxford style shoes, but on the weekends, and whenever he and Tilda and the kids were in Ogunquit, he had liked to wear knee-length cargo shorts, big T-shirts, and Boston Red Sox baseball caps, of which he had a large collection. Tilda routinely begged him to retire the rattier hats but Frank always refused. A hat was serviceable until it came out of the wash in two pieces. That was pretty much the only issue about which Frank was stubborn. He was a sweetheart of a guy, easygoing, everyone who met him agreed. He was genuine and fun and quite simply, likeable. In fact, Tilda thought, there was nothing wrong with her husband, except for the fact that he was dead.

Tilda blinked hard, as if to will away the dark thoughts. And then she heard the crunch of tires on gravel. Her sister Hannah's car, a Subaru Outback much like her own, was just pulling into the long driveway. Good. She was glad for a distraction as the melancholy she had been holding at bay all day was threatening to settle like a sticky, black lump in her chest, something that might choke her.

Tilda walked back up to the front porch of the big old house to await Hannah's arrival.

2

"We got a bit of a late start," Hannah was saying as she dropped one of her travel bags on the kitchen floor. "Our downstairs neighbor's parrot got loose in the hallway again and would not go home."

"I finally persuaded her with some sweet talk and a little treat."

"Why can't her owner handle her?" Tilda asked Susan.

Susan rolled her eyes. "Her owner has issues and let's just leave it at that."

"That bird rules the roost," Hannah added. "Polly really should have a trainer."

Tilda laughed. "Polly the parrot?"

"The owner also isn't very creative."

Hannah McQueen and Susan Sirico had been married for almost three years. Frank had been too sick to attend their wedding in Winchester, Massachusetts. Tilda, Hannah's witness, had worked hard to muster the joy she knew her sister deserved, but with her own spouse dying she had not been very successful. Hannah had even offered to postpone the wedding, at great financial loss, but Tilda wouldn't allow the too generous offer. Her sister had waited long enough for the right to legally wed. Nothing should stand in the way of her big day. Frank had agreed and had written a warm letter of congratulations for Tilda to give to the brides.

The entire McQueen family had attended the service and reception, with the exception of Frank, of course, and of Adam, who arrived after the service was over, claiming he had been held up at the office. At the reception he downed several cocktails in rapid speed and then took off, again claiming work as an excuse. His wife at the time, Sarah, had just rolled her eyes behind his back, but Susan had been visibly angry. She saw Adam's behavior as disrespectful of her union with Hannah. But Hannah had put a lighter spin on things, reluctant, Tilda thought, to admit the possibility of her brother's being as unpleasant and selfish a person as he in fact was.

"Did we miss lunch?" Hannah asked now. She opened the door to the fridge and peered inside.

Tilda shrugged. "I think everyone is on her own."

Hannah emerged from the fridge with a pound of sliced turkey, a pound of sliced Swiss cheese, and a grin.

Physically, Hannah, now forty-four, was clearly her father's daughter. Her hair was a deep, burnished red, just like his had been before it had gone white. She was about five foot six inches tall and had an average build. Her eyes were a blue-green, not the intense blue of her father's, but large and pretty. But where their familial relation really showed was in their mannerisms. Both consistently crossed their legs to the right. Both tapped the tip of their noses with a forefinger when thinking hard. And both liked to eat scrambled eggs with a spoon. Their similarities had been a source of some amusement for Tilda and Craig when they were all growing up, and a source of unexplained annoyance to Charlotte. Adam had never paid much attention to the peculiarities of his family members.

"Here you go." Hannah passed a sandwich to Susan, who eagerly set to her lunch.

Susan was from an Italian-American family who had lived in Falmouth, Maine, for generations. She had dark brown hair and eyes and, in Tilda's opinion, the most enviable skin she had ever seen, even toned and with a natural blush on her cheeks. Susan was a fund-raiser for a family advocacy group in downtown Portland, a job that required a lot of energy and people skills, both of which she had in abundance. While friendly, she brooked no bad behavior. Often the first to laugh at a good joke, she could also be intensely thoughtful. And she was very protective of those she loved, Hannah most of all.

Hannah was a production manager at the Portland branch of a large Boston-based advertising firm. Together she and Susan lived in Portland's West End in a condo that comprised the top floor of an old, restored Victorian home. That meant they had no outdoor space for planting or barbequing, but otherwise their home was exactly what they wanted it to be. They had plenty of access to the great outdoors at Larchmere, only a forty-five-minute drive away.

Hannah put the rest of the turkey and cheese back in the fridge, just as the sound of tires on gravel could be heard. "That's Dad's car."

"He was out playing golf with Teddy," Tilda said.

"Ouch." Susan smiled. "Why does he torture himself like that?"

A few minutes later Bill joined his daughters and Susan in the kitchen. Bill wasn't a very demonstrative man but when it came to Hannah, he could never resist a show of affection. He hugged her warmly.

"How did you do?" Hannah asked, with a grin.

Bill shrugged. "I lost, of course. And no, I'm not telling anyone what I shot."

Bill McQueen was seventy-three years old, a retired Boston businessman. His hair was still thick, though now white, and his eyes were still clear and intensely, piercingly blue. Amazingly his eyesight was still near perfect. The only help he needed he got from the ten-dollar reading glasses he had bought at the pharmacy in town. Bill was just about six feet tall. His taste in clothes was classic, verging on preppy, though Tilda suspected her mother had decided for Bill long ago what he would and would not wear. Tilda doubted her father had bought any articles of clothing since her mother's passing, except maybe socks and underwear. And that dorky hat he liked so much.

Tilda heard the front door open and a moment later her aunt, Ruth McQueen, was in the kitchen. "Greetings all," she said, putting her white, pebbled leather handbag on the table. (Ruth owned approximately one hundred bags of every description.) "I've been to the Bureau of Motor Vehicles and am simply parched. Anyone care to join me in a cocktail?"

"Yes, please," Bill said. "Losing always makes me thirsty for gin."

Ruth laughed. "So that's why you play golf!"

Like her older brother—she was sixty-four—Ruth was a natural redhead, but unlike Bill, she maintained her original deep, burnished shade professionally. She was smallish, about five feet three inches, and slim and strong. She dressed, to use her own old-fashioned expression, "smartly," but always with a bit of drama. Though physically unimposing, Ruth exuded strength of character and a definite individuality. Some people, she knew, found her too outspoken and off-putting. Others thought her eccentric. No one could ignore her. Tilda and Hannah had always been a bit in awe of their aunt.

"So what's new and exciting in your lives, girls?" Ruth asked.

Tilda said, "Nothing."

Hannah said, "Not much."

Susan said, "I've got this very interesting new case. Of course, for the sake of the client's privacy I can't give you details but . . ."

While Susan told her story, Bill, only half listening, sipped his drink contentedly. William McQueen was the patriarch of the family. For the past ten years he had been a widower, living alone in the big house except for the company of his sister, Ruth, now retired. He liked the quiet life they lived, with their small circle of friends—particularly Teddy Vickes and his wife, Tessa, and Bobby Taylor, a lobsterman. But he liked Larchmere better when the house was filled with the sounds of his extended family—his children, now adults, and grandchildren.

When Charlotte was alive, she and Bill had lived at Larchmere as "joint tenants with rights of survivorship." Now that Charlotte was dead, Bill was the sole owner of the house. It had originally belonged to his parents, a plumber and a housewife, who had bought it for a song (relatively speaking) back around 1937. How they had scraped together the money Bill never knew. He did know that the entire undertaking had been for his parents a labor of love. The house was originally only equipped for residence in the summer. Over time, Bill's parents had added a heating system and insulation and electricity. They had replaced the roof and repaired the mortar where necessary and built the guest cottage, which, years later, Bill had renovated.

It was always known that the house would be left to Bill,

not to his sister. Bill had eagerly embraced the legacy of Larchmere, continuing the improvements and expansion, spending more and more time there on weekends and vacations, and eventually retiring to the house when he and his wife were in their fifties. He was never sure that Charlotte entirely shared his commitment to Larchmere. He didn't dare to ask her. It would have broken his heart to know that she would have preferred to live elsewhere, some place more cosmopolitan, some place where the population didn't drastically shrink after Labor Day.

Bill seemed to be the only one who had not been sure of Charlotte McQueen's commitment to Larchmere. She had made no bones about her dislike of the long, quiet winters and her disdain for a good many of the locals, people who had lived in the Ogunquit area for generations. Maybe Bill just hadn't heard his wife's complaints and criticisms. Maybe he had heard but had not been able to bear her opinions. If he had been a different sort of man—his sister would have said a tougher sort of man—he might have confronted Charlotte's discontent. As it stood, Charlotte had gotten into the habit of going off to Portland or Boston and sometimes New York, at least once a week, often for an overnight, leaving Bill alone with his precious house by the sea.

And over the years that precious house by the sea had been grown and improved so that now, instead of being just a two-season house, it was an all-year dwelling, complete with the renovated (it now had a full bath) guest cottage, a gazebo large enough for six people to enjoy a meal, and a three-car garage that housed Bill's 2002 Mercedes S430, Ruth's BMW 3 Series convertible, and a 1961 Volvo P1800, which Bill's friend Bobby just couldn't bear to part with.

No one but Teddy Vickes knew the exact contents of Bill's existing will. Frankly, Bill preferred it that way. Larchmere was no one's business but his own—yet. The one person to whom he would happily have confided the contents of his will refused to accept the confidence. Ruth had told him that sometimes not knowing was best. Bill didn't understand her reluctance to know who would eventually inherit the family house. She had always made it clear that she didn't want to be Bill's heir. Ruth loved Larchmere, but not like her brother did. She had absolutely no interest in taking on the responsibility of a rambling old house, complete with lawns and gardens, and gazebo and guest cottage, especially not at her age.

Ruth had moved in to Larchmere with Bill shortly after Charlotte died. She hadn't asked him if she could, she simply showed up one day, and Bill seemed very thankful for the company. Something had been in it for Ruth, too. She was tired. It was time to take a permanent break from her exhausting career as the senior vice president of a large, international cosmetics firm. Besides, Ruth strongly felt that her brother needed the companionship. Bill had been with Charlotte since they were teens. He had never lived alone. He had never done much of anything without Charlotte besides go to the office to make the money that kept her in tennis lessons, diamond jewelry, and spa vacations.

It had been impossible not to see that though Bill was the breadwinner, Charlotte was the actual head of the McQueen household. She was domineering yet indifferent, difficult, if not impossible to please. There had been little love lost between Ruth and her sister-in-law. For Bill's sake alone they had tolerated each other. Ruth found Charlotte to be mean-spirited, controlling, and parsimonious with her love. Charlotte found Ruth to be vulgar and embarrassing.

Ruth once had found it curious that Charlotte's favorite child was Tilda, a girl so unlike Charlotte herself. By rights, Adam should have been her favorite, self-centered, big-egoed Adam. But then it had dawned on Ruth that Adam could never have provided the near worship that Charlotte required, the near worship that Tilda so readily provided her needy mother. Charlotte must have seen herself in Adam— assuming she was at all self-knowledgeable—and wisely chose her older daughter as acolyte.

Ruth now busied herself with finishing the cocktails and putting out a bowl of mixed nuts (she would fight her brother for the cashews; they had been fighting over cashews since they were children) and a small plate of good olives. She watched Bill chatting with his daughters and daughter-in-law. He was the picture of a contented man.

While some men might have welcomed a solitary existence after so many years with a . . . determined woman, not Bill. He was the sort of man who needed a woman close at hand; it hardly mattered whether it was a wife, sister, daughter, or a friend. In fact, in Ruth's opinion he had always been putty in women's hands, which, she thought, might partly account for his rather poor relationships with his sons. In her experience men didn't respect other men who allowed women to play them like fiddles. But that was only her opinion. And after all, what did she really know about men? Oh, she had had plenty of romantic relationships and she had worked closely with men for her entire long career, but she had never been married, she had never lived with a man other than her father and now, her brother. And daily life with a man you were sleeping with had to teach you lessons you just couldn't learn otherwise.

The cocktails were ready, gin and tonics for Bill and Ruth, a glass of wine for Tilda, and dry martinis for Hannah and Susan.

"To a happy two weeks at Larchmere," Hannah said, raising her glass.

"To my someday winning a game of golf," Bill said, reaching into the bowl of nuts and snagging a few cashews.

Tilda raised her own glass. "To Mom."

"To my brother leaving me a cashew, please."

"To the McQueens," Susan said, "a very interesting group of people."

3

Ruth turned from the sink, where she had been washing salad greens, and reached for a dish towel to dry her hands. Charlotte, with the help of a professional designer, had succeeded in creating a popular room for her family. The kitchen was large and arranged on an open and friendly plan. There was a center island, which included the sink and a cooktop. At the far end of the island the counter was at a higher level, forming a bar top, around which were arranged several stools so that a person could have her afternoon tea there, or a glass of wine while she chatted with the person preparing dinner. A small, round table painted bright blue sat in a sunny alcove, a perfect spot for sipping morning coffee and reading the local paper. A larger, scrubbed pine table was often used for lunch and casual weekday dinners. The walls were a creamy lemon yellow and the cabinets were finished with a honey-colored stain. A rectangular ceramic clock, painted with sunflowers on a vivid blue background, hung on one wall.

"I'm assuming your father hasn't told you about his girlfriend," Ruth said to her nieces and Susan. "He's never been the most communicative man when it comes to personal matters."

They were suitably surprised. Susan shook her head and smiled. Hannah's mouth dropped. Tilda felt as if she had been physically pushed, so off guard did this news take her. "What?" she said. "Dad has a girlfriend?"

"For the past four months or so now. They met a few years ago when they were both on the zoning board. She was married at the time. I seem to recall his talking a lot about her, though. She's divorced now, of course."

"How can you sound so nonchalant?" Hannah asked, her voice rising. "This is a big thing! This is huge!"

Ruth shrugged.

"Who is she?" Tilda pressed. "What does she do? Does she live in Ogunquit? Do we know her? Is she retired?"

Really, Ruth thought. *You would think they'd found out their father was consorting with a terrorist.* "She's hardly retired. She's only fifty. She has a small interior design business. I hear it's successful. What else? Oh, yes, she lives in Portland. I think she has a condo in one of those developments on the pier. When she's in Ogunquit she stays at a B and B. Rather, she used to. Now she stays here. She has no children."

"And this has been going on for how long? Four months? And Dad never said a word to me!" Hannah felt hurt. Why hadn't her father told her about this woman? She had thought they were close. "Wait, what's her name? Do we know her?"

"Jennifer Fournier," Ruth told them. "Some people call her Jen, but not your father. I don't know, you might have met her. She lived in Ogunquit for some time, while she was married. Her husband commuted to Boston every day for work. That can't have helped the marriage, but what do I know."

Tilda put her hand over her heart. "I'm shocked. Really, I can't believe I'm hearing this."

"Why?" her aunt said. "Your father's not a kid but he's hardly in the grave. He's handsome, intelligent, nice, if not the wittiest guy around. Why shouldn't he have a little fun?"

Susan, who had been silent until now, said, "I think it's great. People shouldn't be alone. And yes, Tilda, I mean everyone, including you. If one of my parents died I would want the other to find a companion, remarry, something. I'm not saying it would be perfectly easy for me to accept, but I would accept it."

"She would," Hannah said. "But she's not a McQueen. She's well adjusted."

"I'm well adjusted," Tilda protested. "I'm just surprised. That's normal."

Ruth sighed. "Well, I suggest you girls get used to the idea of your father having a girlfriend. I have a feeling this is pretty serious. Okay, I'm going up to change for dinner. I'll see you all later."

When she had gone Tilda and Hannah stood staring at each other. Neither said a word. Neither had any idea of what to say. Bill's relationship with Jennifer was "serious."

Susan cleared her throat. "If I could interrupt the psycho-path convention here, I'd like to suggest we all go and change for dinner. Hannah?"

Hannah mutely followed Susan from the kitchen. A moment later, Tilda, too, went to her room to change. In the upstairs hall she paused to examine the embroidered sampler hanging on the wall close to the bathroom. Her paternal grandmother had sewn it. On a background of cream-colored linen was depicted a simplified Larchmere as it had looked back around the time of her father's childhood. A rudimentary garden with flowers of faded pink and yellow spread from each side of the house to the borders of the wooden frame. Across the top of the piece Grandma Ruth had spelled out "Larchmere" in an elaborate stitch that Tilda couldn't name. (She had only mastered the cross-stitch.)

She went into her room and closed the door behind her. Her beloved Larchmere! Before Grandpa Will had bought the house, it had been, as far as anyone knew, without a name. But Grandpa Will had decided to call the house Larchmere for, Tilda supposed, the number of larches, a type of pine, rimming the back edge of the property. She knew that "mere" meant a small, standing body of water, but as far as she knew there hadn't been such a thing on the land since before her grandfather's time. Another meaning for "mere"—and she had looked it up as a child—was boundary. That made a bit more sense. The larch pines themselves formed a sort of boundary, and she knew of the remains of an old stone wall in their depths.

The house, built largely of stone, was composed of two floors and a large basement in which Charlotte had installed a small gym and a finished laundry room. On the first floor were the kitchen, a powder room (added by Bill and Charlotte), the dining room, the library, the living room, and a screened-in sunroom (also an addition by Bill and Charlotte). Charlotte, a devotee of the sun, had opened up walls wherever possible and added windows, eager to make the big old house as bright and open as it could be. There was a stone fireplace in the living room, used often in winter, and an iron, wood-burning stove in the library, which gave off a tremendous heat. Across the entire front of the house and around one side ran a covered porch, decorated with wicker chairs and love seats, painted white, and small tables of varying heights. When Charlotte was alive there had also been an ornate, thronelike wicker rocker, hers especially, but after her death, it had been relegated to the basement. Tilda was not sure why, or who had made the decision to remove this very personal piece of furniture from the family's sight. Maybe her father had not been able to bear the sight of anyone but his wife in it.

On the second floor of the house were the master bedroom and bathroom, facing the front lawn, off which sat a small but lovely deck; a second full bathroom; and four bedrooms of varying size. To accommodate extra guests, the library had a big, brown leather sleeper couch. Craig, used to sleeping in his van, on other people's beds—indeed, on any horizontal surface he could find—often bunked down in the library, leaving one of the upstairs bedrooms empty. As he was an avid reader, like Tilda, his retreat to the library made a certain sense.

Ruth's bedroom was, interestingly, as she had had a choice, the smallest of the four, and decorated (some would say crammed) with exotica from her travels. There was a swath of watered blue silk, hung from a rod on the wall, that she had picked up in England. On the floor was an antique patterned rug from Iran. On her dresser sat an intricately carved jade box from China, in which she kept her most precious jewelry. Her many handbags were stored floor to ceiling on custom-made shelves. Tilda remembered these details from a permitted visit years earlier. Ruth kept her door locked, though a cat door had been cut out near its base for Percy, her gray and white, five-year-old longhair, to come and go as he pleased.

Tilda sat heavily on the edge of the bed now. Ruth's comment, that she thought her father's relationship was serious, was weighing on her. Serious meant marriage, especially for a man of Bill's generation and disposition. Marriage meant that what was mine was yours and vice versa. Larchmere was Bill's. Would it someday also be Jennifer Fournier's?

Tilda put her head in her hands. She knew she was being dramatic, imagining the worst possible thing that could happen. But she couldn't help herself. With her father romantically involved it felt as if the very foundations of her life were compromised. Larchmere might soon pass out of the family McQueen. And what would happen to her then?

She simply couldn't imagine Larchmere not being home. She simply could not.

The McQueens met for dinner that evening in the dining room, the only somewhat formal room in the house and only used when family or friends were staying at Larchmere. Charlotte had enjoyed collecting fine china, which she displayed in a tall and unusually deep cabinet she had bought at an antique shop in Kennebunkport. She had also enjoyed collecting expensive linen table settings—cloths, runners, placemats, and napkins. These were kept in a large, low credenza, on top of which was displayed a Murano glass bowl Charlotte had purchased while traveling in Italy with an expensive tour group one summer. It had never occurred to Tilda to ask her father for a tablecloth, or vintage milk glass creamer and sugar bowl set, or the set of sterling silver napkin rings her mother had bought in a SoHo gallery in New York, as a memento of her mother. Tilda's own home furnishings were of a much simpler and less fine sort and she felt that her mother's possessions would be very out of place in her own relatively humble South Portland home.

The family gathered around one end of the oval-shaped dining room table, Bill and Ruth, Hannah and Susan, and Tilda. Percy kept a close eye on the meal from the top of the credenza. If it bothered anyone that a very furry cat chose to be in the vicinity of food, no one had the nerve to complain about this to Ruth. (If Charlotte were alive, however, Percy would have long since been banished from the dining room.)

"Look at us," Hannah said. "We could be a print ad for L.L. Bean." It was true. Hannah was wearing chinos, white boat sneakers without the laces, and a coral colored, light-weight cotton sweater. Susan wore a chino skirt, blue boat sneakers, and a striped linen big shirt tied at the waist. Tilda had changed into fairly new, tan chinos and a lemon yellow cardigan over a matching T-shirt. Bill wore a blue Oxford cloth button-down shirt tucked into pressed chinos. Only Ruth looked urban and out of place, in black linen slacks and a crisp, tailored, very white blouse with the starched collar turned up. Around her neck she wore a bold silver disc on a black silk cord. Her flats were also black silk. She could have been off for luncheon at MOMA in New York City.

Ruth reminded them—not that anyone had forgotten—that Adam, his new fiancée, and his children were due to arrive the next day.

"I'm dying to meet Adam's fiancée," Tilda said. "I can't imagine what she'll be like."

Hannah laughed. "Oh, can't you? I've got a pretty good idea. At least, I know she'll be a whole lot younger than Adam."

"There's nothing necessarily wrong with that," Ruth commented, with a look at her brother. Bill, busily eating, did not seem very interested in the women's speculations.

"Of course not," Susan agreed. "But it won't be easy on Sarah if Adam marries someone much younger."

Ruth, who had remained close to her nephew's ex-wife, shook her head. "I wouldn't worry about Sarah, if I were you. She's not the sort who's easily thrown by such trivia."

"But," Tilda said, "she will be concerned about what kind of person is going to be her children's stepmother."

Ruth nodded. "Of course, as well she should be. Still, she won't be able to prevent Adam from marrying whomever he pleases."

Hannah, who was feeling impatient with the talk of Adam's soon-to-be wife, took it upon herself to move on to the topic she and her sister really wanted to discuss. "So, Dad," she said, with false casualness, "speaking of relationships, Ruth tells us that you're seeing someone. Romantically, I mean."

Bill looked up from his plate and blushed. His embarrassment embarrassed Tilda. But he didn't seem in the least bit ashamed, and that angered her. Her anger, irrational, further embarrassed her. She reached for her wineglass.

"Well, as a matter of fact I am," he said.

Now that the subject had been introduced, Hannah didn't know what else to say. She looked helplessly to her sister. Tilda shook her head. Plenty of thoughts were racing in her mind but none of them was able to emerge as a coherent comment or question.

Susan, who was sitting next to Bill—Ruth was at the head of the table—patted his hand. "Well," she said, "I think it's great, Bill. We look forward to meeting her."

"She'll be here for the memorial, but you'll meet her before that. We see each other pretty often, whenever her business allows."

Tilda was stunned. Her father's girlfriend would be attending Charlotte McQueen's memorial? Ruth was right; this relationship was, indeed, serious. She wondered if Jennifer Fournier enjoyed sailing and then thought: *What a bizarre thing to wonder about!*

Because Charlotte McQueen had died in a sailing accident. She had been out with a friend and had stumbled over a coil of rope that perhaps should not have been where it was. She had fallen and hit her head and that had been that. She was dead instantly. It was a death vaguely romantic and without obvious mess, something, Hannah thought, befitting the rather snobbish Charlotte. Aware of its harsh character, she, thus far, had only shared her opinion with Susan.

"We're all very happy for you, Bill," Susan was saying now. "Aren't we?"

"Yes," Ruth said emphatically. "We are."

Reluctantly, Tilda and Hannah murmured their assent.

Tilda was sitting at the window of her bedroom. The lights were off in the room, which meant that she could see the designs of the trees in the dark outside, branches long and clawing, trunks black against the blue night. She couldn't sleep. She was worried about the uncertain future of her beloved Larchmere. She was worried about her own uncertain future.

What would happen to her if her father remarried and the family home ceased to be the family home? It scared her to think of the house being lost to a stranger. But it also scared her to think about the possibility of her father leaving Larchmere to all four McQueen children. There would be absolute chaos! It would be impossible to negotiate with Adam, who always had to be right, and as for Craig, he would just take off and leave the others to pay his share of the upkeep. Tilda loved her younger brother but she wasn't blind to his faults. As for Hannah . . . Well, Tilda suddenly realized she had absolutely no idea how her sister felt about the possibility of inheriting Larchmere. Hannah and Bill were very close. There was no reason her sister could not be considered a possible sole heir.

And if Hannah were to inherit Larchmere, would she

cherish and protect it the way Tilda knew it deserved? Again, she had absolutely no idea. They had never talked about the house and what it meant to them. They had simply taken it for granted.

An owl hooted. Tilda thought he sounded melancholy. She hugged herself tightly. Was there nothing upon which she could rely? Death took loved ones away. It had stolen her mother and her husband. Time and distance could loosen emotional ties. And now, what if her father remarried and as a result, even Larchmere, her beloved home, was stolen from her?

Life was loss. She knew that. And she had been as prepared as anyone could be for the impending death of a loved one. She had read books and articles in magazines and online. She had bought a copy of Elisabeth Kübler-Ross's classic book, *On Death and Dying,* and dutifully read it through.

She knew all about the five stages of grief. First there would be denial. That would be followed by anger, and then by bargaining. Next would come depression and finally, at long last, there would come acceptance.

She also knew that the stages of grief were not distinct. She knew that they sometimes overlapped and nipped at each other's heels. She was prepared to feel numb. She was prepared for the deep yearnings for Frank that would threaten to overwhelm her. She was prepared for the bouts of awful sadness, for the tears, for the withdrawing from friends and family.

She was as prepared as it was possible to be, which meant that when Frank finally died she was hardly prepared at all.

On the AARP Web site (she had turned everywhere for help) she had been told that grief, like life, doesn't proceed in an orderly fashion. "Mourning," they had said, "cannot happen without your participation." Too bad, she had thought. Because mourning was exhausting and surprising, no matter how prepared you thought you were.

She was tired now. She got up from her seat by the window and crawled into the bed. She still slept on the right side though she could have slept on the left or diagonally, or right in the middle of the bed if she chose. But she didn't choose.

4

Monday, July 16

It was early, not quite seven in the morning, and the air was just beginning to warm. Tilda stood gazing out over the water. The beach was almost entirely empty. A few runners, a few solitary strollers, a few hobby fishermen, and Tilda, who had walked Ogunquit Beach more times than she could ever count.

She began now to walk in the direction of Wells, her eyes fixed to the sand in search of the ever elusive, whole sand dollar. She knew people who had found them, albeit very small ones, on Ogunquit Beach. She just had never found one herself.

"Hello, Tilda McQueen O'Connell!"

Tilda looked up and smiled. "Tessa Vickes!" It was Teddy's wife, another early morning walker. She was walking from Wells, down close to the waterline. She was wearing a cotton-candy pink sweatshirt and her thick, beautiful white hair was tied back in a simple braid.

"Beautiful day!" Tessa shouted as she continued to walk.

"Yes, it is!" Tilda waved and walked on, as well.

Tessa and Teddy had been married for almost fifty years. Tilda thought they were adorable together, still affectionate and clearly happy. She had never heard mention of children or grandchildren. Maybe Tessa and Teddy had not had a family. Maybe a child had died. Tilda knew she could ask her aunt about this but she didn't want to. There was something almost sacred about a couple's past, especially the past of a couple who had been together for so long.

Not that Tilda would ever experience such a long marriage, though she knew she should be grateful—and she was—for the twenty-odd years she and Frank had enjoyed. Those twenty-odd, almost perfect years . . .

Increasingly, Tilda found herself wondering about nostalgia, or, more specifically, about romanticizing her past with Frank. She wondered if the process was inevitable and necessary and if so, she wondered if it had already begun. Was nostalgia destructive if it became extreme? She thought that it might be. Still, at this point, a little over two years after Frank's death, she could barely remember ever arguing with him and what conflict she did remember had no emotional weight.

Like the time a few years back when he had invited his out-of-work cousin, Ben, to stay with them until he got back on his feet—without first asking his wife. Frank had apologized profusely, claiming he had been guilted into making the offer by his aunt. Whatever the reason behind Frank's offer, the reality was that Cousin Ben was entirely ungrateful. He never offered to help with meals, or to clean the bathroom he used. He came home at all hours and more than once he went out while forgetting to lock the front door behind him. Frank had talked to him several times but to no avail. Cousin Ben was with them for almost five months until a friend offered him a better free deal, after which time they had found a few items missing, including a pearl necklace Tilda's mother had given her for her twenty-first birthday.

God, she had been furious with Frank, but now the entire episode seemed unreal, a false memory, meaningless, something that might have happened to strangers.

Tilda passed a group of about seven or eight snowy white and gray seagulls, sitting perfectly still on the sand, looking in the direction of the morning tide. They looked like seven or eight Aladdin's lamps. The thought amused her.

Ogunquit Beach was always alive with animal life— piping plovers, terns, gulls, stranded seals, who were then, mercifully, rescued and rehabilitated by wildlife experts. On occasion, Tilda had even seen an eagle gliding high over the low grassy dunes. But though she searched the sky each time she went down to the beach, she had not seen another eagle since a month before Frank's death.

Tilda heard mad screeching behind her and turned to see the Aladdin's lamps take flight. One had probably spotted a potential meal and the race was on. She turned and continued her walk.

In all the mysteries and ghost stories she had read, contact with the other world seemed to come so easily to the characters. But real people, too, claimed they had communicated with the spirits of the dead and Tilda saw no reason not to believe them. Who was she to say that only what was visible was real? There were more things in heaven and earth than were dreamt of in man's philosophy. Of course, there were cranks among those who swore they had had supernatural experiences. But there were cranks everywhere. You just had to choose to believe and to proceed carefully.

So it made sense that after Frank's passing she half thought that somehow she would be able to contact him, or that he would be able to contact her. Maybe, she thought, they would be able to have actual conversations of a sort. Soon after he died she began to look for signs of other-worldly communication but, to her dismay, found none. But she kept her mind open to possibilities. She talked to Frank in her head and out loud, when she was alone, but it was as if she was talking only to herself. Frank was not hearing her and she was not hearing him. His ghost or his spirit, if such a thing existed—and Tilda believed that it did, though she couldn't say how, exactly—was gone. Tilda was alone, with only the memories.

The silence was deafening. Tilda's soul was stagnant. Of course, she had considered seeking the help of a medium or a psychic. They were in every town. There was one right in Portland's Old Port. But she just didn't trust herself to make an informed decision about who was genuine and who was a fake. She continued to believe, but cautiously.

Then, early in the spring, on the second anniversary of Frank's death and a few months before her mother's memorial, Tilda had made a decision. She decided to believe that Frank would send an eagle to her. It would be his message that it was okay to move on, that it was time to stop mourning and to begin living. He would send it when the time was right. The eagle would be Frank's blessing.

It was a comforting notion. But, Tilda being Tilda, she began to wonder what would happen if Frank failed to send her that blessing. What if she never did see another eagle over Ogunquit Beach? What then? Would she be doomed to live in darkness and sorrow for the rest of her life? Was that what Frank would want?

Tilda shook her head. If Frank could hear her thoughts he would scold her for indulging in unnecessary, negative, superstitious, unproductive thinking. It was true. She did have a dark, even macabre streak, something Frank absolutely had not had. Frank had been deep but he had not been dark. He was a person who could see in the coldest, gloomiest day of winter the opportunity for something good—like gathering the family to learn a new card game or making popcorn and watching a favorite movie.

And, Tilda thought now, there certainly were enough cold and gloomy days in southern Maine, though autumn could be surprisingly warm, at least into early October, when the marshes became golden and sere. Leaf-peeping season was brief but spectacular, usually put to an abrupt end by a violent but majestic thunderstorm that left trees bare and so drenched they felt pulpy to the touch. Bird life was still visible until then. If you watched you could still spot a variety of wild ducks, graceful egrets, loons with their mournful cry, and cormorants, their silhouettes eerily vampirelike when they dried their outstretched wings.

Then came the winters, which were so bad primarily because they were so long, the cold, ice, and snow slowly, slowly evolving into a season of gray, brown, and mud. Most restaurants closed for a month or two, the Ogunquit Museum of American Art went dormant, people left for homes in Key West or Phoenix. It was possible to drive through the entire downtown and then back to Larchmere without seeing one other person, on foot or behind the wheel of a car. It was possible to feel you were going slightly mad. A trip to the Hannaford supermarket in York or Wells, whether or not you needed groceries, became a sanity-saving expedition. People who shunned church during the rest of the year turned up at Sunday services just to hear a voice other than their own.

Of course, there was also a certain charm to winters in Ogunquit. Those who lived there year round had transformed entertaining at home to a fine art. Friends hosted potluck dinners and played board games and cards. The open fields, the town itself, the houses, all was picture postcard perfect, New England at one of its most romantic moments, single white candles in a house's every window and pines sugared with glittering snow.

And then it was early spring, March, when everyone was desperate for sun and warmth and got only mud season, when stretches of marshy land (thankfully, protected from development) were under water and even carefully planned developments, with their big, tasteful houses and perfectly groomed landscapes, seemed ugly and sad.

In April, when warmth began to creep into the air and the sun to shine for a few hours every day, the town, as if desperate for celebration, sponsored a Patriots' Day event in the parking lot of the beach. There were craftspeople selling their wares, and hamburgers and hot dogs sold to benefit the fire department, and sometimes even a band to get people dancing.

May, though still fairly chilly, was a gorgeous month in Ogunquit and the surrounding towns. Late spring was Tilda's favorite time of the year, partly because of the enormous contrast it presented to the barren, brownish-gray damp of March and April. Lilacs were suddenly everywhere, the dark purple French variety, the common pale purple, and the creamy white ones Tilda particularly loved. Stretches of Shore Road presented virtual walls of lilac. The scent could be overwhelming, sweet to the point of intoxication, and Tilda loved it, though the lilacs had made poor Frank sneeze.

Yes, Tilda thought now, as she passed and nodded to another early morning walker—a woman in an electric blue sweatshirt with the cartoonish image of a smiling red lobster splashed across the front—living in Maine, an official Vacationland, was an interesting, sometimes annoying, sometimes exhilarating experience. Living in Ogunquit intensified or concentrated that experience because Ogunquit was, in many ways, the perfect vacation destination.

There was the venerable Harbor Candy Shop on Maine

Street, and fantastic bakeries like Bread and Roses, which made, in Tilda's opinion, the best white toasting bread she had ever eaten. There were fine dining restaurants, such as Arrows on Berwick Road, and 98 Provence on Shore Road. There were more casual eateries, like the Cape Neddick Lobster Pound in Cape Neddick, and Barnacle Billy's in Perkins Cove, where George and Barbara Bush had often been spotted, and down in Wells, there was Mike's Clam Shack on Route 1, which made the juiciest fried mushrooms you could want, and Billy's Chowder House right smack in the middle of a marsh, with excellent steamers and onion rings. And of course, on Post Road in Wells, there was the famous Maine Diner, not to be missed by anyone wanting an authentic "small town" diner experience.

There were local golf courses and scenic cruises like those run by Finestkind, and art to be found in galleries like the Van Ward Gallery and the Barn Gallery on Bourne Lane, the birth of which was spearheaded by the actor J. Scott Smart in 1958. The Ogunquit Museum of American Art, a beautiful white building overlooking the ocean, was esteemed for its large and diverse collection of work by artists from all across the country.

And of course there were more quaint pleasures like the trolleys—Polly, Molly, Holly—to shepherd tourists and the occasional local to and from Ogunquit and its neighboring towns. There were no end of guesthouses and bed and breakfast offerings, as well as family-oriented motels like the Anchorage and grander hotels, like the Cliff House.

Tilda had always had a love/hate relationship with the summer visitors to Ogunquit, complicated by the fact that for a long time she herself had been—and to some extent still was!—a summer visitor to the town. The town's population in winter was a mere one thousand people. In summer it swelled to twenty thousand. There was no doubt that tourists were good for the economy. It was just that traffic became a nightmare from Memorial Day to Labor Day. Once it had taken Tilda forty minutes just to get from her favorite farm stand to Larchmere, a drive that usually took less than fifteen minutes. And that had been on a rainy weekend! But people had booked vacations and, come rain or shine, they would be flocking to Ogunquit and Wells for the beach, family accommodations, and miniature golf, and to Kennebunk and Kennebunkport for a bit more upscale vacation experience, or farther up to Booth Bay to visit the botanical gardens or to Bar Harbor to hike the trails in the Acadia National Park, or farther still to Greenville and Moosehead Lake, where you could take a moose cruise and, if you were lucky, actually see one of the gigantic animals in its natural habitat.

The massive cruise ships would be unloading in Portland through the early fall, their passengers flooding the Old Port's pubs, gift and craft shops, then making their way up into the city to visit the L.L. Bean outlet on Congress Street and then to the Portland Museum of Art, and after, maybe to Victoria Mansion. Others would be day-tripping north to Freeport or south to Kittery to shop at the outlets. Others would take a bus (provided by the cruise line) down to Ogunquit for the day, with maybe a stop at a lobster shack for a lobster roll, a red hot dog, and a whoopee pie.

And there would always be shopping. There would always be husbands and boyfriends hunched glumly on small wooden benches outside the shops on Main Street, Ogunquit, or Commercial Street, Portland, waiting while their wives purchased souvenirs for the kids back home or overpriced T-shirts with slogans like "Lobstahs Rule" and "The Way Life Should Be," and snow globes with plastic mermaids and sand dollars inside. Or they would be pacing nervously outside high-end shops and galleries, the kind that sold one-of-a-kind jewelry, art, and crafts for exorbitant prices, while their wives "treated themselves" for the third time in a week. Tilda herself still wore a gold starfish charm she had "treated herself" to back when she was in college. She had bought it in a shop down in Perkins Cove called Swamp John's. It had been an outrageous purchase for her, but a deliciously satisfying one as most outrageous purchases are.

Tilda suddenly realized that she was almost at the Wells town line. Ogunquit Beach—or Main Beach, as it was also known—ran about one and half miles to Wells, where the temperature of the air changed dramatically. Her father's old friend Bobby, who had been born and raised in Ogunquit, as had his father before him, had explained the phenomenon to her once a long time ago, but Tilda, who didn't have much of a head for science, could not now remember much of what he had said.

She did, however, keep close watch of the tide chart, though it was her habit to go to the beach each morning no matter how high or menacing the tide. The beach had a different beauty and interest every day of the year. It was the one place where Tilda could not imagine anyone ever being bored. In fall came the welcome return to the beach of dogs (and their people), banned from April until October. In the winter came weird drifts and patterns of snow and ice on the sand.

She had walked the length of the beach in all types of weather—in snow and in fog, in rain and in sunshine. Frank had thought she was crazy to go out in subzero weather, even though she was properly dressed against the cold in layers upon layers of fleece and wool. "You're not a mail carrier, Tilda," he would say. "You're under no obligation to leave the house no matter the weather."

But the beach called to her. To walk on Ogunquit Beach was a necessary part of her well-being. It was often inspiring and always interesting. The saddest thing she had ever seen on the beach was a dead dolphin. Tears had come spontaneously to her eyes and she had quickly looked away. The oddest thing she had ever seen on the beach was a roasting pan. A large roasting pan, washed perhaps from some wreck of a pleasure boat. Or maybe an irate wife had thrown it overboard when her ungrateful husband had criticized the meal she had made for him. But who would roast a piece of beef or a chicken out at sea, other than, maybe, a chef on a large ocean liner? And unless he was Gordon Ramsay, why would he toss his kitchen equipment overboard?

A more common site after a storm was the scattering of broken lobster traps. It was illegal, of course, to make off with one to use as decoration for your lawn or screened-in porch, but Tilda had seen people do just that, pick up the tumbled, sandy traps and carry them off to their cars.

Once she had approached an opportunist in the beach parking lot, someone she had watched haul a washed-up trap from the beach to her car. It was a woman who looked to be in her sixties, wearing a pair of skin-tight hot pink shorts and a T-shirt that proclaimed she was a "FOXY GRANDMA." She was definitely not a local, probably not even a Mainer. Politely, Tilda had told the woman that taking a lobsterman's trap was illegal, something she suspected the woman already knew. For a moment the woman had simply stared at Tilda through her spangled designer sunglasses, and then she had shrugged. "Finders keepers," she had said, and put the battered trap in the trunk of her car.

Tilda could have reported her to the police; maybe she should have, but she had not. She had felt bad about that for a long time. After all, Bobby, her surrogate uncle, made his living as a lobsterman. Tilda knew how tough a life he led. She knew he couldn't easily afford the loss—or theft— of his equipment. She had put her silence down to basic cowardice, to an innate distaste for making trouble, even when trouble was just what was called for. Confrontation in any form was not something Tilda ever sought and when she sensed it coming, she turned tail and ran. It wasn't one of her more stellar moral traits, emotional cowardice.

Worse, Tilda had a sneaking suspicion that this cowardice was what was holding her back now, preventing her from really embracing her life without Frank.

At the Wells town line, Tilda stopped and scanned the blue morning sky. No eagle. She turned and began the long walk back to her car. Then she returned to the easy comfort of Larchmere and the good, strong coffee that would be brewing in its kitchen.

5

Adam McQueen, fifty years old, new fiancée and his two children in tow, arrived at the house around eleven o'clock. He swept through the front door with the air of the lord of the manor returning from a successful foray into the larger world. All he needed was a chained, defeated dragon trailing behind and a big bag of booty slung over his shoulder. At least, that was how Tilda saw his entrance.

"Everybody," he announced by way of greeting, "this is my fiancée, Kat Daly."

Ruth, Tilda, and Hannah were left to introduce themselves. Bill was out, no one knew where. Susan had taken a work-related call in her bedroom. Percy, not a fan of greetings and departures, especially those involving children, was absent.

The children, eight-year-old Cordelia and six-year-old Cody, were slightly cranky, maybe from the traffic-choked ride up from Boston, maybe from boredom, though Tilda had recently learned that her brother's family car, a Range Rover Sport, was equipped with a DVD player so Cordelia and Cody could watch movies from the backseat. Cordelia was tall for her age, and like her father, slim. She liked clothes and was already a bit of a fashionista. Cody closely resembled his mother but his eyes were the same change-able hue as Adam's and Tilda's were. Now, when the chil-dren were told they were to sleep in one of the upstairs bedrooms, apart from Adam and Kat, Cody looked like he was going to cry. Cordelia put her arm around her little brother and the gesture almost made Tilda cry. Her own two children were close, too. They were lucky.

"Have you heard the big news, Adam?" Hannah was saying.

"What big news? You're moving to Vegas to be a show-girl?"

"Screamingly funny. No, it's more earth shattering than that. Dad's got a girlfriend."

"He what?" Adam looked both outraged and disbeliev-ing. "What right does he have at his age . . . ? I'll have a talk with him."

Hannah turned to her sister and muttered, "Oh, that'll solve everything."

"Will you people stop," Ruth said. "There is no problem to be solved. Enough."

Adam McQueen was a male version of his mother, Charlotte—handsome, tall, with a slim, muscular build. He had a dashing quality about him that, in his sisters' views, was dampened by a generally annoyed, harried expression. His hair was dark brown and expertly, expensively cut; his eyes were hazel or green, depending on the light, like Tilda's. Adam was known to spend a lot of money on his wardrobe (too much, according to his ex-wife) and his taste in cars was clearly meant to impress the sort of person susceptible to obvious displays of wealth. Currently, in addition to the Range Rover Sport, he owned a Ferrari 460 Spider. At the moment he was wearing a conspicuously designer polo shirt tucked in to crisply creased cotton-blend slacks. On his left wrist he wore a Rolex. It was real; he had made it a point of letting his family know that. Tilda wore a ten-year-old Timex. Hannah wore a Swatch. Craig didn't own a watch and probably wouldn't wear it if he did.

Adam was obviously self-obsessed but entirely self-deluding and unaware. In this way he was also like his deceased mother, which, of course, was not an observation he was capable of making. This similarity did not go unnoticed, however, by his siblings, though Tilda was loath to think or say anything negative or critical about their mother.

Hannah watched her brother not so subtly checking his image in the hall mirror. He seemed like such a caricature. She wondered if he had always been so one-dimensional, or if he had flattened out somewhere along the line, morphed from a three-dimensional person to a cartoon of a being. Hannah didn't know. She realized that she had never paid much attention to Adam when they were kids. Maybe it was the age difference. Six years could be a big divide when you were young.

Once she had asked Tilda about her memories of Adam as a child; they were only three years apart. Tilda had hesitated before saying, "Adam was an indifferent older brother, at best." It hadn't exactly answered Hannah's question but it had revealed something about her sister's feelings regarding him. Still, Hannah found Adam amusing in spite of his being a bit of an ass. Or maybe, she found him amusing because of it.

His fiancée, a woman named Kat Daly, was very attractive in a blond ingenue sort of way. Certainly, she knew how to dress to emphasize her enviable figure. She was wearing tight, white, low-rise jeans; a hot pink halter type top; high, skimpy, silver sandals; and perched on her sleek, shiny head was a pair of designer sunglasses. Her eyes were a suspiciously bright blue (colored contacts, Hannah wondered?) and her nails sported a French manicure. In fact, Hannah thought, she had a bit of a Jessica Simpson thing going on, but she seemed not half as ditzy. Maybe she was a good actress. Whatever the case, it was no surprise that Adam would find her a suitable replacement for his middle-aged wife with her crinkly middle-aged neck. Who cared if she could cook or clean house? Kat looked good on his arm and, as Adam was loudly pointing out to Tilda, she made a good income as a junior account executive in a small but thriving marketing firm in a Boston suburb. *Huh,* Hannah thought. *So Kat has brains and beauty.* Maybe she had underestimated her brother. It was doubtful but stranger things had been known to happen.

Kat and Adam went upstairs to get settled. The children trailed after them, dragging backpacks almost bigger than they were. (That was another thing that puzzled Hannah. Since when had kids needed to lug around so much stuff? They would all be having back surgery before their twenty-first birthdays.)

"What kind of stepmother is she going to be, I wonder?" Tilda was at her sister's side, asking her question softly.

Hannah whispered back, "As long as she can open a juice box, she'll do for his kids. Adam doesn't want another maternal presence in his life. He wants a trophy."

"I wonder if Sarah has met her yet."

"I don't know. Poor Sarah. On second thought, she knows she's well rid of Adam. She'll probably feel sorry for the kid."

"She does seem nice," Tilda said. "She shook my hand."

"Dogs shake hands. Let's wait and see what this girl's really like."

Tilda shrugged. Her sister was right. Only time would tell.

*   *   *

The McQueens, Bill included, regrouped for dinner. Ruth had made pasta with red sauce and clams, which she served with a Caesar salad—Kat picked out her anchovies and lined them around the edge of her plate—and fresh bread from Borealis Breads. For dessert there were Maine blueberries with vanilla ice cream. Neither Adam nor Kat had ice cream. Hannah had a second helping. Bill was the only one to have coffee with dessert. Ruth gave Percy, at his usual perch on the credenza, a small bowl of melted ice cream, which he lapped up immediately, much to Adam's obvious disgust. (Like his mother, Adam was adamantly anti-pet.)

The kids—who had been fed, predictably, gourmet macaroni and cheese that Adam had brought from home, and who had eaten at the bar in the kitchen, which they had declared very fun—had been put to bed with little fuss before the adults' dinner. Tilda couldn't help but think that they welcomed the chance to get away from their father's shiny new girlfriend, who, Tilda had noticed, was awkward with them, though nice enough. Maybe they welcomed the chance to get away from their easily distracted father, too. Tilda felt momentarily guilty for thinking this. Adam was probably a good father, though his parenting style was not half as warm and fuzzy as Frank's had been. Well, Adam and Frank had been entirely different in all respects, opposites really, and though they had never fought (that Tilda knew of) they also had never had more than a completely neutral conversation with each other. "How about those Red Sox last night?" and "Did you see what the market did today?"

Susan said, "I wonder if Craig will show for the memorial."

"He'll show up if it benefits him," Adam said scornfully. "If there's free room and board, he'll be there."

"That's not fair, Adam," Tilda protested. "Craig always pulls his weight when he stays with us. Last time he visited he mowed the lawn and trimmed the front hedge and he fixed the dishwasher. If he hadn't been able to fix it, I would have had to call in a repair service. He saved me a few hundred dollars."

"And how much money did you spend feeding him? He's really got you fooled, hasn't he? Poor Tilda. Always a soft touch."

Tilda couldn't deny the assessment. She did have a soft spot for Craig, her wayward brother. She was aware that their mother had largely ignored him and in some ways Tilda was still trying to make up for that lack of maternal care. When someone criticized Craig, which was often, her stock but heartfelt answer was: "He's my brother and my friend. I don't go looking for his defects. I know they're there. I just don't feel the need to fixate on them."

"Whatever," she said now. "I'm looking forward to see-ing him."

Hannah loved her younger brother, but cautiously. She could never quite decide if he was a decent person or a bum. Still, he did make her laugh and really, he had always been on her side. Hannah remembered when not long after her coming out, Craig had stood up to a kid in his high school who said something derogatory about her. Though a lot smaller than the jerk, Craig took a swing at him in his sister's defense, and wound up with a black eye for his pains. Hannah had to thank him for that. He had been sus-pended from the wrestling team for a month, even missed an important match, but had not once complained.

The puzzling thing to Hannah was that while Craig liked to pretend that he was all free-floating and not to be tied down, he consistently returned to his family, and if that didn't show a talent for loyalty then what did? But if Craig ever felt nostalgia for his childhood at Larchmere, he didn't let on. At least, not to Hannah he didn't.

"I just wish that boy would settle down," Bill said now. "Get a steady job, learn how to pay some bills. He has no sense of responsibility."

"He's not a boy, Dad. He's forty years old and he's done absolutely nothing with his life. He's a waste of oxygen, if you ask me."

"No one did ask you, Adam," Hannah retorted. "And where's all this hostility coming from? What's Craig ever done to you? Except get more girls in high school."

"I just wish he would do something constructive with his life," her father was saying now. "It's such a waste. He showed such promise when he was young. He had a real talent with numbers."

It was sad, Tilda thought, that her father was so disappointed with his younger son. What it was, exactly, that Bill had wanted for Craig Tilda couldn't say, but it certainly wasn't the nomadic life he had been living since college. She thought she understood her father's disappointment. She would not be thrilled if her own son chose Craig's rambling, unsettled way of life. Still, she wished her father could be more loving and less judgmental of her brother. After all, he was an honest, kindhearted person. He didn't do drugs. He wasn't a criminal. He just wasn't—usual.

Ruth kept her mouth shut during this conversation. While she was often inclined to judge, she saw her younger nephew as more sinned against than sinning. She alone knew things about the circumstances of his birth. She alone knew with what tepid welcome he had come into this world.

Kat had been silent throughout the discussion, of course, but Ruth had noticed she looked to Adam every other moment, after every bite of food or sip of wine, almost as if he were the repository of all wisdom, as if she was looking for a clue as to how to behave or maybe as if she was hoping for an encouraging wink or pat on the head. *You're doing just fine, honey. Just follow my lead.*

But maybe, Ruth thought, she was reading into the situation. She didn't know Kat at all. Maybe that almost reverent, almost worshipful look was really her disguised version of disgust. Doubtful, but she would wait and see what developed during the couple's visit before making any big or final judgments.

After dinner, Bill and Ruth each retired, Bill to his bedroom to read, which he did every night until late, Ruth, a lifetime lover of blues and jazz, to the York Harbor Inn with Bobby, where Lex and Joe were playing their usual gig in the downstairs pub.

Kat excused herself before long. Of course she had nothing to contribute to the conversation, which was all about the family, and after watching Kat closely, Tilda suspected that the conversation had been making her uncomfortable. She read that as a possible sign of the young woman's sensitivity. One could wear deliberately provocative clothes and still be sensitive to situations in which one did not really belong. Tilda tried to be careful not to make assumptions about the book based only on the cover.

"She seems very nice," Tilda said, when Kat had gone up to bed. "How old did you say she was?"

"I didn't say," Adam replied. "She's thirty-two. She's never been married."

"Putty in his hands," Hannah muttered.

"Excuse me?" Adam said, frowning.

Susan shot her a look of warning.

"Nothing. I said nothing."

"Has she ever been to Ogunquit before?" Tilda asked.

"No, but enough about her. I want to know about this girlfriend of Dad's."

Hannah shrugged. "You know as much as we know, which is next to nothing. She's divorced, owns her own business, and lives in Portland."

"And has a good eye for an easy mark."

"You don't really think—" Tilda began, then she caught herself. She didn't really want to hear her brother confirm his opinion that their father was being fooled. She didn't really want to contemplate the notion that someone might be out to snatch Larchmere away from the McQueens. Larchmere was essential. It was safety and security. Larchmere was her emotional inheritance. If anyone was to be Larchmere's eventual caretaker, Tilda felt that it should be her. She was aware of her cheeks flushing just slightly.

Adam fixed his sisters with a stern stare. The notion of "home" meant absolutely nothing to him. He was proudly unromantic and unsentimental. And he was proudly a fan of expensive real estate. "I'll do anything it takes," he said now, "to prevent the passing of Larchmere from this family."

"I didn't know you cared so much about the house," Tilda said. She felt a bit angry, a bit confused, even a bit desperate. She wondered if Adam would be her ally or her enemy in the looming, perhaps imaginary, battle for Larchmere.

"Do you know how much money this place could be worth as a luxury bed and breakfast? Or, when the market fully recovers, as a luxury home sale? I'm not letting a financial opportunity like Larchmere get away."

"But the house doesn't belong to you," Hannah pointed out, "not legally."

"It will someday. I'm the oldest child. It stands to reason Dad plans to leave the place to me. And I'm not letting anything or anyone get in the way of my inheritance, especially not some tarty gold digger."

For a brief, awful moment Tilda wondered if her brother

was capable of murder. Ridiculous! There was that flair for the dramatic! Frank used to tease her about the number of gothic and mystery novels she devoured, classics and contemporary stories, anything she could get her hands on. If there was a masked murderer afoot or a nasty demon in the attic, Tilda had to read about it.

"God, you are presumptuous!" Hannah cried. "Really, how did you come by that sense of entitlement?" *Mom,* she thought. *Mom is to blame. She made him think he's entitled to and deserves anything he wants.* "And you know nothing about this Jennifer person," she added. "No more than we know, anyway."

"Which is virtually nothing." Susan stood and stretched. "I'm going to bed. The sea air makes me sleepy. And I think I ate too much."

"I'll come with," Hannah said.

Tilda, reluctant to remain alone with her older brother and his presumptions, also went up to her room.

6

Tuesday, July 17

Marginal Way, a one-and-a-half-mile long walking path along the coast, stretched from Perkins Cove to Ogunquit Beach. It was, in Tilda's opinion as in the opinion of many, many others, one of the loveliest spots on the northeast coast.

It was about nine in the morning and Tilda was making her way along the path. Attractive stone and wooden benches, memorials to former residents, dotted its length. The path was for pedestrians only; bicycles and skateboards and roller skates were not allowed. At places the path was so narrow that baby strollers and wheelchairs gummed up the flow. But a town—especially one that relied so heavily on the tourist trade—could hardly prohibit the passage of baby strollers and wheelchairs.

The craggy cliffs and spectacular whirlpools below the Marginal Way were gorgeous in a romantic sort of way, but they were best kept away from and respected. Still, every summer a few foolish middle-aged men and women (never teens, who, interestingly, seemed to know better) would at-

tempt to climb down the cliffs, maybe to get a close-up
shot of some rock formation, or to capture on film a violent
little eddy, and invariably wind up injured and stranded, at
the mercy of the fire department. It was a bit of a joke
among the locals, the idiocy of people on holiday.

The pines and scrub along the Marginal Way were dis-
torted and scoured and stunted by a lifetime of exposure to
the often brutal wind coming off the water. But the view
out to sea was spectacular, grand, intimidating in its beauty
and scale. In summer the path was alive with dragonflies of
immense proportions and shimmering colors. Tilda had
once read that there were over 113 species of dragonflies
and 45 species of damselflies in the state of Maine alone.
That was a lot of winged creatures.

Tilda finally reached her destination, a small dip off the
concrete path, a natural alcove of sorts, a protected, shaded
little spot before the massive drop of the cliffs. On a drizzly,
summer morning two years ago, just as dawn was struggling
to break, she and Jon and Jane had sprinkled Frank's ashes
from just this spot. She had cried, but soundlessly. Jon, trying hard to be strong for his mother, had remained dry eyed
but Tilda was sure that it had cost him. Jane, sixteen at the
time, had clung to her mother's arm. "Good-bye, Daddy,"
she had whispered when the last of the ashes were lost to
the ocean. "I love you."

How deeply lonely she had felt that drizzly morning, in
spite of her children's presence! And how much more
lonely she had become since then!

Tilda sat on a large gray rock in the little alcove and
looked out at the sea. It was glittering in the morning light.
Unconsciously, because it had become a habit, she twirled
her wedding ring with her thumb. She had kept Frank's
wedding ring, first at home and then in her safety deposit
box at the bank, in the hopes that someday Jon might want
to wear it, if he decided to get married, that was. Of course,

she had not expressed that hope to her son. That would seem like pressure. She didn't want to presume anything about the lives of her children. Maybe Jon wouldn't want to marry. Maybe Jane wouldn't either. Maybe she would never have grandchildren.

Tilda sighed. She knew she was indulging in self-pity, more than ever lately, and she knew it was an unattractive quality, but she just couldn't seem to stop it. After all, she had been virtually dumped by the majority of their couple friends. She wanted to tell them that death was not contagious. "I don't have a taint on me," she wanted to say. Frank's cancer wasn't an infectious plague. Or was it that some people didn't want her around because she was a reminder of death, a reminder of what dreaded possibility they, too, might face? *If it could happen to Tilda McQueen O'Connell, it could happen to me. If Tilda could wind up all alone, then so could I.*

There was an antiquated notion of married women not wanting their single girlfriends around for fear they would try to steal the husbands. But Tilda refused to believe that anyone she and Frank had called friends would indulge in such a dated, sexist stereotype. They had all gone to college. All the women had careers. So what was the problem?

About a year earlier she had read a blog in which the writer, a woman divorced after almost thirty years of marriage, had warned that single women could be "ghettoized" if they didn't "live strong." At first the choice of words had struck Tilda as overly dramatic but as time went on, she had come to agree wholeheartedly with the writer's observation. Only in movies were single women—some of them—glamorous and wanted.

It had been different in the beginning. Soon after Frank's death, friends had reached out and invited Tilda to dinners and card parties and picnics, but the mood at such gatherings was invariably tense, as if no one wanted to be the first to laugh and thereby declare that life went on even after the death of someone special. So then the invitations to dinner and card parties and picnics waned and in some cases, mostly the cases of married couples, eventually stopped coming. Tilda had told herself that she didn't really care. And for a while, she really didn't care. She did nothing to encourage a social life. She stopped making friendly phone calls, stopped replying to e-mails, stopped suggesting lunches or movies or shopping trips to the outlets in Freeport.

Now, two years and some months after Frank's death, she found that she had become alienated from the majority of her old friends and acquaintances. Now, two years and some months after Frank's death, she found that she did care about being alone. She cared very much.

Invariably, weekends were the loneliest. She was hesitant to invite a couple over for dinner, or to ask them out to a movie—wasn't Saturday night date night for most couples? And didn't couples spend lots of time on the weekends hunkered down with their children and running errands and doing chores they had not managed to squeeze in to their hectic work weeks? No one had time for a single woman, divorced or widowed. Or so it sometimes seemed to Tilda, who, as she readily acknowledged, struggled against self-pity but all too often succumbed to its dubious comforts.

She couldn't very well beg Jane and Jon to spend their weekends with her. It would be unfair to them, and unreasonable. The kids had homework and jobs and social lives of their own. She felt she should be thankful they still lived at home, though more and more it seemed that they only stopped by for the occasional meal or to sleep. But their moving away from her was inevitable. Time brought change.

It was just that Tilda had never expected this particular change, that at the age of forty-seven she would be single and alone. Not that every single woman was alone or even lonely. Her college friend, Clarice, had never married, and claimed she had never wanted to marry. She had moved to Seattle after graduation and had been living alone there ever since. She seemed perfectly content to date men without any desire to build a relationship. Not long ago, Tilda, feeling very much the social pariah, had called Clarice and asked if she ever felt the same. Clarice had laughed at the notion. "Maybe," she had said, "some people don't want me around for whatever twisted reasons they have, but I've never noticed any discrimination. I go where I please when I please. And I don't ever feel lonely."

Tilda believed her old friend. She had never known Clarice to be hesitant or indecisive or fearful. She seemed always to be—content. Tilda now envied her. She wanted Clarice to teach her the secret of contentment. There had to be a secret, a magic button she could press, a wand she could wave, something.

Or maybe it was all about hard work and courage. And courage was hard to come by when you were an emotional coward by nature.

Tilda sighed. It was time to get back to the house. She got up from her seat on the rock and made her way back along the path to the parking lot in the Cove. Once there, a small crowd of people in party clothes caught her attention, a photographer and her assistant laden with cameras and other equipment, and most importantly, a bride and her groom. The couple was having their pictures taken against the backdrop of the glittering blue ocean and the gray, rocky shore; no doubt the group would wind its way up onto Marginal Way before long for more spectacular backdrops. Maybe they would gather for a picture just where Tilda had sat that morning.

Tilda stopped to watch. The bride wore a white, strapless dress, which seemed to be the most popular style these days, and her hair was piled high on her head in an intricate updo, interwoven with small pink flowers. She looked very pretty, like a sugar confection. The groom was standard issue in a neat black tuxedo and black shoes highly shined.

Tilda's heart contracted. Weddings had always made her cry, but more so since she had lost Frank. They had married at Larchmere on an afternoon in early October. She had wanted to wear her mother's dress but Charlotte, admittedly not sentimental, revealed that she had sold it years before to a high-end resale shop in Boston. Instead, Tilda had worn a simple, ivory satin sheath with an ivory satin bolero jacket (the woman at the bridal store had insisted that the jacket gave Tilda some much needed "padding") and dyed-to-match kitten-heel shoes. She had danced with her father to "Moon River" and tossed her bouquet of ivory roses and green verbernum to the single women present. (Hannah had declined to participate but Ruth had joined in for the fun of it.) Oddly, now Tilda couldn't remember who had caught it. The next day she and Frank left for a honeymoon in Jamaica, though secretly Tilda had wanted to stay in Maine. Frank had never been to a tropical island before, so for his sake, she went along and of course, they had had a good time.

The bride modestly adjusted her bodice. An older man now stood at her side, in a tuxedo much like the groom's. *Probably her father,* Tilda thought. Her proud, and slightly sad, father. Tilda turned away, tears in her eyes.

Poor Frank. He hadn't lived to see his daughter marry. And poor Tilda! The thought of attending the wedding of one of her children alone, without the father of those children, without Frank, reduced her to something like despair. Weddings were part of the plan. Have children, raise them, send them to college, see them married, be given grandchildren, live out the rest of your life in peace.

But in her case the plan had gone horribly wrong. Well,

she supposed that most life plans went wrong somewhere. Why were people stupid enough to plan what they couldn't control? She had been stupid. So had Frank.

Tilda got into her car and headed back to Larchmere. Frank! How could she possibly walk down the aisle of her daughter's or son's wedding on the arm of just any man, just a friend she knew from town or from work? She wanted that man to be Frank. But that was now impossible. Almost as impossible as it was to imagine attending the wedding of one of her children with someone who was a real partner, a lover, a companion, even, possibly, a husband.

Well, Tilda supposed she could wrangle Craig into being her date, if he was around when a wedding was scheduled to take place, if she could count on him not to take to the road and leave her stranded. That was unfair. Craig was good to her, as good as he could be to anyone, she supposed. He would keep a promise to his sister.

Still, her brother as her date to her child's wedding was an unsatisfactory option. Unless . . . Tilda turned into the driveway at Larchmere, a smile creeping across her face, an idea taking shape in her mind. Yes, she would talk to Craig as soon as he arrived. There might be a solution to this problem of aloneness, for both of them.

7

Craig arrived at Larchmere later that morning in his usual fashion, with a toot of his horn and a call of "The festivities may commence!"

He drove an old, rusty, red van that he had bought from a guy up in Bar Harbor at least twelve years earlier. Tilda didn't know how it still operated. Craig did have a lot of natural "fix-it" talent but even the most inspired and talented amateur mechanic had need of a professional from time to time. Where did he get the money for a tune-up or an oil change or for new tires? He certainly had never asked her for money.

Craig McQueen had always considered himself the odd duck of the McQueen family and indeed, a physical resemblance was hard to pinpoint. He didn't look much like either of his parents or his siblings. His hair was blond and though his eyes were blue, surrounded by very dark lashes, they weren't blue like his father's or like Hannah's. He was about five feet, eight inches, with broad shoulders and a muscular build. His coloring, too, was unlike that of the other members of his family. He seemed to have a perpetual tan while the other McQueens were pale to down-right milk-skinned. Craig had always been very attractive to women—his smile was winning, his features regular, his walk confident—and he had always known it, though he had been a lot less of a cavalier or a Casanova than he let on.

Now he was wearing slouchy jeans, beat-up leather sandals, and a mock bowling shirt. Tilda recognized the shirt as one she had given him for his birthday several years earlier. How, she wondered, and not for the first time, did he do his laundry when he wasn't staying with her? Where did he shower and shave? (He was always clean shaven.) What did he do when he was sick? When was the last time he had seen a doctor? He certainly didn't have health insurance. Her brother's life was a puzzle to her.

But maybe it didn't have to be. She had been mulling over her plan, formulating it, since that morning in the Cove when she had seen the bride and groom. Why couldn't she and Craig be a sort of "couple," sharing a house and chores and meals? Why couldn't they live together like Charles and Mary Lamb—well, without the matricide part? Or like William and Dorothy Wordsworth? Even when William married—which Tilda had no intention of doing, but Craig might, someday—Dorothy had lived with the couple. Most importantly, if she and Craig lived together neither of them would have to grow old alone.

He was barely out of the van when Tilda, the only one there to greet him, said, "Craig, I need to talk to you about something."

"Can't I settle in first?" he asked. He stretched his arms over his head. "I've been driving all day."

"No. This is important."

Craig dropped his arms. "Tilda, I've been on the road for—"

"Please, Craig, it will only take a minute or two."

He sighed. "Okay. What's up?"

Tilda shot a look over her shoulder, but no one had appeared from the house. "Look, Craig, I was thinking. How about you move in with me? In South Portland. You can have Jon's room. He won't mind switching to the den, and he'll be moving away before long anyway, and there's plenty of room in the garage for your van. You know the neighborhood, you know how to get around, and you can be in the Old Port in ten minutes, maybe fifteen. You like to go to Rí Rá when you're in town, right? Doesn't your old friend, the one from college, Jake somebody or other, tend bar there? And—"

"Tilda!" Craig put up his hands. "Please, just stop."

She stopped talking. She figured her brother needed a minute to take in her surprise offer. But Craig wasn't entirely surprised at his sister's offer. He knew she was afraid of growing old alone. He knew she was reluctant to meet another man and maybe start a relationship. He knew she saw him as her easy way out of a painful situation. He felt somewhat flattered by this. He also felt somewhat annoyed. It might not look like it but he had a life, too. He was fully aware that since Frank's death his sister increasingly had been seeking his time and his presence. He knew she was lonely and he was more than willing to help around the house, especially with the chores Frank had once handled, but he also knew that she needed to stand on her own two feet.

"Thanks, Tilda," he said, with what he hoped was a kind, at least a patient, smile. "Really. It's a sweet offer. But you and me living together is just not a good idea. Trust me on this."

"But why not?" she said. "It would be good for both of

us. You could have a home base. I'm not saying I'd ask you never to travel and see your friends and—"

Craig reached out and squeezed his sister's shoulder. "I'm sorry, Tilda, really. Thanks for the offer. It's very generous. Now, I'm sorry, but I really have to use the little boys' room."

Craig hurried off into the house and Tilda stood at the foot of the stairs alone, angry, hurt, but in the end not really surprised at Craig's rejection of her offer. She knew it had been a pathetic cry for help, an act of cowardice and need, rather than an act of real generosity. Still, he might have pretended to consider the offer! He needn't have dismissed it so immediately! Tilda felt like a fool. She knew Craig was a kind person, and knew he would never mention their talk again. Still, she felt embarrassed.

Slowly, she went inside.

"Smartinis!"

Tilda, who had rapidly deemed her earlier embarrassment unnecessary, and who very much wanted to enjoy her younger brother's company, was in the kitchen, as were Hannah, Susan, Adam, and Craig. Kat was taking a nap. Ruth had taken Cordelia and Cody into town with her to pick up more milk. The kids seemed to drink it by the gallon. Bill was in his room, reading.

Craig held a martini shaker in one hand and a bottle of vodka in the other. "Who's up for one of my specials?"

Tilda smiled. All the locals knew, and some remembered, that around 1947 the actor J. Scott Smart had come to live—to preside, some would say—in Ogunquit. At five of an evening he would stand in his doorway and with a cry of "Smartinis!" beckon his friends to cocktail hour.

"I'll have one," Hannah said. "With three olives, please. I need my veggies."

"Me, too, but just one olive. Aren't olives a fruit? Tilda, what will you have?"

"As much as I hate to be a killjoy," she told Susan, "I'll stick to wine."

"Adam?" Craig asked.

"No, thanks," he said curtly.

Craig shrugged and went to work at the kitchen bar.

Next to Tilda, Adam bristled. "I hate it when he does that."

"What?"

"That stupid 'Smartinis.'"

"I think it's kind of clever."

"Clever? It's ridiculous. I'm getting myself a scotch."

Adam went to the liquor cabinet and Tilda to the fridge to retrieve the bottle of sauvignon blanc that had been chilling. She wasn't the killjoy. Adam was.

When the siblings each had a drink, Tilda proposed a toast.

"To what?" Adam asked.

"Uh, to your mother?"

"Good idea, Susan." Tilda raised her glass. "To Mom."

"To Mom," they chorused. "To Charlotte."

Ruth had set the dining room table that evening with pale gray linen napkins against black linen placemats and stark, white dishes. At one end of the table, to allow guests an unobstructed view of each other, sat a tall, silver vase in which Ruth had placed several orange day lilies plucked from the garden.

Tonight, the McQueens would meet their father's romantic partner. Ruth's expectations for the reception were not high. There was nothing wrong with Jennifer Fournier. But only Craig had welcomed the news of her being in Bill's life. Tilda, Hannah, and certainly Adam seemed predisposed to find faults where there were none.

Ruth, herself, found her brother's new girlfriend near perfect. For one, she was not at all like her predecessor, which, in Ruth's opinion, was a good thing. And Jennifer seemed to like Ruth, too. Not that Ruth required her to, but things had worked out nicely this time for her. No more having to put up with a prima donna, just for her brother's sake.

At six-thirty, Bill opened the door for Jennifer and led her into the sunroom where the rest of the family was gathered. "Everyone, this is Jennifer," he said, with a big, proud smile.

Hannah said, "Hi." Tilda gave a silly little wave. Susan gave her a hearty hello. Craig shook her hand. Adam nodded. Kat shyly told Jennifer that she liked her bracelet.

Jennifer Fournier was an attractive woman. She was almost as tall as Bill, taller in heels. Her blond hair was thick, straight, and bluntly cut. She wore minimal makeup and dressed simply but stylishly in black, brown, taupe, and tan. Her jewelry was singular and stunning and she wore very little of it at a time. That evening she was dressed in lightweight, taupe, wide-legged linen pants over which she wore a long, white linen tunic. A large wooden bangle around her right wrist—the bracelet Kat had admired— was her only adornment. Tilda now felt childish in her mint green crew neck sweater and jean shorts, though earlier that day she had caught sight of herself in a hall mirror and thought she looked kind of cute.

Yes, her father's new friend was definitely a standout, and that bothered Tilda. She would vastly have preferred Jennifer to be old and frumpy, maybe even missing a front tooth, maybe even cursed with blotchy skin. Jennifer would be far more acceptable and certainly less threatening if she was visibly flawed. The thoughts were irrational and unworthy, but there they were.

The talk during dinner—lobster risotto, salad, and strawberry sorbet—was vague and general and polite. There had not been a good rain in almost three weeks and people were worried about their crops and their lawns. The president had just returned from a visit to South America and reactions to what had happened there were mixed. When Adam got a bit agitated, the subject of politics was hastily abandoned and Hannah wondered what everyone thought of the new teen trend, in her opinion ridiculous, of having the very tip of the nose tattooed. Weren't nose rings gross enough?

The only awkward moment came when Adam unnecessarily, and apropos of nothing, recalled the fact that their mother, Charlotte, had won a beauty contest when she was seventeen. What was there to say to that, except, "She must have been very pretty."

"She was beautiful," Adam had replied, the implication being, of course, that Jennifer was not.

As soon as the dessert plates were cleared into the kitchen, the group drifted onto the big front porch. (Percy, who had a limited tolerance for company, went up to Ruth's room.) The night was warm. The waves were just audible. Everyone took seats. Craig perched on the wooden rail. He asked Jennifer where she had grown up, and where she had gone to college, and did she miss living in Ogunquit year round.

"Of course she does," Adam said under his breath. "That's why she's with Dad, so she can get her hands on Larchmere."

Craig noted that Tilda had gone to Hampstead College, too, and asked his sister what year she had graduated. Tilda told him and Jennifer said that she had graduated the year Tilda was a freshman. No, they hadn't known each other.

After about twenty minutes of orchestrating the conversation, Craig announced that he had plans to meet a friend. When he was gone, the conversation went dead.

Bill looked down at his cell phone and excused himself to take a call from the minister regarding a detail for Charlotte's memorial service, which was being held at St. Peter's-by-the-Sea in Cape Neddick.

When he had gone inside, Adam, who had not addressed Jennifer since dinner, said: "So, Jennifer, Ruth tells us you have a little design business."

Jennifer smiled. "Yes. I own an interior design firm."

"That must make a nice little pastime."

Ruth shot her nephew an angry look, which he ignored. Hannah shot a questioning look to Tilda, who didn't know how to respond.

"Well," Jennifer said, with great composure, "as a matter of fact it's a full-time job. I work at least forty hours a week. And that doesn't include the time spent commuting from one location to another."

Adam laughed. "Hard to imagine that sort of thing would be profitable in this economy. People tend to cut out what's not necessary and spend only on the important things."

The tension on the porch was palpable. Susan looked as if she could leap from her chair and strangle her brother-in-law. Kat looked confused.

"I do just fine," Jennifer said after a moment, with a tight little smile.

Ruth cleared her throat and said, "Not to change the subject but—"

But Adam spoke right over his aunt. "You don't need a degree for that sort of work, do you? No special training?

Just tell people to paint their walls green instead of orange."

Tilda was mortified by her brother's behavior but felt completely incapable of coming to Jennifer's defense. *Yes,* she thought, *I am truly tongue-tied.*

"Excuse me." Jennifer rose and walked into the house. Ruth got up and followed her.

The moment the women were gone, Susan turned to Adam. "What the hell is wrong with you?" she demanded. "How could you be so rude?"

Adam shrugged. "I wasn't being rude. I was simply asking about her business. I think we have a right to know what our father's girlfriend does for a living."

Kat was looking at her hands, which were flat out on her lap.

Tilda finally said, "You could have been nicer, Adam."

Hannah said, "Yeah."

Ruth came back out onto the porch. She looked furious. "Jennifer is leaving for a B and B. Your father is confused. He doesn't know why she isn't staying here, as usual. I didn't have the heart to tell him it's because his son was an ass to his girlfriend."

"Oh," Tilda said.

"I'm surprised she was able to get a room at this late hour and at this time of year. And by the way, Adam, she has a master's degree from the Rhode Island School of Design."

Tilda felt her aunt's accusing eyes on her. Adam might have been overtly horrid, but Tilda was at fault, too. She should have stopped her brother; she should have said something to alleviate the assault. Hannah, too, should have said something. Kat should have told her fiancé to shut up. They all should have. . . .

Ruth shook her head. "I'm going to bed."

Kat followed shortly after.

Tilda, Hannah, Susan, and Adam remained on the front porch. The night had grown chilly and Tilda was wrapped in a big gray sweatshirt that had once belonged to Frank. He had kept it in the closet of their room at Larchmere for just such occasions. Tilda saw no reason not to keep it for herself.

She still felt bad about what had happened earlier with Jennifer. She could only credit her ill behavior to the fact that she was still in a bit of shock. The thought of her father being with another woman simply had never occurred to her and left her feeling disoriented.

But her bad behavior wasn't the only thing bothering Tilda. She was annoyed by the fact that she felt jealous on behalf of her dead mother. Jealous on behalf of a dead person! She couldn't help but think that if her father had to date and—God forbid!—get remarried, he should have done the seemly thing and chosen a woman nearer to his own age. He should have chosen someone who wouldn't feel like a threat to the family unit, someone who wouldn't feel like a threat to Tilda.

Tilda turned to her sister. Maybe admitting to her unworthy feelings might help her get past them. Maybe Hannah could somehow absolve her. "I thought I was a more sophisticated person," she said. "But I can't help but feel it's an insult to Mom's memory somehow, Dad's dating this much younger woman. . . . And her being around while we're all gathered for the memorial service . . . I know it's been ten years since Mom's death but somehow it just doesn't seem right."

Hannah raised an eyebrow. "You're a tradition-bound

person, aren't you? Everything by the book, everything the way it's always been done. You're a lot like Mom in that way."

"So what if I am? Aren't you even a little bit . . . upset about this relationship of Dad's?"

"Yeah," Hannah said. "I'll admit that it . . . concerns me. Not the fact of the age difference, though. That doesn't seem like such a big deal, not at this point in their lives."

"So, what then?"

Hannah was thoughtful for a moment before saying, "I don't really know."

"The status quo is changing," Susan said. "That upsets everyone initially. Give yourself time to get used to the idea, that's all."

Craig's ancient red van pulled up to the house then, and a moment later he joined his siblings on the front porch.

"What are you doing back so early?" Hannah asked. "I thought you'd be gone all night."

"Me? No way. I'm a one-beer sort of guy when I'm driving. Besides, Kirk had to meet someone else later. What did I miss?"

"Uh—" Tilda said.

"Not much," Hannah lied.

"Actually—" Susan began, but Adam's loudly voiced question interrupted her.

"Is everything all set for Mom's memorial service?"

"Pretty much. I think Ruth handled most of the details." *I certainly didn't participate,* Hannah added silently. *Not that anyone asked me to help.* She wondered if she should have volunteered, for her father's sake. She felt slightly guilty.

"What about the party?" Adam was asking.

"The caterer is booked," Tilda said. "I guess Ruth handled the party planning, too."

Adam nodded. "I thought I'd read something from Ayn

Rand at the service. You know she was Mom's favorite writer."

Of course she was, Hannah thought. Hadn't Rand said, "The question isn't who is going to let me; it's who is going to stop me"? And hadn't she said something about evil requiring the permission or sanction of the victim? Hannah didn't claim to be an expert on the work and teachings of Ayn Rand but what little she did know she didn't much like. Charlotte McQueen's role model had certainly not been Mother Teresa.

"Mom wasn't as good a sailor as she liked to think she was," Hannah said abruptly. "I don't mean that to sound harsh, but it's the truth. Frankly, I wasn't entirely surprised when we got the news that she'd had an accident."

"Hannah!" Susan looked appalled.

"What? I'm just being honest. Mom had a large opinion of herself and her talents." *Much like Adam,* she added silently. "Not that she deserved to die as she did . . ."

"What are you talking about?" Adam said. "Mom was a fantastic sailor. I've always thought there might have been foul play."

Craig barely controlled a grin. "Then why didn't you say anything at the time? I don't remember you demanding an investigation. Hercule Poirot over here."

Adam made no answer.

"Besides," Hannah said, "she was with a friend when the accident occurred. Carol Whitehouse had absolutely no reason to want Mom dead. Really, Adam, since when have you had an imagination?"

Tilda rose abruptly from her chair. "I'm going to bed. It's been a long day."

"And we know you like to be on the beach at dawn. I don't know how you do it."

Tilda just shrugged and went upstairs to her room. The truth was that the critical talk about her mother had upset her. On some level she knew that her mother had not been the warmest or most obliging person but she didn't really want to dwell on that knowledge. She preferred to follow the words of St. Thérèse of Lisieux: "When one loves, one does not calculate." And, Tilda would add, one does not judge. At least, one should try not to judge.

Still, she wondered about emotional cowardice. Selective memory could be a good thing—it was a survival tactic—but it could also be a bad thing, especially when it blocked out a truth that might help you evolve to learn a new and better survival tactic.

Tilda brushed her teeth in the hall bathroom and returned to her room. The only windows looked out on the side lawn. If you leaned out you could see the ocean to the left, but Tilda never bothered. It was enough to know the ocean was there, fully and spectacularly visible from the front rooms and porch.

It was not the best bedroom in the house—that was reserved for her father, of course, who had shared the room with his wife—but it was Tilda's favorite because it was the room in which she and Frank had always stayed when visiting her parents. At first, Jon and Jane had joined them, sleeping on air mattresses or in sleeping bags on the floor. Later, the kids had moved to their own rooms, sometimes to the library couch.

Charlotte had decorated each bedroom in keeping with clean and casual beachfront style, reserving formality and elegance for the dining room and, in a more English country house vein, the library. The walls in Tilda's—and Frank's—room, for example, were painted white, as were the replacement wide pine floorboards. A braided rug in tones of peach, green, and yellow sat on either side of the bed. The sheets, pillowcases, and lightweight summer blankets were white, trimmed with a peach-colored border. The two wooden dressers were painted the color of bells of Ireland.

On the wall were hung three small watercolor seascapes done by a local artist Charlotte had patronized until her interest had waned. The room felt airy and light and peaceful. Frank had always been afraid of somehow dirtying it beyond repair. He wouldn't even bring a cup of coffee upstairs after breakfast. Tilda thought he had been a bit afraid of her mother. Well, a lot of people had been a bit afraid of or intimidated by Charlotte McQueen. But Tilda had only learned about this after her mother's death.

She opened the dresser drawer in which she kept her nightgowns and underwear, and pulled out a thin flannel nightgown. Something came with it and dropped to the floor. Tilda turned on the small lamp atop the dresser and squatted. It was probably a stray penny. But she saw nothing so she reached under the dresser and felt around. (The floor, she noted, was dust free. Ruth and a team of professional housekeepers kept Larchmere in an immaculate state.) Her fingers found the unknown object, something small and round, but thicker than a coin and decorated with raised scrolling. She stood and looked at it. Her heart beat painfully. It was the missing button she and Frank had searched for so diligently. How had it gotten into her drawer? How had it escaped their notice?

Tilda slumped on the edge of the bed, the metal button in her palm. It had fallen off a sweater Frank had inherited from his father. It was the last of the original buttons; all the others had been lost while the sweater was still in the possession of the elder O'Connell.

She closed her fingers over the button. That sweater had meant so much to Frank. When they couldn't find this last original button she had replaced it with one matching the other, newer buttons. And she still had the sweater. It was one of the things she would never throw out or give away. Jane sometimes wore it around the house. It probably made her feel close to her father.

Tilda opened her fingers and looked again at the button. She wondered if it could be a sign from Frank. It wasn't an eagle, it wasn't the sign she had asked for, but it was odd that it had so suddenly appeared after all this time missing. Tilda tried to believe that the button itself meant something. But it was no use. If this was a message from Frank she failed to understand it. She got up and put the button back in the drawer with the other nightclothes. She turned out the light and went to bed.

8

Wednesday, July 18

It was the newlywed couple again. Tilda, on Ogunquit Beach for her morning walk after a restless, dream-filled night, was momentarily surprised at their presence so early in the day. It was barely seven o'clock. She wondered why they weren't sleeping in after the big celebration. But young love had boundless energy. She did remember that.

The woman's hair was now in a simple ponytail; gone were the flowers and curls. She was wearing a pink sundress and white, flat sandals. Her husband was in khaki shorts and a bright, Hawaiian style shirt. They looked clean and neat and happy. They were holding hands.

They must be staying in town, Tilda thought. *So this is where they're spending their honeymoon, pretty little Ogunquit.* No doubt their suite looked out over the ocean. Maybe they would return here every year on their anniversary. Maybe someday they would come with their children. It was a pleasant thought and it made Tilda feel sick with loss.

She remembered a line from *The Dante Club,* by

Matthew Pearl. She had read the book while Frank was ill. The line had struck her forcefully then and had come back to her time and again since Frank's death. A character is confronted with the murder of her husband and, in the author's words, the woman "knew in an instant what it meant to be a widow, what an ungodly jealousy it produced."

How right that was! Through no fault or desire of her own she had been kicked out of the enviable club of married people, and relegated to the club in which no one wanted to be a member—widow.

Gone were all the "companionable endeavors" she and Frank had enjoyed—those comfortable habits every couple shared. Doing them alone seemed unbearably sad. For a while Tilda thought she would have to find some new habits or go mad. Ordering a pizza from the small, old-fashioned shop down the block, and eating it in the living room, sitting crossed-legged on the floor at the coffee table, while watching a Will Ferrell movie (they'd seen *Anchorman* three times) was no longer possible. Without Frank, it was a miserable experience. The rug chafed her legs, the pizza was too chewy, and the movies weren't funny.

The thing was that she still loved Frank. But could you love a dead person, someone who has died? Could she say, legitimately, that she still loved Frank? Or was it the memory she loved, the memory of Frank, not the actuality, which was a scattered handful of ash. . . . Tilda blinked hard. What a macabre thought! How disgusting, revolting, really. But the question remained. Just because Frank had died, must her love for him be dead, too?

Of course not, she thought, almost angrily. Let the philosophers determine the fine points of expression. She loved Frank and she always would, whether he was present in body or in spirit. Tilda looked up into the early morning sun. No eagle.

She looked back at the newlywed couple. They had

stopped and were hugging. The bride rested her head on her husband's chest and he kissed her hair. The last thing on that young bride's mind, Tilda knew, was the thought of her husband's dying and of her being left alone.

Somewhere she had read that every year around eight hundred thousand women in the United States were widowed. That was an awfully big number but only the year before had there been the first national conference addressing the state of widowhood. Tilda had not gone to the conference though she sometimes wondered what would be different now if she had. Anyway, why hadn't anyone been paying attention to all of those women until now? All of those sad and lonely women.

The newlywed couple was walking again. The husband, keeping stride, bent down to pick up a rock or a shell. And suddenly, Tilda had an overwhelming desire to rush up to them, to grab their hands and warn them that their happiness would not, could not last. She wanted to urge them to cherish each other while they could. She wanted to help them and she wanted to hurt them. She wanted to be a memento mori, a reminder of death. She wanted to force them to share some of her pain by confronting them with the dark fact of ending, of nothingness, of being alone and bereft.

Of course, she did not rush over to the newlyweds, to congratulate or to warn or to admonish. Instead, she cut her walk short and headed back to Larchmere, ashamed of the urge to blight the happiness of an innocent young couple, ashamed of her "ungodly jealousy."

9

It was a little after noon and Tilda and Hannah were settling at a table at Chauncey Creek Lobster Pier, in the beautiful, largely rural town of Kittery Point. Tilda had decided, not surprisingly, to order a bucket of steamers, and Hannah wanted a boiled lobster. They had brought a bottle of fizzy water, a bottle of pinot grigio, and a loaf of French bread from Standard bakery. Almost all of the brightly painted picnic tables were occupied. There were several family groups. Four women who looked about Tilda's age had brought for their table a cloth and linen napkins. Two older men had brought their Dachshund, who sat quietly under the table while they ate.

Susan had gone off to spend the afternoon with an old friend in Falmouth. Tilda loved Susan and enjoyed her company. But she wasn't disappointed that it would be just herself and Hannah at lunch.

This was one of the sisters' favorite spots. Across the creek was Cutts Island, its shore thick with pointed firs, birch, and farther inland, oaks and maples. People in kayaks and rowboats and larger pleasure crafts drifted or glided by, often waving at the diners. Teenaged boys, employed by the pound, unloaded wooden crates and equipment from fishing boats moored below the restaurant's deck. Laughter and conversation from the other tables punctuated the air. It was impossible, Tilda and Hannah thought, not to feel privileged at Chauncey Creek, like you had the world at your feet.

The sun was very bright and hot. Tilda reached in her bag for a hat, one of Frank's old baseball caps. She had given most of his clothes to charitable organizations. Some special pieces had gone to Jon, who could just about fit into them; other pieces, like the old sweater, had been adopted by Jane. But Frank's hat collection she had not been able to part with. She didn't like the way she looked in baseball caps, and when Frank was alive she had never worn them. But now, well, there was so little left of her husband. . . .

"You know," Hannah said suddenly, interrupting the sudden, but not surprising, dark drift of Tilda's thoughts, "Susan and I are still talking about starting a family."

Tilda was startled. "Oh. You hadn't mentioned anything in so long I guess I thought that maybe you had decided not to. . . ."

"No. It's still on the table."

"So . . ."

"So what's holding us back?"

"Yes."

"Me." Hannah smiled as if in apology.

"Oh."

"Yeah. Oh."

"Well, why?" Tilda asked. "Are you worried about money? You know that old saying, there's never a right time to have a baby, you just have to do it."

"No, it's not the money. Though the thought of paying for college in twenty years or so does scare the hell out of me."

"Loans," Tilda said. "Scholarships. Work-study programs. Part-time jobs. For the kids, of course."

"I know, I know. It's not the money."

"So, have you talked to Susan about why you're reluctant? Or is that a stupid question?"

"It should be a stupid question. If I can't or don't or won't talk to my wife about something so important, who am I going to talk to? But the fact is that I haven't talked to her, not really. I mean, we talk about the idea of a family and about the fact that I'm not ready for one, but I can't really tell her why."

"Do you know why you're not ready," Tilda asked, "or is it that you can't articulate the feelings? Or maybe you really don't know your reasons."

Hannah was silent for a long moment. And then she said, "I don't know."

Tilda sighed. "I don't mean to preach, Hannah, really, but the most common killer of marriage is emotional distance. You can't shy away from talking to Susan about your fears or hesitations or whatever you want to call them. You owe it to yourself and to Susan."

"I know."

"Look, friendships don't last when people drift apart. How can a marriage, the most intimate and peculiar of friendships, be expected to survive?"

"I know. You're right. You are. And I know I brought up this subject, but let's talk about something else now. Like, about how you're doing."

Tilda smiled. "Besides the disturbing fact that I feel afraid of the future? And that I wish I could go back in time to when my life was wonderful?"

"I assumed as much. For one, you're still wearing your wedding ring."

Tilda looked down at her left hand. The yellow gold ring shone in the bright sun. "I know. I can't seem to be without it. I've tried a few times to leave it at home while I go to the grocery store or somewhere I might not run into anyone I

know. But I can't even do that without feeling all anxious
and guilty. It's like the minute I'm seen without my wedding ring I'll be announcing to the world that I'm over
Frank. That I don't need him anymore, that I don't love
him. I just know I'll feel horribly guilty and judged."

"Do you still need him?" Hannah asked.

"Yes," Tilda said. "I think so."

"How? Or maybe I should ask, why? Or, for what? And
don't say, for taking out the garbage."

"Jon does that. It's been his job since he was twelve."

"Answer the question."

Tilda replied promptly. "I need him because I want him.
I need him because my marriage was a good one. I miss it.
Almost aside from Frank I miss the marriage itself. I don't
know if that makes sense."

"Define 'good.'"

"Excuse me?"

"No, really. I'm not trying to be annoying or provocative. I'm truly curious. For you and Frank, what was
good?"

"It's hard to put into words, exactly," Tilda said. "I don't
know. For one thing, I never, or rarely, felt put upon. Frank
really pulled his share of the load. We respected each
other. We liked each other. It sounds so simplistic or
clichéd but . . ."

"Yeah, it does. But I know what you mean. It's about
partnership. Sharing the burdens and the laughter. I sound
like a greeting card."

The conversation rested a moment while Tilda sipped
her plastic cup of wine and Hannah watched a small pleasure boat drift by the dock. She was thinking about her sister's situation. She knew that Tilda felt alone, almost
friendless. Some of that wasn't her fault. Some of it was.
Hannah and Susan regularly asked her to join their social
activities in town. They asked her to movies at the Nick-

elodeon, to openings at the Portland Museum of Art, where they were members, they asked her to join them at the free summer evening concerts in Monument Square, they asked her to the monthly networking events sponsored by the DownEast Pride Alliance, they asked her to readings and signings at Longfellow Bookstore. Most times, Tilda found an excuse not to go along. Tilda's reluctance to move on with her life was beginning to worry Hannah.

"Hannah," Tilda said then, breaking into her thoughts. "I don't mean to sound naive, though I suspect I probably will. I was wondering. What's—I mean, what would you say is the main difference between our marriages? Aside from the obvious, of course, and aside from the prejudices gay couples face. How is marriage between two women, or two men for that matter, different than marriage between a woman and a man?"

Hannah raised an eyebrow. "Gay couples can share clothes."

Tilda was mortified. "I'm sorry. I offended you. I didn't mean to."

"It's okay. I'm not offended. I'm just still surprised when people ask that sort of question. For me, my life is normal. But for others, I guess it still seems very foreign."

"I'm sorry," Tilda said. "Again. Anyway, I suppose we're all strangers to one another. In the end, I mean. No one ever really knows another person's truth."

"Well, that's a little depressing. What is it with you harshing everyone's buzz?"

"Sorry. Lately I seem to be, I don't know, wallowing."

"Well, stop it. It's not good for your health. Anyway, I want to say one more thing about our earlier topic, relationships. I don't mean to sound too goopy or sentimental, but I agree with you. I believe any good relationship comes down to respect and friendship. The kind of unglamorous,

work-a-day, committed love you won't find in the pages of
a romance novel."

"You haven't read widely in the genre," Tilda said.
"There are plenty of writers who talk about day-to-day
love. It's true that not all of them would call themselves romance writers."

"Well, you know what I mean. I'm not talking about
heaving bosoms, though I've got nothing against heaving
bosoms."

Tilda nodded discreetly toward a guy who was coming
toward them, dragging a cooler. He was technically gorgeous and perfectly built. Tilda could tell because he wasn't
wearing a shirt and his shorts were riding very, very low.

"I know," she said when he had passed. "And I've got
nothing against six-pack abs, though in the end they have
nothing to do with love. But they are nice to look at. Even
though that guy should be wearing a shirt. This is a restaurant, after all. I think there are sanitary laws about such
things."

"You sound like a mommy."

"I am. I'm a middle-aged mommy with no partner."

"Now you're being all self-pitying. Again."

"I know," Tilda admitted. "Self-pity comes easily to me.
I'm not saying I'm proud of it."

"Self-pity and wallowing can kill you. Sorry. I meant,
figuratively."

"I know you did."

"Do you think Dad would ever really consider willing
Larchmere out of the family?" Hannah asked suddenly. "I
mean, if he and this Jennifer person get married. It seems
impossible but stranger things have happened."

Tilda paused before replying. "I've been thinking and
thinking about that. Obsessing, really. I just don't know. I
wish I could say with certainty that I did know. Either way,

then I could deal with his decision. Maybe we're being Nervous Nellies for nothing. I hope so."

"Nervous Nellies? I haven't heard that expression in ages. Didn't Mom used to say that?"

Tilda laughed. "Yes. She used to tell me to stop being a Nervous Nellie every time gym class came around. I think my fears annoyed her somehow."

Of course they did, Hannah thought. Their mother had not tolerated weakness or vulnerability or anything that might vaguely be considered a nuisance or a disruption to her daily life of self-preservation. *My thoughts about her are so harsh,* Hannah realized. She tried to summon even a shred of positive feeling about Charlotte McQueen and could not.

Hannah, disturbed, wanted to get back to the subject of Larchmere. "Sometimes," she said, "it seems to me that Larchmere has a personality of its own, or as if it's a being of its own, not just an inanimate object. I feel sometimes that it's something alive and breathing. It makes me uncomfortable somehow, to think that what is essentially a big pile of stones and mortar and glass has a life independent of its inhabitants. A piece of land or a house isn't supposed to have so much power over a person, is it?"

Tilda frowned. "I guess not. I'm not really sure I understand what you mean."

"It doesn't matter. It's just that I can't deny the power of Larchmere. I feel it now more than ever. Now that I know its future as our home is threatened. I know it's all very romantic of me. You've read *Rebecca,* haven't you?"

"Of course," Tilda said. "Several times. I even taught it one semester. But in the novel it was a person not a house who wielded a bizarre power over the hero and heroine. It was Rebecca herself, from beyond the grave. At least, it was the memories of her and the stories told about her that wielded the power. Rebecca's legend."

"You think so? Maybe Rebecca had a hold on the unnamed heroine but not over Max de Winter, at least not entirely. Don't you remember why he stayed in that god-awful marriage to that god-awful woman?" Hannah asked. "Basically so that no taint of unpleasantness would touch his beloved home. When he comes clean to his second wife, about murdering Rebecca, he admits to something like having loved Manderley too much. He says that that kind of one-way love is doomed to fail, or that it can't grow. He says something like that. One-way, unrequited love."

Tilda nodded. "Yes, I do remember now. His point was that love has to be reciprocal in order to flourish. Do you want the last steamer?"

"No," Hannah said. "You can have it. But about love for the house, or for things, inanimate objects, I wonder. Doesn't, say, a tree, repay your love—your tending to its needs, feeding it fertilizer, watering it—by thriving? Isn't that a form of reciprocity?"

"Maybe," Tilda said. "In a way, yes, though the tree isn't sentient. It's alive but it's not making a conscious, thinking choice about its thriving or failing. It's just—reacting, I suppose."

"Yes," Hannah said, but she wasn't so sure a tree was just reacting to its environment rather than also acting upon it.

"And a house, a structure," Tilda was saying. "What really does it give us in return for our care? In return for repainting its exterior and replacing its old and broken windows and cleaning its chimneys?"

"Shelter," Hannah said. "Warmth. A sense of comfort and security. Adam would say financial security."

"But aren't those qualities really the result of human action? I don't know, the people who inhabit a house seem to me to be the source of all that's good—and bad—about the notion of 'home.' Not the structure around them."

Hannah thought about that for a moment. "So, you believe that home is where the heart is. In other words, that home is an emotional state having little to do with physical realities?"

"Not entirely," Tilda said, "but largely. Anyway, I guess we're not likely to come to any final agreement on this matter of the life—as it were—of the inanimate objects we say we love. I guess it's not important to agree. Well, I guess one thing we can agree on is the fact that we both love Larchmere."

"You're right." Hannah stood and stretched. "Let's get going. I want to call my office when we get back to the house. Just to check in."

It was on the drive back home to Larchmere that the thought first occurred to Tilda. She didn't know why she had not seen the parallel before. It was so obvious. Max de Winter had tried to make the death of his wife look like a boating accident. Tilda's own mother, Charlotte, had died in a boating accident. Or, at least, because of an accident that took place on a boat. Tilda refused to believe that her mother had been anywhere near as horrible and manipulative as the character of Rebecca, but . . . She wondered. Was Charlotte McQueen the abiding—the controlling?— spirit of Larchmere? And if she was, that meant that each of the McQueens' feelings about the house was to some extent colored by the relationship they had had with Charlotte.

Tilda shook her head. These were fanciful thoughts. They were pointless, really. But there was that gothic streak (good-humored Frank had said a morbid streak) again. Still, Tilda was curious. Was Charlotte McQueen indeed the presiding spirit of Larchmere?

10

Adam and Kat had gone up to Kennebunkport to have dinner with one of his colleagues who was vacationing there with his wife. He had not asked that the family watch his children. He had simply announced that he would not be around all evening. Ruth had made Cordelia and Cody hot dogs and beans for dinner. They had asked for seconds and then clamored for ice cream, which Ruth also gave them. Ice cream with chocolate sauce. Then, she settled them in front of the big, flat screen television in the living room and put on one of the loud and cartoonish animated movies they had brought with them. Situation dealt with, problem solved. If Adam wanted his kids to eat organic, then he should stay home and feed them himself.

Dinner then was Bill, Ruth, Craig, Tilda, Hannah, and Susan. Percy, as usual, was lumped on the sideboard, eyes wide. Susan had taken a turn in the kitchen and prepared for them a chicken dish flavored with lime and cilantro. (She had cooked a piece of plain chicken for Percy, who had accepted it as his due.) There was no further talk of Charlotte's memorial or party, except when Bill mentioned that Carol Whitehouse, the woman who had been with

Charlotte in the sailboat on that fateful day, had called to
say she could not be there for the events. Her daughter-in-
law was in the hospital and Carol was going down to stay
with her grandchildren in New Hampshire while her son
went to work.

Tilda thought of the kind of grandmother Charlotte had
been to her children. It had been pretty clear to everyone
that Charlotte favored Jon over Jane, maybe because he
was the firstborn, maybe because he was a boy. Whatever
the reason, her mother's obvious preference for one child
over another had bothered Tilda, though as far as she could
tell, it had not affected Jane in a negative way. Charlotte
McQueen had been good about buying gifts and sending
cards on holidays. And she had been fairly tolerant of having Jon and Jane underfoot during their visits to Larchmere. But, and Tilda felt almost disloyal remembering this,
she had not been very willing to visit the children in their
South Portland home. She had never offered to babysit,
even for a night. Tilda had never felt comfortable asking
her.

Of course, Charlotte had never known Adam's children,
as she had died before they were born. Would she have
been closer to her son's progeny? It was impossible to
know. And how would she have felt about Hannah and
Susan's children, assuming they had any someday?

After putting the kids to bed, Ruth went to her room,
claiming exhaustion. In fact, she was eager to get back to
the book she had started reading earlier that day, a shamelessly sexy novel by a new young writer who claimed to
have worked as a high-class call girl. Susan, who had
brought along her laptop because she had a project dead-
line looming, went off to the room she was sharing with
Hannah to work. Plus, although she would never admit it,
not even to Hannah, she was a big fan of InStyle.com and
wanted to check the Look of the Day.

Tilda, Hannah, and Craig were in the kitchen, loading the dishwasher and scrubbing pots, when Jennifer came by. Tilda was acutely aware of her own rather messy appearance after a long day in the sun and kitchen cleanup. Jennifer, in contrast, looked rested and fresh; her beige blouse was crisp and unwrinkled and her hair was neat. A quick and hopefully furtive glance at Jennifer's feet indicated that she had had a pedicure recently, maybe even earlier that day. Her gold tone sandals looked expensive. Tilda wondered if Jennifer owned a pair of baggy jeans or ratty sneakers. She chided herself for being snippy and jealous, even if it was just in her head. Thoughts were real, too, in their way.

Jennifer and Bill went into the library to play chess. Tilda had never mastered games and puzzles. She couldn't play chess, couldn't remember how to play checkers, didn't play cards. While she could handle a word search, crosswords left her stumped.

"I'm glad Dad has someone to play chess with," Hannah was saying, bending down to replace a pot in its proper cabinet. "He never did find a chess partner after Mom died, did he?"

Craig shook his head. "Not that I know of. I do know he plays against himself but that has to get boring. I know that he and Bobby used to play poker. There was a whole group of guys who would play. They'd move from house to house, Larchmere one month, someone else's the next."

"That's right," Tilda said. "I remember now. Mom would put out chips and dip for the guys."

Hannah looked to Craig. "The other wives put out sandwiches and cole slaw and Maine shrimp salad."

"And desserts," Craig said. "I remember Dad telling me that Teddy's wife made the best blueberry cobbler he'd ever tasted."

"Even Bobby, who's not exactly Mr. Domestic, put out a good spread."

Tilda frowned. "What are you saying? That Mom was cheap?"

"No. I'm saying that Mom didn't really care about Dad's poker nights. She didn't want all those men in the house. Obviously, she thought that chips and dip would deter them. But they came, anyway."

"Because Dad would bring out the good scotch when she went up to bed!" Craig added. "He knew how to treat his guests, even if Mom didn't."

Tilda felt uncomfortable. She knew that memory was unique to each individual, that time and psyche tended to distort what had occurred into what you wanted or needed to think had occurred. Siblings who grew up under the same roof each grew up in a different family. She knew that.

Still, it bothered her when Hannah and Craig said disparaging or critical things about their mother, even if for them, these disparaging or critical comments described the truth. But Tilda's truth about her mother was different. At least, it was partly different. Adam's truth was different, too.

"How about a nightcap?" Hannah suggested.

"Sounds good," Craig said. "Let's go out onto the porch. It's chilly. I could make us Irish coffees?"

"Perfect!"

Tilda chose not to join her sister and brother. Instead, she went upstairs to her room and sat again at the chair she had drawn to the window the other evening. She could hear Hannah's voice, and Craig's, but just barely, as a murmur. Then, Craig laughed and Hannah hushed him.

She wondered if this was the first time she had really listened to her siblings talk about their mother. She felt as if so much of what she was hearing this week was new. Charlotte hadn't liked her father's poker games or his buddies. Why hadn't she known that? She was older than Hannah and Craig. She should have been more aware of family dynamics. She wondered if she was the only one who cherished good memories of Charlotte McQueen. She wondered what Adam would have added to that conversation in the kitchen.

Tilda sighed and decided that she didn't really want to know. She closed the window to block out the sound of her siblings' voices.

11

Tilda was on the beach. It was a little later than she liked to walk but Jon had called that morning to say that the air conditioner that serviced most of the downstairs, the kitchen and living room at least, was on the fritz. He wanted permission to call the repair guy, which, he knew, would cost money. "I'd fix it myself if I could," he had said, "but I'm not Dad."

Nobody is Frank O'Connell, Tilda thought now. *Not even Frank O'Connell is Frank O'Connell anymore.*

She remembered how horrible it had been when Frank was finally gone and the simple yet devastating realization hit home—that never again would Frank's hand touch hers. The loss of his physical body and of their long habit of living together in all its physicality just struck her down. While he was dying their physical relationship had altered, of course, but his being entirely gone was a tremendous blow. No one told her how deep and meaningful the affection for the parts of a loved one's body could be, so that when the loved one was gone, you would ache to see just once more the shape of his fingernails, the pattern of hair on his wrist, the freckles on his nose, all the little things that made the loved one utterly and entirely unique. All of these peculiarities would be gone and it would hurt so badly at times, the missing.

"'Quoth the raven, "Nevermore."'" Tilda said the words aloud. There was no one to hear but the seagulls. The line was from Edgar Allan Poe's most popular poem. Almost everybody knew "The Raven" but how many people knew, as the poem's narrator did, just how deep grief and loss could take you?

It was simply all over. Frank was dead. There were no ifs, ands, or buts, no second chances, no do-overs. If only she could say: No, I didn't like the way this turned out, it isn't fair, let's start again.

Tilda suddenly remembered something else she had read, something else that had stuck in her head. It was from *Kafka Was the Rage,* Anatole Broyard's memoir of his years in Greenwich Village. In one chapter he talked about the early death of a good friend. About receiving the bad news of his friend's illness, he had said: "We never believe such things until they're over." Tilda had found that observation to be stunningly true, at least in her case. You knew it was going to happen. And then, it happened and you were surprised, as if you had had no clue.

But it was time to get over the surprise and the shock and the sadness. She didn't want, like Poe's narrator, to be mired in—to use Poe's own words—"Mournful and Never-ending Remembrance." She was not interested in torturing herself by obsessing over her loss. She was not. But healing was hard. Moving on was a process fraught with controversy. She had graduated from the grief-counseling sessions, she had been to see a therapist, she had tried the antidepressants the doctor had given her, and she had flushed them down the toilet when nothing much changed.

What was the next step, then, in recovery? If only someone would tell her exactly what to do!

She scanned the sky over the beach before heading up to the parking lot. It was empty, except for two whirling, cawing seagulls.

She would call her son as soon as she got back to Larchmere. She hoped he had been able to book the repair guy. She hoped the bill wouldn't be outrageous. She was not good at arguing with repairmen. That had been Frank's job.

It was late morning, around eleven o'clock, and Tilda was in the sunroom. Lots of people found it the most pleasant room in the house, as, perhaps, it was meant to be. The floor was made of old, rescued pine boards, sanded and painted a gentle gray. The walls were white. A long, low table against the back wall had been painted robin's egg blue, as had the trim around the large windows. The furniture—a couch, several chairs, and two small occasional tables—were suited for life by the beach. The cushions were upholstered in heavy linen, striped navy and white. On the back wall and between the windows were hung simple watercolor prints depicting various kinds of seabirds. It was a restful, clean room.

Tilda was sitting on the couch, trying to focus on the novel in her hands. It was *The Sea, The Sea,* by Iris Murdoch. But even though the book was one of her favorites, and Iris Murdoch one of her favorite writers, her thoughts kept slipping away to dark places, to loss and loneliness and petty jealousy and the outrageous cost of air-conditioning repair bills. She sighed loudly, surprised that she had done so.

Hannah, who was seated on a chair, and who had been flipping through a local paper, looked up at her sister. "You okay?"

"Yes. Sorry."

"In a bad mood?"

"Not bad, exactly. More like a grim mood."

The sudden appearance of Adam and Kat prevented further conversation on the topic of Tilda's mood. Kat was wearing another halter top, this one a blue paisley print, and a pair of tight, white shorts. The day was cool (though the sunroom was warm) and Tilda had a not very nice urge to suggest that Kat put on a sweater and long pants, preferably something bulky. The sight of so much young, firm flesh made her feel grumpy. Poor Kat. She was innocent of everything but youth.

It seemed that Adam and Kat were in the middle of a conversation, because Adam now said, as he sat in the cushioned chair next to Hannah's, "Larchmere is a perfect party venue. It was practically designed for weddings."

Tilda wasn't sure about that but she was sure—or almost sure—that her brother wanted to have his second wedding at Larchmere because it would be a good way to flaunt the family's prestige and his own wealth to the locals, as well as to his new bride and her family. It wasn't a nice thing to think about her brother, but the truth was that Tilda didn't much care for Adam. She never really had, and since his, in Tilda's opinion, senseless, utterly selfish divorce from Sarah, her dislike for her older brother had grown. Her own marriage had been strong and now that Frank was dead she found herself even more committed to the idea of a lifelong union. She did not want to be judgmental but when it came to Adam she found it hard not to be.

"We could have a tent, do the whole thing outdoors," Adam went on. "And we could clear the furniture out of the living and dining rooms in case of rain. I know several excellent caterers. As for the flowers, I know this guy in Boston who does fabulously exotic stuff. Leave it all to me."

Kat shot a shy and nervous glance at Tilda, who was

staring at her book, pretending not to listen. "I'm sure it would be very nice, Adam," she said, her tone tentative, "but I've always dreamed of a wedding in my hometown. You know, so my parents could invite some of our neighbors and my relatives who are too old now to travel and—"

"Framingham is a dump compared to Ogunquit, you know that, Kat."

"Don't be mean, Adam," Hannah said. "It is not a dump. Besides, I agree with Kat. A hometown wedding is a nice idea."

Tilda looked up now; there was no point in pretending that the conversation was a private one. Kat looked tense, as if Hannah's support had made her uncomfortable.

Adam frowned. "It's not your wedding we're discussing."

"It's okay," Kat said suddenly. "If Adam really wants us to get married here, that's fine. Ogunquit isn't that far from home."

"Our brother is Bridezilla," Hannah commented sotto voce, though she was pretty sure Adam had heard.

Kat finally sat, and reached to the closest table for a magazine. It was an old copy of *Living*. She began to flip through it but Tilda doubted she was really interested in Christmas cookie recipes and directions on how to make your own wrapping paper. Was anybody interested in making her own wrapping paper, especially when you could get it in discount bulk at the supermarket?

Cordelia appeared in the doorway of the sunroom, Cody in tow. Ruth was just behind them, carrying a cup of coffee. "Dad?" Cordelia said.

"Hmmm."

"Me and Cody want to go to the beach now."

"Cody and I," Ruth corrected.

"In a minute." Adam tapped Kat's arm. "Cordelia will make a perfect flower girl. Cody will be ring bearer, of course."

Kat opened her mouth as if to protest—What if, Tilda thought, she had her own nieces and nephews? What if she didn't want a lot of attendants?—when Cody wailed, "What's a ring bearer?"

Adam explained.

Cody stamped his foot. "I don't wanna be a stupid ring bearer. Everyone's gonna laugh at me."

Adam stared sternly at his son. "You'll do as I say, young man."

Cody's face went slack and his lips quivered. Cordelia said, dubiously, "A flower girl? Does that mean I have to wear one of those dorky gowns in some gross color?"

Ruth stepped past the children. "This is not the time, Adam," she said quietly.

"I'll say when it's time to talk to my kids," he replied angrily. "What do you know about being a parent?"

Ruth let him wait a moment before saying: "I know about common sense."

Tilda looked at Kat. Her eyes were on the magazine page again and her cheeks were flushed. Tilda felt sorry for her. But she also felt that Kat should learn to speak up for herself before it was far too late.

Ruth turned back to the children. "Get your bathing suits, kids. I'll take you to the beach."

Jennifer arrived for lunch at a little after one o'clock. Tilda had not known she was coming. She had brought with her—after checking first with Ruth, it turned out—a large bowl of crabmeat salad. Ruth had prepared salad greens and together the women assembled a platter of food and put it out on the kitchen bar top.

Cordelia and Cody had eaten sandwiches in the sunroom and were now watching a movie until someone would take them back to the beach. Tilda was hungry but she wanted to refuse Jennifer's offering of food. She wanted to go off alone. But she stayed in the kitchen, annoyed and guilty, and ate some of the crabmeat salad, which was very good, very crabby, with a pinch of Old Bay seasoning and not too much mayonnaise. She wanted to hate it. She fought against the desire for more.

"The crab salad is very good," she blurted. "Thanks."

Jennifer smiled. "It's my mother's recipe. It's very simple but it's a crowd pleaser."

"Jennifer is a wonderful cook," Bill said proudly.

Hannah, perched on a counter out of easy sight, made a face. Susan frowned at her.

"Well, I wouldn't say I'm a wonderful cook," Jennifer demurred. "I do some things well."

Adam and Kat came into the kitchen.

"Adam, do you want any salad?" Bill asked.

He looked disdainfully at the half-empty platter. "Kat and I already ate."

The sudden puzzled—and hungry—look on Kat's face told Tilda that Adam was lying.

"Hey, nobody told me it was time for lunch! Hey, Jen. Nice to see you again." Craig came loping into the kitchen, squeezed Jennifer's arm in passing, then reached for a plate. After taking a bite, he exclaimed, "Whoa! Excellent crab salad. Who made this?"

Adam rolled his eyes. Hannah made another face. This time Ruth caught them both and frowned, along with Susan. Tilda reached for her water glass. Bill was oblivious to the tensions.

The awkward meal was soon over. Ruth disappeared without an explanation. Jennifer left, empty bowl with her, claiming a meeting with a client in Cape Neddick.

When she had gone, Craig turned to his brother. "Really, dude, what would it cost you to be a human being? Just once. You stood there like there was a pole stuck—"

"So, what do you kids think of Jennifer?" Bill had returned from seeing his girlfriend out.

"She's great, Dad," Craig said quickly, almost as if he were defying the others to contradict him.

"Yes, she is," Bill said. "I'm a lucky man to have met her."

There was a silence that Tilda—and probably others—found hugely uncomfortable. Susan looked grim.

Finally, Hannah spoke. "I wish you'd told me, told us, earlier about this . . . relationship, Dad."

"Why?" Her father sounded perplexed.

"Well, no reason," she said lamely. "Just that it would have been nice to know about something so important to you."

"I'm sorry, honey. I certainly didn't mean to hurt your feelings." Bill was genuinely contrite. He hated to cause his younger daughter any pain. Come to that, he didn't like to cause anyone pain, though in his business he had known some people who did.

"It's okay, Dad," she said. "But promise that if something else big happens in your life you let me—us—know right away. Okay?"

"Sure," he said. "It's a promise."

"You are being cautious though, Dad, aren't you?" Tilda asked then. "How long have you known Jennifer?"

"Long enough." Bill's tone brooked no argument. "We were on the zoning board together for a few years when she still lived in town. She's a lovely person. I might be old but I'm still a competent judge of character."

"What were the circumstances of her divorce?" Tilda pressed. "I mean, did she initiate the divorce or did her husband? Was it a case of infidelity?"

Craig said dryly, "Enquiring minds want to know."

"I don't see that Jennifer's divorce is any of your business, Tilda. Really, it's not even my business. What she's told me she's told me of her own free will. I simply don't press her for details."

There didn't seem to be anything more to say, not at the moment. Hannah and Susan left to take a drive. Craig said he was meeting a friend in Old Orchard Beach. Tilda went off to try once again to do some reading. Kat, who had grabbed a carton of yogurt once Jennifer was gone, now dropped it in the recycling bin in the corner and went off.

Adam remained behind in the kitchen with his father. When Bill made to leave the room, Adam detained him. "Wait, Dad," he said. "We need to talk. I'm not happy about this turn of events."

Bill frowned. "Excuse me? What turn of events?"

"This relationship of yours with this Jennifer person. Dad, she's twenty-three years your junior."

Bill looked closely at his older son. "And you're dating a woman significantly younger than you," he said. "Don't tell me age is the issue here. What's really upsetting you about my relationship with Jennifer?"

Adam hesitated. Of course, the age difference was not the real issue. The real issue was the threat a potential wife posed regarding the inheritance of Larchmere. But he couldn't come right out and say that, not yet, anyway. Not unless he had to.

"It's a small town, Dad. Everybody talks. I don't want you to look like a fool, a laughingstock."

Bill felt himself flush. He couldn't remember the last time one of his children had angered him. He was always disappointed by Craig, but not angered. "I could say the same about you," he told his older son. "But I won't. Now, if you'll excuse me . . ." He turned again to leave the room.

"She doesn't care about you, Dad," Adam said loudly. To hell with diplomacy. He was a man of no patience, anyway. There were bigger things at stake here than his father's feelings. There was Larchmere. There was Adam's financial future. "She just wants your money," he said, unable or perhaps unwilling to conceal the contempt in his voice. "She wants Larchmere. And you're too foolish to see that."

Bill stopped and slowly turned back. "You've just added insult to injury," he said. "This conversation is over." And then he did leave the room.

12

That night the McQueens hosted a casual dinner party on the front lawn. In addition to Jennifer, Bobby, and the Vickes, Bill had invited the local librarian, Nancy, and her partner, Glenda; the guy who owned the landscape company that kept Larchmere perfectly groomed (he came with a wife and two teenaged sons); the owner of a small but influential gallery on Route 1 (he, too, came with a wife); and a scattering of other people with whom he and Ruth had become friendly over the years. Percy had been secured in Ruth's bedroom with a good supply of water and treats so that he wouldn't be annoyed by people drifting in and out of the house.

It was a cool evening so Tilda had worn a heavy cotton sweater, navy, over a white, man-tailored blouse, jeans, and navy sneakers. Heels of any sort were a ridiculous choice for a lawn party, but Tilda noted that Kat was wearing purple kitten-heeled sandals. They would be ruined by the end of the evening, the heels scraped and stained with grass and mud. She wondered briefly if she should offer Kat a pair of sneakers or flats, but then rejected the idea. None of her footwear could be called fashionable and she just knew that Kat would reject the offer on that basis alone. More rejection, Tilda did not need.

She was standing a bit apart from the guests, who were still arriving or milling about, feeling a bit like the lady of the manor and enjoying it. Suddenly, she felt a soft little whisper of movement and looked down to see a garden snake slithering past her, almost but not quite brushing the toe of her sneaker. The little fellow made it safely under the hostas, which ran rampant along one side of the house. She smiled. At least tonight he wouldn't be an owl's midnight snack.

While life in Ogunquit was not exactly life in the backwoods, it had its share of rural features. Wild turkeys roamed the wooded areas, the strutting male and the female shepherding her brood. On occasion coyotes, the bane of local cats and small wildlife, could be heard barking, and of course there were deer, herds of them, that would destroy any kitchen garden they could get into. Hedgehogs routinely ate flowers off their stems and black bears had been known to prowl around a house in the dead of night, looking for a snack. Wild ducks made way too much noise during mating season, the males furiously chasing each other in flight while the bored-looking female waited in a pond for one of her suitors to return. For a while an owl had made its nest in a tree close to Larchmere; several times Tilda had seen the beautiful bird in daylight, swooping low over the driveway, which, she thought, was unusual as owls were known to be nocturnal hunters, not often seen in the day.

And crows! There seemed to be a preponderance of crows in Ogunquit—a murder was right! For weeks on end it sounded to Tilda as if the birds were killing each other, their shrieks becoming moans and screams as they wheeled in the sky. More annoyingly, if the lids on the trash cans weren't properly set down, the crows would toss the lids aside and wreck havoc with the contents. While Tilda had never actually seen crows tossing lids, she had witnessed them sitting atop an open can, tearing through plastic bags with determination, and she had no doubt that those big, glossy black birds could do anything they set their minds— or their stomachs—to. She would take the tiny, pretty piping plovers any day, even though in an effort to secure their breeding grounds and nests local environmentalists had succeeded in getting the Fourth of July fireworks display cancelled for several years in a row. It would do the tiny birds no good to be trod upon in the dark by revelers, quite possibly on the far side of inebriation, strolling the beach.

And the peepers! Tilda loved the sound of peepers, those tiny, inch-long male tree frogs whose chorus in mating season could drown out the sound of a television behind closed windows. When the peepers began their song, spring was not far behind. And the deep croak of the solitary bullfrog was another sure indicator of warm weather before long.

The sudden appearance of her older brother interrupted her pleasant musings. "I can't stand that guy," Adam said, his voice thick with distaste.

"What guy?"

Adam nodded in the direction of the grills. "Bobby. I don't know what Dad sees in him. And the idea of Aunt Ruth consorting with him makes me green around the gills. But she's a whacko so what can you expect."

Tilda was shocked. "Ruth is not a whacko. And Bobby is a great guy, Adam. Mom loved him, too."

Adam looked down at his sister as if she were crazy. "No, she didn't. Mom hated the sight of him. For Dad's sake she tolerated him being around, but barely."

This was disturbing news, shocking really. Her mother had hated her father's best friend? Why had she not seen that? Maybe Adam was lying. But why would he lie?

"Bobby is like an uncle to me," she said, her tone defiant.

"What could he and Dad possibly have in common? Talk about an odd couple. The guy reeks of fish."

"He does not!" Tilda cried. Then, embarrassed that she might have been overheard, she spoke in almost a whisper. "That's a totally mean thing to say, Adam."

Adam shrugged. "I'm going to get another drink," he said, and walked off in the direction of the bar that had been set up on the porch.

"No, thanks," Tilda muttered. "I'll get my own." She looked back to where the grills were set up and saw Bobby handing Jennifer a burger. She said something and he laughed heartily. It looked like Bobby approved of his friend's new girlfriend. And if Bobby approved of her, maybe even liked her, Tilda thought, maybe Jennifer really was okay.

Tilda turned away. Why did things have to change? She would have preferred not to know that her mother had disliked Bobby. She would have preferred that her father had never met Jennifer. She would have preferred that Frank be at the grills, presiding, like in the old days. Like in the wonderfully innocent old days.

Bill McQueen was wearing that awful hat, the one he had bought after Charlotte's death. Hannah thought it made him look kind of goofy, but in an endearing way. He was talking to Bobby, his old friend. At first glance they seemed an unlikely duo. Bill was tall and slim where Bobby was short and stocky, a virtual wall of muscle. Bill's skin was relatively unlined, and pale. Bobby's face was a map of deep creases and the color of caramel. Bill had gone to college, then graduate school. Hannah knew for a fact that Bobby, though fantastically well-read, had dropped out of high school. Bill had made a living in an office, wearing a suit and tie. Bobby made his living in rough clothes, out on rough waters. Bill had had a family. As far as Hannah knew, Bobby had never even been married. Still, it was clear to Hannah that the men shared a deep bond. Maybe it was a case of opposites attracting. Maybe their mutual love for Ruth was the bond. She didn't know and she supposed it didn't matter.

Hannah sipped her beer. What she did know was that she had an awful lot of wonderful memories of big summer parties on the lawn, and of more intimate winter parties around a decorated tree, and an awful lot of wonderful memories, too, of small, random, seemingly insignificant moments. There were the summer nights when she and sometimes Craig, too, had camped out in the gazebo, scaring themselves silly with ghost stories and gory tales of campers being eaten by bears and trampled by moose. They had never run back to the protection of the house, though. She and Craig had had guts, not like Adam and Tilda, who rarely, if ever, broke the rules or challenged themselves physically.

Maybe, in the end, Adam and Tilda were the smarter ones, not taking chances. But boy, Hannah had had fun! Once she had attempted to build a tree house, all on her own, in the biggest oak on the property. It was a rudimentary structure when completed but she was very proud of it. Until the floor gave way and she came tumbling to earth with it. She broke her wrist and was in a cast for what seemed like forever to a ten-year-old. She remembered her mother being very, very angry about the incident. Her father had promised to help her build another tree house, when she was all mended, but somehow, that particular thrill had worn off.

Bill caught her eye now and waved. She smiled and waved back.

Hannah was aware of her father's preference for her. She assumed that he tried to hide it, for the sake of his other children—he was a fair man—but it was obvious all the same. She was sure pretty much everyone knew that she was the favorite. And her father was the parent she had always loved best. She really had had no choice. She had never felt close with her mother, ever. Their relationship had been tepid from the start and had only grown cooler when Hannah had come out while in college.

As Charlotte increasingly lost interest in her younger daughter, Bill, in contrast, began to show Hannah even more affection, as if to prove that he loved her unconditionally, as if to make up for her mother's lack of concern.

Charlotte had been perfectly, distantly polite to the girl-friends (not that there were many) Hannah had brought home on occasion, but after a while, Hannah had stopped bringing anyone home, friends or lovers. She had come to realize that being virtually ignored hurt more than being openly vilified. Someone had said that indifference, not hate, was the opposite of love. Hannah agreed.

But things had changed after her mother's death. Hannah had felt free to visit Larchmere more frequently. The house felt warmer, more welcoming, without her mother's chilly, silently critical presence. And then she had met Susan, who immediately fit seamlessly into the McQueen family, which only made visits to Larchmere that much more appealing.

Now Hannah watched as Susan crossed the yard, walking in her direction. She looked lovely that night, dressed in a lilac, ankle length, spaghetti-strap dress in some crinkly fabric. She wore flat, silver sandals and her hair was piled up in a messy, sexy twist. She was smiling.

"Your dad looks like he's having a good time," she said when she joined Hannah.

"Yeah."

"But you look distracted. What are you thinking about?"

Hannah smiled. "Oh, nothing. Just how glad I am that you and I are here, at Larchmere, together."

Susan smiled back and squeezed Hannah's hand. "I'm glad, too."

13

"Kat seems entirely out of her element," Craig commented to his sister. They were standing together on the lawn. Craig was on a break from grill duty. Hannah was on her third beer. "Of course, I have no idea what her natural element is, or where it is, for that matter. I just know that she looks like she wants to bolt."

"I know. And poor Cordelia. Look at her, she's practically clinging to Kat but Kat hardly even seems to notice."

Maybe Kat didn't like children all that much, Hannah wondered. Maybe she didn't like Cordelia in particular, though the girl was pretty sweet. Or maybe the fact of Cordelia's being Adam's daughter disconcerted her. Whatever the reason, Hannah felt bad for the little girl.

Teddy Vickes joined them. He had been Bill's lawyer, and friend, for as long as Hannah could remember. He had to be in his eighties by now, though his mind seemed as sharp as ever. Teddy's benign, friendly manner belied the fact that he was a tough and fair-minded and dedicated lawyer. His wife, Tessa, had made a career as a homemaker and seemed to enjoy taking a backseat to Teddy's popularity. She seemed, Hannah thought, very proud of her husband. When not cleaning house (it was spotless) and cooking and baking (she was very good in the kitchen) Tessa volunteered at York Hospital in whatever capacity was needed, sometimes in the café, sometimes in the gift shop, on occasion in the wards themselves.

"Hard to believe it's been ten years since Charlotte passed," Teddy said, with a shake of his totally bald head. "Seems like only yesterday."

Craig murmured something unintelligible. Hannah nodded.

"I'll never forget how she always wore a scarf around her neck or her shoulders, even on the hottest days. And I don't think I ever saw the same scarf twice! I'll bet she had hundreds of those things. Silk scarves, some flimsy material that was maybe chiffon, my wife would know, fur scarves in the winter. Charlotte loved her scarves."

"Yes," Hannah said. "She did have a flair with clothes." *And if she had loved her children as much as she had loved her scarves, then maybe . . .* Hannah knew she was being unfair to the memory of her mother—how could Charlotte fight back against the accusations?—but right then, she just didn't care.

Ruth joined their little group. She had just set out plates of cookies, brownies, and lemon squares, all made by Tessa Vickes, on a nearby table. Cody and his sister had been rooted there since Ruth appeared, burdened with goodies. It happened in a split second, as lots of accidents do. Cody, reaching for a cookie, put his hand a bit too close to the flame of one of the low, and supposedly "safe," candles.

"Ow!" Cody stared down at his finger and started to cry, which struck Craig, Hannah, and Ruth as the perfectly normal thing to do.

Adam and Kat seemed to appear from nowhere. Kat yelped and put her hand to her mouth. Adam put his hands on his hips. "What were you doing, putting your finger so close to the flame? Haven't I taught you better?"

"It was an accident, Daddy!" Cordelia, ever the protective big sister, protested. "He didn't mean to do it!"

Kat still had her hand pressed to her mouth. Now she put it down and cried, "Oh, my God, what do we do? Is he going to be all right?"

Jennifer, who had been hovering, watching, closer to Adam and the children than to Craig and the others, now stepped in. "Of course he's going to be all right," she said. "It's only a tiny little burn. It probably won't even blister. Come on, Cody, how about I take you inside and we put some cold water and a Band-Aid on that finger?" Jennifer reached out and Cody quickly, gratefully took her hand. They went off toward the house. Together, Adam and Kat drifted away, seemingly glad to let someone else solve their problem. Cordelia tagged behind her father, a cookie in one hand and a brownie in the other. It seemed that Adam had forgotten to reprimand her for eating sugar.

Hannah and Craig shared a meaningful look. "Adam's going to have to hire a nanny," Hannah said. "That's clear."

"Jen seems to be good with children, though."

Or she's just sucking up to her boyfriend's grandkids, Hannah thought. "Mmm," she said.

Ruth nodded. "She told me that she and her ex-husband had tried to have a baby but it just wasn't going to happen. He refused to adopt. That was years ago." Ruth, herself, had never wanted a family, but being of an empathetic nature, she thought she could begin to understand how the disappointment of not being able to have children could damage a person for a long, long time.

"That's too bad," Craig said.

"Yeah." Hannah was beginning to get uncomfortable with the conversation. She wondered if Jennifer's divorce had been one of the results of the failed attempt to have a family. She looked around for Susan, whom she had not seen in a while. She spotted her chatting with Nancy, the town's librarian, across the lawn.

"Excuse me," she said to her brother and her aunt. She went to join her wife.

As the sun faded and the evening grew darker and cooler, sweaters were fetched from cars and the house, candles were lit, and someone—probably Craig, Hannah thought—put on a selection of jazz music.

An owl was hooting in the darkened trees and the lapping of the tide could just be heard if you listened hard enough. The gazebo was lit with strings of tiny lights and several small candles in glass holders were set on the table within. Much of the food was set out there. The corn on the cob was from New Jersey, as Maine corn came in best late in the summer. Tessa Vickes had brought the mammoth pot of fish chowder, which was, as usual on such occasions, the first to go. Just enough cream, big chunks of haddock and halibut, a perfect sprinkling of black pepper—the chowder was agreed to be excellent.

Though not really party food—they were pretty messy as a rule—there were steamers, courtesy of one of Bobby's friends, who dug them out of the water right in front of his house and sold them to a select few. Tilda considered the first steamers of the summer—not lobster—the real start of the season. Mainers ate lobster all year round. It was only those "from away" who considered lobster a warm weather indulgence.

Tilda, who had settled in a chair with a plate on her lap, thought again of Frank's traditional role at these McQueen family summer events. He really had been the grill guy extraordinaire. If it could be eaten, Frank could find a way to cook it on the grill. He had even mastered grilled desserts.

Tilda missed his grilled fruit pizzas, but most of all she missed his specialty, the dessert he was happy to make whenever she asked for it, a grilled peach melba served with vanilla ice cream and homemade balsamic raspberry sauce. She knew that if she asked Bobby to follow Frank's recipe he would make the dessert for her, but she never asked him to. It would feel too much like trying to substitute Frank. Frank could not be substituted.

Tilda had loved when Frank would come to bed after a party smelling all smokey. He had always offered to take a shower first but she had always told him not to bother. There was definitely something sexy about a man and his grill. She even knew a woman whose husband had gotten a first date with her by building a grill in her backyard. Now, that was a very smart move.

The big charcoal grill at their—at her—home in South Portland had stood unused, under its black leather cover, since a few months before Frank's death when he had last had the strength to use it. His baseball style cap with the word "Grillmeister" on it, a gift from Jon, hung unworn in the hall closet.

Tilda looked down at the untouched plate of food on her lap, and then over to where Bobby and Craig were sharing grill duty. Adam had never been one to enjoy getting his hands dirty or his clothes smelly. Her father, Bill, had abdicated to Frank years before. She wasn't sure if Teddy even knew how to grill, what with Tessa being such a fantastic cook.

Suddenly, Tilda felt overwhelmed by sadness. She got up, tossed her plate in one of the garbage bins Bill had provided on the lawn, and escaped into Larchmere.

14

The library was quiet, at the back of the house, away from the party out on the front lawn, but Tilda could still hear the distant din and hum of voices and music. Tilda loved Larchmere's library. This room alone seemed to belong in an English country manor, not in a house near the beach. (For the first time Tilda wondered if the decor and atmosphere of the room had been her mother's or her father's decision.) A large, old, colorful but almost threadbare Asian rug covered much of the floor. The wall-to-wall bookshelves were stained a dark brown. The leather sleeper couch was also dark brown. Two high-backed armchairs, one, faded chintz, the other, faded green velvet, settled on either side of the wood-burning stove. A portrait of Larchmere hung over the stove, painted by a friend of her father's long since dead. Black and white, framed photographs, sitting on a large wooden desk, showed Tilda's grandparents, both sets, on their wedding days. Her parents' wedding portrait was in her father's room.

Tilda turned on the lamp that stood on the desk. It had a brass stand and a green glass shade. She angled the shade so she could better see the books on the shelves to the right of the desk. She found what she had hoped to find. There was a Book of Common Prayer in Larchmere's library, as well as a copy of the King James Bible, the Book of Mormon, and the Koran. Craig had contributed a copy of the *I Ching* back when he was in college and interested in such things. Tilda took down the Book of Common Prayer. Its red leather covers were clean and the edges straight. No one in the McQueen family could be considered overly religious. Somewhat interested in religions, yes, but not religious.

A minister of the Unitarian Universalist Church had married Tilda and Frank. Frank's parents had wanted them to be married in the Catholic Church, in which he had been raised. But Frank just didn't feel deeply about the religion of his youth. Now, twenty some-odd years later, Tilda couldn't recall the exact words of her own marriage ceremony. They had written their own vows but Tilda had not looked at her wedding book, where they were recorded, for years. Had there even been prayers, in the traditional sense?

She opened the red leather book and found what she was looking for. She read in a soft voice, almost a whisper:

"Matilda, will you have this man to be your husband; to live together in the covenant of marriage? Will you love him, comfort him, honor and keep him, in sickness and in health; and forsaking all others, be faithful to him as long as you both shall live?"

There was another version of the vow, and Tilda read that, too.

"In the Name of God, I, Matilda, take you, Francis, to be my husband, to have and to hold from this day forward, for better or worse, for richer or poorer, in sickness and in health, to love and to cherish, until we are parted by death. This is my solemn vow."

If she had spoken those words, it seemed that she would

be let off the hook, now that Frank was gone. Why should she feel scared or nervous about meeting another man? Why should she feel guilty about marrying again? She had kept her marital commitment to stay with Frank until one of them died. He had died. She had not.

Tilda closed the book and returned it to the shelf. She knew that the vows she and Frank had written had not mentioned illness or death. Love, of course, respect, and compassion. But nothing about dying.

She turned and walked to the other side of the room, where her wedding portrait was displayed. Someone— her father, she assumed—had put it away when Frank died, probably in an effort to spare her more pain. Which, of course, was ridiculous. Out of sight did not always mean out of mind. Tilda had soon rescued it from a drawer in the desk and returned it to its usual place, propped on a shelf against some of the least read books in Larchmere's library. (In her own home, the portrait hung in the living room, amid graduation photos of her kids, formal family Christmas portraits, and Hannah and Susan's official wedding photo.)

Tilda looked carefully at the photo in its silver frame. How young she had looked—how young she had been! And even skinnier than she was now! And Frank . . . She had never noticed it before but looking at the portrait now she thought that Frank looked absolutely terrified! The awful thought struck her that maybe he had been unsure of marrying her, hoping for a last-minute escape, a reprieve. Ridiculous. He had probably just been uncomfortable in his tuxedo, scared he would pop a button at a wrong moment, or spill red wine all over his starched white shirt.

His parents were gone now, dead within a year of each other, victims of cancer, about three years before Frank got sick. They had been in their forties when Frank, their only child, was born, a late and a surprise baby, a cherished gift neither had realized they had wanted so dearly. Abundant and unconditional love had helped Frank become the happy person he was, the smile of joy to Tilda's frown of worry. It was sad that such good and generous people, all three of them, had died such miserable deaths. But good didn't mean lucky, or exemption from life's harsher realities.

Her own parents had never been close with the O'Connells. They had little in common and met only once or twice a year at some celebratory occasion, like Jon's or Jane's birthday or Thanksgiving or, very rarely, at a July Fourth barbeque at Larchmere. Tilda had always thought the O'Connells, Margaret and John, found Larchmere too grand, maybe even intimidating. Maybe it was Charlotte they found "above their station," maybe Bill, too. Tilda had done her best to make her in-laws feel welcome at Larchmere but her best, she was afraid, had not been quite enough.

"There you are."

Tilda turned toward the door. She had not heard it open.

"You're being missed out front," Hannah said. "Tessa Vickes wants to talk to you about her book group. She's a little tipsy though, so don't expect much literary insight."

"Oh. Sorry."

"Are you okay? You were thinking of Frank, weren't you?"

Tilda smiled halfheartedly. "Guilty as charged. I'm sorry."

"First, stop saying you're sorry. Second, come back outside. Maybe you should get a little tipsy, too. You've got that melancholy look on your face again."

"Alcohol will make me feel sadder than I already do. Plus, I haven't eaten much all day. I'd probably fall down."

Hannah sighed, feigning exasperation. "Well, all right, there's strawberry shortcake."

Tilda felt enormous and sudden relief that she had this person in her life, that this person, with her good heart and her tousled red hair, loved her. "Thanks, Hannah," she said, though words were inadequate to express what she felt. "I'm really glad you're my sister."

"Oh, come on." Hannah grabbed Tilda's arm and tugged her toward the door. "I hate when people get all sentimental on me. Besides, Tessa is waiting. You need to talk to her before she falls to the ground!"

15

It was the morning after the barbeque. Though tired from staying up too late the night before, Hannah had come with Tilda for a walk on the beach. She felt she needed some exercise after all she had eaten at the party. Frank had been the Grillmeister, no doubt, but Bobby wasn't shabby, either. She defied anyone to pass up one of his burgers. (There had been hot dogs, too, in addition to the chowder and lobster and steamers and corn and strawberry shortcake. And beer.)

All morning, and prompted by her reading in the Book of Common Prayer in Larchmere's library, Tilda had been thinking about her colleague Bea Harris. Bea taught geometry, had one young daughter, and was recently divorced. According to Bea, the whole mess was her husband's doing. He had cheated. He had used money from their joint account to take his mistress on vacations. He had broken Bea's heart and her spirit. Bea claimed that she had it much harder than Tilda, who had "only" had to deal with death, not with betrayal.

"Let me ask your opinion," Tilda said to her sister. They had walked about a quarter mile down the beach in silence, until now. It was almost nine-thirty (they had come out late in deference to Hannah) and the beach was filling with people lugging chairs and coolers and Boogie Boards and kites. "Who do you think suffers most—someone who's lost a loved one to another person or someone who's lost a loved one to death?"

Hannah raised her eyebrows. "That's a big question. I'm not sure I can say. On some levels all loss is equal, I suppose. All loss is hard to bear. What do you think?"

"I think," Tilda said, "that you can qualify or quantify loss only theoretically. I don't think that loss as experienced can, or should, be qualified or quantified."

Hannah nodded.

"I think that the intensity of a particular loss can be determined only by the person experiencing the loss," Tilda went on. "I'm sure that for particular people the loss of a grandparent might be far harder to bear than the loss of a parent. It all depends on the individual and her circumstances."

"I guess I'd have to agree," Hannah said now. "But what brought up this happy topic?"

Tilda told her about Bea. Hannah agreed that the woman had no right to judge the size or the weight of Tilda's loss or to compare it to her own. But to be charitable, and Tilda always tried to be, Bea's words had probably come from a deep and dark chasm of pain. There was a very good chance that Bea had not really intended to wound her friend; there was a very good chance that someday she would regret speaking as she had. Emotional pain made one do and say terribly hurtful things. It was to be expected and understood and even, if possible, forgiven.

"Chances are you didn't want your husband to die," Tilda said now, musingly. "Chances are you didn't want him to go away. I won't say that I don't feel angry with Frank and at—at the universe, I guess, for allowing this to happen, for allowing Frank to die at the time and in the way he did. But I'm not angry with Frank—or the universe—in the same way I would be if he'd left me for another woman because of some ridiculous midlife crisis."

Hannah laughed. "The person experiencing the midlife crisis wouldn't call it ridiculous. It's probably all too real and awful for him, or for her. Why else would an otherwise sane and reasonable person disrupt his or her life so entirely, which is usually what people suffering a midlife crisis do? Look at all those cheating, adulterous male politicians who have been in the news these past few years. Every one of them made a public fool of himself. Which is why we laugh at them at the same time we're praying like mad that it will never happen to us."

"You'll never have a midlife crisis, Hannah," Tilda said. "You're too smart and levelheaded."

Was she really? Wasn't she having a midlife crisis at that very extended moment—debating whether to start a family or to—to what? To run away? "Let's hope so," she said with false cheer in her voice.

They walked a bit farther in silence, each occupied with her thoughts.

"I don't know how to 'create the conditions for affection,'" Tilda said suddenly. "I read that phrase recently, in a book, in a novel by Alexander McCall Smith. Do you know him? Of course you do. Everybody does. It's a good phrase. It struck me very forcefully. With Frank, it was so easy, right from the start. Our relationship came so naturally. I didn't have to create anything. Neither did he. It took almost no effort to fall in love, to get married."

"Maybe that can happen again," Hannah said. "Maybe another relationship can come naturally. If you, what was the phrase—'create the conditions for affection'—which I

take means to be open to other people. To be open to possibilities, to be imaginative."

"But can you really be open when it's a choice? I mean,
can you force yourself to be open to others? It sounds very
hard. I stumbled onto Frank all those years ago. And I was
so young. Now . . . now I have to decide to be willing to
stumble onto someone. That's very different, isn't it? You
don't intend to stumble. You just do."

"I don't know." Hannah shrugged. "People seem to be
stumbling on purpose all the time if you believe the claims
of eHarmony and Match.com and all those other dating
sites."

"I can't meet someone online," Tilda said firmly. "It
seems so . . . I don't know. It's just not me."

"You are so old-fashioned. How do you do it? How do
you survive in the twenty-first century?"

"I do just fine, thank you," Tilda said. "I use the Internet.
I do my banking online. I just have—preferences—for getting to know people."

"Well, all I know is that you can't go on like some, I
don't know, some medieval widow who shuts herself up in
a convent for the rest of her days. You have to live your
life."

"Why?" Tilda countered. "No, really. Why can't I just—
I don't know, endure life?"

"You're right," Hannah said. "You could choose to endure life rather than to live it, but how self-pitying is that?
And doesn't it seem like a crime against—I don't know,
life itself—to choose the path of least resistance? Life isn't
one of those novels where it's noble and romantic to waste
away, to pine for the man lost at sea or whatever. Not for
me, anyway. And I don't think it was for Frank, either. Not
the Frank I knew as my brother-in-law. And as my friend.
The last thing he would want is for you to be a martyr to his
cause."

A martyr to Frank's cause! That doesn't sound very appealing, Tilda thought. That sounded like something the narrator of "The Raven" would do, martyr himself to the cause of his dead loved one. She did not want to be a martyr!

"Let me ask you something," she said now. "When you met Susan, did it feel right immediately? Did it feel natural to be together, right from the start?"

"Well, you have to remember we'd been set up by a mutual acquaintance," Hannah said. "At least someone thought we'd be compatible, so we had a pretty good shot of success going in. So, yeah, there was definitely immediate attraction. I don't know about 'natural,' though. I was a nervous wreck. Can you be natural and nervous at the same time?"

"Sure. Of course. I remember the very first time I saw Frank. I hadn't met him yet, but just the sight of him across the classroom made me want to throw up."

Hannah laughed. "Well, there's the basis for a good relationship! Vomit!"

"Very funny. You know what I mean. I was just immediately attracted and immediately felt all funny inside."

"I know," Hannah conceded. "If you don't care, you can't be nervous. Well, on that note, I have to get back to the house. Mother Nature—Ms. Natural herself—is calling."

They hurried back to the parking lot and Tilda's car. Just before Tilda got into the driver's seat, she scanned the horizon. Nothing.

16

It was later in the day and Hannah and Susan had driven down to the beach. Hannah was wearing a large brimmed hat, one of those hats with some sort of magic sun protection woven right in. It had cost her a small fortune but she was not eager to get skin cancer. Red-haired people, she had read, were much more likely to get skin cancer than people with other hair colorings. Susan's head was bare. Her skin had been bronzing since May, in spite of her using sunscreen. She looked fantastic. Hannah was just a little bit jealous. It felt weird to be jealous of your spouse so she tried not to notice the appreciative stares sent Susan's way.

It was just after noon and the beach was crowded. They walked to the right, around the bend of land where the ocean became the Ogunquit River, and settled on a blanket, their backs to the dunes.

Off to the right was a family with, it seemed to Hannah, every accoutrement you could possibly buy for "fun in the sun." Mom was sitting in a super-duper portable chair made of canvas; on one side was a cup holder, and on the other was a sort of tray for food or magazines or books.

She wore a hat with an elongated visor and flap that covered the back of her neck. (Hannah preferred her own hat.)

The boy, maybe about nine years old, had a Boogie Board
(which was pretty useless on this part of the beach; there
were no substantial waves on the river), a water shooter
(with which he soaked his father, who was reclining in his
own super-duper portable lounge, every few minutes), an inflatable raft (in purple and neon green), and a disc that made
a screeching noise when he flung it (though there was no
one interested in catching and returning it).

The older girl, maybe about eleven, was trying in vain
(there was no wind) to launch a huge kite in the shape of a
butterfly. It was pink and purple. She had set up her own
umbrella (pink) and blanket (purple) several feet away
from the rest of her family. She was wearing wraparound
sunglasses better suited to a lifeguard and a bikini (pink,
naturally) that Hannah would blush to wear out of the
dressing room.

The baby of the family, a girl about three, was wearing
floats around her upper arms, an inflatable tube around her
middle, and jelly shoes. (*Okay,* Hannah thought. *You can't
fault her parents for protecting their baby.*) Dad was hooked
in to his iPhone. Mom's nose (covered in zinc oxide) was in
a book. Beside Dad sat an enormous cooler, the biggest
cooler on wheels Hannah had ever seen.

Hannah turned to Susan. "Remember when you were a
kid and all you brought to the beach was a pail and shovel?
Maybe swim fins or a play scuba mask. What's with all the
stuff people lug to the beach these days? Aren't the sand
and sun and water enough?"

"You sound like an old curmudgeon."

"I am an old curmudgeon."

"They seem like a nice enough family."

Hannah frowned. "How can you tell?"

"I don't know," Susan said. "I just can."

"What about the bikini on the girl? That's uncalled for. It's unseemly."

"Unseemly?" Susan looked at Hannah with puzzlement. "What's with you today? Anyway, all adolescent girls dress more provocatively than they used to. I'm not saying it's right or wrong. I'm just saying it needs to be recognized and managed. By the parents, not by you."

Hannah shrugged. She could have her opinion. When—if—she ever had a daughter there was no way in hell she would be wearing a bikini before the age of . . . well, eighteen might be pushing things a bit, but her point would be made.

"I would love to have a boy and a girl," Susan said then. "One of each. That would be perfect."

"You are so traditional!"

Susan shrugged. "So? And I'd like them to be pretty close in age. I think there's a better chance of their growing up to be good friends that way. Look at my family. We're all eighteen months to two years or so apart. And we're all friends."

"Yeah, but look," Hannah said, nodding toward the family to their right. "That mother has a babysitter right in her own family." Not that the eleven-year-old looked like the most responsible kid around. Or the smartest. Now she was trying to jump rope on the shifting sand. "The older sister or brother can help out with the younger kids. That seems like a pretty good deal."

"Oh, I'm sure it can be, if that's what you want. But not for me." Susan turned to face Hannah. "I'm already thirty-four, Hannah. I don't want to be giving birth into my forties. Not if I can help it."

Hannah felt the guilt again. She knew she was putting a

strain on the relationship by prevaricating. She had been up front about her love of children. She had said she was open to the possibility of a family. She did not want to be judged as a liar. And she did not want to lose her marriage.

"I'm sorry," she said. "I'm sorry I'm still hesitating about this. About starting a family."

Susan turned to her but Hannah couldn't see her eyes behind her dark glasses. "I know it's a tough decision. I just wish you'd talk to me about what exactly is holding you back."

"I know," Hannah said. "I'm trying."

Susan turned back to face the water. "John. Or James. Maybe Stephen."

"What?"

"The names I'd consider for a boy. Nothing oddball. For a girl, maybe Elizabeth. Or Margaret, after my aunt. Something classic. Catherine is nice."

"I wonder what Kat's real name is."

"Kat. I asked her."

"Oh." Hannah shifted, trying to get comfortable on the blanket. "I've got to remember to bring a beach chair next time. My back is killing me. I'm too old to be sitting crossed-legged on the sand."

"You're not too old for anything. Except maybe miniskirts. Really, Hannah, why do you talk as if you're about to toddle off to the nursing home?"

"Sorry. I don't know." She didn't know, not really. She did know that old people shouldn't be talking about starting a family. *Oh, crap,* Hannah thought. *Am I trying to sabotage this whole family thing? Am I trying to convince myself that I'm too old to take on that sort of responsibility?* No. That wasn't it at all. Her hesitation was not about being too old. It was about being too Charlotte.

"Race you to the water?" Hannah said suddenly.

Susan grinned. "Loser buys winner a present?"

Hannah leapt to her feet. "You're on!"

It was late that afternoon. Hannah (who had won the race and chosen a bag of nonpareilles from Harbor Candy as her treat) had come out to the front garden to clip flowers for the house. The hydrangeas were fat and vividly purple and would look wonderful in the squat blue glass vase Susan had given Ruth last Christmas. Hollyhocks—magenta, orange, pink—were stunning but too tall for an inside display. At least, Hannah couldn't see what to do with them, but she wasn't the most creative person. A handful of black-eyed Susans would look fun in the kitchen (anyone could see that!), and maybe a white rose in a slim vase for the sunroom.

Before she began to clip the flowers she spotted her younger brother sitting cross-legged on the lawn, staring out over the ocean. She immediately assumed he wanted to be alone, but she found herself approaching him anyway.

"Wouldn't a chair be more comfortable?"

Craig looked over his shoulder, then back out to sea. "I'm fine."

Hannah dropped down next to him. "What are you doing?"

"Thinking."

"About what?"

"The meaning of my life. And no, I'm not joking."

"Since when are you so ruminative?"

"I've always been ruminative. Though I'm not sure I've ever used that particular word—ruminative—to describe myself. I've always been thoughtful. Full of thought if not always attentive to the needs of others."

"Is that why you haven't gotten married, because you can't be properly attentive to someone else's needs?"

Craig was visibly taken aback.

"I didn't mean that as an insult," Hannah said quickly. "I think it's smart to know your limitations. It's smart to admit to your own flaws and faults."

"And strengths," Craig said. "Let's not forget my strengths, vague as they may be. But that's not why I haven't gotten married." He hesitated to go on. He really didn't want to have this conversation, not now, maybe not ever.

Hannah knew when she wasn't wanted. "Well, I'd better go," she said, standing. "Ow. I still think a chair would be more comfortable. What is it with people like you and Susan and your flexibility?"

Craig smiled a bit. "We're younger than you."

"Don't rub it in." Hannah walked back up the lawn to the front garden to gather her flowers.

Craig continued to stare out over the ocean. It looked intensely blue that afternoon. He didn't blame his sister for conjecturing the reason for his single status. He was pretty sure most of his family wondered about his choice to live on his own, to roam, to take each day as it came. For that matter, he wondered, too, sometimes, more now than ever before, why he lived the way he lived. He wondered why he didn't—why he couldn't—make a commitment to a woman, to a job, to a place with four walls, a floor, and a roof.

Craig got up abruptly. He wanted to go swimming. He hoped the water was very cold.

17

Tilda was in Perkins Cove. It was crowded, of course, and Tilda felt torn between annoyance and tolerance for the tourists and day-trippers. She wanted the Cove to herself all year round. She knew she was being selfish but it was hard not to feel possessive of beauty and of a place that held so many good memories.

And Perkins Cove was chock-full of good memories for Tilda. She smiled to herself as she remembered the time she and Frank and the kids had been having lunch on the deck at Jackie's, Too and a gigantic seagull had swooped down and grabbed her paper basket of fries in its beak. Tilda had screamed and Frank had roared with laughter and the kids had ducked under the table. A few minutes later another basket of fries had appeared, on the house.

There was the time, years after that, when she and Frank had come to Larchmere for a weekend in early November, just the two of them. The town was virtually abandoned and the roads were virtually empty. They had walked along Shore Road to the Cove, which was eerily, but not unpleasantly, quiet. The air was cold and damp, the sea was flat and silvery, the rocks a mottled gray. They had brought with them thermoses of hot chocolate and drank them while sitting huddled together on one of the wooden benches facing the water. It had been a perfect afternoon.

And then there was the time, one spring, just after an icy rain, when Frank had scrambled down onto the rocks to retrieve what he thought was a perfect snail shell, only to badly twist his ankle (that icy rain!) and discover that the snail shell was really only a battered old golf ball. He had had a good laugh at himself, in spite of having to hobble around for the rest of the weekend. That was typical of Frank. He was always ready to find the good in the bad, the humor in the adversity.

Yes, there were so, so many memories. And there were all the conversations and events she had forgotten, moments Frank might have remembered for her. His memory had always been better than hers. Why couldn't a person retain every little detail of a life! But maybe that would drive a person mad. Maybe some degree of forgetting was necessary for living in the present and planning for the future. Maybe. But the fact remained that with Frank gone, gone too was a big part of Tilda's past.

Tilda walked along, stepping aside for a double-wide stroller and then for three elderly ladies, walking arm in arm and wearing matching T-shirts (the shirts declared them to be members of the First Church of the Righteous in Villa, Maine; Tilda had no idea where that was and wondered if "righteous" people should be advertising their righteousness). She stopped outside a small, new shop and looked distractedly at the window display.

About a month before he died Frank had made her promise that she would find a good man after his death. He wanted her to be happy. He wanted her to get married again. So, after some protest, she had promised, just to make him happy. And now, the last thing she wanted was to keep the promise she had made to her dying husband. What kind of a person did that make her? She had lied for the sake of her own convenience.

Tilda turned from the store window she had been staring at, without having noticed much of anything inside besides a toy puffin and a rubber lobster, to see two young men, probably in their twenties, ambling along. The one on the right was in great shape and cocky about it, wearing a tight T-shirt and slouchy jeans, his hair cut close to his head and fixed there with product. His sunglasses looked expensive. Maybe they were knockoffs. Maybe they were the real thing. A lot of young people had a lot of money these days. His buddy, the guy on the left, was not quite as pumped or as pampered. He was a guy, Tilda thought, who was probably hoping for his friend's castoffs. He had that manner of a sycophant.

How judgmental I've become! Tilda thought as the two came toward her. Suddenly, inexplicably shy, she turned to look back at the window display. As the two young men passed behind her, one of them laughed. It wasn't a nice laugh. It was derisive. She knew it was the cockier of the two. She knew he had laughed at her, in her loose linen blouse and shorts down to her knees. Maybe she was being paranoid or overly sensitive. Maybe she wasn't.

Tilda walked on. Outside the next T-shirt and souvenir shop stood a handsome, nicely dressed, middle-aged man. *He's waiting for his wife, no doubt,* Tilda thought. He was just another bored husband on vacation, wondering when he could next catch a ball game on television. She began to smile to herself when she saw this man openly, overtly ogle a teenaged girl coming out of the shop. True, she was ogle-worthy, with her short shorts, long tanned legs, tight little T-shirt showing off a taught, tanned stomach, and long, shiny blond hair. But still! Did he have to be so blatant? He was old enough to be her father! Her older father!

Tilda watched as the girl wiggled off to join her friends, who were gathered around the Cove's little monument. The man followed her with his eyes. Tilda wondered if the girl was aware of the effect she was having on this man. She decided that she was, indeed, aware. A moment later a middle-aged, very attractive woman came from the shop. She was wearing an outfit similar to that of the teenager. An enormous diamond glittered against her tanned chest. Another one glittered from her left hand. Her hair was expertly platinum. Her breasts looked store bought.

The woman slipped her arm through the man's and together, they walked off toward MC Perkins Cove. Tilda stared after them in fascination. Did the woman know that her husband blatantly ogled younger women? Did she care? Had she given up caring? And why was the husband even bothering to ogle other women when his own wife was such a knockout, albeit a knockout off an assembly line?

Because the wife was not a teenager, that's why! Tilda felt furious on behalf of the wife, unsuspecting or not, and on behalf of all middle-aged women, herself foremost, who were mocked by young men and betrayed by men their own age. She felt her whole body tingle with rage.

Why was it that the physical signs of aging on a man were so often seen as a positive, as indications of experience and wisdom, of acquired gentleness and kindness, while the physical signs of aging on a woman were so often seen as—as a failure somehow, as something grotesque? "What's wrong with that woman?" Tilda imagined young people saying about her, that she could not—or would not—retain her firm chin and her smooth skin? Doesn't she know that a woman is supposed to be young and beautiful and of some pleasure to us, the observers observing an ob-

ject? Of what use is a woman past her physical prime? Oh,
sure, she might still be good for maintaining a household
or going to the office and earning a living. But could she
please do all that while wearing a mask to hide her saggy
jowls and a caftan to cover her bulging middle?

Calm down, Tilda told herself. *You're getting way too
angry. Anger isn't pretty. Frowning causes more wrinkles
than smiling.* Hadn't her mother told her that? And God
knows, Charlotte McQueen had known what she was talking about. She had fought the approach of aging like a sol-
dier in combat fights off the armed enemy. And to a great
extent, she had won. That is, until she had died.

And if only Frank hadn't died, Tilda wouldn't be single
again at forty-seven! Almost fifty. It was easy, and unfair,
to blame Frank. But it wasn't entirely true that if Frank
were still alive she would be feeling sexually attractive in
the eyes of the world. She imagined that every woman—or
almost every woman—over the age of forty felt keenly the
loss of her younger physical self, even if she was in a good
and loving relationship. Because the bottom line was that
love had little if anything to do with one's self-image. It
was strange but true. Frank had always heaped compli-
ments on her; what's more, he had meant them. But her
husband's love and sincerity had not been enough to prevent Tilda from looking in the mirror and criticizing the
ruin she found there.

She tried to remember what, exactly, the British author
Graham Swift had said in his wonderful novel called *Last
Orders.* Something about "fading beauty" and how, depending on the viewer, it could be seen as a source of further affection. Tilda didn't know about that. Love among
the ruins indeed! Even Chaucer's oft-married Widow of
Bath bemoaned the loss of her youth and beauty, albeit
without a trace of self-pity. With a few words she dis-

missed her former companions—"the devil go therwith"—
and resumed the business of living. *If only,* Tilda thought, *I
could be more like the Widow of Bath, just without the
gapped teeth!*

She went into Swamp John's, hoping to find distraction
in expensive jewelry and crafts and immediately caught a
glimpse of herself in a seashell-rimmed mirror. She was
startled. *I'm too thin,* she thought. *I'm starting to look
scraggly and scrawny. And old. I'm starting to look old. I
need a better face cream. I need some plumping. I need
some ice cream.* Tilda felt a rising panic and dashed back
outside.

Ice cream. Yes. That was a good idea. Comfort food was
a middle-aged woman's best friend, or so it often seemed.

The little ice cream shop was crowded with customers,
parents and children and grandparents, teenaged girls and
boys. She got on line and was jostled by a woman to her
left, laden with shopping bags, trying to leave the shop.
Tilda tried to step out of her way and felt herself bump into
someone. She turned. It was a man, holding a cup of ice
cream in one hand. In the other he held a paper napkin.

"Oh! I'm so sorry!" she exclaimed.

The man smiled. "That's quite all right. No harm done.
That's why I get my ice cream in a cup. No chance of losing it."

He was taller than Tilda, maybe a bit over six feet, and
slim. His hair was entirely gray and stylishly cut, close to
his head. He wore nondescript summer slacks and a short-
sleeved, crisply ironed shirt, tucked in. A pair of sunglasses, aviator frames, peeked out from his shirt pocket.

"I'm sorry," Tilda said again. She felt more embarrassed
than the encounter warranted. She didn't know why.

The man smiled again, said, "Enjoy your afternoon,"
and left the shop.

Tilda got her ice cream (she dared to get a cone) and carefully picked her way down onto a relatively smooth rock overlooking the water. The water was very still at that moment, and very blue. Slowly, her nerves began to calm. Before long she was no longer interested in criticizing every member of the male sex and no longer—for the moment, at least—inclined to rant and rave. An expanse of blue water could soothe just about any bad mood. Tilda felt the warmth of the rock beneath her and she felt almost at peace.

Finally, cone finished and her butt sore from sitting (the view was spectacular but the seat was hard), Tilda got up and carefully made her way back up to the parking lot. She tossed the crumpled napkin in a trash bin. She thought she heard her cell phone ringing and, head bowed over her bag, began to rummage. And she walked right into the back of a tall, slim man.

The man turned around.

"I'm so sorry!" Tilda cried. And when she recognized him, she said, "Again. I guess I've been a bit distracted all day. . . ."

"We've got to stop meeting like this," the man from the ice cream shop said. Tilda liked his smile. And his eyes were nice, very brown, with very long lashes for an adult male.

"How was your ice cream?" she asked.

"Butter pecan is always perfect," he replied. "Yours?"

"Double fudge brownie. I'm a chocoholic. If you like interesting flavors you should try Goldenrod Kisses in York Beach."

"Thanks. I'll keep that in mind. My name is Dennis, by the way. Dennis Haass."

"I'm Tilda McQueen O'Connell. I'm visiting my family. We have a house here. It's my father's house, officially."

"Nice," he said. "I've rented a small house for a month. It's off Grey Road. I've already been here for a little over two weeks."

"Oh. Where do you live? I mean, where's home?"

"Mostly I live in Florida but I have a condo in Phoenix," he said. "My son and his wife and kids live out there. I like to spend time with my grandchildren whenever I can."

There was no mention of a wife. Nor was there mention of a girlfriend or fiancée, but why would there be? *Besides,* Tilda told herself, *I don't care about his romantic situation.*

"I've been to Ogunquit before," he said now, "but it was years ago. If you have a moment I'd appreciate a recommendation on some good restaurants."

Tilda did have a moment. She named a few places, steering him away from the more touristy joints, which, she suspected, he wouldn't care for, and the places that catered to the wild and crazy twenty-something crowd.

He thanked her and then cleared his throat. "So, you're visiting with your husband?"

Tilda automatically began to twirl her wedding ring with her thumb. Of course he would think she was in Ogunquit with her husband. She could be accused of false advertising, couldn't she? "No," she said. "I'm a widow, actually."

"I'm sorry."

Tilda smiled vaguely. "Thank you. It's been a little over two years now."

"I'm sure it's still difficult."

"Yes," she said.

There was a bit of an awkward pause. Tilda realized she had no idea of what to say next. She realized she had no idea of how to graciously take her leave.

And then Dennis said: "Forgive me if I'm out of line, but I wonder if you would like to meet me for dinner this evening."

She was stunned. Had she just been asked out on a date? So, there was no girlfriend or fiancée? What the heck was she supposed to do now? She felt sweat gathering under her arms. "Um," she said. "Um, no. I'm sorry, I have plans."

Dennis smiled and shrugged. "Okay, that's fine. Enjoy the rest of the day. And thanks for the recommendations."

He turned and had walked a few yards before some odd impulse made Tilda call out. "Wait! Mr. Haass! Dennis!"

He stopped and turned. Tilda hurried forward to him.

"I'm sorry," she said. "I'm a little out of practice. Socially speaking, I mean. I am available for dinner this evening. If the offer is still open. Thanks."

Dennis smiled. It was another genuine, nice smile and they made plans to meet at the Old Village Inn on Maine Street at seven o'clock. When he had walked off again, Tilda suddenly remembered the conversation she had had with Hannah on the beach, the conversation in which she had mentioned the phrase "conditions of affection." She had told her sister she didn't know how to create "conditions of affection." But maybe, after all, she did know. She felt both immensely proud and terribly scared of what she had just done. She had just accepted a man's—a stranger's!—invitation to dinner.

What would everyone say? Was it possible to keep the date a secret? Suddenly, Tilda was in a paroxysm of confusion and embarrassment and fear and excitement. The ice cream in her stomach did a slow and not entirely pleasant dance and Tilda hurried to her car.

The Cape Neddick Lobster Pound, which was immediately across the road from the Cape Neddick Campground, was open for lunch. At the Pound, Craig's old friend Chip Morrow was tending bar.

Back when they were teens, Craig and Chip had waited tables together at Mike's Clam Shack, on Route 1 in Wells. Chip had never moved away. He was married to his high school sweetheart and had three kids. The oldest was already almost twenty. Chip had not changed much in the years since he and Craig had first met. He was a little balder and a little heavier, but otherwise, he was still the same slightly wild, slightly lazy, entirely good-hearted guy he had always been. Chip was reliable in that way.

Craig shook hands with his old friend and ordered a beer and a turkey club. It was just noon. He was the only person at the bar; the tables in the big room behind him were only just beginning to fill. In the evening every table would be occupied, mostly by families from the campground.

"Word has it your father's pretty serious about this woman Jennifer," Chip said when Craig's sandwich arrived.

"He might be," Craig said. "I don't really know."

"Well, your brother's been talking. Not that that's much of a surprise. He's always liked to hear himself talk."

Craig smiled. "So, what's he been saying?"

"That no one not a born McQueen is getting Larchmere. Making threats, nothing too specific. Being a blowhard."

"That sounds like Adam."

"What do you think about the house?" Chip asked.

Craig put down the sandwich he was about to bite. "What do you mean?"

"I mean, you ever think about inheriting that big old place?"

"Me!" Craig laughed, a bit too loudly. "No way. Who wants that sort of responsibility? I'd probably only sell it, get it off my hands as quickly as I could. The upkeep alone could bankrupt a person. And the taxes? No, Larchmere isn't for me."

Besides, he thought, *I don't deserve it. Someone like me doesn't deserve that sort of privilege.*

Chip sighed. "It is a beautiful place, though. Wouldn't mind that sort of house being in my family. Can see the ocean from your own front porch!"

"You can see the ocean from a fishing shack. The ocean is everywhere, Chip."

"Maybe so. But a big house like that . . ."

"Sometimes," Craig said, wondering who he was really trying to convince, "big, spectacular-looking things are more trouble than they're worth."

"Maybe. No point in thinking about it anyway. My father's got nothing more than a rusted old plow to leave me!" Chip laughed, obviously not in the least bothered by the fact of his meager inheritance.

Other customers came in then, a vacationing couple in matching polo shirts (why did some couples do that, dress alike?), and Chip moved off down the bar to serve them. Craig quickly ate the rest of his lunch, left the best tip he could afford, and went home.

While her brother was having lunch at the Cape Neddick Lobster Pound, Hannah was driving down to see her father's car mechanic in York Beach. Her car had been making an odd sound and she was eager to get it looked at. Herbie did just that, adjusted something or other, and the odd sound was gone.

On the way back to Larchmere she had decided to stop at Billy's Chowder House, less for something to eat, though she was hungry, than to visit the marsh that spread behind the building. She loved marshes, in all weather and at all levels of tide. There was something compelling about a marsh, something mysterious. Marshes made her think of ancient times and bogs and ritual burials in the mud under the green and yellow and brownish grasses and tall, sturdy cattails. Besides, at high tide you could paddle a canoe through a marsh and that was a totally enjoyable, almost spiritual experience.

Hannah took a seat in the bar area where she had a full and unobstructed view through the large wall-to-wall windows. She ordered a bowl of haddock chowder and a beer. While she waited for her lunch, she gazed out at the marsh spreading behind the restaurant. The tide was low. It would begin to come in soon. She noted the striations of earth below the grasses and above the muddy ground. To herself, she recited these lines:

> "You sit and wait for another tide.
> And then, another.
> You are dead, alternately,
> asleep.
> You have no wings."

She rarely remembered poetry—back in grammar school it had been hell to memorize even short poems, except the famous one about the purple cow—but those particular lines had stayed with her. They were from a poem by a Maine writer. The title was "Marsh at Mid-Life." She had read the poem in one of the small, local papers back in Portland.

At first Hannah couldn't figure out why the lines—pretty depressing, she thought—had stuck with her, especially since she had made no effort to learn them by heart. And then she had got to thinking. Those lines kind of described her own life at that moment in time. She was waiting, but for what, exactly, she didn't know. Answers? She was stagnant, like the marsh at low tide. She was stuck, mired in indecision and fear. She was in the middle of her life. There was no going back but the idea of moving forward just inspired confusion.

Her lunch came and Hannah ate it but without enthusiasm. As soon as she was finished she paid the check and left. She did not look back at the marsh, now slowly filling with the incoming tide.

18

The moment Tilda had gotten back to the house from the Cove she sought out Hannah, who had just returned from the mechanic's and her solitary expedition to the marshes in Wells. Tilda told her about the date she had made with Dennis Haass, if only so that someone knew where she was going and with whom. She had read enough mystery fiction not to meet with a stranger without some sort of witness—even though she and Dennis were meeting at the Old Village Inn where almost every staff member knew her and her family by name. And that fact, too, had given her pause. What might the local gossips make of her having dinner with a man other than Frank, other than her father or brothers?

She had come very, very close to canceling. Dennis had given her his cell phone number. She could simply call and say that "something had come up" or that she had forgotten a prior family obligation. She sensed that Dennis would be a gentleman about her cancellation and not press her for details or make her feel badly. But she had not cancelled, partly because Hannah threatened to drag her to the restaurant by force if she tried to back out and partly because—

and this surprised her—she actually wanted to play the evening through.

Tilda went up to her room and opened her closet. Deciding what to wear took an agonizing hour. She tried to remember the last time she had struggled to choose her clothes. She couldn't. She had not dressed for someone in years and years. Maybe she never had. She had always been so entirely comfortable with Frank. She couldn't now recall if in the very beginning she had dressed to impress or to attract him. She doubted that she had. But maybe Frank would remember differently. If he were alive. God, she wished she could ask him to clarify her own life for her, to help her to remember! With Frank gone, so much of herself was gone.

Tilda surveyed the limited selections in her closet. All she had to choose from was what she had brought for the two weeks at Larchmere and a few other staples she kept at the house. Not that her entire wardrobe, if it could even be called that, contained anything appropriate for a first date. But was this a "first" anything? Was it even a date? And what did forty-seven-year-old women wear on dates these days, anyway? If it involved anything cleavage baring, she was out of luck. She had very little cleavage to begin with and certainly nothing designed to show it off.

Finally, finally she chose a pair of wide-legged, cuffed, chino trousers—they required that she wear her one pair of sandals with heels—a white blouse, and a navy cardigan with gold tone buttons. It wasn't a sexy outfit but none of Tilda's clothes were sexy. She had brought only one bag with her, an oversight, and it certainly was too bulky for a dinner date. Then she remembered something. She dug in the back of the closet for the cardboard box that contained an assortment of accessories that had belonged to her mother. She found what she was looking for—a simple, woven clutch with brown leather trim. She had never before used it. Maybe, she thought, it would bring her luck, or ensure a nice evening.

She had about an hour to kill before it was time to leave for the restaurant. She was loath to encounter any of her family (other than Hannah) because then she would be compelled to explain why she was wearing heels and makeup, so she stayed in her room. She sat in the seat by the window and looked out but didn't see much. Her thoughts, as they were almost always wont to do, circled around the two most significant events of her adult life—the death of her mother and the death of her husband. Even the birth of her children, whom she dearly loved, could not touch these other two moments in significance.

In a matter of eight years she had lost the two most solid anchors in her life. It was strange and awful to feel so unmoored, even at the age of forty-seven. Age and maturity didn't entirely erase the need for the comfort, the surety of maternal love, and it didn't necessarily strengthen you against the brutal fact of being widowed.

She thought about how after both losses it had been hard to take interest in the things she had once enjoyed. That was normal, she was told. She was told to be patient. But the experiences had been hard to bear. For example, after Charlotte's accidental death, Tilda found that she no longer cared about knitting. She had loved to knit since she had learned, on her own, when she was ten years old. Over the years she had made lots and lots of scarves and mittens and sweaters for her family but mostly for her mother. Some of the sweaters she had made Charlotte were, Tilda thought, really beautiful. (Where had all those things gone? Funny. Tilda hadn't seen any of those sweaters or scarves or mittens in her mother's closets when she and Hannah had cleaned them out after Charlotte's death.)

Ten years later, and she still had no interest in knitting. Recently, she had asked Jane if she wanted her collection of needles and yarn (mostly scraps), had even offered to teach her or pay for a few lessons. Jane had nicely but firmly rejected the offer. Knitting wasn't her thing. The needles and bits of yarn had gone to a local thrift shop.

And then, when Frank died . . . Well, things had been much worse. Tilda found that she could no longer read. Knitting had been an enjoyable hobby. Reading was a necessity of spirit. Reading was to Tilda akin to breathing, something natural and necessary. It was unthinkable, not to be reading several books at a time, not to be going to the bookstore and the library every week to restock her personal shelves. The problem wasn't a lack of focus. She could concentrate on her lesson plans and she could reread familiar material for her classes. She could read the local paper and the national and international news online. But books, ones she had not yet read, proved impossible. She felt a frightening sense of disability, as if she simply was not capable of taking in or comprehending anything new. After six months she forced herself to go back to her book group. The experiment failed. She found the reading choices of the other members unsatisfactory but she couldn't say why. She tried to read new gothic novels, new mysteries, and found them all insipid. She was getting desperate. It was torture.

Finally, finally, after almost a year, her ability to read came back, slowly at first, then rapidly and completely. How and why this had happened Tilda didn't need to discover. It was enough that her greatest passion—aside from her love for her family—had returned.

But some things still hadn't settled or resolved. There were still things—seemingly small things—that appeared insurmountable, incomprehensible to her. Like going to the movies by herself. In college she had loved to go to the movies on her own, and for a few years after that, too. But once married to Frank, she had gotten into the habit of renting the movies she wanted to see and Frank didn't. That way, they could at least be in the house together, though in separate rooms. That had seemed important. Now, the idea of going out to a movie—or, for that matter, to a restaurant other than Breaking New Grounds for a cup of coffee!— seemed monumental, virtually impossible. What had happened to her independence? What had she allowed to have happen to it?

The therapist she had seen for a while had encouraged Tilda to take a trip on her own, nothing major, maybe just a weekend away. "A change of scene would do you good," the therapist had said. A change of perspective might ensue. But Tilda had stayed home, paralyzed. It wasn't fear, exactly, that held her back. It was more a failure of imagination. She simply could not imagine traveling without Frank.

The last big trip they had taken was to Montreal for their tenth anniversary. Because it was October and the kids were in school and too young to stay by themselves, Hannah had stayed with them. Charlotte was supposed to have come down for a day to relieve Hannah but for some reason that Tilda now could not remember, she had cancelled her visit.

Tilda and Frank had splurged and stayed in a fancy hotel, one ordinarily beyond their means, and eaten at five-star restaurants two of the five nights, though Frank, a basic sort of guy who preferred his food basic, too, wasn't as impressed by the cuisine as was Tilda. But they had loved the city and often talked about going back someday. They never did make it.

Nor had they made it to Paris. They had been planning the trip, a delayed celebration of their twentieth wedding anniversary. But plans had come to an abrupt halt when Frank got sick. There simply was no money to spend on travel or other things not strictly necessary. Anyway, before too long Frank had been too weak to travel farther than Maine Medical, a fifteen-minute drive from their home.

Tilda sighed, got up from the chair, and stretched. She wondered if she would ever be able to break out of the uncomfortable comfort zone she had somehow fallen into.

She looked at her watch. It was time to leave for the Old Village Inn. It was time to start regaining some of her old independence and sense of adventure. Yeah, right! Her stomach was jumpy. She felt a bit sweaty, in spite of the deodorant and powder she had liberally put on. She felt more like she was going to an execution than on a date. An execution! Really, how melodramatic could she be? She would drive into town, have dinner, and drive home. That was all there was to it, she told herself. That was all there was to it. Step one, step two, step three.

No one was around when she got downstairs. She could leave the house unnoticed. She checked her image in the hall mirror for one last time before leaving the shelter of Larchmere and closing the door behind her.

The Old Village Inn was crowded, no surprise there. Built in the nineteenth century, it was a warren of dark, cozy rooms decorated with quality antiques and Americana. Tilda passed through the front hall and peered into the bar. The bartender waved to Tilda. One of the waitresses, a veteran of crazy Ogunquit summers, nodded to her as she wove her way around the small and charming dining room off the bar, dish-laden tray on her shoulder. One of the OVI regulars, in his corner stool, shot glass in front of him, smiled in her direction. Tilda had never seen him anywhere else but on that bar stool in the corner. Not on the street or on the beach or in the corner market. She wondered where he lived. She wondered if he had any family or friends. She realized she didn't know his name. She smiled back.

"Tilda."

She turned to find Dennis a few feet behind her. He was wearing a navy blazer, pressed chinos, and a white dress shirt open at the neck. He looked trim and sporty and handsome.

"Hello," she said, with a smile. She felt surprisingly calm, now that the big night had officially begun. She did not feel sick to her stomach, not like she had when she had first glimpsed Frank.

"I made a reservation this afternoon," Dennis said. "I wasn't sure what luck we'd have getting a table without one."

"Good idea. I should have thought of it." *But,* she added silently, *I was too busy having an emotional crisis and wallowing in my misery.*

They were given a table for two in a corner of the smallest dining room. A quick glance around told Tilda that the other diners were strangers. Good.

They discussed the menu, selected wines, and ordered. Dennis told her that he was sixty-two. He had been divorced for about six years. His wife had left him for another man.

"That's so sad," Tilda said. "Actually, it's more than sad. I think it's horrible."

Dennis smiled. "It wasn't fun, I'll say that much. I'd be lying if I said that my ego didn't take a bruising. But you work things through. You get past the negative feelings. You have to."

"Yes. But I'm sure that some people just can't let go of those negative feelings. Don't you think?"

"I suppose. But those people aren't my concern. I don't mean to sound cold. It's just that going through the divorce taught me that I needed to focus on me before anyone else. Again, I really don't mean that to sound off-putting. But I do think that everyone should cultivate a healthy level of selfishness, or self-centeredness. If you don't live your own life, who else will do it for you?"

The words hit home with Tilda. "Well," she said vaguely, "I suppose that's true." You just have to be ready and willing and yes, capable, of living your own life, and that was a tall order, especially for emotional cowards!

They talked about their children. Dennis had the son, Dan, in Arizona and a daughter in Florida. "I get to see her pretty often," he said. "I like to cook and Marie can't boil water. She's getting a doctorate in marine science. Don't ask me to explain anything about her particular specialty because I can't. I do worry, though, that she won't find a job in her field. With the economy the way it is, I think she's going to have a hard time."

"Do you think we'll ever stop worrying about our children?" Tilda asked then.

"Never!" Dennis laughed. "It's a life sentence, this thing called being a parent. It's not for the faint of heart."

Tilda thought of Hannah and her hesitation to start a family. She had always thought of her sister as brave. But did Hannah feel otherwise about herself? Did she doubt her ability to be a good parent?

They talked about what sort of books they liked to read (Dennis was into nonfiction and spy stories) and what sort of movies they liked to watch (Dennis, unlike Frank, did not care for Will Ferrell). They talked about their careers. Dennis had retired early. He had made a good deal of money in systems management, whatever that was. They talked about Ogunquit. Dennis's wife had preferred spending summer vacations at the family's house on the Jersey shore and it was only after his divorce, when he was no longer welcome at his in-laws' home, that he'd first come to Ogunquit. They talked about its charms and Tilda told him, from an insider's point of view, about its more difficult aspects, like summer traffic jams and bleak Februaries.

Finally, a check was brought to the table. Dennis reached for it immediately, as if there was never any question of who would be paying. Tilda opened her mouth to protest or to offer to pay half, she wasn't sure which, and then closed it. She had not been out with a man other than Frank in over twenty years. What were the rules? What was the etiquette? Should she offer to pay next time? But that would be presuming a next time!

"Thank you very much," she said when the waiter had taken Dennis's credit card. It would have to suffice.

"You're welcome," he replied.

They both had parked in the small lot around the corner from the restaurant, and now walked there side by side. Their arms did not touch. Tilda wondered what would happen if they did touch, accidentally. Would she flinch?

They stopped next to Tilda's car. "Thank you," Dennis said. "I had a lovely evening."

He put out his hand. Tilda put out hers and they shook. "I did, too," she said. Their hands released.

"Be careful getting home. Do you want me to follow you?" he asked.

Tilda shook her head. "Oh, no, thank you. I'll be fine. I know the roads by heart."

He asked if he could call her. Perhaps, he said, they could get together again? Tilda said yes, she would like that, and gave him the house telephone number.

"Well, good night then," he said, and went off to his car at the end of the lot.

Tilda got in her car. She felt strangely let down. She was vaguely disappointed that he had not kissed her. Even a kiss on the cheek would have been nice. And then she was surprised by her disappointment. Only a day ago she had entirely rejected the idea of being with another man ever again. Did things really change that crazily, that quickly? And she wasn't even in lust with Dennis! But a woman wanted to be wanted. She wanted the right to reject a suitor. This train of thought surprised her, too. The right to reject a suitor? She had not thought in those terms since before Frank had come into her life. Maybe she had never thought in those terms. So, why now? Wasn't she too old to be wanted, too old to have a suitor, too old to be sought after? *Apparently,* she thought, *I'm not too old for any of those things!*

She started the engine, pulled out of the lot, and made her way back to Larchmere, watchful, as always, of frightened deer, wandering cats, and drunken drivers.

19

It was morning, the horizon was dimmed with haze, and Tilda was walking the beach. She was hardly aware of her surroundings, though. She was thinking about the previous night.

Hannah had been waiting for her when she got home and had grilled her for detailed information. What had they talked about? Had Dennis paid for the meal? Had he been presumptuous or rude in any way? Had he asked her questions and listened to her answers? What had he worn? Was he divorced, widowed, had he never been married? Did he have children, grandchildren?

"What did he order for dinner?" Hannah had asked then.

"Why does that matter?"

"I'm just curious."

"He had the halibut special. So did I."

Hannah had nodded. "Huh. I see. Did he order coffee after dinner?"

"He doesn't drink coffee."

"Interesting."

Tilda had not bothered to pursue the topic of food and its special indication of character. But she had talked about how nervous she had been at first, and how gradually, over the meal, words had flowed and they both had laughed and how, by the end of the evening, she was sorry it was all over. She had even admitted that she was disappointed there had been no kiss.

What she had not told Hannah, however, what she had not really been able to put into words, was how it had felt to be perceived as a couple after two years of being on her own. She had seen the glances, meaningful ones from people she knew, and casual glances from strangers who were merely, almost unconsciously registering "couple." She was embarrassed to admit to her sister that she had felt something like elation, almost a feeling of pride. For a moment she had felt as if she were once again part of that elite club of people who came in pairs. People who came in pairs were attached. They were grounded. They were held in place by bonds of affection.

"Do you think Ruth knows where I went?" Tilda had asked Hannah, just before going up to bed.

Hannah had shrugged. "I don't know. She's been at Bobby's most of the night."

"Do you think anyone else knows?"

"Well, Susan, of course. Dad is pretty oblivious to lots of stuff. Adam doesn't care about anyone but himself. If Craig knows, or suspects, he won't make a big deal of it." Hannah had grinned. "Besides, with the gossips in this town, by morning everyone in a twenty-mile radius will know you were on a date. You'll just have to deal with it."

Now, on the beach the morning after the momentous event that was her first date post-Frank, she thought again about the notion of being "attached." There were many fine organizations that fought for equal rights for "the unat-

tached." And while she admired and supported their efforts, she didn't at all like the term "unattached." She was
without a romantic partner but she was certainly attached.
She had children and a father, and an aunt and siblings. She
had colleagues and friends. She had her students. She had a
neighbor whose garden she watered when the neighbor
traveled out of town on business. She even had the memory—the fact—of a husband.

No person was an island. Poets and preachers had established that long ago. At least, she, Tilda McQueen O'Connell, was not an island in the sea of life and it was unfair that
she was considered by some people to be "unattached," as if
she were incapable of normal human intercourse and com-
munion. She was more than capable!

Though Tilda wasn't a big fan of the Internet, she had
spent a good deal of time online after Frank's passing. Her
therapist had urged her to do so, in the hope that she might
find contact with a community of grievers helpful to her recovery. And Tilda had found all sorts of sites on the Web on
which or through which widows and widowers could talk
and share advice and sympathy and even meet for friendship or romance. There were sites for widowed pagans,
witches and Wiccans, to find comfort with others in their
world. There were sites devoted to helping widows in under-
developed countries. There were sites for war widows and
young widows and widows of convicted felons. Every con-
ceivable type of person seemed to be targeted as worthy of
friendship and support. There was no excuse for isolation,
at least not online. Everyone, thanks to the Web, was in
some way "attached."

A young gay couple was walking from Wells, hand in
hand. They smiled and waved as they passed Tilda, up higher
on the beach, in the softer sand. She smiled and waved back.
Another young couple in love, death the furthest thing from
their minds.

She had read somewhere that it usually took one to two years for a person to recover from a major bereavement like the death of a spouse. Well, it had been two years since Frank's death, a little more than that. Could she consider herself "recovered"? Could you be cured of grief like you could be cured of a minor disease? Or was grief like alcoholism or any other addiction, something that afflicted you and that never really stopped afflicting you, even when all outward examples of peculiar behavior had been put away?

A father and his young son (at least, she assumed that was their relation) were tossing a plastic ball off to her left, on higher sand. The son's latest toss went wild and the ball rolled down the beach toward Tilda. She hurried forward, picked it up, and returned it to the boy. The father thanked her, they wished each other a good day, and Tilda walked on.

She knew she was one of the lucky ones, if any widow could be called lucky. She and Frank had made peace with each other and with their relationship long before his final diagnosis. She had been with him when he died. The moment of his passing had been calm.

Yes, in a way she was one of the lucky ones. She lived with no haunting, unresolved issues except, of course, for the fact of her husband's early death. It was a pretty big fact but facts didn't haunt like issues haunted. Facts hit you on the head, smacked you in the face, forced you to deal with and acknowledge them. They didn't sneak around and take you by surprise when you least expected them.

Tilda checked the sky for the eagle that was never there and decided that when Dennis called, as promised, she would suggest they take a drive to Kennebunkport. And, she thought, it might be nice to go to the party at the Ogunquit Museum with someone. Craig might come with her if she asked him but . . . No. She would ask Dennis to accompany her. She would ask him to be her date. And maybe at the end of the evening he would kiss her cheek. Maybe, she would kiss his.

"I want to talk to you."

Jennifer looked up from the interior design magazine she had been reading, slightly startled. She had not heard Adam come into the sunroom. He stood now before her, hands on his hips, legs slightly apart. It was an inappropriately combative stance.

"Yes?" she said.

"I think it would be best for you to back away from this relationship with my father."

"Excuse me?"

"You heard what I said."

She had heard. Her comment had been an attempt to buy time and process what she had heard. "For whom would it be best?" she asked.

"For everyone."

"Not for me."

"Look, let's be civilized about this. I—"

"Civilized?" Jennifer stood and tossed the magazine on the chair behind her. She was only about three feet away from Adam. He had been looming over her while she sat. "You have no right to tell me what to do."

"I have a responsibility as the oldest McQueen to protect my family's interests. And those interests include Larchmere."

"Your father is the oldest McQueen," Jennifer retorted. "And how dare you assume I'm with your father for his money. That's an insult to me and to your father."

"My father is an old man. He doesn't know what he's doing. And he's always been a sucker for a pretty face. But I'm not going to let you steal my inheritance. Understand that."

Adam turned and left the room as abruptly as he had entered. Jennifer sank back into the chair. Her hands were shaking. What the hell had just happened? It was like a scene out of a cheesy soap opera. People in real life didn't threaten each other like Adam had threatened her. He had actually threatened her, hadn't he? Yes, Jennifer decided. He had. His intent had been to frighten her, to run her off the property.

She would tell Bill. No, he would be furious. She would deal with Adam's . . . threat on her own. But how? She would tell Ruth, ask for her advice. No. She didn't want to drag any of the other McQueens into this craziness. She would ignore Adam, that's what she would do. And she would ignore the suspicious glances from Tilda and the inquiring frowns from Hannah. Thank God for Craig, though she wasn't at all sure that his kindness outweighed the antagonism of the others.

Jennifer stood again and left the sunroom, though she had no idea where she was going. And she wondered what she had gotten herself into as a result of this relationship with Bill McQueen.

20

It was mid-morning and Craig, feeling oddly restless and unfocused, was taking a solitary walk around the Larchmere grounds. He had slept badly the night before, which might have accounted for his current state of mind. He had been dreaming that he was traveling in the USSR of all places, and had been detained at the airport on his way back to the United States. The police, or state officials, or whoever they were, refused to tell him on what charge or suspicion he was being held. They tore open his bags and began to fling the contents all over the seedy little room. Craig had watched as objects from his childhood came to light—a floppy rabbit, a favorite book, a blanket, even a lamp with a pale blue shade and puppies painted around its base. He had not seen or thought of those objects in years and years. Even in the dream he was surprised to see them. He had struggled back to consciousness and sat up in bed, spooked. He had been lugging his past around with him. People had refused to let him go home. But what people?

A dragonfly, with its needlelike body and glittering wings, zoomed past Craig, inches from his face. A large blue jay chattered loudly from the rim of the stone birdbath. In the front garden, yellow and orange lilies stood tall and proudly. Looking at them now, lines popped into Craig's head, surprising him since it had been years since he had last read them in the New Testament. "And why do you worry about clothes? See how the lilies of the field grow. They do not labor or spin."

Well, Craig was not a flower, nor was he a bird. Yes, he knew what the historical Jesus—or his pitchmen—had meant by those lines; at least, he thought he knew. But lately, well, for a year or more, Craig had been worrying, and the worrying was about the "big stuff."

What did he have to show for his life? Was it necessary to have "something" to show, to display? Wasn't being a fairly decent human being, not consciously harming others, wasn't that enough? Maybe. But maybe not. Being actively good and productive might be better than being passive and inoffensive. Doctors vowed to do no harm. But they were also expected to do some good.

Craig laid his hand against one of the stones of the house. It was warm to the touch; it could be said to feel alive. He realized now, almost against his will, how much affection he felt for the house, for Larchmere, in spite of its associations with his mother—and to a lesser extent, with his father.

He walked on and noted that the rose trellis needed painting. He remembered the first night he had climbed out of his bedroom window and down the trellis to the ground. It must have been the summer he was either eight or nine. He had been scared silly to do it but the trellis was so tempting and climbing down it was the easiest way to get out of the house unseen. The trellis held and he had made it to the lawn in one piece, if a bit scratched by thorns. The second and third and twentieth times he had practically skipped down the wooden slats. He had always suspected that his aunt knew about his nocturnal rambling—she had an uncanny ability to know secret things—but if she did know, she had never told on him.

Maybe, in Ruth, he had a true friend, someone he could talk honestly to about his place in the family. Maybe. But to risk inclusion was to risk a subsequent exclusion. To risk acceptance was to risk rejection. He knew that. His attitude toward the notion of "home" had been largely distrustful for as long as he could remember. Most often it was a place to get away from, a place to leave behind, when it wasn't a place he could barely tolerate.

He remembered dreaming about, even planning for an independent, on-the-road existence since he was in fourth or fifth grade. He had run away, of course, several times. Once, when he was about eleven, he had made it as far as York Beach (on foot) before being spotted by a friend of his father's, someone Bill knew tangentially through Teddy Vickes. The guy had called the McQueens, while keeping a surreptitious eye on Craig, who was sitting on a bench reading a comic book, until Bill showed up, Bobby in tow for extra muscle if needed. (When he was a boy, until he went to college, Craig was known for an occasional but disruptive bad temper.)

And yet, for all of the running away, he always returned to Larchmere. Why was that? Why did he always, inevitably, feel the need to come home?

He often thought of Robert Frost's famous line: "Home is the place where, when you have to go there, they have to take you in." Whether or not they actually had to, they, the McQueens, always did take him in. There might be some grumbling about the welcome, but he always got a welcome. At times, he had wished his family had slammed the door in his face. At least that would have put an end to the frustrating and seemingly unproductive cycle of leaving and coming back.

The hummingbird feeder outside the sunroom needed to

be filled. Craig made a mental note to check the supply of feed and pick up more if necessary. And the wooden gate to the small herbal garden needed to be repaired, quite possibly replaced. He would pop down to the hardware store and pick up anything he couldn't find in his father's rudimentary workshop in a corner of the basement. He would make the repair or do the replacement himself, save his father a few hundred bucks, earn his keep for the two weeks at Larchmere. He knew that his father disapproved of the way in which he had lived his life so far. He also suspected that his father harbored ideas about his son's life that were patently untrue. Craig was not a criminal. He was not a drug addict. He was not dishonest. He was tired of trying to prove himself as worthy. He should just go away and stay away.

And yet, he knew that he would come back. He recalled now an article he had read somewhere online, in which the author, a psychologist maybe, had explained why people hated leave-takings. It was, she said, because no one can exist without the recognition of other people. In other words, Craig thought, you are no one if another person doesn't acknowledge that you are there, that you are present.

"And who of you by being worried can add a single hour to his life?" That was another line from that same New Testament passage. And it was very, obviously true. Worrying—thinking—could only take him so far.

Craig went inside, to the basement, to look for tools.

Ruth stood at the window of her room, watching her younger nephew wandering the perimeter of Larchmere. Percy was lumped on the windowsill, purring loudly. Every so often, Ruth gave his furry cheeks a scratch.

She saw Craig put his hand against the house and peer closely at the stone. She guessed he was checking the condition of the mortar. She knew, and always had known, that

Craig was a bit of a lost soul. But she refused to believe that he was so far gone that he couldn't allow himself to be accepted back into the family he had semi-abandoned. The family that had semi-abandoned him. Her sister-in-law, Charlotte, had virtually ignored her youngest child. But what else could have been expected, given the situation?

Ruth shook her head. She remembered, very clearly, all those years ago, when Charlotte found out she was pregnant with Craig. She had been furious with everyone—though maybe not with herself; Charlotte was not the sort to take blame for her actions. She had been hell to live with for those first weeks. One evening, while paying Larchmere a brief visit, and fed up with her sister-in-law's foul mood, Ruth had suggested that Charlotte just shut up and get an abortion. Charlotte had fixed her with a cold eye and proclaimed that while she didn't want this fourth baby, she found the idea of an abortion "distasteful." Ruth would never forget that moment. *Distasteful.* Imagine! Not repugnant, not morally wrong, just distasteful. Like bad behavior in public, like blowing your nose at the dinner table or failing to hold the door for the person behind you, nothing more. The subject of abortion had been dropped.

Two things of many about Craig's childhood came to Ruth's mind, watching her nephew from her window. The first were the flares of temper, seemingly random, though to Craig, no doubt caused by some perceived injustice or by some intense frustration. He would hit something with his fist or throw something across a room, rarely causing physical damage but upsetting whoever was witness. He never yelled or cursed. His rages were silent. Bill had wanted to take Craig to a child therapist. Charlotte had vetoed that idea as a waste of money. "He'll grow out of it," she had said. And the rages had, indeed, stopped around the time Craig went to college. Ruth often wondered where all that anger and frustration had gone.

The second thing about Craig's childhood that came to mind now was the running away, which might have all started the first time he climbed down the rose trellis outside his window. He had not gone far that first night, just around the lawn a bit before climbing back up the trellis and into his room. Eventually, though, Craig's nocturnal excursions had become longer and more far flung, until he was disappearing for hours at a time. Not all disappearances were bona fide instances of running away. Some were just jaunts into town to hang out with friends. But some were deliberate attempts at leaving home "for good." He had always left a note, though. He had been good about that.

Ruth sometimes wondered what might have been different for Craig if she had been around more often. But there was no point in wondering at this late date. Her job had kept her very busy and often on the road. Still, she had visited her brother and his family as often as she could, first at their house in a Massachusetts suburb and later, after Larchmere became habitable year-round, in Ogunquit.

Not that every McQueen had enjoyed her visits. Charlotte had barely tolerated her. And Ruth was convinced that Adam saw her as an enemy. Anyone could see that she made him uncomfortable, though Adam himself would never admit to that. He routinely argued with her or put her down to the other McQueens (she wasn't stupid; she knew what went on) or, most infuriatingly, treated her as someone beneath his notice. Why she should be such a problem for him was unclear, however. She seemed to aggravate every insecurity he had been trying to bury, ignore, or deny since he was a boy. His negative attitude toward his aunt couldn't be entirely due to his mother's antipathy and disdain. Ruth was sure there were other factors at play, but life was too short to waste too much time contemplating her nephew's state of emotional retardation.

The girls, on the other hand, loved and even admired Ruth. She was grateful for this; at the same time she felt as if she deserved such love and admiration. Ruth had always had a sturdy sense of self-worth. She was also brutally self-critical.

Tilda and Hannah had always looked forward to their Aunt Ruth's visits. She was a breath of fresh air, funny and irreverent where their mother was neither, making their father laugh with silly jokes and outrageous stories. And she always brought gifts, odd and exotic things acquired on her travels. There were the turquoise bracelets from New Mexico and the jade animal figurines from Vietnam (that had been a pleasure trip with a short-term romantic partner), the lace from Belgium and the plaid woolen kilt (for Tilda) and polished wood shillelagh (for Hannah) from Ireland. When Ruth had gone to Peru she had brought back native musical instruments for the boys. Adam, she remembered now, had accepted his gift without thanks and dropped it on the sofa, where it sat for the duration of her visit. Craig had thanked her, and though without musical talent, had tooted on his pipe for hours. Charlotte had not been pleased.

Craig, too, had seemed to enjoy hearing about his aunt's travels, though it was clear to Ruth that by the time he could talk, which was very early, especially for a boy, he was already feeling a bit removed from his family. As if he were an afterthought, or a mistake. As if he were someone not intended for too close a relationship with the other McQueens. Craig stayed on the outside of the family circle and watched. Ruth, figuring that he might not want to invest much emotional energy in his aunt, assuming that she, too, would find him unnecessary, had always tried to bring him closer, or, at least, to indicate that it was okay for him to make a move toward emotional intimacy. But he was slippery even as a boy and ultimately Ruth had simply respected him for being who he needed to be.

Yes, there was no point in wondering about the "what ifs." She had done her best for her family. She had attended graduations though she had missed numerous recitals and plays. She had tried to be with her brother's family for Thanksgiving or Christmas each year and for a few days or weeks each summer. On the whole she thought she had done a pretty good job of being an aunt. At least, she had done what it was in her to do.

Craig was out of sight now, gone around the other side of the house.

Ruth looked down at her fur child. "Well, Percy," she said, "is it time for a tuna treat?"

Percy said that yes, it was.

21

Hannah and Susan were at the arts and crafts fair on the grounds of the Ogunquit Playhouse. Going to arts and crafts fairs wasn't Hannah's favorite thing to do, but Susan loved them so Hannah went along. It was funny, she thought, how love broadened your horizons, whether you wanted it to or not.

They recognized a few of the craftspeople from the year before. The guy who made simple but beautiful wooden toys was there, as was the woman who made very delicate, silk-screened scarves. Hannah had bought one for Susan last year, and if Susan wanted another one this year, she would buy her another one. Several people were selling their handcrafted jewelry made of gold, silver, beach glass, and beads; one older woman was selling gorgeous quilts and intricate wreaths constructed of all sorts of pinecones, made by members of her church. A local farm was selling various honeys, homemade soaps, and fragrant sachets to stash among sweaters and lingerie. (What lingerie? Hannah wondered. Does Hanes brand count? Did underwear really have to smell anything other than clean?)

After a half hour of wandering, Susan excused herself to

visit the ladies' room in the Playhouse. Hannah waited for her under a big, shady tree out front. Before Susan had been gone a moment, a woman walked by that Hannah thought she recognized.

"Karla?" she said.

The woman turned and smiled. "Hannah!"

They hugged. "Wow, I haven't seen you in years!"

"I know," Karla said. "I think the last time we ran into each other was just before your mom died."

"That's why I'm here right now. I mean, staying at Larchmere. We're having a memorial for my mother. It's been ten years since the accident."

Karla frowned in sympathy. "It must still be tough on you all. You always seemed like such a close family."

"Mmm." *Close is relative,* Hannah thought. *Pardon the pun.*

"How is your father? And your aunt? What fun she used to be!"

"My dad is great, thanks. And Ruth is Ruth. She never seems to change. She never seems to get any older, either."

Karla laughed. "I'd love to know how she pulls that off!"

"You're not the only one! Oh, and I'm married now. I'd love you to meet Susan but she's in the ladies' room at the moment."

"Hannah, that's wonderful!" Karla cried. "I don't hear much about the old gang now that we live in New Hampshire. Congratulations!"

"Thanks," she said. "So, what are you doing in Ogunquit?"

"Howie and I are up for a week with the kids. We're staying at the SeaStar Motel in Wells. It's pretty basic but who needs anything fancy when you've got the beach?"

"And Billy's Chowder House right there on the marsh."

"Onion rings! Remember how we used to go there Sunday afternoons after working all Saturday night at the restaurant and gorge on onion rings?"

"Those were fun days. Now I have to take a Tums before I eat onion rings!"

"Oh, gosh," Karla went on, "remember that time when that guy who used to wait tables at Billy's came to work with us at Two Boats and the first night he was on the floor all of our tips went missing? I was so upset! Remember, he was caught red-handed. I never understood how he could be so stupid!"

And there it was, a memory that Hannah had managed to keep from coming back for some time now, tapping noisily at her brain. She had been a sophomore in high school. An answer key for a final exam had been stolen. Another girl had accused Hannah. Hannah, of course, was innocent and had protested her innocence to her parents. Charlotte had come around to believing her only after much persuading and many tears. They were scheduled to meet with the principal to discuss the situation. The night before the meeting, Charlotte announced that she would not be able to attend. She had "another appointment." Bill and Hannah had gone alone to the meeting. In the end, Hannah was believed and her name cleared, but her mother's lack of support and then of her abandonment had scarred Hannah.

What kind of mother didn't believe in her own daughter's innocence? What kind of mother didn't fight tooth and nail for her child? Her own mother, that's what kind. And Hannah was her mother's daughter. Well, Tilda was Charlotte's daughter, too, and she seemed to be a kind and attentive parent but that didn't mean . . .

"Oops," Karla was saying, "I'd better go! See that little boy over there, the one running in circles? That's my youngest. He's about to fall down any minute. I don't know why he likes to make himself dizzy like that! It was so good seeing you again, Hannah."

"It was good seeing you, too, Karla." Hannah mustered a smile and Karla hurried off to where her son was now staggering to the ground.

Hannah watched her old friend lift her son to a standing position and hold his arms until he steadied himself. She watched as Karla smoothed the boy's hair and kissed his cheek. She turned away, moved and disturbed. She was deeply afraid of imitating her own mother's lackadaisical and at times downright dismissive parenting. She was so deeply afraid that she couldn't seem to admit to the fear out loud. If she said it—"I'm afraid I'm going to make the same mistakes my mother made"—it might somehow come true. She knew she was being ridiculous, even superstitious. She couldn't help it.

Susan was striding toward her, her coral-colored crinkly cotton skirt happy in the breeze it created. There was an inquiring smile on her face. "Who was that you were talking to?" she said when she joined Hannah. "I didn't recognize her."

"Oh, no one. Just Karla Goodhue. We used to wait tables together, back in the old days. I hadn't seen her since before Mom died."

"Did she say anything to upset you?"

"No," Hannah said. It wasn't really a lie. "Why? What's wrong?"

Susan looked at her closely. "That's what I'm asking you. You look . . . down suddenly. Distracted."

"I'm fine. What? You're looking at me weird!"

Susan sighed. "All right, have it your way. Come on, let's get out of here. I know what will cheer you up."

"I don't need cheering up."

"Yeah, you do. Because if you don't snap out of the weird mood that came over you while I was in the ladies' room, I'm going to toss you into the ocean. And you know how much you hate cold water."

"We're nowhere near the ocean."

"Hannah."

"Okay," she admitted. "So I'm in a bad mood. Memories of my less than saintly, coldhearted mother tend to do that to me. What will cheer me up?"

"A rum punch at Barnacle Billy's."

"It's only eleven o'clock. I'm too old to be drinking before noon. Not that the idea doesn't have appeal. Not that I don't make exceptions."

"This is a time for radical measures. I'll buy you some food, too."

"All right, you convinced me. But if I get tipsy, you're driving us home."

"Of course."

They walked, hand in hand, to the parking lot. "Do you know," Hannah said, "Barnacle Billy's was once an art supply store called the Brush and Needle, back when Ogunquit was an important center for American art?"

"No. I didn't know. How do you know?"

"I read it in a book called *A Century of Color.* It's about all the old art colonies in Ogunquit. There's a copy in the library at home."

"Oh. Maybe I'll take a look at it."

They reached their car. Susan went around to the passenger's side. "I guess Ogunquit still is an important center for art," Hannah said, opening the doors. "At least, in some respects. Michael Palmer still lives and works here. Beverly Hallam lives in York. Just last year the museum mounted a show of her work. Isabel Lewando is still around. All artists. The Barn Gallery is thriving. It's nice to be in a place where history feels so alive."

Susan smiled. "See? You're in lecture mode. That means you're already in a better mood. Just the thought of a rum punch helped!"

22

The cocktail party at the Ogunquit Museum of American Art was an invitation-only event. Founded in 1953 by Henry Strater, a painter and philanthropist, the museum's permanent collection now included almost sixteen hundred pieces of art. A long, low building with huge windows overlooking the water, it was designed by architect Charles S. Worley Jr. It was a dramatic building in a dramatic setting. Many believed the museum to be the most beautiful small museum in the United States. The grounds included the Victory Garden out back, and on the front lawn, a reed-rimmed pond and several large wooden sculptures of animals by Bernard Langlais. When they were kids, Jon and Jane liked to climb and clamber all over the sculptures, in spite of Tilda's admonitions not to touch.

Tilda and Dennis arrived about half an hour into the cocktail party. It was inevitable that she would know or at least recognize the majority of the attendees, as year-round locals or as longtime summer residents. She was prepared for questions about her father and her aunt, for mentions of Frank, for questions about her own state of well-being. At least, she hoped that she was prepared.

She wore a blue and white, vertical-striped blazer, navy linen slacks, a white T-shirt, and navy canvas espadrilles. The gold hoop earrings had been a birthday present from Frank. So had the slice of green Maine tourmaline she wore on a slim gold chain around her neck. Of course, she was wearing her wedding ring.

Dennis went off to get Tilda a glass of wine. She warned him, with a smile, that the drinks line would be long. A lot of wine was consumed at these museum events. One evening Frank had counted one old geezer's total as ten glasses in two hours. The man had left the museum on foot and un-aided, a real professional.

"Tilda McQueen O'Connell! It's so good to see you!"

Tilda turned to see a peculiarly short man in a blue and white seersucker suit fast approaching.

"Alan Horutz! Hello!"

Alan Horutz was one of Ogunquit's more pleasant characters. His age was indeterminate; Tilda thought he could be anywhere from fifty to seventy years old. The strange thing was, he had always looked exactly the same as he did now. He lived in a little house on Agamenticus Road and owned a successful little shop that sold all sorts of quirky objects, from funky kitchen utensils to contemporary hand-crafted jewelry to antique dolls. He had never been married or been known to have a partner. When the weather was right his pet parrot, a monstrously large bird named Hugo, would stroll the town with Alan, perched on his shoulder. Come rain or shine, in winter and summer, Alan Horutz always wore an immaculate blue and white seersucker suit.

"How have you been?" he asked with genuine interest and sympathy. "I haven't seen you since, well, I think it was last summer."

"I'm doing okay, thanks. It's been a rough couple of years but . . ."

"Yes, I imagine. You know, just the other day I was

thinking about Frank. What a great man. I was remembering the time when I came down with that dreadful summer
cold and was flat on my back. Well, there was no way I
could run the store, and do you remember Frank filled in
for me! He sacrificed an entire week of his vacation for
me! How many people would do that sort of thing for another person? I ask you."

Tilda mustered a smile. "Not many," she said.

Alan chatted for another moment and then took his
leave. Tilda stood there feeling a bit dazed. She knew that
Alan Horutz had not intended to make her feel guilty for
being at the party with a man other than Frank, but inad-
vertently, he had. What man could hold a candle to Frank?
That was what Alan had implied. No man. So why was she
bothering to spend time with Dennis?

Maybe, she thought, *I shouldn't have come tonight.*
There were so many vivid reminders of her life with Frank.
She had spotted one of his fishing buddies, a guy named
Mark who owned a high-end craft shop in town and who
spent the winters in Key West. They had caught each
other's eye and waved. Neither had made the effort to cross
the room.

There was Frank's favorite painting in the main gallery,
a Marsden Hartley work called "Lobster Pots and Buoys,"
painted in 1936. There was that sculpture Frank liked, the
one of men playing boccie ball on the beach. (He had
bought a boccie set after first seeing the piece and had
quickly become good at the sport.)

It had been over two years but it was almost as if Frank
was still with her—even if he wasn't communicating directly. She knew that this feeling of closeness, of presence,
could be a good thing—she had been hiding safely in the
emotional proximity of the past—but for the first time she
felt a bit stifled by it. For the first time Tilda wondered if
life in Ogunquit was a healthy thing for her. What if

Larchmere was left to her, and not to Adam or Hannah or, God forbid, Jennifer? Would the weight of the memories suffocate her?

Tilda wondered. When you died, maybe the most important way you lived on was in other people's memories. Memories were your most intimate legacy. But if those memories were compromised in some way, would your continued existence be compromised, too?

What would happen to Frank if she started to forget things about him? Would he, in effect, die again? She desperately wanted to keep him alive . . . but recently, really, just since coming to Larchmere this summer, she had begun to wonder if she was clinging too closely to his memory and to the memories of their life together. Would such clinging wind up killing her, in a metaphorical if not a physical way? Still, she was afraid that letting Frank go, letting him ease away just a bit, for her own selfish sake, would be cruel, a sort of moral crime or a betrayal.

Her father, clearly, had let go of his wife, enough to be romantically involved with another woman. But Tilda didn't feel she could ask him about his process of healing—and of forgetting. Besides, Bill McQueen wasn't the sort of man to talk much about his feelings. Maybe his reticence was more a generational behavior. Either way, she would probably never know what, exactly, her father had experienced in his ten years as a widower.

She saw Dennis now across the room, neat and trim in his navy blazer and tan pants, a glass of wine in each hand. He had stopped to study a painting from the permanent collection, one that Frank had hated. Tilda couldn't remember the name of the artist or of the painting. She wondered why.

Tilda looked away from Dennis and saw her coming. It was Louise Sherman, a longtime local resident no one much cared for, a rather aggressively gossipy woman who owned several small and very successful family restaurants in Ogunquit and Wells.

There was no escaping her. The crowd was too thick for Tilda to easily slip away. In a moment Louise was up against her. She put her hand heavily on Tilda's forearm and closed her bony fingers around it. She was painfully thin, something her choice of clothing accentuated rather than hid, and was doused in a heavy, cloying perfume. Tilda found Louise Sherman macabre. She fought the urge to shiver in disgust.

"So," Louise said by way of greeting, "what's going on with your father and that fashionable girl from away?"

"Hello, Louise."

"I think her name is Genevieve or Jocelyn or—"

"Jennifer," Tilda corrected. "What do you mean about what's going on?"

"Are they serious? Are they going to get married? I remember when she first came to Ogunquit, years ago. That was with her first husband. They're divorced now—well, of course you know that. She lost the house in the divorce, or maybe they sold it, I don't know. The husband, ex-husband I should say, isn't around anymore. I heard she has some sort of condo in Portland. Or maybe it was Portsmouth. I—"

"Portland," Tilda said, and wondered why she had bothered to continue this awful conversation.

"Well, I wonder what his plans are for Larchmere. I mean, if he marries her, you and your brothers and sister might very well be out of a summer home. If I were a McQueen I'd be in a state about it all! The thought of losing that big, gorgeous house to a—"

"Excuse me," Tilda blurted, finally done with this horrible woman. "I must be going." She wrenched her arm from Louise's death grip and forced her way through the crowd of revelers. In the smaller gallery she now saw Dennis and hurried to his side.

"What's wrong?" he asked immediately, handing her the glass of wine he had fetched. "I'm sorry I abandoned you. The line was long and I got waylaid. . . ."

"Nothing is wrong," Tilda said. "Just some horrid woman. It was nothing."

"All right."

Tilda took a sip of white wine. She was suddenly, painfully aware of the eyes of other guests upon her, questioning, probing. Who was this strange man she was with, this newcomer? Was he her date, a boyfriend, something more? She was not being paranoid. She knew all about life in a small town. She had felt relatively safe and secure in the dimly lit rooms of the Old Village Inn. But here, in this bright and open space, she knew she was a center of attention and it bothered her.

"I'm kind of rattled by this evening," she said now to Dennis. "That woman . . . I think I had better just go home. I'm sorry."

Dennis managed to look disappointed and understanding at the same time. "Of course," he said.

Tilda put her hand lightly on his arm for a moment. "You came to Ogunquit to enjoy a vacation. I'm sorry. You don't need to be dragged into a stranger's drama."

"I am enjoying my vacation," he insisted. "Don't apologize, please. And to be honest, you don't feel like so much of a stranger."

Actually, Dennis didn't feel like much of a stranger to Tilda, either, but she was not prepared to admit that. Dennis following, they wove their way through the crowd and out into the golden evening sun.

23

Sunday, July 22

Tilda was still out of sorts the morning after the party at the Ogunquit Museum. That awful Louise Sherman! But by the time she got down to the beach and began to walk along the waterline, sneakers in hand and pant legs rolled up, she felt calmer. Better. The water was very cool. She found a piece of a sand dollar (she had never found a whole one, except on a visit to South Carolina) and put it in her pocket.

About a quarter of the way to Wells, Tilda stopped to chat with a local man named Wade Wilder. He was a retired contractor who loved to fish, which was what he was doing now, as he did every morning. The interesting thing about Wade was that he hated to eat fish. He was a strict meat and potatoes kind of guy. So he either threw his catch back into the ocean or gave it to a friend or passerby.

"Anything today?" Tilda asked, looking up at Wade's friendly face. He was very tall, probably, Tilda thought, close to six feet five inches, and very thin.

Wade smiled down at her. "Nope. Not yet, anyway."

"How's Molly's mother doing?" Molly was Wade's wife. Her mother, who was well into her eighties, lived with them. Lately, Tilda had heard, she had been failing.

"Not so good," Wade said with a shake of his head. "Had to put the old girl in a nursing home just yesterday. Broke Molly's heart but it was time."

"Oh, I'm so sorry," Tilda said. "I hope she'll be happy there. Well, at least all right."

"Not much choice about it now. I'll tell her you said hello, if you like."

Tilda said that yes, she would like it if Wade gave her greetings to his mother-in-law, and she resumed her walk, leaving Wade to catch and release to his heart's content.

Wade's story made her think. Presumably, her father, Bill, would die before his younger sister, Ruth. Maybe. If Tilda inherited Larchmere, there was a good chance that in time she would become her aunt's primary caregiver. Then again, even if she didn't inherit Larchmere, as the oldest niece it might very well become her duty to care for an aged Ruth. Adam certainly wouldn't. There was no question there.

The idea had never occurred to her. Of course, she would never abandon her aunt but it might be difficult to care for her from South Portland if Ruth insisted on staying at Larchmere. . . . Tilda cringed. She felt guilty for even considering her aunt as a problem to be solved. Besides, knowing Ruth, she would probably live to a fine old age and quite independently, too.

Not like Frank. Near the end he had announced, several times, that he had had a good run. It would bother Tilda that he could think that way. After all, he was dying before he could see his children graduate from college. He was dying before he could have a midlife crisis, before he could lose his hair, before he could need bifocals! Never had the indignities of middle age seemed so precious to her.

But to her objections he would answer, how many guys could say that they had married their dream girl, had two great kids, worked at a job they enjoyed, owned their own home . . . ? Tilda had blocked out Frank's rationalizations. She had argued with him, too.

"But you'll never get to see your grandchildren," she had said. "We won't get to grow old together."

"Those things are lousy, Tilda," he had admitted, "especially the fact that I don't get to grow old with my best friend. But what's it going to get me to dwell on what I can't have? I don't have the time to be miserable and angry. I just don't. I want to die with some peace of mind, with some dignity. So, please, let me do that."

Those conversations had been coming back to Tilda a lot lately. For Frank, dying with dignity had meant dying without kicking and screaming. It had meant going gently into that good night, refusing to rage against the dying of the light, Dylan Thomas be damned.

Maybe because of what she had experienced with Frank, Tilda was no longer afraid of death and dying. At least, she didn't think that she was, not in the way she had been before Frank's illness and death. She wondered if this lack of fear was a good thing or a bad thing. She wondered if it was a sign of resignation, of giving up on life, or a sign of maturity.

What was it, exactly, that most people feared about dying? Tilda often thought about that. Was it the process itself that scared them, the anticipation of pain and discomfort, the mental anguish of knowing that your time was up and that you had not accomplished half of what you had intended to accomplish? Was it the anticipation of the emotional trauma involved in taking leave of loved ones? Was it the anticipation of the grief surrounding the loss of favorite habits and haunts, of the changing seasons, of holidays, even of the first satisfying sip of coffee in the morning?

No doubt for some the fear of dying involved a spiritual concern regarding the afterlife. What if there was no afterlife and you had spent your entire life banking on the belief that there was something better and happier after death? What if there was an afterlife and you had spent your entire life banking on the belief that there was nothing after death, no reward and no retribution?

Big questions for which Tilda had no answers. Maybe nobody had the answers.

On the way back to the parking lot, and walking higher up on the beach in the softer sand, she passed behind Wade. He would be there for hours and he would be back the next day and the one after that. She wondered if Wade was afraid of dying and almost immediately thought that he was probably not afraid of anything.

Before slipping into the driver's seat of her car, Tilda performed her own daily ritual and scanned the summer sky. But there was nothing.

"There's Sarah's car. Down by the turn."

"You can see that it's her car?" Tilda asked, squinting and making out only a glint of metal. They were on the front porch of Larchmere. "Boy, your eyesight is good."

Craig shrugged. "Guess I take after Dad."

Sarah Wilder McQueen, driving a Honda Odyssey, pulled up the drive a few minutes later. She was there for the memorial service. Tilda and Craig knew that but neither was sure that Adam did. Yet. Their brother's divorce had been acrimonious, though Sarah's conduct throughout had been an awful lot more mature than Adam's. Which was interesting, given the fact that she was the one being left for a mistress who, shortly after the divorce was made final, disappeared from the picture. No one but Adam knew what had happened to her and no one wanted to ask.

Sarah parked her car, got out with her travel bags, and with a wave, walked toward Tilda and Craig. Over time she had lost some of her sharpness and urban chic but was still an attractive woman, now forty-five. Compared to her ex-husband's young fiancée, some might judge her a bit old and worn. Not that Sarah was the sort of person to dwell on the importance of appearance. Her only remaining vanity was a visit to her hair stylist every two months for a color touch-up. Gray hair was the one concession to age that she would not make.

For all of Kat's physical perfection, Craig thought, watching his former sister-in-law, Sarah was the sexier woman. Difference attracted Craig, not the standard. Uniqueness, a real individuality, those were attractive qualities in people. Like Sarah's recent habit of wearing colorful, oversized beads (several strands at once) and consciously dorky glasses. The beads and glasses suited her.

Sarah greeted Tilda and Craig and together, the three went into the house. "So," she said softly, "what's Adam's fiancée like? I've heard a bit from the kids but I'd love to know your opinions."

"See for yourself," Craig murmured.

Kat and Adam were coming from the living room. Both stopped short at the sight of Adam's ex-wife standing in the front hall. Tilda realized that Kat must have recognized Sarah from photographs. Neither said a word.

Sarah stepped forward, hand extended. "Hello, Adam," she said, but she turned toward Kat. "And you must be Kat. It's nice to meet you."

Poor Kat. She looked completely baffled by the situation. Sarah kept her hand extended and a smile on her face until finally, Kat extended her own hand and blurted, "Your children are very nice."

The brief, awkward handshake over, Sarah said, "Yes, I know," and stepped back to join Tilda and Craig.

"Why don't I take your bags to the cottage," Craig said. "You can get settled and come back to the house for something to eat."

Sarah thought his suggestion a good one and together they left the house, her bags in tow. Tilda noticed Kat slip away upstairs. Adam looked apoplectic.

"What is she doing here?" he hissed.

"Ruth invited her."

"What the hell for?"

Tilda sighed. "Just because you divorced Sarah there's no reason for the rest of the McQueens to ignore her. She's still a part of this family, Adam. You made her a part when you married her and had the children."

Adam frowned. Tilda wondered if he thought a frown made him look important. "I'm going to have a word with your aunt about this."

No doubt you will, Tilda thought. *But it won't do you any good.* She went off to the kitchen. Sarah liked tea. Tilda thought she would put out a selection of tea bags and local honey. She didn't mean to eavesdrop. But after a moment or two she heard two voices in the hall, Adam and Sarah. She had not expected Sarah back at the house so quickly.

"Look, Adam," she was saying, "I just talked to Cordelia. The kids want to stay with me in the guest cottage."

"Absolutely not. That's ridiculous."

"No, it's not ridiculous. Cordelia said they feel—uncomfortable."

"Are you saying they don't like Kat?" Tilda, in the kitchen, flinched.

"Keep your voice down, Adam. What I'm saying is that the situation isn't ideal for them."

"No way. The kids are mine this weekend, Sarah. That's the law. You want to take it up with a judge, be my guest."

Sarah paused before answering. Tilda imagined her sighing in frustration. "Don't be an ass, Adam. You know I don't want any more legal wrangling. But Cordelia and Cody are unhappy being with you and Kat. And I'm not saying anything bad about your fiancée. She seems like a very nice young woman. But they would rather stay with me in the cottage. You'll still spend time with them. I'm not spiriting them away to Argentina. We'll just be in the backyard."

"What made you say Argentina?"

"Nothing. I don't know. I saw a PBS special the other night. Come on, Adam, let the kids stay with me in the cottage."

"All right." His tone was begrudging. "But I'm making note of this occasion. I deserve time with my children. I have rights."

"Yes. Thanks. Now I'll go and get them packed up."

Tilda heard Sarah's footsteps, retreating. She prayed that Adam would not come into the kitchen. He would know for sure that she had overheard his capitulation and he would be angry. Her prayer was answered. A moment later, she heard the front door slam.

24

Tilda and Dennis were spending the afternoon in Kennebunkport. Tilda was glad to be away from Ogunquit for a while, and the prying—or simply curious—eyes of her longtime neighbors. Small towns provided a strong sense of community. They also, at times, were stifling.

She had chosen to wear a pair of off-white chinos and a fitted black linen blouse that had once belonged to her mother. She had found the blouse among her mother's wardrobe and, though Tilda rarely wore black, had saved it for herself. She had not worn it until now. She wasn't sure why she was wearing it.

Susan, upon seeing her sister-in-law preparing to leave the house, had asked her to wait a moment. She had run up to her room and returned promptly with a multistrand bead necklace in lime green. "Put this on," she ordered. "It will really make your eyes pop and it's a perfect contrast to the black." Tilda had protested, saying that she wasn't used to wearing that sort of jewelry, by which she meant anything costume and funky. But Susan had insisted and Tilda was glad about it. Dennis had complimented her the moment she had fetched him at his house. He said she looked vibrant.

They had stopped at a quaint, old cemetery (it was not hard to find one in New England) and were wandering along the crooked aisles of battered and worn headstones. The grass had been recently mowed and at a few of the newer graves (still a half or full century old) there were small vases of flowers.

"I find it heartening," Dennis said, "to see how people so wanted to remember their loved ones. There's something soothing about these old cemeteries." Dennis turned to her. "I'm sorry. Maybe I shouldn't have said that."

"No, no, I agree actually," Tilda said. "Maybe it's the fact that they're so old. . . . We're so removed from the people buried here . . . and yet, we're so connected. All these years later, and that baby there, Constance Morrison, is known to us somehow. She lived for only a month but almost two hundred years later we're bearing witness to her life."

"Yes, that's exactly what we're doing, bearing witness."

Tilda smiled at Dennis. She was amazed to find that she could talk about important, even personal things with a man who was virtually a stranger. The experience made her feel a bit hopeful, even happy.

"Are you a superstitious man?" she asked then.

"I don't think that I am, though I don't make it a point to walk under ladders. Why?"

"Well," she said, "it's funny, but not long before Frank got sick I suddenly found myself thinking, totally out of the blue, that my life was too good, almost perfect, and that something bad was bound to happen."

Dennis nodded. "I suspect lots of people have experienced that kind of moment. Most adults know that nothing lasts forever. I'm not sure I'd call that being superstitious."

"Maybe not," she said. "I know that until that moment

I'd never considered myself a superstitious person. Well, Frank would have argued otherwise! Anyway, I got the bad feeling one day while I was walking the path around Back Cove in Portland. I was kind of daydreaming as I was walking, admiring all the colors of the marshy land and the herons among the grasses, and the ducks in the water close to the shore. The weather was perfect. I remember the air feeling very soft and fresh, and the sky being very clear. There were a few clouds but they were the light and puffy kind, nothing threatening. And then, bam, it hit me like a slap to the face. My life was too good, everything was too good, and it wasn't going to last much longer."

"Maybe you intuited a message from the universe. Don't laugh," Dennis said quickly, though Tilda had no intention of laughing. "I'm serious. Or maybe deep down a part of you sensed that Frank was sick. You said you were very close. It could happen, a subconscious knowledge."

"Yes," Tilda said, "maybe." But whatever the cause of that revelation or intuition, it had taught her one big lesson. Nothing good could come of perfection. Nothing good could come of perceived perfection, anyway. If nothing could be better, then everything could be worse.

They continued to stroll through the cemetery. They noted particularly interesting headstones and the occasional grandiose family mausoleum. Her mother was buried in the McQueen family plot in a cemetery in York. Her father was to be buried there someday, too. But what if he married Jennifer? Would that change everything that had been planned?

"Frank was cremated," Tilda said suddenly. "My kids and I scattered his ashes off the cliff on Marginal Way."

"But he's still remembered." It was not a question, but a statement.

"Oh, yes. On his birthday last year the kids and I had a little party in his honor. You're told to do that kind of thing, you know. Celebrate the life of the one who's died. You're supposed to remember as a way of getting past grief. I baked his favorite cake. Duncan Hines chocolate cake with vanilla icing from a can."

Dennis smiled ruefully. "I wish I could say that I still celebrate my ex-wife's birthday. But that's another way a divorce is different from death. At least, in my case. I don't hate my ex-wife—I don't think I've ever hated anyone— but I certainly have no desire to celebrate her life. Not even at first, when I still actually missed her."

"She hurt you. Frank didn't hurt me. It's not like I could blame him for dying. It's not like he did it to wound me."

"Yes," Dennis said. "I'm sure you were wounded by his passing but it's not as if he intended that. It's all about in-tention."

Tilda smiled. "Are we intending to get something to eat?"

"Of course! What are you in the mood for? I'm pretty flexible when it comes to feeding time."

"I would love a crab roll. And some fries."

"Done and done." Dennis grinned.

It was a beautiful evening after a perfect summer day. (They deserved as many perfect summer days as they could get, Hannah had remarked. It was compensation for the long and lousy winters Mainers had to endure.) The sky was clear and a few early stars were visible. Hannah and Susan decided to take a drive to Nubble Lighthouse. Sit-ting on tiny Nubble Island close to the rocky shore of the mainland, the picturesque, red and white lighthouse, built in 1879, was probably the most photographed lighthouse on the coast of New England. Check any gift shop in Maine and you would find its image on postcards, mugs, coasters, even T-shirts.

Craig came out of the library as they were preparing to leave. Hannah thought she had never seen anyone look so obviously lonely. She wasn't used to Craig looking anything but . . . fine.

"Where are you guys headed?" he asked.

"The Nubble Lighthouse," Susan said. "I know, how clichéd, but it's so beautiful."

"Why don't you come with?" Hannah suggested.

"Yeah, do."

Craig hesitated. "Are you sure I'm not going to be in the way? Three's a crowd and all."

"Craig," Susan said, taking his arm, "we're an old married couple. We're not going to make out."

"We're not?" Hannah said, feigning huge disappointment.

"Hilarious. Now, come on."

Craig shrugged. "Sure, thanks."

The drive to the lighthouse was uneventful; they passed only one car pulled to the side of the road by the police. Hannah parked the car in the gravel lot and the three got out into the night.

They were not the only ones who had decided to visit the Nubble Lighthouse that evening. There was a family of four, two parents and two children. The children were shouting and chasing each other. The parents ignored them or just didn't care what the kids were up to. Neither looked particularly happy to be there. They stood feet apart from each other, as if strangers. The father's hands were in his pockets.

To the right of the young parents was an older couple in matching, crazy patterned sweaters. The man was taking pictures of the lighthouse while his wife shouted into her cell phone. "What a nice meal we had!" Hannah heard her say. "You and Ralph really should come with us next year. What? I can't hear you—"

Hannah smiled ruefully at Craig and Susan. "Well, so much for a peaceful experience."

"It's summer," Craig said. "You can't expect a private experience in July."

"And not everyone appreciates a beautiful night sky," Susan added.

A beautiful night sky . . . "Remember when Dad got that telescope for Mom?" Hannah asked suddenly. "It was huge. I don't think she ever used it. I wonder what made him buy it in the first place. I don't remember Mom ever having an interest in astronomy. Astrology, yes, but not astronomy."

Craig frowned. "I know exactly why he bought her that telescope. Because Carol Whitehouse had gotten one, some super fancy setup, and Mom just happened to mention it to Dad, who, of course, ran right out and bought an even more super fancy setup for Mom. It was all about one-upping her friend."

"How do you know about that?" Susan asked.

"I heard Mom and Dad talking one night. And no, I wasn't purposely spying. But once I heard Mom whining about how Carol thought she was so special, blah, blah, blah, well, I just had to stay and listen. For the sheer entertainment value of it all, of course."

"Poor Dad," Hannah said. She doubted he had really understood his wife's motives. "What ever happened to that telescope anyway?"

"Adam made off with it."

"Why?" Susan asked. "He has no hobbies. If it's not related to his job he doesn't care about it. I bet he hasn't read a novel since college."

Craig shrugged. "It's worth a lot of money. Maybe he sold it."

They were silent for some time and then Craig spoke again. "Adam might not have hobbies," he said, "but he's perfect. Tilda, too. They're the perfect children, I mean, at least as far as Mom was concerned. They're both professionals, they both got married, and they both had two children, a boy and a girl. Okay, Adam got divorced but nobody considers that much of a big deal anymore. In some circles it's almost de rigueur. I doubt Mom would have cared."

"And then look at us!" Hannah said with a laugh. "We're the oddballs, the outcasts. I'm gay and—"

"Married," Susan interrupted.

"Gay trumps married, I'm sorry to say. And Craig's a wandering minstrel, as it were."

"Dad doesn't care that you're gay," Craig said to his sister. "You're golden in his eyes. I'm the embarrassment in this family. I'm the one who makes people lower their voices when my name is mentioned. Oh, Craig McQueen," he said in an exaggerated whisper, his eyes wide. "He's the troubled one. We don't know what went wrong with that boy."

Susan swiped his arm. "You two have an inferiority complex. Craig, I'm sure nobody thinks you're an embarrassment. We certainly don't."

"Thanks, Susan. I appreciate your vote of confidence. But I'm not asking for pity. I've made all the choices that have gotten me here—forty years old and virtually homeless. I must have wanted what I got."

"But now?" Hannah asked. She looked carefully at her brother. She couldn't read his face; the night was too dark. She couldn't tell if he was really mocking himself or just playing a game.

Craig shrugged. "Now nothing."

Susan opened the cooler at her feet. "I think it's time for some champagne."

"You guys really know how to live!" Craig said. Hannah thought he sounded relieved to be off the topic of his unusual life.

Susan popped the cork and poured them each a glass.

Hannah raised her plastic cup. "To us."

"To family," Susan said.

"Must we?" Craig asked.

Hannah said, "Yeah. Do we have to?"

"Yes." Susan looked from her wife to her brother-in-law with that formidable look she reserved for the most stubborn of her family services clients.

Craig sighed. "I know when I'm beaten."

He and Hannah said, "To family."

25

Monday, July 23

The beach seemed more than usually crowded that morning. Families were already beginning to settle in for the day. A group of about ten gay men had set up blankets and chairs and lounges in a large semicircle facing the water and had erected a flag that read "Happy Birthday, Eric!" Tilda spotted Tessa Vickes on her own morning constitutional and waved but Tessa didn't see her. Wade Wilder was there, too, chatting with someone Tilda didn't recognize, maybe a summer visitor. Wade would chat with anyone who cared to chat back.

Tilda walked at the water's edge—the tide was coming in—enjoying its coolness. Jon and Jane would be joining the rest of the family soon at Larchmere. She was looking forward to their arrival, but one little thing was nagging at her. Just before she had left South Portland the other day, both of them, separately, very casually, had mentioned the possibility of her dating. Too casually, Tilda thought. She wondered if they were cooking up some scheme to force her into the dating world. Would they secretly sign her up on a dating Web site? Or, horror of horrors, bring home someone they had scouted out on their own?

She wondered if her children would have been so eager for her to date if their father had died suddenly. Maybe not. But Frank had been sick for a long time and Jon and Jane had witnessed the difficulties Tilda had endured. Taking on most of Frank's chores around the house. Driving him to and from the hospital. Caring for him in the awful days after a round of chemotherapy. Tempting him with all of his favorite foods, only to have him turn his head, barely able to hold down water.

She kicked a bit at the water rolling in and remembered a *New York Times Magazine* article she had read the year before. Deborah Solomon had interviewed Joyce Carol Oates. Ms. Oates had described widowhood as "physically arduous." Tilda understood that. While Frank was sick, she was already in a way widowed. She had had to assume so many of Frank's responsibilities, as well as shoulder the burden of care for him. And then, when Frank was gone, well, the burdens became all too real and permanent.

Anyway, Tilda thought, she was pretty sure both Jon and Jane believed that their father would want their mother to be happy, and if that meant remarrying, then so be it. In life, Frank was nothing if not generous, affable, and kind spirited. Why should he be any different in death?

And there was also the fact that both Jon and Jane would soon be setting out on the adventures that would be their own lives. Tilda suspected they would be a lot happier if Mom was being looked after by a husband and not by them! The truth was she was meeting no resistance from her children regarding dating. She almost wished they did object, and strongly; it would give her an excuse not to move on. Excuses not to act were underrated. Because what if you acted—what if you tried—and you simply didn't get what you wanted? What if, in spite of her best efforts, she never again achieved a real, settled kind of love like the love she had had with Frank? It took time to develop that kind of love, a love in which two people were completely comfortable with each other. Maybe it was too much to ask for.

She stopped. She looked up to the sky, turned from left to right, and then she looked behind her. Except for the wheeling gulls and one lone pigeon, the sky was empty.

Ruth was in the library, dusting shelves and the spines of the books on them. Percy was asleep in a corner of the brown leather couch.

"Ruth?"

She swung around to find Adam's fiancée standing just inside the door. She wore a cap-sleeved, very fitted, hot pink T-shirt and an above-the-knee wraparound denim skirt. Ruth wondered if she owned anything with long-sleeves—a blouse, a sweatshirt, something! Certainly in the winter she must cover up?

"Do you mind if I ask you something?" Kat said.

"Of course not," Ruth replied. She put the duster on the desk. For an awful moment Ruth wondered if this young woman was going to ask her opinion of Adam. What if she asked for advice about marrying him? What in the world could Ruth say?

Kat took a few steps into the room. "I was wondering, why are there corks all along the wall in the sunroom? I mean, obviously someone put them there but—why?"

Ruth looked at her nephew's fiancée keenly. "You're not a craftsperson, are you?"

"No," she admitted. "I mean, I took a pottery class once but I was awful at it. But what I mean is, how is lining up corks—how is lining up anything, shells or rocks or whatever—how is lining up stuff along a shelf a craft? I'm sorry. I don't mean to sound critical. I just don't understand."

Ruth shrugged. "There's not much to understand. You see, every time I finish a bottle of red wine I put the cork on a shelf, right next to the cork from the last bottle of wine I finished."

Kat's face betrayed confusion. Ruth assumed she was debating whether to laugh or to wonder if alcoholism ran in her fiancé's family. "Oh," she said.

"And someday," Ruth went on, "when the wall is filled with corks, when I can't squeeze one more cork onto a shelf, that's when I'll be ready to die. Not before, mind you."

Kat put her hand up against her heart. "What do you mean," she said, her voice a bit squeaky, "that you'll be ready to die? You're not planning—anything, are you? I mean you're not . . ."

Ruth smiled blandly. "What you're trying to say is that I am in complete control over the placing of the corks. You're trying to say that I can quite easily calculate the number of corks it will take to fill those final shelves and that I can drink bottles of red wine as fast or as slow as I please, knowing that when I fill that final shelf I'll be ready to die. You're trying to say that my statement sounded . . . poetic, but that in reality I am planning—drawing out or hurrying toward—my own demise."

There was a moment of silence. "Uh," Kat said finally, already turning toward the door of the library, "I think I'd better be getting back to Adam."

Ruth smiled to herself. *Poor kid,* she thought. *So easily rattled. Spooked by the crazy old spinster aunt.* She supposed she should have been nicer to her a moment ago. She was going to be a member of the family—unless she smartened up and dumped her jackass of a fiancé. Ruth knew she shouldn't talk about a family member, her own nephew, in such negative terms, but blood didn't make one blind. At least, in her case it hadn't.

Hannah appeared in the library then, mumbled something about a book she had been reading having gone missing, and then noticed her aunt's expression. "You look thoughtful," she said. "What's up?"

"Kat was just here. She's very young, you know. Emotionally. Adam is going to destroy her within a month of the wedding. Poor thing. She's clearly incapable of saving herself. But I don't know how I can be of any help. You know how I don't like to interfere. It seems . . . immoral somehow. Or maybe unethical is the more appropriate term. Something one isn't supposed to do."

Hannah shook her head. "How could it be unethical to advise someone against a danger she might not see, a danger that you see quite clearly? How could that be wrong? It would be wrong not to say anything."

"Yes," Ruth agreed, "it would be wrong, in most cases. If I see a car barreling down on a pedestrian, I'm under every moral or ethical obligation there is to shout out a warning. But in Kat's case . . . It's difficult to warn someone about a danger you sense, a danger that's intangible, even though, in your own opinion, it's real. Like Adam's voracious ego."

"Yes. I suppose you're right. Though I do wish there was something we could say to her. But any word of warning against a marriage to Adam would be suspect, coming from his own family, wouldn't it? Kat might very well think we just don't want her to be a McQueen because of something wrong with her."

Ruth sighed. "We are in an untenable position. Besides, in the long run it probably is in Kat's best interest to make up her own mind about a future with Adam. Everyone's got to grow up sometime, don't they?"

"Tell that to Craig."

"Now that's unfair," Ruth said forcefully. "Your brother isn't entirely immature, you know that."

"Maybe not," Hannah admitted. "I'm in a charitable mood. But I don't know why he can't accept responsibility for anything. I mean, I don't think he's ever paid rent on a place to live."

"Don't be ridiculous. Of course he's paid rent. In some form or another, maybe not in cash but certainly in services."

"I know for a fact he doesn't have a checking account."

Ruth laughed. "That hardly makes him a criminal. At least he's not the sort to pass bad checks."

"That's true." Hannah didn't say that only the night before, at the Nubble Lighthouse, her brother had seemed on the verge of expressing discontent with his wayward lifestyle. But maybe that was something she had imagined.

"Well," Ruth said, "I don't want to go on defending your brother to you. You'll feel about him what you feel, no matter what I say."

"Probably. By the way, what made you say that about Kat's being emotionally young?"

"Oh, nothing. Just that I explained about the corks."

"Ruth, you didn't!"

"I did," Ruth said. "She didn't seem to understand."

"You're incorrigible." Hannah was unable to restrain a smile.

"I think I saw your missing book in the living room."

"Nice change of subject. But thanks."

Hannah left the library and Ruth went back to her dusting. Percy stretched, yawned, put a paw over his eyes, and went back to sleep.

26

Tilda stood staring at the ruins of the fairy house. The ruins themselves were ruins. They were ruins of ruins. If she had not known there had been a fairy house at the site, she would not have been able to recognize the few remains as such.

She was in one of the black moods—worse than the gray moods—that occasionally descended and enveloped her. They didn't come as frequently as they had in the months just after Frank's death. But they still came, often out of the blue. Black moods out of the blue.

Time passed, she thought now, staring down at the dirt and bits of old, brown leaves, and everything fell into ruins. Relationships, civilizations, lives. A random breeze made its way through the trees and Tilda shivered. Maybe the breeze foretold rain. Frank had loved rainy days. He had never found them depressing.

Frank. With one brief and unmemorable exception, he was the only man with whom she ever had had sex. That was not a complaint. Their sex life had been good. But, now single again, it did seem like a bit of a burdensome fact, her relative lack of sexual experience. But it wasn't her biggest concern by far. In her experience, admittedly not vast, sex took care of itself. It was the heart that needed coaching and support. But not when you were young. Then, the heart seemed to know exactly what to do.

She had been a little bit younger than Jon was now when she met Frank. She had been a little bit older than Jane. Her children were in possession of a youth they entirely took for granted, as did most young people. At any moment either of them might meet a soul mate, someone with whom they would spend the rest of their hopefully long lives. Or, they might meet the first of several soul mates. It could happen. This afternoon, tomorrow, the day after could mark the start of an entirely new and unexpected life path.

So, then, could the same thing happen for her? Or was she too old, had she had her big chance, was she being self-ish, hoping or reaching for another great love at her age? She was almost half a century old.

Tilda kicked at a clump of dirt. It was all well and good for celebrities of a certain age to date gorgeous men in their twenties and thirties, but what about a forty-seven-year-old schoolteacher who had not been on a date in over twenty years? Well, unless she counted dinner and a drive to Kennebunkport and the party at the museum with Dennis as dates, and Tilda wasn't really sure that she did. What was she supposed to do with her decidedly unglamorous self? Should she get Botox injections? Did she even have the money for Botox? And wasn't it actually a poison? Was she desperate enough to inject poison into her face just to get a date? Was she supposed to be?

Should she join a gym to firm up the flab that had mysteriously replaced muscle? Should she get a new haircut? Maybe try a new color, some highlights? What about a new personality, one less prone to black moods? A new wardrobe? But she liked her clothes, mostly! An eyelift, a tummy tuck, a butt lift? It was exhausting, this attempt to reenter the world of single men and women, this attempt to stave off old age and yes, death. Exhausting and in the end, futile.

Of course, she thought again of Dennis. Dennis seemed to find her company welcome, but did he find her attractive, too? Or was he just being nice to a clumsy, middle-aged woman? Was she just a pity project? He hadn't yet kissed her. But neither had she kissed him. There was a reason for that.

She liked Dennis. He was smart and funny and kind and she enjoyed spending time with him. But she didn't have intense feelings for him, in spite of his good qualities, and in spite of the fact that he was, by any normal standards, handsome. She wondered if his age had anything to do with her lack of sexual interest. Maybe. But she was reluctant to admit that she found the fact of his age, of his being fifteen years older than her, disconcerting. No, more than disconcerting. Unappealing?

But why should she feel this way? Jennifer was in love with a man twenty-three years her senior. She seemed very happy. But Jennifer—as far as Tilda knew—had not nursed a dying husband. Was that it? Tilda wondered. Did she, too, now associate age with death and dying and decay?

Suddenly, her own prejudice appalled her. She was the first to accuse older men with younger girlfriends—her father included?—of discriminating against women their own age. And here she was mentally rejecting the idea of forming a long-term relationship with an older man because he was statistically more likely than a younger man to get sick and die and make her life messy and difficult.

It was all too ridiculous, Tilda thought, this "moving

on" business. She gave the clump of dirt one last kick, turned, and walked rapidly back to the house.

Hannah and Susan had driven to the outlets in Kittery. Hannah, Susan informed her, needed some new T-shirts, which they could pick up cheap at Old Navy. (Hannah tended to spill things on her clothes, so there was no point in paying full price.) Susan had a discount card for the Zales jewelry store and wanted to "just take a look." That meant, of course, that by the end of the day she would have a new piece of jewelry, nothing too expensive, just a little something nice. Maybe a small gold charm with a tiny diamond accent. She was collecting charms with the intention of someday creating an individualized bracelet.

Also, Susan reminded Hannah, their friends Moire and Colleen, already mothers of a little boy, were pregnant with a second child. The baby shower was in two weeks and Susan wanted to buy something special, a keepsake gift, in addition to the package of onesies and the wee pairs of socks she had already purchased. Maybe an engraved rattle or a silver-plated "ceremonial" cup. Maybe a silver teething ring or a little box made of fine china. There were a few stores in Kittery that sold such things.

Susan wanted to get the baby's gift first, so they went into the Lenox outlet. Susan, a professional shopper, immediately began to examine the items for sale. Hannah, who didn't much enjoy shopping, watched the other people in the store. There was an older couple, maybe in their seventies, vacationers, Hannah thought, looking around desultorily, probably killing time until the early-bird special at a local, family-style seafood restaurant. There was a man about her own age, wandering aimlessly, clearly befuddled by the choices of pretty objects for sale. Maybe, Hannah thought, he was looking for an anniversary gift for his wife. The man hailed a salesperson, who expertly took him in hand. And then, through the front door came a man, woman, and two small children. The man was clutching the hands of the two children, practically dragging them along behind him. The woman, who looked pale and haggard, was heavily pregnant.

Hannah tried not to stare but it was hard. How, she wondered, was this woman even walking! She was massive! Her back must be a sheet of pain. Her feet must be in agony. Her hands, Hannah noticed, were red and swollen.

One of the children—they were both girls—began to howl. The father yanked on her arm. The mother flinched and put her hand to her head. *She probably has a headache,* Hannah thought, *and she isn't even allowed to take an aspirin!* Pregnant women weren't supposed to take drugs of any sort unless prescribed. How ridiculous! How did they stand it!

The howling went on until the father dragged the little girls back out of the store. The woman looked around at the elegant picture frames and stacks of holiday-themed table settings and displays of delicate figurines. She looked, Hannah thought, helpless. And then she, too, left the store.

"You were watching that woman."

Hannah was startled. She had not heard Susan come up to her.

"Yes," she admitted. "She looked so . . . miserable."

Susan put her arm through Hannah's. "I know this is lousy timing," she said. "I'm sorry. But is it my safety you're worried about? Is it my health?"

"What?"

"Is that what's holding you back from agreeing to start

our family? Are you worried about my health through all the procedures and then the pregnancy and then the birth?"

"God, Susan," Hannah said, "of course I worry about your safety. No medical procedure is without some risk. Ruth once said that the only minor surgery is surgery done on someone else. And pregnancy is no picnic and child-birth . . ."

"So, that's the big reason? Concern that I might get really sick or die?"

Hannah shook her head. "No. No, it's not that. I mean, oh boy, of course I'm concerned about you but—"

"I'm sorry." Susan withdrew her arm from Hannah's. "I knew this wasn't the time or the place."

"That's all right."

Susan went back to examining the selection of baby presents. Hannah trailed after her. How could she admit to Susan that her biggest fear was that she would repeat the same mistakes her mother made with her? How could she admit to her fear that no matter how hard she tried to be different she would treat her own children with noncha-lance, even, to some extent, negligence?

Susan would grow to hate her. Of course she would hate her for not being a loving enough parent to their children. She would have every right to leave the marriage and take the children with her. Hannah would have destroyed every-thing.

Suddenly, a horrible, horrifying thought occurred to her. What if she was afraid to admit her fear of being like Char-lotte because she might be cured of, or talked out of, the fear? Maybe, deep down, she didn't want to be talked out of it because maybe, deep down, she really didn't want to have children of her own!

She took a deep breath. She was panicking, overreact-ing. She was being a drama queen though only in her head, which was embarrassing enough. She had to get out of that place, walk it off, something.

"I'll meet you in Old Navy," Hannah said abruptly, and she hurried off.

"Here, let me help you with that."

They were in the Cove. Bobby was unloading his boat. Craig reached down for the heavy trap Bobby hoisted up to him. He was aware of a small boy on the dock, in shorts and a buzz cut, watching them with fascination. There was, Craig knew, a certain mystery to lobstermen and their craft.

"Thanks," Bobby said. "I'm not as young as I used to be."

"Who is? Still, you're in better shape than a lot of guys I know who are my age."

Bobby climbed up out of the boat and onto the wooden dock. "Clean living, Craig, clean living. Work hard, eat right, cause no harm, do good when you can, drink the finest whiskey you can afford. No magic to it."

"You ever live anywhere else but Ogunquit?" Craig asked. "Just wondering."

"Nope. Lived here all my life. Never wanted to live any-place else. Why would I?"

"You never wanted to travel? See other countries?"

"I read the magazines and watch the television shows. I'm what you might call an armchair traveler. No desire to get on a plane. I went to New York City once. That was enough."

Craig grinned. "What took you to New York?"

"Rather not say."

"Fair enough." Craig paused and then said, "I guess I got the rambling bug somehow. I just can't seem to stop moving."

Bobby, who never wore sunglasses, squinted up at Craig. "Voltaire—you know him? He said that a man should cultivate his own garden. Guess I'm with him on that."

Craig nodded. He would have to think about that.

"Well," Bobby said, "I best be getting on. Lobsters don't sell themselves."

Craig said good-bye to his father's old friend and walked up through the parking lot to stand at the top of the rocky slope that led to the water. The sun was very strong—he didn't know how Bobby could open his eyes without sunglasses, let alone set out to sea. He thought about what Bobby had said.

A man should cultivate his own garden. A man should take care of his own concerns, and family, and responsibilities. A man should learn his own mind. Voltaire might have meant all of that or something else entirely. He would have to go back and read the work. He was pretty sure there was a selection of Voltaire back at the house, and it probably included *Candide*. But for now, he asked himself where his own garden was to be found. The answer was easy. It was Larchmere.

Until this visit, the notion that Larchmere might someday cease to be "home" had never once occurred to Craig. Now, with that idea pending, he was beginning to realize just how important Larchmere was to him and, maybe more importantly, to whatever sense of self he retained. Who you are is where you are. Or something like that. Maybe, who you are, or a big part of it, is where you are from.

The reality was that he had never been content anywhere else but Larchmere. Time and again he had told himself that he didn't want to settle anywhere, that he was happy wandering aimlessly across New England, that Larchmere was merely a place to which he returned, briefly, on occasion.

But that made Larchmere a touchstone. And touch-stones were important. So, for Craig McQueen, was the real truth, or a big part of it, that no place could possibly match the attraction of Larchmere? Was his fate inextrica-bly wound up with the fate of the big old house and lands?

The thought was powerful and disconcerting. He didn't want to deal with it just yet. He walked away from the water and back to his old red van.

27

Hannah, Tilda, Kat, Susan, and Adam were scattered about the sunroom, waiting out a passing thundershower. Adam was reading the financial news online. Kat was staring out at the heavily falling rain. Tilda and Susan were talking quietly.

Suddenly, Hannah tossed the local newspaper she had been glancing through onto a side table. "Hey," she said, "I've got an idea. Let's go out to dinner tonight, maybe catch some live music. All of us here, and Craig, of course."

"That sounds like a plan," Susan said. "I'm sure Bill and Ruth could use a break from us clattering around the kitchen."

"Good. How about we go to The Front Porch? I love that place. Everybody always seems to be having such a good time. The fun is catching."

"Like a cold," Adam muttered, eyes still on the screen of his laptop.

"What's The Front Porch?" Kat asked, turning from the window and its dreary view.

"It's a very popular restaurant and piano bar. You must

have seen it on your way to Larchmere. It's right on the corner of Main and Beach Street. A big white building, smack in the center of town."

Kat nodded. "Sure. Piano bars are fun. I haven't been to one in a long time, not since college, I think."

"Me, neither," Susan said. "Let's do it."

"That place is far too loud," Adam said.

"Not on the first floor, in the dining rooms. And the food is very good."

Adam snapped shut his computer and sneered. "According to who? Look, piano bars are just excuses for a bunch of pathetic people to make asses of themselves singing show tunes off key. Why don't we go to Arrows? I'll call and see if we can get a reservation. That or MC Perkins Cove."

Hannah laughed. "Arrows? You've got to be kidding me, Adam. Susan and I can't afford Arrows. We can barely afford MC after replacing our oven and our fridge last summer."

"I'm with Hannah," Tilda said. "I like The Front Porch. Susan does, too, and Kat should have the experience since she's going to be a regular in Ogunquit before long. Come on, Adam, be a sport. We promise we won't make you sing. It's not karaoke."

Adam sighed as if grievously put upon. "Fine, we'll go to The Front Porch. But I am not paying for Craig."

As if summoned—or maybe Adam had caught a glimpse of his brother, hence his comment—Craig appeared in the doorway of the sunroom. "I'm paying for my own dinner, thanks. I just did a job for Harold, the guy with the old farmhouse on Pine Road."

"Just make sure you wear a clean shirt," Adam said, without humor. "I'm not being seen in town with someone who looks like he's been on a construction site all day."

"No worries," Craig replied jauntily. "I'm on my way to the creek with my laundry right now."

At the last minute, Kat claimed a bad headache and announced her intention to stay at Larchmere. It wasn't hard to see that she felt uncomfortable with her fiancé's family. Tilda could hardly blame her. Though he easily could have joined his siblings, Adam drove himself into town, leaving Hannah and Susan to ferry Tilda and Craig in their serviceable Subaru.

Tilda was wearing beige linen pants, a lime green T-shirt, and a light, beige cotton sweater. She had thought about draping a scarf around her neck—she had brought one to Larchmere, a gift from her children—but rejected the idea. She didn't have the flair for scarves her mother had had. Hannah wore chinos, and a classic Levi's jean jacket over a black T-shirt, and Susan had on an ankle-length, bright aqua summer dress with silver sandals and silver bangles around her wrist. With her tanned skin and dark hair Susan looked exotic, more obviously sexy than the other two women. Tilda thought that Craig looked jaunty in a French blue, Oxford style shirt, sleeves rolled up and open at the neck, worn out over jeans. Adam, who had never approved of his brother's sartorial choices, wore a white dress shirt under a navy blazer, gray dress slacks, and shiny black shoes.

Traffic stopped them in front of a new nightspot on Shore Road, a place called Accent. Hannah, Susan, and Craig were debating the relative benefits of some new computer technology. Tilda, seated behind Hannah, and not interested in the conversation, looked out the window. Accent was small but the open-air deck in front was packed with people in their twenties and thirties. Not a family joint, she noted, and just as she was about to turn away, she thought she spotted a familiar face at a table by the front railing. Tilda peered more closely and carefully. Oh, yes. It was Kat! She was leaning across the table, talking to a young, handsome man, someone clearly closer to her age than Adam was. In front of her on the table stood a frosty, bright pink cocktail. She watched as Kat tossed her long blond hair over her shoulder and laughed.

"Damn traffic!" Hannah complained. "Damn tourists!"

But Tilda didn't mind being stuck. She wanted to watch her brother's fiancée, who must have slipped out of Larchmere just seconds after they had gone. But how had she gotten into town? Cabs were virtually nonexistent in Ogunquit! Had someone arranged to pick her up? Transportation was only part of the mystery.

Tilda frowned. Did Kat want to be caught, if indeed she was doing something wrong, and it certainly looked like she was doing something wrong? When you claimed a sick headache, you stayed home. You didn't go out, dressed in a cleavage-bearing, figure-hugging mini-dress, and sit chatting and sipping a cocktail with a man not your fiancé! Tilda fought an urge to tap on Craig's arm, point in Kat's direction, be sure someone else witnessed the scene. But she fought that urge. Adam and Kat's relationship was none of her business. And for all Tilda knew, the guy with whom Kat was chatting was her cousin or an old, platonic friend who had called her cell, found out they were both in town, and arranged a reunion. It was unlikely, but it was possible. Wasn't it?

The car rolled forward, slowly. "Freakin' finally," Hannah muttered. Tilda kept her mouth shut as they left Kat behind.

They met Adam in the restaurant. Tilda scanned his face for a sign that he had seen his fiancée on the deck at Accent, but Adam's expression was its usual slightly harried or annoyed one. If Adam were truly angry, everyone would know.

They were shown to their table (Adam complained about its location but there were no other tables available for at least a half hour) and Craig excused himself to visit the men's room.

He was making his way through the bar area and back to the table when a tall, slightly overweight woman in a low-cut floral top with pretty, long dark hair blocked his path. She was not unattractive. Craig smiled and made to move aside but the woman blocked him again.

"Excuse me," Craig said. He wondered if she was a little drunk, maybe unsteady on her feet.

"You're Craig McQueen," the woman said.

"Yeah," he said. "I'm sorry, do I know you?"

The woman's eyes, which were fixed down on him, seemed to grow darker. "Think hard."

For a moment, Craig continued to draw a blank. But then, as he looked at the woman, some tiny bit of recollection began to tickle at his brain, the vaguely familiar shape of her very dark eyes, and he said, "Mary." And then, "Vermont. What was the name of that town? Yeah, Green River. Wow. It was a long time ago. How've you been?"

"You said you'd call me when you got back into town."

Had he said that? He really didn't remember. It had to have been at least eight years since he had seen this woman. Mary. "I never did get back to Green River," he said honestly.

"You had my number." The woman's voice was tight, angry. "You could have called to tell me you weren't coming back."

Why, he thought, *would I have done that? I knew her for about two weeks and then we had a one-night stand.* No commitment, no promises. Other than the one he didn't remember making, the one about calling.

"I'm sorry," he said. There was no point in arguing his

case. He couldn't imagine why she had wanted to stop him and talk.

"You should be. You got me pregnant."

Craig's mouth went dry. "We used condoms," he said automatically. Had they? That was something else he couldn't quite remember. Was anyone in the bar listening to this horrible conversation?

The woman, Mary, laughed unpleasantly. "Well, they didn't work. I had to borrow money from my sister to have an abortion. I had no way to find you and no job, so there was no way I could have had the baby. I was a mess and it was all your fault!"

Could he believe her? He wasn't sure. He had hardly known her all those years ago. He hadn't even known her last name. Maybe she was lying now as a sort of revenge for his having left her. There was no way he would ever know for sure. He felt sick to his stomach. He felt ashamed.

"I'm sorry," he said. "I don't know what else to say."

"There is nothing else to say. Except, screw you."

And then she—Mary Something or Other—was gone into the crowd at the far end of the bar. Craig wondered if her boyfriend or husband was going to emerge next, to pop him in the nose. But an abortion as a result of a one-night stand was hardly the kind of thing a woman was likely to reveal to the new man in her life.

Craig couldn't move for a moment. He wanted to sneak off on his own but he knew that if he did Tilda would be upset with him. He didn't want to be responsible for disappointing another woman. He made his way back to the table and took a seat.

"Why the long face?" Adam asked. "Did you find out it's illegal to panhandle in downtown Ogunquit?"

"Something like that," he said quietly, and picked up the menu the waiter had left for him.

They ordered from their waiter, a young gay man whose name was Rob and who told them he had come from New Jersey to work for the summer before starting college. After a wait that Adam declared far too long, the meals arrived. Adam sent his fish back, claiming it was overcooked. Maybe it was, Tilda thought. But maybe it wasn't. Adam liked people to know he was in the room. (Rob was professionally gracious about it.) Tilda enjoyed her pasta primavera. Craig, usually a voracious eater, left half of his meal on the plate. Hannah and Susan, who had each gotten the pork chop with mashed potatoes, announced themselves pleased.

Conversation during the meal was light and noncommittal. Tilda allowed herself to think that the night was, indeed, going to be declared a complete success. (Barring the strange absence of Kat.) In fact, it wasn't until coffee and dessert had been served (none for Adam, just coffee for Craig) that the tensions always flowing just under the surface of the relationship between Susan and Adam began to rise. Wine had been consumed, as had predinner cocktails. *I should have known,* Tilda thought. *Don't tempt fate with assumptions of happy endings. Especially not when alcohol is involved.*

Susan had been tapping her coffee spoon against her cup for about thirty seconds when abruptly, and apropos of nothing they had been discussing, she turned to Adam. "You know," she said, "I haven't forgotten that you blew off our wedding."

Hannah's eyes widened in surprise and, Tilda thought, concern.

Adam shrugged. "I showed up at the reception."

"But you missed the ceremony," Susan pointed out. "The ceremony is the most important part of the celebration."

Tilda agreed but this was not her argument. She sipped her coffee and took another bite of the crème brûlée.

Adam sighed. "Look, I had to work. I'm not going to apologize for my career. Some things just take precedence over others."

"A few bucks take precedence over your sister's wedding?"

"Susan, it really doesn't—"

But Hannah's attempt at calming her wife was rejected.

"No, Hannah, he should take responsibility for his actions in this family. Really, Adam, it was very disrespectful, not only of your sister but also of our union." Susan looked at the others for confirmation. "Am I right?" she asked.

Again, Tilda agreed with Susan but, fearing Adam's wrath being turned against her, only murmured something unintelligible. Hannah, also clearly unwilling to add to the argument, gave a quick nod. Craig, usually the first one to take the side of anyone fighting against Adam, was oddly silent and unresponsive. In fact, Tilda thought he seemed to be miles away, toying with his napkin, looking vaguely at nothing.

"Well," Susan prodded, her voice raised, "am I?"

Tilda was increasingly uncomfortable with the situation. She wondered if she should finally say something to end the argument—but what?—when Adam's hand hit the table with a thud that made her coffee spoon rattle against her cup. Tilda shot a look around but no one at neighboring tables seemed to have noticed Adam's display of temper. Everyone but the McQueens seemed to be having a good time.

"Look," Adam hissed, eyes fixed on Susan, "I've had enough of this. We are not having a scene in public. Everyone in this town knows the McQueens. They respect us.

There's a certain decorum we keep. So keep your voice down."

In one swift move, he drew his wallet from his back pocket, tossed some cash onto the table, and stood. He did-n't say good-bye to the others.

Tilda watched him weave his way out of the main dining room, wondering how he reconciled slamming his hand on the table with not making a scene. She found herself hop-ing that Kat got back to the house before Adam did. It was odd to feel more loyalty to a virtual stranger than to her own brother, her own flesh and blood. It was upsetting.

Rob the waiter appeared (tactfully, he had stayed away from the table during the heated argument), and they paid the bill. Tilda put in an extra five dollars for Rob's tip (she had waited tables in college and knew how depressing and difficult the job could be) and she and Craig walked out to the car, followed a few minutes later by Hannah and Susan, who had stopped in the ladies' room before the drive home.

Hannah took Susan's hand. "Well, that was a bad idea," she said. "What was I thinking?"

"I'm sorry. I didn't mean to let fly at Adam like that. I guess my anger's just been building."

"Oh, Adam can take it. It's my fault, really. I feel like such a fool. Why did I suggest we all hang out together like normal people?"

"Only Adam causes problems," Susan rightly pointed out. "Tilda and Craig aren't troublemakers."

"No. But what was up with Craig tonight? When he came back from the men's room he looked like he'd seen a ghost or something. He hardly said a word after that."

"Ssshh. They'll hear us."

Hannah and Susan and Craig and Tilda climbed into the car and drove back to Larchmere in weary silence.

28

Tuesday, July 24

There was another newly or about to be wed couple on the beach that morning. This bride, older than the other Tilda had seen, and fashionably slight, wore a slinky ice blue satin sheath. Her groom, also middle-aged, wore a navy suit, expertly cut. Tilda guessed that they had money. The photographer, whose hair was a flamboyant orange, was calling out directions to the couple. They moved and posed as if professional models. Tilda wondered if people took lessons in posing for their wedding pictures. People took dancing lessons for the wedding reception. Why not lessons in assuring beautiful photographs?

She began her walk to the Wells town line, and left the couple and their photographer behind. Since when, she wondered, had Ogunquit become a wedding destination? She thought that it probably always had been a wedding destination but that, given her relatively new status as widow, she was now hyperaware of the presence of summer brides.

Tilda had been thinking a lot about weddings and marriage and, in particular, about wives. There was a Hebrew proverb that said, "Whosoever findeth a wife findeth a good thing." She had been thinking a lot about that.

What did it really mean to be a wife in today's culture, in the United States in the early twenty-first century? Did the role of "wife" have any validity? Well, so much had changed, and mostly for the better. Now both Hannah and Susan could be a wife, a legally recognized entity with rights and responsibilities and public standing. But Tilda wondered if marriage itself was really necessary any longer.

No. Well, maybe for some it was, those who followed a religious system that required—or strongly urged—women to marry. But for those for whom marriage was not an economic or religious necessity, was it still preferable to the other options? It seemed that it might be. Marriage brought with it social privileges. It shouldn't still be that way but it was. Marriage meant respectability. No matter what the sordid or boring truth was behind the closed door of the married couple's home, the fact that they were legally married conferred upon them greater status than that afforded to single people.

Married people were offered discounts on everything from car insurance to vacation packages. Single people, no matter what the reason for their single state, were considered less stable and mature and successful than married people. Two was better than one. It was ridiculous and unfair but that was the way it was.

When she was married, when Frank was alive, Tilda had never once given any thought to the plight of the single person—widowed, divorced, living alone by choice or by chance. She hadn't passed judgments; she just never had given the position of the single person a thought. She was a bit ashamed of that now, ashamed of her lack of concern or interest in everyone "else" or "other." Had she been one of those self-satisfied, even smug people, who simply failed to empathize with those in a situation not her own? She was afraid that she might have been.

At the Wells town line, Tilda turned and began the walk back to the parking lot. Along the way she ran into Nancy Brown, Ogunquit's librarian. She and her partner, Glenda, had been at the recent party at Larchmere.

"Oh, did you see the bride?" she cried, rushing up to Tilda and grabbing her arm. "The one in the pale blue dress?"

"Yes," Tilda said. "I did."

"Oh, isn't she exquisite! I honestly don't think I've ever seen a more beautiful bride in my entire life. I really don't!"

Tilda extricated her arm from Nancy's grip and forced a smile. "Yes," she said, "she is lovely. But I really must be getting home now. Give my love to Glenda."

Nancy continued on toward Wells and Tilda walked rapidly back to her car, eager to be at Larchmere. The bride and groom were gone. Just before getting behind the wheel she scanned the sky. Nothing.

Tilda was sitting at the kitchen bar drinking a cup of tea and leafing through a catalogue of out-of-print books. With a pen she was marking off books she might like to buy. It would all depend, in the end, on money. Still, it was fun to dream about owning rare first editions and peculiar books long out of print. She made a mental note to visit Cunningham Books when she got back to Portland, a wonderful bookshop at Longfellow Square that sold old and rare books.

Footsteps—the sound of high heels—alerted her to the fact that someone had come into the kitchen. Tilda turned.

Kat stopped midstride. "Oh. Hi," she said. "I'm just getting something to drink."

Tilda thought Kat sounded embarrassed, almost guilty, for being in the kitchen when someone else was there. As if she were invading McQueen territory.

"Sure, of course," Tilda said. "There's some iced tea in a pitcher in the fridge if you'd like. Ruth made it earlier."

"I'll just have water. But thanks."

Kat went to the sink, where there was a water filter, and poured a glass.

"So," Tilda ventured, "how long have you and Adam known each other?" *If Kat is going to be my sister-in-law,* she thought, *I really should try to know more about her. I don't even know if she has brothers or sisters.*

Kat smiled and took a seat at the bar. Tilda thought she might be grateful for Tilda's interest in her life.

"We met at a networking event about a year ago," she said. "He didn't call me for a while and I was pretty upset, because I really liked him. But when he did call we started seeing each other all the time. And after a few months he proposed. I couldn't believe my luck. I still can't!"

Well, Tilda thought, here was a woman who seemed to be marrying not for economic or religious reasons. Here was a woman who was marrying for love. "It's a lovely ring," she said. It was lovely, if a bit ostentatious for Tilda's taste.

Kat held out her left hand and admired the platinum and diamond monster on it. "I know. I absolutely love it. There are three carats total. All my friends are jealous, even the ones who are already married."

Adam had to make a statement, Tilda thought, had to be the biggest and the best. Well, if it made him happy to conquer, or, at least, to think he had conquered, then so be it. Tilda's mind flashed again on the young man with whom Kat had been having cocktails the night of the Front Porch expedition and wondered if Adam had, indeed, really conquered in this case.

"I'm sure the ring is insured," Tilda said, and then wondered why. Adam's insurance was none of her business.

"Oh, yeah. Adam won't tell me what it's worth, exactly, but I know it has to be a lot!"

Tilda only nodded, not knowing what else to add to the subject of the ring.

"We're going to have a family, you know," Kat said suddenly. "Adam promised we'd start trying to get pregnant just after the wedding."

"Oh," Tilda said. She was taken aback. The idea that Adam might want more children had never occurred to her. She had just assumed he was marrying again for the trophy aspect of it. She tried to sound enthusiastic and believing. "That's very nice," she said.

Would Kat be one of those sexy pregnant women who showed their belly in skintight tops, one of those women who continued to wear heels well into the third trimester? Of course she would. Tilda felt oddly jealous, again. During her pregnancies she had taken to wearing Frank's shirts over stretch maternity pants. They were comfortable and concealing. She had not looked sexy.

"Yeah," Kat was saying. "I've always really wanted kids—I'm an only child—but I really wanted to have a career first, you know? But when I have my first baby, that's it, I'm done, I'm staying home."

"And Adam understands what you want?" The question was out before Tilda realized that it probably shouldn't have been asked.

Kat looked surprised at the question. "Sure. I think so. I mean, I talked to him about it."

"Oh. Then he must know what you're expecting. That's good." Again, Tilda had meant to sound reassuring but was afraid she had failed. Kat's face was registering big doubt.

"Yes," she said, her eyes flickering away from Tilda.

"I'm sure he understands." There was a moment of silence and then Kat said, "Well, I should be going."

She left the kitchen in a hurry, brushing past Hannah, who was on her way in. Hannah looked at her sister inquiringly.

"Well, I just had an awkward conversation."

"I'm guessing it was with Kat."

"Yes, it was with Kat." Tilda lowered her voice. "She told me that she's planning on getting pregnant right after the wedding. And that Adam is fine with the idea of starting another family."

Hannah's expression tightened. "He should not be having more children," she declared. "He's barely a father to the ones he's already got."

"But Kat has a right to children of her own," Tilda said.

"Of course. All I'm saying is that she might want to choose a different father. Someone who actually gives a damn."

"Oh, I think Adam loves his children. I just think he didn't realize they would be so much work."

"What kind of a person has kids without accepting the full responsibility of their care?" Hannah asked rhetorically. "A selfish, irresponsible person, that's what kind of person."

Hannah's voice rose as she spoke. She was visibly angry. Tilda's imagination made a sudden leap. She thought that by talking about bad or inadequate parents her sister might be referring not only to their brother, but also to her own fears of being a bad or inadequate parent. Was that the real reason she had been putting off making a decision to start a family?

It didn't feel like something she could ask about, not yet, anyway. "The children don't seem to be suffering," she pointed out. "And Sarah makes up for so much. She's a wonderful mother."

"Be that as it may," Hannah replied, "I just don't believe that Adam should be having more kids. For that matter, I don't believe that he even wants more kids. I think he's lying to Kat, stringing her along. Oh, he'll marry her, but then he'll find all sorts of excuses why they shouldn't start a family. By then, she'll be totally in his thrall. And if she tries to divorce him, he'll threaten to leave her with nothing."

"You really think he's lying to her?" Tilda asked. "Well, of course, it's a possibility. Adam lies. But about something as big as wanting another family?"

"Yes, I think he's lying."

Tilda sighed. "Well, I guess I think so, too. I feel awful about this, Hannah, but I kind of hinted—very subtly—to Kat that she might want to make extra sure he means what he says."

"Don't feel awful. Women need to protect each other."

"But Adam is my brother."

"Adam," Hannah said, "isn't a very nice person."

29

It was later that day, before dinner, and Hannah was stretched out on the bed in the room she shared with Susan. It was decorated much the same as was the room Tilda occupied, with the exception that the watercolors on the walls depicted pines and oaks and maples throughout the four seasons, and not seashells. Above the bed was a large framed quilt, all subtle colors and hues, which Charlotte had bought at an auction. Hannah had never understood why they had not been allowed to actually use the quilt. After all, it had been made as a practical item, something to keep a person warm on cold winter nights. But even now, ten years after her mother's death, Hannah would never dream of taking the quilt down from the wall.

Hannah yawned. She felt unaccountably tired. She felt that if she fell asleep now she would sleep through the night. She knew she should get up soon and change for dinner. Her clothes were rumpled and slightly sweaty. There was a fan on the dresser but she felt too lazy to get up and turn it on. She continued to lie there, almost motionless. This, she thought, is lassitude.

The door to the bedroom opened and Susan came in. She shut the door behind her.

"Hey," Hannah said.

"Hey yourself. What's going on?"

Hannah wanted to tell Susan that Adam claimed—through Kat—that he wanted more children. There was no reason to hide the information from her wife. But any mention of children would, inevitably, lead to another no doubt fruitless discussion about starting their own family and Hannah, recently feeling very cowardly, did not want to talk.

"Nothing," she said.

Susan sat on the bed next to Hannah. She lowered her voice when she spoke. "I was wondering," she said, "has anyone said anything to you about Larchmere? I mean, about what's going to happen to it when Bill . . ."

"I don't want to think about my father dying," Hannah said quickly, sitting up against the pillows. "It makes me very uncomfortable. He's always been my anchor, you know that. I don't like to imagine life without him."

"Of course you don't," Susan said. "But someday he will be gone. He's going to leave Larchmere to one of his children. It's only smart to think ahead in case you turn out to be the heir. And if you are the heir, naturally, that affects the both of us."

Hannah nodded. "Of course. I know. But please, could we not talk about it right yet? Please? I promise we'll talk soon. When we get back home. Not here."

Susan sighed. Hannah wondered just how much more putting off she was going to tolerate.

"All right. When we get back to South Portland then." Susan got off the bed. "Dinner is at seven, don't forget. Ruth and I are making a seafood stew." And then she was gone.

Hannah slid down again until she was prone on the bed. Inheriting Larchmere. Until this week, until learning of her father's romance, the idea had never even occurred to her. Why? she wondered. Why hadn't she ever thought about what would happen to the family home when her father died?

Well, she thought now, *what if Dad does want me to have Larchmere? What then?* How could she ever afford to keep such a huge house and estate? She would have to steal Adam's idea and convert the house into a bed and breakfast just to pay for basic maintenance. But if she did that she would need financing. No bank would lend her all the money she would need. She might have to consider asking her aunt to be a business partner. And that would be tricky. Hannah figured that Ruth might have some money tucked away, but she would not want to put her aunt on the spot. True, Ruth was tough enough to say no to a request she didn't want to fulfill, but still . . . asking for money, even a loan, from a family member, was scary. She thought she knew why even Craig, who was always short of cash, didn't do it.

Hannah sat up again, restless. Of course, she thought, running a bed and breakfast might mean having to live in Ogunquit year round, as neither she nor Susan had a taste (or the money) for a winter home in Florida, where many Ogunquit residents went for the worst of the winter months.

And they so loved their life in Portland! There were the museums and galleries and the great bookstores like Longfellow and Cunningham, all within walking distance of their home. What would they do if they couldn't have dinner every Wednesday evening at the Pub, with all the other regulars she and Susan had gotten to know and love? And the Sea Dogs! Hannah would not be happy without easy access to the Sea Dogs' games. And Ogunquit off-season was so deadly quiet; Hannah really didn't know if she could handle it. And what about her job? Would she have to quit (and then where would their health insurance come from!) or would she be able to maintain basically two careers? And what about Susan's career? She absolutely loved her work in social services. Sure, they could commute to Portland daily—they knew someone who did just that—but commuting was a physical as well as a financial strain. It would mean they would need a second car, a backup, and that was yet another expense.

Hannah got up from the bed and went to the window. A massive blue jay was perched on a branch of an oak tree, screaming his unpleasant scream. She thought of screaming children and of that family she had seen in Kittery, the little girls being dragged along, the mother massively pregnant. She thought of the big issue looming in her life: the notion of having a baby in the near future. She and Susan had agreed they wanted to raise a child in an urban environment, not tiny little Ogunquit no matter how beautiful and serene.

Hannah sighed. She loved Larchmere but she really hoped that Tilda inherited the house. It would make things so much easier for Hannah and Susan. Their lives wouldn't be totally disrupted. But she doubted that Tilda could afford the ownership and upkeep of a house the size of Larchmere, either. What then? Only Adam—and maybe Ruth—had the money to take over the responsibility of the estate without having to resort to drastic measures. Ruth didn't want Larchmere. Adam wanted it for all the wrong reasons.

It was all a muddle. The only thing Hannah did know for sure was that if her father did leave Larchmere to her, there was no way she would reject the gift—and there was no way she would ever sell the house. She felt enormous gratitude toward her father for being the supportive parent he had always been, especially in light of her mother's indifference. She believed that it was her duty as a grateful daughter to accept any responsibility he chose to give her.

But how would Susan deal with the privilege—and the burden—of Larchmere? Hannah wondered if she would be forced to prioritize, to choose what was more important: her own life with Susan, her wife, or the maintenance of her family's physical legacy. The question frightened her.

Slowly, she turned from the window and went to take a shower.

"Did Sarah finish that degree she was going for? What was it, a master's in management?"

Craig and Adam were in the kitchen. Craig was brewing a pot of tea. He had a sudden craving for Lapsang souchong, with its heavily smoky flavor, which was odd because he usually preferred to drink Lapsang souchong in the fall and winter. Adam was mixing some sort of protein shake. It was a bright, acid green. Craig shuddered. He was all for healthy eating but he preferred to chew his calories. And he preferred them to be colors found in nature.

Adam looked surprised. "How would I know? I don't talk with her about anything other than the kids. I've got enough on my plate."

Craig was shocked. He knew he shouldn't be—he knew what his brother was like—but he was. "How can you just ignore someone you were married to?" he said. "She's the mother of your children. Don't you care even a little about her as a person?"

"Who are you to talk?" Adam shot back. "You've never made a commitment to a woman in your life."

"Maybe so." Craig thought of the woman from Vermont, Mary, and cringed a little. "But at least I didn't dump my hardworking wife for a woman twelve years her junior.

Come on, Adam, your divorce was a classic midlife crisis thing. It's pretty lame stuff. It's been done to death."

Adam glared at his brother. "You know nothing about the circumstances of my divorce. No one does. Except Sarah, of course. And my lawyers."

Craig was not intimidated. "Have you told Kat how you refused to give up half of your CD collection, even though Sarah is the music lover? Or about the time you keyed that car—what was it, the one Sarah got in the divorce—so that she couldn't get its full worth when she sold it?"

"My past is none of Kat's business," Adam said. His voice was cold.

"She's going to be your wife. You have to be honest with her." And, Craig wondered, if Kat knew the entire, gritty truth, would she still want to be Adam's wife?

"Selective honesty is all that's required in this situation. I don't need to know every minor little detail of Kat's past. In fact, I'd rather not."

"As long as her credit is good, right?" Craig laughed. "Don't want to be responsible for someone else's debts."

"Her credit is impeccable."

"Did you check for a criminal past as well?"

"Of course. She's clean."

"And she's hot."

Adam shrugged. "What's wrong with that? It doesn't hurt my professional image to have a beautiful, well-dressed wife."

"You're a caricature," Craig said. "Straight out of central casting for middle-aged male panicking over the loss of his youth and virility."

"My virility," Adam replied coldly, "has never been an issue."

Craig smirked. "I'm not sure I'd go around admitting that."

"Grow up, Craig."

Craig put down his cup of tea, untasted. "Why are you even bothering to get married again?" he persisted. "Doesn't the single life suit you better? Or is this new marriage all about appearance? It doesn't look good for a guy in your professional position to be footloose and fancy-free, does it? You need to look respectable, dependable, like a politician, get yourself a wife, go to church on Sundays. Marriage makes sense for someone like you."

Adam slammed his almost empty glass on the bar top. "Someone like me? Oh, right, you mean someone who accepts responsibility for his actions. Someone who has a career, someone who pays his bills. Someone who's not living in a disgusting, rust-ridden van at the age of forty. Someone who has some real value in the world, someone who contributes to society. You might think I'm worthless, Craig, but I'm the one paying taxes. I'm the one contributing to charities. I'm the one raising children. When was the last time you voted? Wait, I bet you're not even registered to vote! When was the last time you showed up for a town meeting? Oh, wait, you'd actually have to live in the town to go to its meetings."

Craig was silenced.

Adam laughed. "That's right. Got nothing to say to that, do you? Talk to me when you get a life." Adam, leaving his empty glass on the bar top, picked up his laptop and left the room.

Craig slumped onto a stool. He felt shaken. He felt badly that things had gotten so heated. He acknowledged that he had spoken with unnecessary ill intent. He also acknowledged that some of Adam's criticisms, some of his charges, while harsh, were also valid.

What was his value in the world? Did anybody need him, did anybody want him around? Well, Tilda needed him but that need wasn't entirely healthy. Could a person have value when he lived isolated from human responsibil-

ity? Well, yes, life itself was sacred, Craig thought he believed that, but . . . Wasn't a life of service to others more
valuable than a life of—of what? Avoidance?

Not for the first time Craig wondered if he was even
serving himself by the way he was living his life. Was he a
selfish person? No, he didn't think that he was. Not selfish,
not really, not grasping or greedy at all. A shirker. Maybe
that's what he was, a shirker of responsibility, a shirker of
duty. You couldn't be proud of being a shirker.

His father, Bill, wasn't a shirker. Neither was Bobby,
nor Teddy, for that matter. Frank had been one of the most
responsible guys Craig had ever known. Those men were
brave. He respected them all. They all were deserving of
respect.

The question for Craig was, was he?

Craig dumped the now cold tea down the sink, washed
his cup and his brother's glass, and went out to his old red
van. *Maybe,* he thought, *this is where I really do belong.*

30

It was about an hour after his confrontation with Craig and Adam was in the sunroom, his laptop open in front of him. His face wore a frown of concentration.

Kat knew it was not the best time to bring up an important topic, not while Adam was working—which he almost always was—but she felt as if she might burst if she didn't talk to him soon. Her earlier conversation with Tilda about her and Adam starting a family was weighing on her. She needed to be reassured. Adam had sworn he wanted more kids but maybe, just maybe, he had lied about that in order to . . . She could hardly think the words.

"Adam?" she said.

"Mmm."

"Are you busy?" It was a stupid question. Obviously he was busy.

Adam didn't answer. Kat perched on the chair next to him. "I just wanted you to know that I'm really glad we're going to try to get pregnant right after the wedding."

"Mmmm."

"I mean, I'm not getting any younger!" Kat laughed a

little nervously and fought an urge to bite a fingernail, something she had not done since she was eleven.

Adam finally looked up from his laptop. He never went anywhere without his laptop and iPhone. He was a very plugged-in person.

"I'm sorry," he said, with a vague smile. "I wasn't really paying attention. What were you saying?"

Kat swallowed hard. She still got a thrill when she looked at his beautiful, strangely colored eyes. Right then they were bright green. He was such a handsome man. His jaw was so firm. She spoke with some difficulty. "I was saying that I'm glad we're going to start a family right away, once we get married. Like we talked about."

Adam shifted in his seat and crossed one leg over the other. He looked somehow professorial. "Yeah, about that," he said. "I've been thinking and, really, what's the rush? You're young and I'm in great health. These days, women can safely have kids at forty and fifty, no problem."

Kat folded her hands and squeezed them together in her lap. *Oh, God,* she thought, *this can't be happening.* "But I thought you said—"

"I'm sure I meant whatever I said at the time I said it." His tone was a bit impatient. "But I've thought more about the whole kid thing and I just don't think it's a great idea for us to rush into it. Don't you want to spend some time alone together before we start schlepping to doctors and changing diapers and getting up at all hours every night to deal with a screaming baby? Believe me, I've been there and it isn't a hell of a lot of fun."

Kat didn't reply. She couldn't, not then, anyway. She didn't want to fight; she didn't feel angry. She felt slightly sick to her stomach. Sick, and disbelieving. They had talked about private schools. They had talked about how best to save for college. She had made a list of names she liked, for boys and for girls. She had thought she would write a mommy blog and make some personal spending money. She had told her parents and though they had reservations about her marrying a man of fifty, they were happy about the prospect of being grandparents.

"And come on," Adam said now, "what about your job? You've got a nice little career going. You don't want to jeopardize it by taking maternity leave, not until you've moved up the ladder a bit and are really invaluable. Not in this economy, anyway. Quitting now would be stupid."

Kat's head began to buzz and her stomach felt all jumpy, almost as if she was going to faint. She had only fainted once, right after giving blood at a drive, but she remembered very clearly how it had felt just before she had lost consciousness. "Yes," she managed to say. "The economy is bad."

Adam smiled indulgently, the smile of the victor very used to being the victor. "Look, I'm sorry, honey, but I've got to get back to this document. Maybe we'll drive down to Blue Sky this evening for a drink, okay? You can wear that nice dress I got you, the black one with the skinny straps. Just think. If you were pregnant you wouldn't be able to wear it! Or have a cocktail!"

Kat left the sunroom. She wasn't sure that Adam had even noticed her leaving.

It was later in the afternoon. Adam had gone out to meet an old friend for a drink; he promised he would be back in an hour or so. Kat made sure he was gone before she sought out Tilda. She found her in the sunroom, with Hannah. She hesitated at the door. She liked Tilda and she was pretty sure that Tilda liked her. But Hannah made her a little nervous. She wasn't quite sure why.

"Kat, hi." Tilda smiled and gestured for her to join them.

Kat summoned her nerve. *What the hell,* she thought. *The McQueens are going to be my family before long. Or, I'll never see them again after this week.*

"I hope I'm not bothering you," she said, taking a chair.

Hannah shook her head. "No. We were just plotting to take over the world. Nothing major."

Kat managed a small smile.

"What is it, Kat?" Tilda asked, her voice kind.

Kat shot a look at Hannah before beginning. "Do you remember what we talked about, in the kitchen? About Adam and I starting a family?"

Tilda nodded. "Of course."

Again Kat felt that awful, old urge to bite her nails. Instead, she clasped her hands tightly together in her lap. "Well, I got to thinking and . . . I mentioned it again to Adam, earlier today."

Tilda knew exactly what poor Kat was going to tell them. "And what did he say?" she asked gently. Out of the corner of her eye she thought she could see Hannah frowning.

"He told me he thought we should wait a few years before starting a family. He told me he'd thought it all through and he didn't think we should be in a rush. He said I'd put my career at risk by having a baby now."

"And what did you tell him?" Tilda asked, masking, she hoped, her supreme annoyance with her brother. "Did you tell him you don't care about your career as much as you care about having a family? Like you told me?"

Kat closed her eyes for a moment. "I told him . . ." She opened her eyes and cleared her throat. "It's embarrassing. I didn't really say anything. I guess I just was—noncommittal."

"You were upset. You were taken by surprise. That's okay."

"Are kids a deal breaker for you?" Hannah asked, leaning forward toward Kat. It was a tough question for her to ask. She dreaded the question being asked of Susan. She believed Susan would stay with her no matter what, but the thought of Susan's giving up something so meaningful to her for the sake of her wife made Hannah feel awful.

"I don't know," Kat replied. "I think so. I love Adam but . . . but he promised we would have a family. God, I'm already thirty-two! If I wait too much longer I—"

Hannah interrupted her. "If you acquiesce to Adam and delay getting pregnant and then in two or three years he's still putting you off, what then? Do you want to have to go through a divorce and start looking for Mr. Right all over again? You could be forty by the time you meet someone special, forty-two or -three by the time you're ready to have a baby with him."

"Hannah! Don't—"

"I'm just being honest here, Tilda. She should seriously reconsider this marriage. Now, before she wastes any more time." Oh, God, Hannah thought, did that mean she believed that Susan should reconsider her commitment to her . . . ?

Kat stood abruptly. "I'm sorry. Adam is your brother. I should never have involved you, either of you."

"It's all right," Tilda said with what she hoped was an encouraging smile. "Don't apologize. Talk to your girlfriends, Kat. Hannah is right. You have to believe in what you want from your life."

With a weak smile in return, Kat left the sunroom. Tilda's maternal instincts had been aroused and she thought about how terribly young and vulnerable Kat had seemed. She wondered what Kat's parents had to say about their daughter's impending marriage. She suspected she would never know.

"Are we being horrible people, trying to break up the engagement of our own brother?" Tilda asked her sister.

Hannah sat back and sighed. "We've been through this

already. We're not trying to break anyone up. We're simply encouraging a young woman to think for herself. And hoping she dumps the loser."

"Hannah, don't. We really don't know what goes on between those two. Maybe Adam really and truly loves her." *And if he does really and truly love her,* Tilda thought, *then why had Kat snuck out for a private meeting with another man?*

"Think what you like, Pollyanna. If it were ethically acceptable I'd pay her to leave him."

"Since when do you hate Adam? I always thought you two got along."

"We did. We do. Sort of. It's just that I think he's all wrong for that girl."

"Young woman," Tilda corrected.

"Whatever. Call it intuition. And now he's trying to back out of a major promise!" The moment Hannah spoke those words, she felt it again—that awful, cringing guilt and glaring self-awareness. Was she the proverbial pot calling the proverbial kettle black? When was she going to make good on her promise to Susan to have a family?

Hannah rose abruptly.

"Are you okay?" Tilda asked.

"Yeah, fine. I just need to stretch my legs."

Hannah left the house and walked swiftly down the driveway to Shore Road. And then she began to run.

31

It was early evening. Tilda was reading on the front porch when her father drove up to the house. She watched as he got out of the car, shouldered his golf bag, which had been in the trunk, and climbed the porch stairs. He set his golf bag against the railing. He was back from a game with Teddy.

"Should I bother to ask?"

"No," he said. "You can rely on past experience." He sat heavily in the chair next to Tilda's.

Tilda grinned. "That bad. Why do you continue to play?"

Bill shrugged. "I like golf. I don't have to be good at it to like it. And Teddy puts up with me. Even though I'm no competition whatsoever."

"Mom was pretty good, wasn't she? At least, I remember her as being good."

"She was a good golfer, yes. But she wasn't really interested in the game. It just came naturally to her, I guess. It was the same with tennis. She never took a lesson and yet she was the star of her college team."

Yes, Tilda's mother had been, to a great extent, a natural

athlete. She golfed, she played tennis, she swam, she sailed. But in Hannah's opinion Charlotte had overestimated her athletic skills. Maybe she had, but Tilda really didn't think so. The sisters' memories of Charlotte would always differ. To Tilda, and she guessed, to Adam, Charlotte was golden. To Hannah, she was brass. And what was she to Craig, Tilda wondered. Rust?

"What did you do with Frank's clubs?" Bill asked.

"They're in the garage. Jon might want them someday."

Jon was good at sports. Jane, like her mother, had no interest in sports whatsoever. Frank had been more of an armchair athlete, until he had discovered boccie ball. The golf clubs had been a gift from Charlotte and he had used them only rarely.

"I think you should get married again, Tilda," her father said, breaking the comfortable silence. "I don't like to see you alone. You're still so young."

Tilda was taken aback. They had never talked about her personal life before. She didn't really want to talk about it now. "I'm fine, Dad," she said. "I've got my job and the kids and you and—"

"A job doesn't give you a hug when you're feeling sad." Her father's intense blue eyes held her own. "Jon and Jane will be gone before long. And Tilda, I've got Jennifer now, and my own friends. I love you, you're my daughter, but there's a limit to what I can be for you at this point in our lives. You know that."

"Of course I know that, Dad. But lots of people are fine living alone."

"True. Your aunt lived alone for years and years and she thrived. But you're not Ruth. You should be with someone, Tilda."

Tilda felt insulted. Why should she be with someone? Because she was weak? Because she wasn't capable of living on her own?

As if he had read her thoughts, her father said, "You're a very loving and giving person. You're a caretaker. Living alone is a waste of your best gifts."

She was mollified, a little. But she didn't know what to say. Then: "I have been seeing someone, you know. He's spending a few weeks here, in Ogunquit. We've been out together a few times."

Her father nodded. "I heard about it from Teddy, who heard about it from Tessa. Lord knows whom she got the news from. I think it's a good thing, Tilda. But it's only a start. A good start, but this man isn't your next husband."

"How do you know that?" Tilda asked. She was surprised by her father's tone of certainty.

"I'm old," he said simply. "I know some things."

They were silent again for a moment and then Bill sighed and got up from his chair. "Well, I'd better go inside and get cleaned up. Think about what I said, Tilda. Oh," he added. "Your aunt is making a seafood pie for dinner. I hope you have a good appetite."

Tilda managed a small smile and nodded.

Bill had just showered and changed into fresh clothes. He came into the kitchen to find Hannah on one of the stools at the bar top. She was drinking a glass of iced tea and leafing desultorily through a magazine.

"Mind if I join you?" he said.

Hannah smiled and closed the magazine. She hated magazines, all of them, even *The New Yorker.* She found them all somehow disappointing. Why did she even bother to pick one up? "Of course not, Dad," she said. "There's iced tea, if you want some."

Bill poured himself a glass, added two teaspoons of sugar—he had a sweet tooth—and sat at the stool beside Hannah's. "I was talking to your sister earlier," he said. "I told her she should consider remarrying. I don't think she was very happy to hear my opinion."

"I know. She's struggling. She's still mourning Frank."

"Frank isn't coming back."

"She knows that, Dad. It's just hard. Well, you should know. You lost your wife. You've been through the grieving process."

"Yes."

"Anyway, she has been seeing someone. A summer visitor. I think she said he lives in Florida."

"I know." Bill smiled. "Everyone in town knows. It's a good sign, a positive step. But then he'll go back to Florida or wherever it is he lives and Tilda will be on her own again. I want her to have the courage to keep moving forward."

Hannah hesitated. She did not want to pry but she was interested. "Dad?" she said. "Before Jennifer, was there anyone else? I mean, after Mom died, of course."

"No," Bill said immediately. "Your mother was a hard act to follow. And—" Bill frowned down at his iced tea.

"And what?"

"I was a bit—tired—from that marriage." He now looked up at Hannah. "I'm not saying anything bad about Charlotte, you understand that. But, well, life with her could be a bit exhausting. And then Ruth came to live at Larchmere so soon after her death, and I didn't feel lonely like I might have, rattling around this big house on my own."

Hannah was surprised at his revelation. She knew her mother had been a difficult woman but she had never been sure her father had been fully aware of his wife's difficult nature.

"So, then what changed when you met Jennifer?" she asked.

"I don't know, exactly," Bill said. "Time had gone by.

And I was immediately drawn to her, even though she was married at the time we met. I suppose you could say I had a crush on her! I never thought she would get divorced and that we might actually have a chance together."

"So, things just sort of—happened."

"Yes. I suppose you could say that."

"That's what I told Tilda she should hope for," Hannah said. "Something to just happen, like it did with Frank. I told her it's still possible she could meet the second love of her life when she least expects to meet him. I hope I wasn't wrong to say that. What if she never does meet anyone special?"

"You weren't wrong to encourage your sister to live her life, not just sit back and watch it pass. No one can promise her happiness but she knows that."

"I wonder what Mom would tell her, if she were alive now. What do you think, Dad?" Hannah asked. "What advice would Mom give Tilda?" *And what advice would she give me?*

The question gave Bill pause. In fact, it upset him in some way. Finally, he said, "I don't think she would have had much advice to give. I don't think she would have had much sympathy, either, for Tilda's mourning. Your mother wasn't—she wasn't a terribly emotional woman. Oh, she had lots of good qualities. Just—well, being warm and fuzzy wasn't one of them."

Hannah took a sip of her tea. *Charlotte McQueen was cold. That's what you mean to say, Dad. That's what you want to say. But I understand that you can't.*

"Jennifer seems very different from Mom," she said carefully. "Aside from both being stylish."

"Yes. Jennifer is quite different."

They were silent for a moment, drinking their tea.

"You're not your mother, Hannah," Bill said suddenly. "In fact, you couldn't be less like her."

Hannah was stunned. It was as if her father had been reading her mind all this time. She didn't know what to say. Finally, she asked, "Am I like you, then?"

Bill smiled. "You're better than I am. You're braver. You've had to be. And you're a heck of a lot prettier."

Hannah laughed. "Gee, thanks, Dad!"

"Seriously, Hannah, I'm very proud of you. I hope you know that."

Hannah blinked back tears and took her father's hand in her own. "Thanks, Dad. I do know it."

32

Wednesday, July 25

Tilda had gone for her usual morning walk on the beach, and then would be visiting a yard sale in the hopes of finding some good books. Bill was playing golf with Teddy. Craig had driven off just after dawn, no one knew where. Kat, who seemed not to be much of a morning person, was still in the room she was sharing with Adam. Ruth had gone to the outlets in Kittery and Susan was on the phone with one of her colleagues. Hannah was on her own and bored.

"What's going on?" Hannah asked. She had come into the kitchen to find Cordelia and Cody and Adam. Adam's arms were folded across his chest. Cody looked near to tears. Cordelia, displaying something of her father's toughness, was frowning.

"Daddy won't take us to Wonder Mountain," she said.

"The miniature golf place in Wells?"

"Those places are for white trash in bad clothes they bought at a Walmart sale."

"Personally," Hannah said, "I prefer Target. But that's

beside the point. Look, Sarah could use a break. Susan and I will take the kids."

"How about I could use a break?"

"Yes, Adam, you, too. You and Kat go get into your bathing suits and head down to the beach. You looked very stressed."

Hannah's sarcasm was lost on her brother. "Fine." He took out his wallet and handed her some cash. "If they act up bring them right home."

Adam left the kitchen and Cordelia's frown became a wide smile. "Thanks, Aunt Hannah! Come on, Cody, we're going to play miniature golf and I'm going to win!"

"No, you're not!" he shouted. "I am!"

Hannah followed the running kids out of the room. She hoped that Susan would be as enthusiastic as they were.

She was. The four drove down to Wells—typically, traffic moved at a crawl—and by the time they got to Wonder Mountain they were all a little cranky. But Hannah rallied her troop and before long they were happily playing the first game, Hannah purposely messing up so that Cordelia could win, and encouraging Cody when he failed to make a simple shot. A second game was agreed upon and this time Susan and Cody played against Hannah and Cordelia. Somehow, miraculously, the game was declared a tie.

The adults decided that it was time to move on and Cordelia volunteered to return the balls and clubs. Cody helped her while Hannah and Susan watched from a short distance.

"You're so good with them," Susan said.

Hannah gave a little, dismissive laugh. "That's because they're not my children."

"No," Susan said firmly. "Because you're good with kids, period. You told me you had a thriving babysitting business when you were young. You told me you loved spending time with the kids."

Suddenly, Hannah felt weepy. Behind her sunglasses she opened her eyes very wide, hoping to forestall tears. What was going on? Her period wasn't due for another two full weeks. It couldn't be PMS. It was this whole kid issue.

Cordelia and Cody were running back to them. "Hey, guys," she said, quickly wiping her right cheek where she suspected a telltale tear, "how about we get some ice cream on the way home?"

"Dad doesn't let us get ice cream and stuff when we stay with him," Cody said. "He says we'll get fat."

Hannah rolled her eyes, not that anyone could see that, either. Her brother was an idiot. "Then we just won't tell him we got ice cream."

"Cool!" the children chorused.

"What is his problem?" Susan muttered as they ushered Cordelia and Cody to the exit. "The kids are fine! He's going to give them an eating disorder if he's always so restrictive."

"And let's get chocolate sauce and sprinkles on top," Hannah called ahead. She smiled at Susan. "An aunt is allowed to spoil."

"It was very good of Hannah and Susan to take the kids to play miniature golf."

Sarah and Craig were sitting side by side on the front porch. Only a moment earlier they had watched as a mother deer led her two Bambi-like young ones across the lawn and into the woods. One of the babies walked with a limp. Craig worried about its ability to survive on its own. Damaged children held a special place in his heart.

"They like kids," Craig said. "And Hannah is killer at miniature golf."

"But she'll probably let them win."

"Yeah. At least a few games. Susan beat her once last

summer and Hannah was grumpy for days. It was pretty amusing."

They sat in companionable silence for a while. The day was hot and still. Craig felt almost sleepy, though he wasn't actually tired.

"What about that master's degree you were going for?" he asked.

"Got it. Thanks for asking. Now let's hope it gets me a better job."

"I asked Adam about it but he didn't seem to know."

Sarah laughed. "That's Adam. Out of sight, out of mind."

"Doesn't it bother you that—"

"That what?"

Craig wondered how to ask this question. "That he has so little interest in you?"

Sarah looked down at her lap for a moment. "It's complicated. Yes, it bothers me. And no, it doesn't."

There was another few moments of silence before Craig said, "What made you marry my brother? Really, this is not a trick question. What was it?"

"Nothing made me marry him," Sarah replied promptly. "No one forced me to marry Adam. I fell in love with him, short and sweet. And before you make a face or snort or do something equally disgusting and childish, let me assure you, Craig, that everyone has a lovable self. Even if it's very small or sporadic, even if it's occasional, everyone has a lovable self. Everyone. Even your brother."

Craig wondered about that. Presumably his mother had had a lovable self. His father had married her. What was more, he had stayed married to her, though staying with Charlotte might have been more about fear or apathy than love. He would probably never know.

"So," Sarah asked then, "why haven't you settled down with a woman? It can't be for lack of options."

Why indeed! That was a loaded question. Lately he had begun to think that in his wanderings and refusal to settle down with anyone he was being ridiculously passive/aggressive, trying to punish his parents for the lack of love he felt as a child by continuing to disappoint them—as, of course, they expected he would. But he wasn't entirely ready to admit that, certainly not to his former sister-in-law, whom he respected very much.

Craig shrugged. "You know what Sartre said. Hell is other people."

Sarah eyed him keenly. "I don't think you really believe that."

"Well, maybe if I'd met someone like you."

"Spare me."

"Sorry. But it's a bit of a sore subject with me lately."

"Why lately?"

"I don't know," he said quickly. "No reason."

"Of course you know. But that's okay. You don't have to talk about it."

Craig smiled. "Did Adam ever get how smart you are?"

Sarah smiled back. "Yes. And when he did get it he divorced me."

"He thrives on competition with men. With women, he needs to be king."

"Yeah. He does seem to be a bit of a throwback in that way. Not like your father, anyway."

"My father lets women dominate him. Well, until now. Jennifer doesn't strike me as the sort to need dominion over anybody."

"So, she's not a Charlotte?" Sarah asked.

"Not that I can see. And Ruth likes her."

"That's a valuable stamp of approval. Ruth likes you, too. In fact, I think you're her favorite McQueen."

Craig felt embarrassed and disbelieving at the same time. "I don't know about that," he said.

"Why? Aren't you worth a special place in someone's heart?" When Craig didn't answer, only stared straight ahead over the lawn, Sarah said, very softly, "I see."

Ruth was in the kitchen unloading a bag of produce she had brought home from a local farm stand, when Adam accosted her.

"When was the last time Dad updated his will?" he said by way of greeting.

Ruth looked at the tomato she was holding. It was damn near perfect, and what a fragrance. She put it in a large white ceramic bowl with the other, less perfect, but probably equally as delicious, tomatoes.

"Hello, to you, too," she said. "And I have no idea."

"You must know where he keeps a copy. In the library? In his bedroom? Did he ever install a safe like I told him to?"

Ruth gave her nephew a look of mock horror. "You're not going to go searching for it, are you?"

"Of course not. I'm sure Teddy has a copy filed safely away."

"Then why do you care about your father's copy? What's this all about, Adam?" *Ah,* she thought, *just look at these green beans! Lightly tossed with garlic and good olive oil and they'll be heaven to eat. And these shallots are a work of art. How rosy they are!*

Adam took a step closer to his aunt. "I want to know what Dad plans to do with the house."

Ruth carefully folded and put away the reusable shopping bag before responding to her nephew. "First of all," she said, facing him again, "it's none of your business, nor is it any of mine. Second, even if I did know Bill's plans, I wouldn't tell you. I wouldn't tell anyone."

"It's your duty, and mine, to protect the family's interests," Adam argued.

"You mean the family's property, which, technically, isn't the family's at all, it's Bill's and Bill's alone."

"Not forever. Not for long. He's seventy-three."

Ruth leaned back against the sink. She was finding this conversation both inappropriate and amusing. "Our father died at eighty," she said. "Our mother lived to be ninety-three."

"That doesn't necessarily mean that Dad will live to be that old."

"Planning to kill him, are we?"

"Don't be ridiculous," Adam said, now sounding angry. "I just want to be sure he's done the right thing."

"Which is?"

"Which is leave Larchmere and its holdings to me, the eldest son, the only one with good financial sense and expertise."

Ruth sighed. It was clear that he was deadly serious. He really and truly felt due the legacy his father and grandfather had worked so hard to establish, the legacy they had cherished.

"Adam," she said, her tone neutral, "I don't much like you. I never did and it's a good bet I never will." Ruth started to leave the room.

"Come back here," Adam demanded from behind her. "I'm not finished!"

Oh, she thought, *but I am.*

33

It was later that afternoon, after Tilda's visit to the yard sale, where she had found no books of interest to her. She was in the kitchen getting a snack when her cell phone rang. She didn't recognize the number. It was the guy from the air-conditioning repair service. She had told Jon to have him call her about the price he had quoted. She seemed to recall that the last time the air conditioner had broken down the price for repair was a lot lower. She wondered if Jon had properly explained the problem.

Tilda told the repairman what, exactly, had gone wrong. At least, what Jon had told her had gone wrong. The repair guy quoted his original price. Tilda suggested that it seemed rather high. This push and pull went on for several minutes.

"Look," the guy finally said, with a big, put-upon sigh. "Just let me talk to your husband, all right?"

"My husband," Tilda replied, shocked at being so dismissed, "is dead."

There was another sigh, this one not quite so dramatic. "I'm sorry about your husband. But the job costs what it costs. You don't want to pay, you can find somebody else."

Tilda didn't know what to do. She could ask Jon to call other repair services for quotes. Or she could do it herself. That could take time. She would probably have to deal with other dismissive, sexist men just like this one. "Oh, all right," she blurted. "Fine."

"Tell whoever is going to be home to have a check for me."

The call ended. Tilda no longer wanted that snack. She gripped the bar top. Her face felt hot. She felt angry and, at the same time, vaguely sad and lost.

For a long time after Frank's death Tilda had felt anonymous. It was the best word she could find to express how she felt. If the person who knew you best was gone, no longer there in the physical world to validate your existence by his own existence, then who were you, where were you to be found? What was your name? Who was there to recognize you?

And who was she now, a little more than two years since her husband's death? Not the same Tilda McQueen she had been before her marriage. Not Mrs. O'Connell, Frank's wife, the person she had been for over twenty years. And not quite the anonymous person she had been right after Frank's death.

What—where—was her identity? She was a widow. It was a grim word that brought with it too many fiercely negative cultural associations. Throughout the history of the western world, at least throughout its literature, widows had been portrayed in a bad light. Her schooling had taught her that.

Take Chaucer's Wife of Bath. For many women she was a figure of courage and individuality, but she was also a figure to mock, admittedly deceitful and manipulative, even emasculating. Black widows were killers of men, liars and cheats, sexually and morally depraved. Villains in movies had widow's peaks, that telltale V-shaped hairline that, in folklore, predicted a wife would outlive her husband.

Widows and orphans were to be protected and pitied. Widows were to be married off to a reluctant brother-in-law. They were to be tucked away in attic bedrooms and expected to serve the resident family in exchange for the tiny airless room and meager board. Widows were a burden. Widows spent their evenings alone. Widowers were invited to dinner and served hearty meals and good brandy. Widows were to be taken advantage of by unscrupulous repairmen!

Tilda's obsessively negative thoughts, which she had made no attempt to check, were interrupted by the sudden appearance of Jennifer in the kitchen. Tilda had not heard the front door open and close. Jennifer was wearing a milk-chocolate colored linen A-line dress, and darker brown sandals with heels. A large, sculptural brooch was pinned by her right shoulder. Her bag was from Coach. Tilda recognized it from the window of the Coach store in the Maine Mall. The bag, which was new this season, cost several hundreds of dollars. She could not afford it.

"Hi, Tilda," Jennifer said. "What a beautiful afternoon."

"Hi," Tilda replied.

"How's it going?"

"Fine."

"I just stopped by to drop off a magazine for Bill. It's about chess. There's a good article in here I thought he might like to read."

"Oh."

There was a moment of awkward silence before Jennifer said, "I've been meaning to ask if you've been to the day spa in town, the one in the old, converted church on Maine Street. I was wondering about their massages. I'd really like to get one soon, it's been ages."

"I wouldn't know about the massages," Tilda said, turning to face the sink and thereby turning her back to her father's girlfriend. "I don't have the money to be going to spas."

There was a moment of heavy silence and then Jennifer said, "Oh. I'm sorry. Well, I've got to be—"

Jennifer picked up her expensive bag and left. Tilda immediately felt like a jerk. She considered, just for a moment, going after her to apologize. She could say she was in a bad mood, that she had been snapping at everyone since breakfast, that it was her period or the onset of menopause. But that would be a lie.

Tilda sank into a chair at the little table in the breakfast nook. She felt ashamed. The ugly, embarrassing truth was that she was jealous of Jennifer Fournier. Her father's girlfriend was beautiful and poised and had her own successful business (at least one that afforded her massages and bags from Coach!) and most significantly, she was romantically involved with a good man. That the man was Tilda's father was almost beside the point.

Being jealous of Jennifer would get her nowhere. Tilda knew that. It wasn't Jennifer's fault that she was lonely and had less disposable cash to spend on herself. If she wanted a new life, then it was up to her to make one. To make new friends, which she did think she should do, people who had not known her as Frank's wife. To earn more money if that was important to her, though she wasn't really sure that it was. To find love—if that was, indeed, what she wanted. According to her father, that was what she needed.

Tilda got up from the table. She would have to call Jon and tell him where she kept the checkbook.

Craig had found the old wooden fanlight in the basement. He vaguely remembered his aunt having brought it home with her a few years before. He had no idea where she had gotten it. The glass was long gone but that was all right. Painted a bright white, he thought that it would look nice in the living room, maybe over the antique chair with the pale green plushy upholstery.

He had carried it out of the basement and around the back of the house to examine it in sunlight. First, it would need to be scraped, which, given its condition, would take some time, then primed and repainted. He didn't know if it was worth the effort—if anyone really cared about the old piece—but it gave him another project, something to keep his hands busy while his mind was under siege.

There had been the fight with Adam, in which, to a certain extent, he had rightly been denounced as—though Adam had not used the term—a shirker. There had been the brief conversation with Bobby, the one they had had at the Cove, about life and location and meaning. And then there had been the talk he had had with Sarah, on the front porch, while Hannah and Susan were with the kids playing miniature golf. She had asked him if he felt undeserving or unworthy of a special place in someone's heart. He had not answered. His silence had spoken for him.

Craig sighed and turned the old fanlight so that he could assess the damage to its other side. He would never forget the woman who had accosted him at The Front Porch and accused him of getting her pregnant and, in effect, of forcing her to have an abortion. He had forgotten her once but now he would always remember, even be haunted by her—and by the child he would never know. His child, if the woman could be believed, and somehow Craig had come to the conclusion that she could.

"What are you doing?" It was Bill. He had come around the back of the house and upon Craig with the old fanlight.

Craig thought he detected a note of suspicion in his father's voice. He wondered if his father had a right to be suspicious of him. Had he ever given him a reason not to be?

"I thought I'd fix up this old fanlight," he said.

"It belongs to your aunt."

Craig wondered if his father thought he was going to sell it and make off with the money. "I know," he said. "I thought it would look nice in the living room, over the green chair. After I fix it up."

Bill looked at his youngest child for a moment. Craig waited. "Yes," he finally said. "It would look nice there."

He turned to go, where, he didn't say.

"Dad?" Craig called.

Bill turned. "Yes?"

But Craig had no idea what to say or why he had called out to his father. "Nothing. Sorry."

His father went off. Craig turned back to his project and his thoughts.

"What do you think this is?"

Tilda observed the wooden object Dennis was holding up. It was about two feet long, most of which was handle—she guessed—and at one end there was a bowl-shaped object attached, dotted liberally with small, round perforations. "I have absolutely no idea," she said finally. "Some kind of sieve? Let's ask the owner."

They were in an antique shop along Route 1 in Wells. It was a big old barnlike structure, though Tilda wasn't sure it had ever actually been a barn. She liked this particular shop because its collection was so eclectic and its prices were generally affordable.

Frank had hated to go antiquing. He thought the whole notion of browsing, for anything, was insane. Early in the marriage Tilda had dragged him along on a few expeditions but he had been so obviously miserable—and no fun to be with!—that afterward she had let him stay home. She had begged him to stay home.

It felt strange to be enjoying one of her favorite activities with a man other than Frank. It felt almost like cheating, though of course, it wasn't.

She and Dennis, who was carrying the mysterious object, walked up to the central counter at which the owner presided. Their arms brushed against each other. Tilda wondered what it would be like to have sex with Dennis. She tried to imagine him naked. She tried to imagine herself naked with him. She shivered in embarrassment though nobody in the shop could read her thoughts. The thoughts were pleasant, even a little bit exciting. So what if he was in his sixties? Sixty was the new forty. Could sex be a part of her life again? For the first time since Frank's death—and in an antique store of all places!—she could sense this as a real possibility.

"Excuse me," Dennis was saying to the shop's owner. He was a middle-aged man wearing a pair of oversized, heavy, black-framed glasses, behind which his eyes were huge and swimming. "We were wondering what this is meant to be?"

The owner cocked his head and seemed to be considering the object for some moments before he said, "What do you think it's meant to be?"

"A sieve of some sort," Tilda ventured. "Like a big colander?"

"Well," the owner said, "then I guess that's what it is."

Dennis laughed, then Tilda, then the shop's owner. "Seriously," the man said, "my wife brought that in. Don't know where she got it and she has no more idea than I do what it is or where it came from. Thought someone might want it though. You can have it for fifteen dollars."

Dennis graciously declined the offer. Tilda watched him walk to the back of the store to return the mysterious object to its place. She thought of how she had snapped at Jennifer earlier in the day. She determined to apologize to her father's girlfriend as soon as she could. It was never right to begrudge someone her happiness. Your own unhappiness was a burden you had a duty to bear alone. At least, you should not use it as a weapon.

Dennis returned and Tilda took his hand as they left the shop. It was as natural as putting one foot in front of the other.

"I can't believe you actually read that rag! It's garbage! It's all lies and innuendo. You're even more of an idiot than I thought!"

"Don't call me an idiot. You're a fool if you don't worry about socialism encroaching in this country. You've got your head in the sand and you always have!"

Susan was in the kitchen, alone. The loud voices she was hearing belonged to Hannah and to Adam. She guessed they were in the living room. It didn't matter. They should not have been shouting as if they were in an open field.

A door slammed. A moment later, Hannah stomped into the kitchen. "My brother," she said, "is an ass."

Susan frowned. "Be that as it may, did you really need to scream at each other? You could have woken the dead."

Hannah, who was rummaging in the fridge, looked around at Susan. "What?"

"You were screaming at each other."

"We were angry." Hannah emerged from the fridge with a yogurt and plopped down on one of the stools at the bar top. Susan handed her a spoon.

"You've never heard of rational discussion or negotiation?"

"You get mad. You have a temper."

"Yes," Susan admitted. "I do. But I just can't imagine fighting with my sisters and brothers the way you McQueens can go at it. I just can't."

"What do you do when there's a conflict?" Hannah asked. "How do you solve problems?"

"We don't have conflicts. We don't have problems with each other."

"Oh, come on, Susan. I really find that hard to believe."

"Have you ever seen one of us tense with another?" Susan demanded. "Have you ever heard me complain about my sisters and brothers?"

"Well, no," Hannah admitted. "But I have heard you complain about your parents!"

"But with understanding. They still think we're all ten years old. When they overstep their boundaries it's only because they love us so much. They can't get out of the habit of being overprotective."

Hannah laughed. "My mother never got into the habit of being overprotective. It might have been nice if she had."

"At least you have your father. But let's get back to the point. Look, Hannah, if we do have a family, I really don't want us to engage in a dynamic of nastiness and fighting and judgment and dissension and—"

"Okay, okay, I get it." Hannah put down the spoon and empty yogurt container. She felt hurt but chastened, too. This coming together of two people who had grown up in very different households was tough. She wondered if the adjustments and negotiations would ever come to a peaceful end. She hoped that they did. "We'll make our own rules," she said. "New rules, and new guidelines. I promise."

Susan gave her a long, enquiring look. "We'll see," she said finally. "Maybe we shouldn't make any more promises to each other just yet." She took the yogurt container to the recycling bin, put the spoon in the dishwasher, and left the kitchen.

Hannah sat very still. She had heard Susan say "if" they ever had a family. And she knew what Susan had really meant by those last words. She meant that she, Hannah, should stop making new promises until she fulfilled the ones she had already made. Susan, her wife, didn't trust her. Hannah thought she might be sick right then and there. She was destroying her marriage by her hesitation, by her inability to confront and conquer her demon.

She continued to sit very still for a long time, until the nausea passed.

34

Thursday, July 26

It was around eight-thirty in the morning. Predictably, Tilda was taking a walk on the beach. Bill had gone for a half round of golf with Teddy. Hannah was sleeping in and Susan was online, in their bedroom, keeping up with the case of one of her more difficult clients. Ruth was out, no one knew where. Percy was sunning himself—he liked to get an early start—in the sunroom. Craig, too, was gone somewhere in his old red van. Sarah and Cordelia and Cody were playing a game of catch on the back lawn. Kat was on the front porch, busily sending text messages to people unknown and drinking iced coffee.

Adam was alone in the kitchen when he heard the front door open, then shut, and high-heeled footsteps approaching.

"Oh," Jennifer said when she walked into the room. "Good morning. Is Bill around?"

Adam took a long sip of coffee before answering. "No."

Jennifer adjusted the shoulder strap of her tan leather

briefcase. "Please tell him that I was here," she said, and she turned to go.

Adam banged his empty cup onto the bar top. "This isn't going to happen, you know." He spoke loudly. He meant to sound menacing.

Jennifer knew that she should just keep on walking but an old fighting spirit made her turn back. "What's not going to happen?" she said.

"The little invasion you've planned into the life of the McQueens. Your little scheme to take over Larchmere."

For a brief moment Jennifer wondered if Adam was mentally ill. "What?" she said.

Adam took a step closer to her. "If you insist upon hanging around our father, I will make your life hell. I have the means to do it. Do you understand me?"

Jennifer clutched the strap of her briefcase more tightly. She had no idea of what to say. She felt threatened. She wondered if they were the only two people in the house. She had seen Kat on the porch but she would be no help if Adam attempted to harm her physically.

Adam's voice was a roar. "I said, do you understand me?"

Jennifer, now terrified, found herself nodding.

The front door opened, then closed. "I'm back!" It was Bill, returning from his golf game.

Adam left the room quickly and quietly, brushing against Jennifer hard enough for her to stumble. He avoided his father by slipping into the living room until Bill had passed the open door on his way to the kitchen. Then, Adam left the house.

Bill came into the kitchen and propped his golf bag against a wall. "Hi, Jennifer," he said. "What a nice surprise to find you here."

"Bill," she said, her voice trembling, "something's come up. I'm afraid I have to go away for a while."

* * *

Tilda was just back from the beach. She went immediately to the kitchen for a glass of water. Hannah was there, leaning against the sink. Susan stood next to her. Ruth stood by the fridge. Her expression was grim. Bill was sitting at the table, his hands on his lap. He was very still.

"Dad," Tilda said, alarmed. "Are you okay?"

Bill's voice was flat. "Jennifer is gone to Portland."

"Oh. Why? When will she be back?"

Her father looked down at his hands. "She told me she got a call from an important client about a job in the city. She said she had to go. She said she probably won't make it back for the memorial service."

Tilda felt her face go hot. She avoided meeting her aunt's eyes. Jennifer's excuse for leaving Larchmere was so clearly a lie, Tilda was sure that her father, an intelligent man, had not believed it, either. What had happened? When had it happened? "Oh, Dad, I'm so sorry," she managed to say, finally. "I'm sure she'd rather be here, with you. . . . You know how work can be. . . ."

Bill gave his daughter a weak smile, got up, and left the kitchen.

"What happened?" Tilda asked, looking now from Ruth to Hannah to Susan.

"I'm not quite sure," Ruth replied. Her voice was tight. "I got back from the store—we were low on milk again—and found your father sitting right where he was a moment ago. Jennifer had just left."

So, Tilda thought, *whatever had happened to finally drive Jennifer away from Larchmere had happened this morning.* Who had been home? Had someone said something awful to her? Had it all just been too much, the McQueens and their difficult personalities?

Her poor father! He had looked heartbroken. Tilda thought again of how she had snapped at Jennifer when she had asked about the day spa. She felt guilty. She was pretty sure that her behavior since first meeting her father's girl-friend had contributed to Jennifer's feeling unwelcome. And she had not had the chance to apologize to her. "I think it's partly my fault that she's gone," she said now to Ruth and Hannah and Susan. "I'm sorry. I feel very badly."

Hannah felt a bit badly, too, but she was not about to admit that. She was more concerned about the possibility that Jennifer's love for her father wasn't really as strong as he believed. She wondered if Jennifer was just bailing on him the moment things got rough. She would try her best to comfort her father. She owed him that much.

Craig came into the kitchen then, followed a moment later by Adam.

"What's wrong with Dad?" Craig said. "We just passed him in the front hall. The poor guy looks like he got sucker punched."

When neither Ruth nor Hannah nor Susan spoke, Tilda told her brothers about Jennifer's sudden defection.

"Ouch." Craig winced. "Poor Dad. That doesn't bode well for their future."

"Well," Adam said, "I, for one, am glad she's gone. Good riddance to bad rubbish."

"His command of the English language is so fine and subtle, isn't it?" Craig said.

Ruth took a step forward. "We all know that excuse about an important client was just a lie," she said. She was angry now. "Jennifer left because none of you—none of you except Craig and Susan—made her feel at all wel-come. Adam, you were downright rude to her. I don't blame her one bit for leaving though I'm sorry for your fa-ther." Ruth took a deep breath. It wasn't entirely the kids' fault that Jennifer had left. Her brother could be a weak man. "And," she said, "Bill should have seen what was going on and shielded Jennifer from all the crap Adam tossed at her. And from the hostility you girls betrayed."

No one said anything. Adam looked bored. Tilda and Hannah looked guilty and worried at the same time. Susan looked as if she might cry. Craig looked embarrassed. He was not used to praise, no matter how faint. He felt he could have done more to make Jennifer feel welcome. At least he should have made Adam shut up.

Ruth sighed and reached for her black linen Kate Spade tote bag, which was sitting on the bar top. "I'll be back later," she said.

"Where are you going?" Tilda asked, wondering for a moment if her aunt was going to drive up to Portland and bring Jennifer back to Larchmere with her.

"To see Bobby."

35

Not long after Ruth's departure, Jon and Jane pulled into the driveway at Larchmere. Tilda was happy to see them but at the same time she was very aware that she was not as desperate for their company as she had been only days earlier. This surprised her. She wondered if it was because of Dennis's recent companionship. Probably. Maybe.

Jon got out of the car and waved to his mother. He was looking more like his father every day, husky though not fat, his eyes the same cow brown, his hair the same light brown. For Tilda, the transformation was both wonderful and painful to witness. She supposed, she hoped, that the painful part would lessen over time. Time healed all wounds. Time made the unusual usual and the new, old. Or so it was said.

Time had not made Frank's changing appearance easier to bear. At least, it hadn't for Tilda. When it was first clear that he had lost a significant amount of weight as a result of the illness, drugs, and other treatments, Frank had joked that he was in the best shape of his life. Then, after a beat, he would add: "Except for the cancer." No one had really found it funny, least of all Tilda, but everyone, Tilda included, would laugh or share a falsely happy, conspiratorial smile.

After a few months of continued weight loss Frank stopped making this joke. It was no longer possible for anyone to pretend that it was funny. The face of illness was never amusing. In *The Historian,* a novel by Elizabeth Kostova, a character looks down on the face of his beloved mentor. The mentor is, in a manner, dying. He had become "the unbearable beloved." Tilda knew exactly what that meant.

Jane followed her brother up onto the porch. Unlike Jon, she closely resembled her mother. She was as tall and slim as Tilda and shared her longish face. Unlike her mother, though, she wore her dark brown hair to her shoulders, and her eyes were a very definite, unambiguous green.

Jane smiled and gave Tilda a hug. "You look good, Mom. Better than you have for a while. You're not slouching."

"Maybe it's the fresh ocean air." Tilda felt sheepish. Maybe it was the fresh ocean air. Or maybe it was the fact that a man, a nice, handsome man, was paying attention to her. But she couldn't tell that to her daughter. For now, maybe for always, Dennis Haass would remain a secret. That is, unless one of the locals gabbed and she would deal with that when and if it happened.

"Maybe," Jane said. "Well, whatever you're doing, do more of it. Where's Craig?"

"I don't know. Craig is his own man."

Together the three went into the house and headed straight for the kitchen. Though Jon and Jane were quite capable of getting themselves something to eat, Tilda put out a snack of grapes, a round of goat cheese, and crackers. Jon reached for a bottle of water and Jane opted for cranberry juice.

Tilda told them about their grandfather's romance. She

also told them that Jennifer had been suddenly called back to Portland on business.

"Grandpa's the man," Jon said with a grin. "Dude."

"So, when is she going to be back?" Jane asked. "I'm dying to meet her."

Tilda felt her face flush. "I'm not sure, exactly. The client in Portland is an important one or something."

Jane eyed her mother, who had always been a terrible liar. "What's wrong? Why did she really leave?"

Tilda was embarrassed. "Ruth thinks she didn't feel particularly . . . welcome. She also thinks it's our fault. Mine and Hannah's and Adam's, I mean. I do feel terrible. It was just so . . . surprising to learn that Dad was involved. We all could have been nicer."

"Is she hot?"

"Jon!"

"Answer the question, Mom," Jane said.

"Well, yes," she admitted. "She is hot. Attractive, I mean."

"I bet Uncle Craig was nice to her."

"Yes, he was."

Jane sighed. "It's your generation of women. You're all so prejudiced."

"Prejudiced!"

"If Jennifer was ugly or fat you wouldn't have minded so much that she was dating Grandpa."

"I'm prejudiced against attractive women?" Of course, she was. "That's crazy," she said.

"Yes, you are prejudiced. Women can be their own worst enemies. Women are all too ready to turn against each other. It all comes down to jealousy."

Jon guzzled the last of his water and grabbed a fistful of grapes. "I'm out of here," he said. "I'll be down at the beach for a while if anyone needs me."

Her brother loped off and Jane set to the food.

It was not a generational thing, Tilda wanted to tell her daughter. It was a middle-aged thing, the anger over the loss of your looks. And the anger at yourself for being so upset about something that should be trivial! Sagging chin? Who cared when there was world hunger to remedy! Flabby middle? How could that really matter when global warming was destroying the planet! Jane would know all about it when she was forty-seven. Or maybe she wouldn't. Maybe she would escape the insanity. (Sarah seemed to have. So did Ruth.) Maybe she would figure out what an incredible waste of time it was to lacerate your fading appearance and to feel jealous of other women who were more physically attractive. Maybe she would be comfortable in her body. Tilda hoped that she would.

"I'm going to see if Craig's around," Jane said, startling her mother from her thoughts. "Thanks for the snack."

Jane picked up her plate but Tilda said, "I'll clean up." Jane smiled and Tilda watched her daughter leave the kitchen. She so prayed for her happiness.

Tilda knocked on the front door though she knew it was never locked. It was later that day and she had gone to Bobby's house on an errand for Ruth. In her left hand she carried a shopping bag filled with "used" books Ruth had bought for her friend. It was well known that Bobby was a great reader. Tilda had peeked at some of the titles. There was a pristine copy of *Run to the Mountain: The Journals of Thomas Merton*. There was a hardcover copy of *Harold Bloom's Shakespeare: The Invention of the Human*. And there was an old paperback copy of Joseph Heller's *Catch-22*.

Bobby opened the door and nodded. Tilda followed him inside.

"Kids get in okay?" he asked.

Tilda set the bag on the kitchen table. "Yes. Jon's already at the beach and the last I saw Jane she was following Craig around like a puppy dog."

Bobby smiled. His house was minuscule compared to Larchmere and neat as a pin. The kitchen contained no fancy appliances and most of the furniture had come from his parents' house. The floors and countertops were immaculate. Bobby was someone who still beat his throw rugs with a stick. Books were stacked floor to ceiling along one wall of the living room. There was no dust.

Tilda wondered when Bobby had the time to read all that he did, and to work as hard as he did. She suspected that he was far more disciplined than most people.

"You know that Jennifer went back to Portland," she said now, suddenly feeling the urgent need to confess.

Bobby took a pitcher of iced tea from the fridge and set it on the kitchen table, next to the bag of books. "Ruth told me."

"I feel really bad about not making her feel more welcome. It was nothing about her. She seems very nice. It was all about me. My fears. My insecurities."

Bobby put two glasses on the table and poured them both a drink. "I'm sure she understands she did nothing wrong."

"I hope so. And I so hope we—Hannah, Adam, and I—haven't put her off Dad entirely. Craig, of course, was nice to her. I wanted to apologize to her but she was gone before I had the chance."

They sat at the table. After a moment, Bobby said: "Things will work out if they're meant to."

"Yes," Tilda said. But she wasn't sure she believed that. So, she and Frank had not been meant to grow old together? Who had ordained such a horrible thing?

It was as if Bobby had read her mind. He looked at her and then up at a framed print on the kitchen wall. It was a copy of a van Gogh painting. "You don't know this, Matilda," he said, "but I lost my wife. It was a car accident that did it. Your aunt and your father are the only ones outside of my family who know the truth. And now, you know. And some old-timers, who remember when it happened. But they don't talk about it. There's no point in talking." Bobby looked back at her. His gaze was steady.

Tilda felt tears prick at her eyes but rapidly blinked them away. "I'm so sorry, Bobby," she said.

"It was a long time ago."

"What was her name?"

"Janet."

"It's a pretty name."

"I want you to listen to something, Matilda." Bobby began to quote something, a prayer or a mantra, Tilda thought. The words were vaguely familiar.

"All shall be well,
And all shall be well,
And all manner of things shall be well."

"That's beautiful, Bobby," Tilda said, truthfully. "Who wrote it?"

"A thirteenth-century woman. Dame Julian of Norwich."

"Of course. I thought it sounded familiar. I must have come across it in college, medieval literature or history. But I'd almost completely forgotten it."

"It's deceptively simple, that prayer. It bears repeating. It might do you some good. Or not."

"Thanks, Bobby," she said. "I'll try to keep it in mind. Really."

Tilda got up from the table and Bobby followed her to the front door.

"Thank your aunt for the books," he said.

Tilda promised that she would and got into her car. She was profoundly grateful for Bobby's presence in her life.

Hannah was in the library. She was paging through an old family photograph album. This one chronicled about two years of the McQueens' life. Adam looked about ten, which meant that Tilda was about seven, Hannah about four. Yes, and there was Craig, appearing about midway through the book as an infant. But after that . . . Hannah paged to the end of the album. There were very few pictures of Craig. There weren't all that many of Hannah, either, at least not compared to those of Tilda and Adam. But maybe that was normal, just the way things went in large families. The thrill of yet another new baby simply wore off. The first baby is a miracle. The second baby makes a cute sidekick. The third child was extraneous. The fourth child was redundant.

Still, Hannah remembered a happy childhood. Look, the photographs proved something. There she was smiling, laughing, blowing out birthday candles, soaring down a slide in the playground. She certainly didn't look emotionally deprived or neglected. And maybe she really hadn't been, not in the early years. Maybe her perception of her mother's relative indifference to her third child had come only later, when Hannah's awareness of herself as a real person, an individual, took hold. Adolescence. Yes, that was probably about the time that things changed in her relationship with her mother. At least, that was when she became aware that her relationship with her mother was not what it could have been. It was not what Hannah needed or wanted it to be.

Was that why she had loved babysitting? Had babysitting given her an opportunity, no matter how limited, to give to another child what she, herself, had wanted so badly?

Maybe. She thought now about what Susan had said about her own close family, how they never fought, how they hugged and kissed when they met and departed, how they loved their parents. Maybe truly happy families were real, after all.

Hannah looked up to see Craig enter the library. She noted immediately that his shirt was tucked into his pants and that he was wearing a belt. In place of his usual worn leather sandals (which he wore until Thanksgiving or so) he was wearing decent brown loafers with socks. *Where the hell did he get the loafers?* she wondered. They were easily circa 1980.

"Where have you been?" she asked.

He shrugged. "Nowhere special."

She didn't believe him. "You're lying. Or being elusive."

"I don't lie. Not when I don't absolutely have to. Not when it's not a social obligation."

"Okay. But you're up to something, that's clear."

"You have a suspicious mind, Hannah Banana."

He went over to a section of the large bookcases and began to scan the rows of books.

"What are you looking for?"

"Nothing."

"Mr. Evasive today!"

"Sorry. I was wondering if we had a—a book about bees."

Another lie. "I have no idea. But if you come over here I'll show you a very cute picture of you when you were just a few months old."

"Strolling down memory lane?" he asked, joining her.

"More like stumbling. Look."

Craig bent to look over his sister's shoulder. It was a picture of Tilda, age seven, sitting on a couch, and holding baby Craig on her lap. She was smiling into the camera. His eyes shifted to the facing page of the album. There was a similar picture, though in this one it was Hannah holding her new brother.

"Let me see something," he said. He flipped back through the earlier pages, and then forward, to the end of the book.

"What are you looking for?" Hannah asked.

"There's not one picture of me with Mom," he said.

"Oh."

"Not that I'm surprised." Craig straightened up. "Well," he said, "guess I better get out of these clothes. I promised myself I'd clean out the garage today."

"Okay," Hannah said. Craig left the library. She felt awful for her brother. Charlotte had not been particularly fond of her younger daughter, but she really had virtually ignored her younger son. And Hannah had had to go and remind Craig of that! Hannah shut the photo album and put it away.

36

Friday, July 27

Charlotte's memorial service was held at St. Peter's-by-the-Sea on Shore Road in Cape Neddick. Founded in 1897 by Nannie Dunlap Conarroe, in memory of her husband George, St. Peter's was an Episcopal chapel for summer residents and visitors. It was a beautiful stone building that sat atop Christian Hill. Per George Conarroe's wishes its cross was visible to fishermen at sea. Dignified St. Peter's was one of Maine's most popular locations for baptisms, weddings, and memorials of all sorts. Charlotte's funeral had taken place there, too.

The weather was good, with bright skies and no forecast of rain. At a little before ten o'clock the attendees of the memorial service filed into the church. Tessa Vickes, standing at the door, gave each person a red rose to hold. Not surprisingly, red roses had been Charlotte's favorite flower. Tilda was touched that Tessa had remembered.

Tilda wore a lightweight, cream-colored silk pantsuit she had bought years and years before at Talbots. Under it she wore a dusty blue silk blouse. She was thankful it wasn't a brutally hot day because she already felt warm in the small, un-air-conditioned church. *Maybe,* she thought, *I should reconsider dresses and skirts. At least my legs could breathe.* Had she ever seen her mother look uncomfortable in the heat? She didn't think that she had. Charlotte had always been self-composed.

Jon and Jane sat to her right. Jon wore a navy blazer, white shirt, no tie, and chinos. Jane had on a flowery chiffonlike top in pinks and purples and a darker pink skirt that came just above her knees. Adam, sitting in the pew directly across the center isle in a dove gray suit and pale yellow tie, seemed to have abandoned his idea of reading a passage from Ayn Rand's work. Maybe he had forgotten. He looked distracted. Kat looked grim. In honor of the occasion she had chosen to wear a little sweater over her sundress. She didn't exactly look modest but Tilda appreciated her effort at looking appropriate.

Hannah, to Tilda's left, was wearing a pair of enormous sunglasses. Tilda had not seen them before on her sister. She guessed they were protection against more than the bright sun, which was why she was wearing them in the church. Susan's crinkly cotton dress was a vibrant pattern of pinks and oranges. She carried a straw clutch with a faux-jeweled clasp. Craig sat alone in the pew behind them. He was wearing his best clothes. His expression was inscrutable. His hands were folded in his lap.

Sarah, sitting in the row behind Adam and Kat, wore her consciously dorky glasses and four strands of wooden beads around her neck. Cordelia was adorable, also consciously, in a black and white flower print dress and black patent leather shoes. Cody looked massively uncomfortable in a blue Oxford shirt buttoned almost to the neck, and tucked neatly (for now) into pressed jeans. It was good of Sarah to have come. Tilda smiled over at her sister-in-law. She was glad they were still friends of a sort, no thanks to Adam.

Her father, in a sober suit and tie, sat in the first row, just in front of Adam and Kat. Ruth, also in a sober, well-cut suit, sat to his right. The Vickes and Bobby Taylor were to her right. Bobby had worn a tie for the occasion, but no jacket. Tilda wasn't sure he owned one.

Tilda looked behind her. The pews were empty. She wondered why her mother's special friends weren't in attendance. Carol Whitehouse, the woman who had been with her when she died, had called with a valid excuse not to be there. But where were— Tilda stopped short. Where were who? She tried hard then to recall her mother's friends but she couldn't recall a single one other than Carol. Maybe her memory was bad. Maybe her mother had not really had personal friends, like her father had Bobby and Teddy. For the first time Tilda wondered if Charlotte had even liked Tessa Vickes.

Tilda looked over at Tessa. Outwardly, she was the antithesis of Charlotte McQueen, in her sensible flat sandals and voluminous sundress that looked as if it dated from the seventies, and her hair in a braid down her back. Charlotte had always been perfectly groomed and coiffed. She had worn tailored clothing. She had not cared for flats. And inwardly? A few moments spent with each woman would prove that Tessa Vickes and Charlotte McQueen had been as unlike as two women could be. Tilda doubted there had been a close friendship between them.

Tilda tried to pay attention to what the minister was saying but her mind continued to wander. Who had been at her mother's funeral? Tilda couldn't remember. She had been in shock. She had nodded and shaken hands and accepted condolence cards and then, mercifully, it was all over. She could ask Ruth about the attendees. She was sure to remember. But Tilda wasn't sure she wanted to know that her mother had died virtually friendless.

The minister's tone changed. He was winding up his

talk. Tilda realized she had missed everything he had said about her mother. Had he said that she was loved and popular? Had he said that she was universally missed?

"Almighty God," he was saying now, "we entrust all who are dear to us to your never-failing care and love, for this life and the life to come. . . ." The words, Tilda thought, were most likely from the Book of Common Prayer. She wasn't sure that she believed in God, but now she found herself silently repeating those words of entreaty and thinking of her beloved and much lamented Frank.

The party was held at Larchmere in the early evening. Bill had sent an invitation to everyone he knew, no matter how slightly, in the towns of Ogunquit and Wells and Cape Neddick. Tilda wondered how many of the guests had really known or cared for her mother. She suspected that many if not most people had come for her father's sake.

Once again the gazebo was lit with strings of tiny white lights. Food was set up on a long table inside, and on smaller tables on the front porch. Adirondack chairs, painted white, sat in small groups around the lawn. Other chairs, a variety of styles, were stacked against the house for the use of whoever wanted one. In the front hall of the house, on a wooden easel that had once belonged to Charlotte (she had taken up painting for about a month one summer), sat a formal portrait of her, taken the year before she died. Charlotte had liked to have formal portraits taken. In this one she was wearing a crisp, white cotton blouse with the collar upturned. Around her neck was tied a small navy silk scarf. She wore pearl studs in her ears. Her face was captured as if she were gazing off into the distance in contemplation. Her hair was slicked into a classic French twist, showing her firm jawline. The photograph had been retouched, but not by much. The Charlotte of the portrait looked expensive and self-contained and utterly self-satisfied. It was, Tilda thought, a very good picture of her mother.

Tilda wandered the lawn for a while, drink in hand, listening to her father's guests in conversation. She passed a very old man, someone whose name she couldn't immediately recall. He was talking to another very old man. Tilda knew him as Turkey Mike but had no idea why he was called that. "I remember when Bill's father was still alive," the nameless old man was saying. "My own father helped him build that guest cottage back in, oh, it must have been 1930 some odd, I'd say."

"Lots changed since them days," Turkey Mike replied, with a shake of his head. "Lots changed."

Tilda walked on, determined to ask her aunt how Turkey Mike had come by his name.

"I don't see that nice Jennifer Fournier here, do you?"

"No. That seems a bit strange, don't you think? With she and Bill such an item."

The speakers were the elderly Simmons sisters. Martha and Constance lived together in a tidy white farmhouse that had belonged to their parents. Neither had ever married. They were very nice and, as all "spinsters" were said to be, a bit batty. Both were wearing white cotton gloves and straw hats with silk flowers around the brim.

Tilda vowed to pay the sisters a visit and moved on.

"Poor Bill looks a bit worn out. The memorial must have been a strain for him." That speaker was a longtime member of the zoning board. Tilda couldn't remember his name, either.

"I wonder when Matilda is going to find herself a new man. A woman shouldn't be alone like that. It isn't right." And that was Mrs. Reed, who had been married four times and who now was rumored to be looking for husband number five.

Tilda smiled again, and wondered if Mrs. Reed had ever

tried to snag Bill McQueen. That, she thought, would have been a disastrous match!

"Remember when Charlotte wanted to put that god-awful addition on the house?"

Tilda paused at the mention of her mother. She was behind the speaker and his friend. She recognized them as more Ogunquit old-timers. One had worked in local construction. The other had been a house painter. She wanted to hear what they would say. She grabbed her cell phone from her pocket and pretended to study it, as if she were reading a text message.

"She fought the zoning board like a, well, like one cat fights another cat invading his turf. But she lost in the end."

The former house painter laughed. "I remember Bill was pretty embarrassed about the whole thing. That addition wasn't his idea, I heard tell. But no one ever blamed Bill for any trouble his wife caused. That time or any other. He needn't have worried that anybody would turn on him."

Tilda snapped the phone shut and hurried away from the men.

37

Adam had left Kat sitting by herself near the gazebo. She had been out of sorts all day, cranky when she spoke and sullen-faced when she didn't. He did not like her this way. He wondered what had happened to change her usually placid, good-natured personality so abruptly. It was probably something hormonal, he decided. Well, if this is how she got from a bad period, there was no way in hell he was going to let her get pregnant!

He was hunting out his father's lawyer. He spotted him on the front porch and strode rapidly ahead. He was still in the suit he had worn to the memorial service. He was the only one at the party formally dressed.

"There you are," he said, bounding up the porch stairs. "I want to talk to you."

Teddy, drink in hand, looked at him with some amusement, which Adam interpreted as confusion. "You do, do you?" Teddy said. "What about?"

"I want to know the contents of my father's will."

"And I want my hair to grow back but that isn't going to happen either."

Adam frowned. "This is not a joke, Teddy. I need to know before things get further out of hand."

"Things seem to be just fine to me. Except," he said pointedly, "for Jennifer's not being here, that is."

"Forget about her. If she knows what's good for her, she won't be coming back."

Teddy took a long sip of his drink before saying, "Adam McQueen, your behavior is appalling. I thought your father raised you better."

"My father was too busy working to raise anyone. My mother was responsible for everything. But that's beside the point. Tell me what's in my father's will. I have a right to know."

"Son," Teddy said, drawing himself straight and tall, "you aren't going to get a word out of me about your father's personal business so you might as well save your breath on trying."

Teddy went off to get himself another gin and tonic. For all he cared, Adam McQueen could go to Hades.

Tilda opened the door to the restaurant and peered into the bar area to the left and ahead. Dennis waved. He was sitting at the very end, by the back wall. He had saved the stool next to him, no easy feat on a busy summer night.

Tilda walked rapidly to the back of the bar. "Thanks so much for coming," she said. Almost without thinking she had called him on her cell phone soon after overhearing those men talking about her mother. She had asked if he was free for a quick drink. She had told him that she felt stifled by the crowd at home and needed to slip away for a while. He had said that, yes, he was free. They had agreed to meet at Five-O.

"I'm glad you called me," he said. "I'm glad I can be of some help."

"I can't stay long."

She felt a bit reckless being there with Dennis, like she had snuck out of her parents' house—which, in fact, she had—when she was supposed to be in bed. She felt as if she was breaking a law. It wasn't a bad feeling.

"Just too crazy back there?" Dennis asked.

"Mmm," she said and sipped her drink, which he had thoughtfully ordered for her before her arrival.

"Emotions must be riding high. A memorial is meant to bring back memories, good and bad."

"Yes."

"They're meant to be cathartic somehow. Though I'm not sure they always are."

Tilda managed a smile. "I wonder if they ever are. Thank you again for meeting me. I hope I didn't spoil your evening."

"Not at all. This is the highlight of my evening."

They talked a bit longer about not much at all and then Tilda said that she had to get back to Larchmere and the party. Dennis walked with her to her car, which she had parked in the lot behind the restaurant.

Without premeditation they kissed. It was passionate. It went on for some time.

Tilda eventually pulled away, but with reluctance. "I feel like a teenager," she whispered, "kissing out back in the dark."

Dennis stroked her face with his thumb. "So do I. Thank you."

"Thank you, too. I had better get back. . . ."

"Of course," he said. "And by the way, I was wrong when I said back at the bar that that was the highlight of my evening. This was the highlight, right here with you in this parking lot."

Tilda got behind the wheel of her car. In the rearview

mirror she saw Dennis watching her until she was out of sight.

Tilda got back to Larchmere a few minutes later to find the party still in full swing. No one seemed to have missed her. Hannah and Susan were chatting with the Simmons sisters. Craig was lighting sparklers for the children at the party, careful to keep them away from danger. Jon and Jane had reunited with some people they had worked with in past summers and were chatting and laughing happily. Tilda had noted, earlier, that Adam had made no effort to talk to her children since their arrival at Larchmere. Greetings had been exchanged and Kat had been introduced, but, as far as Tilda knew, there had been no further involvement. She was not surprised. Adam had never been a particularly attentive uncle.

Tilda now spotted Adam and Kat over by the gazebo. They were arguing. Anyone could see that from their quick and abrupt hand gestures, their bent shoulders. She wondered if the argument was about starting a family. She felt bad, again, for having interfered in their relationship and turned away from the unhappy pair.

Sarah and the kids had already retired to the guest cottage. Ruth and Bobby were still at Bill's side. It seemed that neither had wanted to leave him alone that night. His sadness was obvious. Tilda wondered how much of her father's grief was for his dead wife, Charlotte, and how much was for the fresh loss of his girlfriend, Jennifer. She thought that she knew the answer to that question.

She walked over to where Bill, Ruth, and Bobby were sitting in a grouping of Adirondack chairs. She leaned down and put her hand on her father's arm. "How are you, Dad?" she asked. She hoped he believed in her concern.

Bill smiled feebly but gamely. "Just fine, thanks, Tilda."

She opened her mouth to say something comforting, anything, but just at that moment a big, wide man came lumbering up to the group. It was Pete Strout, former owner of a successful musical venue in York Beach, now comfortably retired.

"Bill McQueen," he bellowed. He always bellowed. "Sorry I got to the party so late but let's make up for lost time!"

Tilda stepped back from her father. She had lost her chance.

It was almost one in the morning before the last party guest had gone home. What food was left—not much—had been hastily put away and the McQueen family had retired for what was left of the night.

Tilda was in her room, preparing for bed. She knew she would have trouble falling asleep. She felt all wound up after the events of the last few days. She felt as if her emotions were bouncing against the walls. The memorial. Jennifer's defection and her own complicity in it. The boisterous crowd at the party. Her dates and excursions with Dennis. The time she had taken his hand. Their unexpectedly passionate kiss. Her father's strained face and palpable sadness. Her aunt's, and her daughter's, accusations of bad behavior.

And what she had overheard at the party about her mother had upset her. She knew her mother had not been perfect—who was?—but to speak ill of the dead at their own memorial seemed wrong. Not that the two men had really said anything that bad or insulting. They had simply been recounting an episode that clearly had stuck in the memory of the town. It was an episode that showed her mother in an unflattering light.

It was that nostalgia problem again, Tilda realized. For some people death seemed to erase a loved one's every flaw and raise him to the status of saint. But should it? No. Well, maybe not.

Tilda got into bed and yawned. Suddenly, she felt that sleep was, indeed, possible. She was just about to drift off when she heard a strange noise from downstairs. It had sounded like something large falling. . . . Tilda threw off the covers and raced into the hallway. Hannah and Susan were a few steps in front of her and Ruth's door was just opening.

"Dad! Craig!" Hannah called as they hurried to the first floor.

"In here, in the kitchen!"

The four women crowded through the doorway to find Craig kneeling over his father, who was prone on the floor. Bill was wearing his pajamas and a robe. One slipper had fallen off a foot.

"I was in the library. I heard a noise. I've called an ambulance."

Craig began to check for a pulse and signs of breathing. Ruth rushed to his side and put her hand lightly on her brother's head. Susan and Hannah clutched each other, staring. Tilda's hands were over her mouth.

Only when the ambulance was gone and Bill was off to York Hospital did Adam emerge from his room, annoyed and hungover.

38

Saturday, July 28

"I called Jennifer at her Portland apartment about five-thirty this morning," Tilda told the others. "I let her know that Dad's going to be fine. She was going to pack a bag and be on her way."

It was a little after seven o'clock. After learning that Bill had suffered not a heart attack, as was feared, but a panic attack, albeit a big one, Tilda, Hannah, and Susan had gone back to Larchmere for quick showers and coffee and were now sitting on plastic chairs in a waiting room. Craig and Ruth had spent the night at the hospital; Craig was in his father's room. Adam had only just arrived, leaving Kat back at the house. Sarah, Jon, and Jane were on their way; they would leave for the hospital when Bobby showed up to watch the children. He had forgone his boat that morning to be at his friend's side, and had only just left the hospital for Larchmere.

"Jennifer!"

Tilda hurriedly got to her feet at her approach, as did Ruth and Hannah. Adam stood off to the side, arms folded.

"I got here as fast as I could," Jennifer said. Her eyes looked puffy—she obviously had been crying—but she was as impeccably dressed as always.

Ruth reached out and hugged her. Hannah gave her an awkward pat on the arm. Tilda gave her arm a squeeze. "I'm sorry," she said.

But Jennifer didn't seem to hear. She walked over to Adam. "I want to talk to you," she said. "Away from the others. Now."

Adam rolled his eyes and half turned away from her. "I said now," Jennifer repeated. To Tilda's amazement, he followed her down the hall.

Tilda looked from Ruth to Hannah to Susan. "What is that all about?" she asked.

"Payback," Ruth said. "She's going to ream him for abusing her. Good. Not that it will do much good in terms of Adam's behavior—he'll never change—but at least it should make her feel better."

What happened between Jennifer and Adam was this.

"What do you want?" he said. "I thought I told you to get lost."

"Teddy told me that you hounded him about Bill's will at the party last night. How dare you treat people like they're inferior to you, just children to be bossed around, and threatened, and manipulated. And don't you ever again even dream of speaking to me the way you spoke to me the other day. If you even come close I will go directly to the police. Do you understand me?"

"I—" Adam began but Jennifer went on, her voice tight with fury.

"Shut up, Adam, and listen to me. I will never forgive you for trying to stand in the way of your father's happiness, let alone my own peace of mind. Do you hear me? Never."

Adam attempted a grin. Since Sarah, no one had spoken

so angrily to him. He was slightly amused. "I suppose you'll go running to my father and accuse me of all sorts of crimes against him. Isn't that the way you people work?"

Jennifer looked up at this man, the oldest child of the man she loved. How could father and son be so different? She actually felt pity for Adam, along with disgust. What a miserable human being he was! "On the contrary," she said calmly. "Your father will never hear a word of your behavior from me. It would be cruel, and I'll leave the cruelty to you."

Jennifer walked back to where the women stood. A nurse came over to guide her to Bill's room. Adam followed her in. Craig was already inside. Craig hugged Jennifer and she hugged him back.

"I'm glad you're here," he said. Then, he stepped back to let her sit on the bed by Bill's side. Adam stood stiffly by the door.

Jennifer took Bill's hand and smiled down at him. Her smile was a little wobbly but she refused to cry.

"How are you feeling?" she asked.

"Fine. Better. Thank you for coming."

Of course he sounds so formal, Jennifer thought. *He doesn't really believe I'm here because I love him so. He thinks I've come back out of courtesy; he thinks I'm paying a courtesy visit to the former partner.* She would have to convince him otherwise.

"Bill," she said, "believe me, the only reason I left Larchmere was for your sake. I thought it would be better for you if I weren't around for the memorial. Everyone seemed . . ." Jennifer took a deep breath. She remembered her words to Adam in the hallway. She would not speak badly of Bill's children to him. "I felt that I was out of place. I felt that I was interfering. Well, maybe I was wrong. I'm sorry. I should have stayed by your side."

There was a moment before Bill could speak. He

squeezed her hand and smiled. "No, no," he said, his voice breaking. "It's my fault for not seeing what was going on, for not shielding you, for not protecting you. I let you down, Jennifer, and I'm sorry."

Jennifer smiled. "Let's just say our communication skills could use some work. I love you, Bill McQueen, and I will never leave you again."

"Good," Bill said. His voice was stronger. "Because I wouldn't want my wife anywhere but right at my side." He reached into the drawer of the bedside table and took out a blue velvet box. "This is for you," he said, "if you'll have it. It was in the pocket of my robe when I collapsed. I've had it for about a month but I just couldn't find the right moment to propose."

Jennifer took the box and laughed. "Nice," she said. "So you wait until you're in the hospital. . . ." Carefully, she opened the box, and then the tears did flow. She held out her left hand and Bill slipped the ring onto her finger.

"If you don't like it—" Bill began.

"Sshhh," she said. "Don't even think such a thing. It's a lovely ring and I love it and I love you."

The door to Bill's room slammed. Adam was gone.

Craig quietly slipped out after him. "I thought I should give those two lovebirds some time alone," he said to his brother, who was very red in the face.

"I think Dad is mentally incompetent. Someone not mentally competent isn't considered capable of contracting marriage. That's the law."

"He had a panic attack, Adam, not a psychotic break."

"We'll see what my friend John has to say about it. He's a professor of psychiatry at Harvard Medical School. I'm going to give him a call today. He'll give us a break on a complete psychological evaluation."

Craig struggled to keep his temper. "No one is having my father 'evaluated.' Don't be ridiculous, Adam."

"Don't tell me I'm being ridiculous!" Adam shouted. "Do you know what's at stake here? Do you?"

"Uh, our father's happiness?"

"Who gives a shit about his happiness! I'm talking about the house, the money, the—"

A nurse suddenly appeared. He was large. His neck was covered with tattoos. "Sir," he said to Adam, "if you can't keep your voice down, I'm going to have to ask you to leave."

Cool, Craig thought. *The hospital has bouncers.* He watched his brother stalk off down the corridor. And he felt a stab of sorrow.

39

The house was very quiet. It didn't occur to Adam to wonder where his children were.

He went straight up to the second floor. He felt he had not shaved properly that morning and was eager to examine his face in the bathroom mirror. Nothing irked him more than a sloppy shave.

He passed the door of the room he was sharing with Kat. It was closed. He thought that Kat might still be asleep but then he became aware of noise from within, a dresser drawer closing, and he opened the door.

"What are you doing?" he said immediately.

Kat, whose back had been to the door as she stood by the bed, turned and gasped. "You startled me," she said.

"What are you doing? Why is your travel bag on the bed?"

Kat reached deep down for every bit of confidence she possessed. "I'm sorry, Adam," she said. "I can't do this."

"Can't do what? What are you talking about?"

"I can't marry you!" she cried, frustrated with his inability to see, to hear, to listen.

Adam closed the door to the bedroom behind him. "What do you mean you can't marry me?"

"Just what I said. I can't marry you. I'm leaving. I'm going home."

Adam took a step closer to Kat. "Look, what's this all about? Close that bag and talk to me. What's gotten into you?"

Kat's blood rushed just a tiny bit. He was a sexy man. He was handsome. Were his looks all that she had fallen for? The thought shamed her. She took a deep breath and a half step back.

"Nothing's gotten into me. It's just . . . I . . . I thought I loved you but . . . and then there's the kids, Cordelia and Cody . . . and I feel so uncomfortable here, with your family. I need to leave, Adam. I'm sorry."

Adam chuckled in that annoyingly patronizing way he had perfected. "Kat, don't be ridiculous. I demand you stay and get this nonsense about leaving out of your head."

"You demand?" Now Kat was angry. "I'm not your kid, Adam. You can't order me around. I don't love you anymore, you lied to me about wanting a family, and I'm not marrying you and I'm going home. I've already called my parents."

There was a dead, scary silence. Kat wondered who would hear her if she screamed. She desperately hoped she would not have to scream.

Finally, Adam spoke. His voice was hard and cold. "Then I want my ring back."

Kat, stunned, clutched her left hand in her right protectively. "It's mine," she said. "You gave it to me."

"Under the condition that you marry me. Now, give it to me."

He took another step toward her. Kat felt menaced. Instinctively, she retreated a step, then jerked the ring off her finger and threw it at him. It hit the floor by his feet.

"You idiot!" he hissed. "You could have damaged the diamond! I'll never get my money back if it's damaged!"

The loud sound of a car's horn made Kat reach for her bag. "That's my ride," she said. She did not meet his eye as she dashed toward the bedroom door.

Adam followed her down the stairs and out the front door.

Teddy and Tessa Vickes were there in their old green Cadillac.

"Mr. and Mrs. Vickes are driving me to Portsmouth," Kat said as Teddy got out from behind the wheel of the car. "I'll get a bus back to Boston."

Teddy nodded curtly to Adam and helped Kat stow her bag in the trunk. "You ready?" he said kindly to her.

"Yes. Thank you." Kat climbed in the backseat and Adam saw Tessa Vickes turn to give her an encouraging smile. No doubt, he thought sneeringly, she would also have a bag of home-baked cookies for Kat.

Adam stood, rigid. He watched the old green Cadillac pull off and head down the driveway to Shore Road. He watched the woman who had promised to be his wife leave him. She did not turn to look back at him. His hands were clenched at his sides. When the car was out of sight he became aware of children's laughter, followed by the booming laugh of a man. It was coming from the direction of the guest cottage. His children. He remembered now that Bobby had been sent to Larchmere to watch them. He knew he should go and fetch his children from Bobby's care. Instead, he went back inside, up the stairs, and into the room he had once shared with Kat Daly. He lay down on the unmade bed.

* * *

It was a little after noon. Tilda, Hannah and Susan, Ruth, and Jennifer were in the kitchen, having arrived a little earlier from York Hospital. Bill was being kept for further observation but his doctor, a man who had treated Charlotte, too, had promised that he would be home either that evening or the following morning. Craig had stayed on, washing up in the men's room and grabbing a sandwich from the cafeteria. He swore he would return to Larchmere some time that afternoon, at least to change clothes. Jon and Jane, with their mother's blessing, had gone to meet some old friends. Sarah had taken her children to Jackie's, Too for lunch. Nobody wanted to scare them unnecessarily so their routine was proceeding as normally as possible.

Tilda and Hannah could not stop apologizing to Jennifer and asking for her forgiveness.

"I'm sorry for not being more accepting," Tilda said.

"Me, too." That was Hannah. "And for not standing up to you that night when Adam was such a jerk about your business."

"And I should never have snapped at you when you asked me about the spa in town. I felt so awful about that." That was Tilda, again.

Jennifer laughed and held up her hands. "Enough! All is forgiven. Let's start over."

"Fine by me," Hannah said.

Tilda nodded. "Thank you."

Susan asked for a closer look at Jennifer's engagement ring. Jennifer put out her hand. "It's an Edwardian style but the ring itself is new. Bill said he helped design it!"

"Dad?" Hannah said. "A jewelry designer? Wow. He really has got a new lease on life!"

Ruth, who had been opening a chilled bottle of Prosecco, sensing a celebration in the air, said, "I say we have a nice lunch, just us gals."

"I'm starved!" Susan put her hand to her stomach. "I forgot to eat breakfast in all the excitement."

"Me, too," Tilda said. "I know there's dried pasta in the pantry. And we've got excellent tomatoes and a bag of frozen peas. And there are fresh herbs in the garden. And there's a ball of fresh mozzarella, if Craig didn't eat it. You know how much he loves it. How about I make a big cold pasta salad for lunch?"

"I'll get the Miracle Whip," Susan said, heading for the fridge. "If no one objects. I'm addicted to the stuff."

"And let's have some of this Prosecco." Ruth held up the bottle. "I think we could all use a glass."

Jennifer laughed. "Or two!"

Adam came into the kitchen as Ruth was pouring out glasses of the sparkling wine. No one had seen him since he had stormed out of the hospital that morning. He looked angry and cold and strange.

"What's wrong?" Tilda asked. "You look upset."

His voice was expressionless. "Kat's gone," he said. "She broke the engagement."

Tilda and Hannah shared a look of guilt. Susan, in an attempt to hide her smile, turned toward the sink.

"Oh," Tilda said. "I'm sorry." Silently, she regretted that now she would never find out just who Kat had met the night she and her siblings had gone to dinner at The Front Porch. Had a mystery lover had anything to do with Kat's defection?

Hannah nervously cleared her throat. "Yeah. Me, too."

"It's for the best," Ruth said, turning to put the bottle in a bucket of ice. "I'm sure."

"Teddy Vickes and his wife took her to the bus station in Portsmouth. You know the mouth on Tessa Vickes. The whole freakin' town must know by now."

Jennifer continued to say nothing. Her placid expression

hid the fact that inside she was laughing at his obvious embarrassment.

Adam looked pointedly at Jennifer now. "I won't be around for dinner tonight," he said.

"Okay," Ruth said. No one asked him where he was going or when he would be back. Tilda supposed he needed some solitude. That, or he just couldn't stand the sight of his family any longer.

Craig sat on the cushioned guest chair by his father's hospital bed. He was tired but didn't want to sleep. He sipped his third cup of coffee since noon and considered buying a chocolate bar from the vending machine in the cafeteria. He wanted to comb his father's hair—it was uncharacteristically messy and it made him look old—but he felt too shy to attempt it.

Bill stirred and opened his eyes.

"Hey, Dad." Craig put the cup of coffee on the bedside table and went over to his father. "How are you feeling?"

Bill shifted to a sitting position and Craig helped him adjust the pillows behind his back.

"A little embarrassed, to tell you the truth."

Craig smiled a little. "Since when are you such a macho guy? Everyone is vulnerable at some time."

"Be that as it may," Bill said, "I'm sorry I caused everyone such worry."

"You were just paying me back for all the worry I've caused you over the years."

There was a moment of fairly awkward silence. Bill toyed with the edge of the sheet. "Thank you, Craig," he said suddenly.

"For what?"

"For taking charge when I passed out. Ruth told me all

about it. And for staying with me all last night. You didn't have to do that."

Craig felt an acute mix of embarrassment and pleasure. He thought that he might cry. "I wanted to stay. Really, it was no big deal, Dad."

"It was a big deal to me. Thank you."

Craig cleared his throat, patted his father's arm, and sat back down in the cushioned guest chair. "You'd do the same for me."

Bill looked fondly at his son. "Yes," he said. "I would."

40

Sunday, July 29

During the course of the morning Larchmere emptied of many of its inhabitants. Sarah and the children headed back to Massachusetts. (Obviously, Adam had given up more of his visitation rights. He also wasn't there to see them off.) Tilda had told Sarah the night before, at dinner, about Kat having broken the engagement. In fact, aside from updates on Bill's condition (which was fine, though his doctor had suggested he stay the night in the hospital), the conversation over dinner had been mostly about Adam's new status as single. Sarah had not been surprised at the turn of events but she had not stooped to gloat. Mostly, she was concerned as to how Kat's sudden departure might affect her children. They had not been in love with Kat but they had, to some extent, gotten used to her.

Craig, whom Bill had sent back home to get a good night's sleep, had been very quiet at dinner. Tilda and Hannah each thought he looked more reflective and pensive than usual. He had gone to bed immediately after the meal and had left for the hospital first thing that morning to fetch his father.

Not long after Sarah left for home, and Tilda had returned from her walk on the beach, Jon and Jane took off for Portland and their summer jobs.

"You'll call us if something happens to Grandpa, right?" Jane asked her mother from the passenger seat of Jon's car.

"Of course," she promised. "But I think he'll be fine now."

"And you'll continue to be nice to Jen, right?"

"Of course!" Tilda felt a twinge of embarrassment. "I learned my lesson, don't worry."

"Oh, and one more thing, Mom." That was Jon, leaning over his sister.

"What?"

Jane smiled. "We know about you and your Florida mystery man. I just hope you're being careful—if you know what I mean."

Tilda blushed furiously as her children laughed and pulled away. She recovered enough of her composure to wave them off, watching until the car was out of sight along Shore Road. She felt the anxiety she always felt watching them go away. She also felt very proud of her children. And so much for secrecy in a small town!

Adam had not shown himself at breakfast time. Tilda thought she heard someone—presumably Adam—come in well after midnight. She hoped her brother would be all right. She did not hate him and she was not enjoying his discomfort as Hannah and Susan and maybe even Ruth and Jennifer seemed to be.

Tilda turned back to the house. Suddenly, she felt incredibly tired and fought the urge to go up to her room and lie down. But she had made plans to see Dennis around eleven so instead she made another cup of coffee, showered, and got dressed.

* * *

Tilda and Dennis had driven down to York Beach. He had expressed a desire to try an interesting flavor of ice cream at Goldenrod Kisses, maybe the caramel with sea salt. And he wanted to buy a few souvenirs for his grandchildren. Together, they strolled the main street, crowded with tourists. Dennis bought a plushy lobster for two-year-old Leah and a stretchy bracelet made of aqua-colored shells for four-year-old Laura. They were waiting until after lunch to have ice cream.

"Your father is a lucky man," Dennis said, when they were settled at a table at Inn on the Blues. "I mean, to have a family that loves him like you do."

Tilda thought about that for a moment. "Well, I don't know about lucky. He earned our love and respect. He was, he is, a good father."

"That may well be, but not everyone who earns love and respect gets it. There are such things as ungrateful children. And ungrateful spouses, and ungrateful friends."

Yes, Tilda thought. *Like Adam is an ungrateful son. Will Jon turn out to be an ungrateful child? Will Jane?* She believed in her children but only time would tell.

They ordered fish and chips and chatted about the McQueen and the Haass families. Dennis revealed that when his wife had left him for the other man, his son refused to talk to her for months. "I found myself advocating for my cheating wife," he said with a wry smile. "I didn't want my son's relationship with his mother to be permanently compromised."

"The things we do to keep the peace. That was good of you."

Dennis shrugged. "Parents put their children before themselves. At least, they should."

"Forever, do you think?" Tilda asked. "I mean, shouldn't

there be a time when it's legitimate for a parent to think of him- or herself first?"

They discussed this thorny issue for a while, without coming to any hard and fast agreement on the limits of parental responsibility, then left the restaurant and went around the corner to Goldenrod Kisses. They took their ice cream down to the beach and settled side by side on two large rocks. The tide was low and the sand stretched ahead of them for what seemed like miles.

Dennis ran a finger along Tilda's cheek. "I've been thinking about that kiss," he said, "in the parking lot."

Tilda blushed. "Me, too," she admitted. And she had been, when not worrying about her father.

"Would you like to try it again?"

Tilda nodded. She took off her sunglasses, turned, and moved closer to Dennis. His lips met hers. His kiss was expert. She tasted sea salt and sweetness. It was not unpleasant. But it was not like it had been in the parking lot.

"That was fantastic," he said, when they had each, gently, pulled away. His voice was husky.

"Mmm," she replied. It had been nice for her, not fantastic. But she could hardly tell the truth. She put her sunglasses back on, hoping to hide a telltale sign of her real feelings.

They left the beach soon after. Dennis dropped her off at Larchmere. Tilda managed to make the parting kiss a quick peck. She gave him a big smile and if he was disappointed, he didn't let on. She watched as he drove off in his rental car.

Tilda went up to her room. She flopped onto the bed and wondered to what extent the circumstances of their first kiss had colored and heightened the experience. When she had run away from the party she had been feeling hurt and somehow adrift and in need of contact and reassurance.

Dennis had been there for her. It was night. No one knew where she was. She had drunk some wine. The right elements for romance had been in place. Did that make the experience of that kiss any less valid? No. Tilda knew she would remember it for a long time.

She got off the bed and went to the bathroom to wash off the sand and sunscreen. Dennis's vacation in Ogunquit was coming to a close. She knew that for her it would be a natural end to their brief but happy romance. She hoped that for him, it would be the same.

Susan found Hannah in the library. She was sitting in the middle of the big, brown leather couch. "What are you doing?" Susan asked. She sat down next to Hannah, facing her.

Hannah smiled. "I'm doing absolutely nothing. Do you ever find that all you want to do is nothing? Not read or listen to music or go for a walk or even meditate or think about things. You just want to do nothing."

Susan raised an eyebrow. "Uh, not really. I don't like doing nothing. I like to keep busy and productive."

"Oh, busy and productive is good, too. But sometimes I like to just sit and vegetate."

"Speaking of vegetating . . . Hannah, I want to talk a bit about the family issue." Susan's tone was gentle but firm.

Hannah's smile faded. "Oh."

"Yes, oh. I'm trying to be patient and understanding, Hannah. I really am. But it's been two years now. I'm beginning to feel . . . concerned."

"I'm sorry."

"I believe you are. But the apologies aren't getting us anywhere."

"I know."

"I was thinking that maybe we should see a marriage counselor. We don't seem to be making any progress, just the two of us. What do you think?"

Hannah felt raw panic. Marriage counseling meant failure. That was what her mother had said, time and again. It led to separation and that led to divorce. People only went to marriage counseling as a last resort. Were she and Susan really in such a desperate place? And she wondered: Why had her mother talked so negatively about marriage counseling? Had Bill asked her to go and had she refused? Her father had told Hannah that she was nothing like her mother. She needed to believe him. "Okay," she said, aware that she sounded less than enthusiastic.

"Are you sure?"

"Yes," she lied. "I'm sure."

"Okay. I can find someone through my work connections. Or if you'd rather research someone, that's fine, too."

"No, no. You can choose a therapist for us. I trust you."

"All right. I think we're doing the right thing, Hannah."

"Yes."

Susan wanted to say more but decided not to. She squeezed Hannah's hand, got up, and left the room. Hannah sat in the middle of the big, brown leather couch for a long time. She had never felt so afraid.

Tilda found her younger brother repairing the old wooden gate to the herb garden. It was a hot afternoon and his T-shirt was soaked with sweat. She offered to bring him some water but he told her that he was almost done with the job.

"Dad seems good," she said. "He's resting but only because Jennifer ordered him to. He said something about calling Teddy for a game of golf tomorrow morning."

Craig stood up and stretched. "I'm glad Dad's doing well. And I'm glad he didn't need CPR the other night. I'm certified but I've never had to perform it on anyone other than the dummy in class."

Tilda was surprised. "I didn't know you knew CPR."

"There are a lot of things people don't know about me."

"Because you never tell them about yourself. You don't let them see the whole you. I'm sorry," she said. "Maybe that was unfair."

Craig looked at his sister. "No. It's partly true. Maybe mostly true. I've spent a lot of time hiding. When I wasn't running, that is."

Craig made an adjustment to the gate and tried the new latch he had installed. "Done," he said. "Not that a gate keeps out the deer, but at least it looks nice."

"I'm sorry I underestimate you, Craig."

Craig looked around at his sister again. "Do you? I kind of thought you were the one person who didn't underestimate me."

Tilda smiled. "Let's just say there's room for improvement in my attitude."

"There's room for improvement in everyone's attitude. We're all just human."

"Too true." Tilda kissed her brother on the cheek and turned to go.

"Where are you off to now?" Craig asked.

"I've got something I need to tend to. Some old business I let slide. I'll see you later."

Tilda went around the house and into the woods where the ruins of the old fairy house were barely visible. She knelt on the ground and began to clear away debris. She had decided that she would reconstruct the old fairy house, and that she would maintain it. Maybe she would even build a second house, and a third. She could create an entire village for the fairies.

Because who could truly say that fairies didn't exist? Maybe they could be imagined into existence. People

imagined all sorts of things into existence and then sometimes even came to believe that those things had created
their creators! Angels and gods, spirits and goblins. And
who could say that miracles didn't happen, or that people
didn't make miracles happen when the universe seemed
not to be listening to their pleas?

Tilda picked up a small, smooth rock. It was gray with a
scattering of tiny white lines. She had a vague memory of
having found it on the beach, many years ago. She would
use it again in this new fairy house. And she would find
new materials, too. New materials for a new construction.

Something was beginning to change. Dennis's friendship and that first, important kiss; her father's unexpected
romance, and then his illness and recovery; the destruction
of Adam's engagement; Craig's periods of obvious sadness
or depression, which seemed to portend a crisis; Hannah's
struggle with the decision to start a family. Things were in
motion. Things had been wrenched up from their places on
the ground and tossed into the air and Tilda had no idea
where they would all decide to land. She was afraid. She
was, she realized, also excited. She went back to work.

41

Monday, July 30

Bill McQueen and Jennifer Fournier had decided to marry without further delay. Well, they would have to wait until Wednesday—there were some preparations that took a bit of time. And, more importantly for the McQueen family, Bill had decided to reveal the contents of his will. The severity of the anxiety attack had frightened him. Life could be snatched away at any moment. Bill wanted his family to be prepared, and he wanted to be happy for his remaining days on earth. Teddy was summoned and was at Larchmere by late morning.

The family was gathered in the library. Bill sat behind the desk, his hands folded before him, and Teddy was perched on its edge. The others—Tilda, Hannah, Susan, Craig, and Ruth—were seated around the room. Jennifer, too, was there, at Bill's invitation. She stood at his side. Adam, who was standing apart from the others, made no acknowledgment of her, but by this time no one, probably not even Bill, expected him to treat her with anything like respect. Percy, as if another witness to the scene, was sitting upright on the desk, across from where Teddy sat.

Tilda felt dread and anticipation and fear and a little bit of excitement. Hannah clutched Susan's hand. She didn't know it but she was feeling the same crazed mix of emotions her sister was feeling. Craig's face was inscrutable, as it had been at his mother's memorial, but his arms tightly folded across his chest betrayed his discomfort. Only Ruth and Jennifer looked entirely at ease and without expectation.

Teddy began to read. There was a life insurance policy for Ruth, and the grandchildren were given small monetary gifts. Certain particular objects that had been in the McQueen family for generations were bequeathed. Tilda inherited her maternal grandmother's diamond solitaire necklace. Craig got his grandfather's handmade wooden tool chest and all of its interesting contents. Adam got his grandfather's monogrammed silver cuff links. Hannah got her grandmother's gold locket and chain. There was even provision made for Jennifer after Bill's death, something Bill had had added only since their engagement in the hospital. Bill's Mercedes, which was paid for, and his old and expensive complete collection of Shakespeare, were to be passed on to Bobby. There was a monetary donation to Bill's favorite charity. Teddy was given Bill's golf clubs. "But you can't have them until I'm gone," Bill said. Everyone, except for Adam, chuckled at that.

And then, the most important part of the document was read. When Teddy finished reading, there was a silence that roared in their ears.

Adam, his face purple, broke that silence. "You what?" he shouted at his father. "You're leaving Larchmere to Hannah? You're leaving our family home, our legacy, to a lesbian?"

"Adam!" Tilda cried, horrified, outraged, almost as if the insult had been aimed at her.

But he ignored her. He turned to Hannah, who had risen from her chair and now stood rigid with shock, Susan's arm tightly around her shoulders.

"And your 'marriage'?" he spat. "Please. It's a total sham, a disgrace. What a joke."

Percy bared his teeth at Adam and hissed loudly. Craig's hands were in fists by his side and his jaw was clenched. For the first time in over twenty years he wanted to hit someone—and hurt him.

"How dare you say—" Ruth put her hand over her mouth, as if afraid of what words might come out of it. It was an unusual gesture for a woman who was very good at speaking her mind.

Bill rose from his chair behind the desk and Tilda moved forward, scared that her father would have another attack. "How dare you talk to your sister this way!" he said, as if picking up where Ruth had left off. "You should be ashamed, Adam. What would your mother say if she were here to listen to such—to such—to such hateful talk?"

"Mom?" Adam laughed meanly. "Please. She totally agreed with me. She wouldn't have even bothered to show up at that farce of a wedding. She hated the fact that her daughter was gay. And she would have been disgusted that you chose to leave Larchmere to her and not to someone normal," he said, pointing at his chest with his long forefinger, "not to the oldest son, not to me."

There was another horrible, heavy silence in the room after this display. Adam looked from one to the other of his family though no one but Bill and Craig met his stare. Teddy was rigid, his eyes lowered to the document he still held in his hands. Jennifer had sunk into Bill's abandoned chair. A low and awful moaning was coming from Percy's chest.

Finally, with a shake of his head meant, Tilda was sure, to exhibit his righteous disgust, Adam stalked to the door of the library. "If this insanity is going to stand," he said, "I'm out of here." He slammed the door behind him.

"He's getting very good at dramatic exits," Craig noted dryly, finally releasing his fists. "Maybe he should have gone into acting instead of finance."

Nobody laughed.

"I'm so sorry, Hannah." Bill went to his younger daughter. Susan released her protective hold so that he could give Hannah a powerful hug. "So very sorry."

Hannah managed a smile. "It's okay, Dad," she said, her voice gruff with emotion. "Everyone is entitled to his own opinions."

"Not if they're contemptible," Craig muttered.

Contemptible. Yes, Hannah thought, that was a good word to describe her older brother's opinion of her. Well, fine. If he found her so distasteful, as the new owner of Larchmere she would simply refuse him access to the property. He would be persona non grata. Adam didn't approve of her? Well, fine, she didn't approve of him.

Hannah took a deep, steadying breath. No. No, she would not ban Adam from his childhood home. There had been enough family dissonance already. Hannah had always tried to be a person who created love and closeness, not hate and distance. Still, it was clear that her relationship with Adam would never be the same. So be it. Life was not all about happy endings. In her opinion, Adam didn't deserve one.

Ruth rubbed her temples as if she had a headache. Her brother's decision to leave Larchmere to Hannah had not surprised her; Adam's grotesque behavior had, in spite of all she knew about him.

Jennifer finally rose and came around the desk to where

Bill stood. She put her arm through his, more to steady herself than to assist him.

"Dad," Hannah said now, "are you sure about this? Are
you sure you want to leave Larchmere to me?"

"I have no doubts, Hannah. I never have."

"But how . . . It will be hard to . . . When do you want
us to . . . ?" Hannah looked to Susan for help but for once,
Susan seemed without words.

Bill's expression grew puzzled, even, Tilda thought, a
bit hurt. "What's wrong, Hannah?" he asked. "I thought
you would be glad to have Larchmere."

Hannah clutched her father's hand. "Oh, Dad, I am glad.
And I'm grateful, more than you can ever know, but I
would be lying if I said I wasn't also overwhelmed. Larchmere is a huge responsibility. It means so much to all of us.
I just . . . I just hope I can be a worthy keeper."

Susan had regained her voice. "It's just that there are so
many things to work out, Bill, details, logistics." She
turned to Teddy. "We'll need some help, some advice."
Teddy nodded.

Craig stepped forward a bit and cleared his throat.
"Dad," he said, "Hannah, listen to me for a minute. I've
been doing a lot of thinking lately, not just since coming
here two weeks ago. And now, with all that's happened,
well, I've made a decision. I'd like to stay on in Ogunquit
and help Hannah run the house in whatever way she
chooses."

Tilda looked at her father. He seemed stunned. His face
was expressionless.

Hannah wanted to laugh and to cry. "You mean, give up
your glamorous life on the road? No more nomadic existence? You want to sleep in the same bed every night?
Clean toilets and fix leaking pipes?"

Craig smiled. "Toilets, too? Well, if I have to . . . Seriously, I've been thinking. I'm tired and I'm lonely and I want to make this commitment. It's a commitment to my family but also to myself. Besides, the van is on its last legs. Or tires."

Tilda felt a twinge of hurt. After all, she had asked Craig to live with her and he had refused! Now he was offering to live with—in whatever capacity—Hannah. But then the twinge was gone. She had come far on this visit to Larchmere. Maybe she even had grown. Craig was doing the right thing for Hannah, just as he had done the right thing for Tilda when he had refused to take responsibility for her life.

Susan wiped tears from her eyes. "Craig, you're a real sweetie," she said.

"Are you sure you know what you're getting into?" Hannah asked him. "You're making a really big commitment, Craig. Frankly, while I'm grateful for the gesture, I'm not entirely sure I believe it."

Craig shrugged. "What choice do you have, Hannah Banana? You're just going to have to trust me."

Hannah turned to Susan, who was still leaking tears. "Well, all right then. We accept your offer. And we thank you."

Ruth felt a rush of love and admiration for her younger nephew. She had known all along that he could come home and mean it. "Bravo, Craig," she said. He blushed and Ruth thought he suddenly looked about ten years old.

Bill's eyes were shining now and he shook his son's hand. "I seem to have done you a disservice all these years. This is a wonderful thing you're doing for the family."

Craig's blush became furious and he turned to Hannah. "Hannah," he said, "remember that time earlier this week when you asked me where I'd been and I said nowhere? Well, I'd been talking to Guy Cokal—you know, he's got a small accounting firm on Pine Road. He's promised me a job while I study for my CPA. He's going to train me, get me started."

Susan laughed now. "Mr. Never Had A Job doing people's taxes! There's more than a little irony there, Craig."

"I've had plenty of jobs," Craig said, grinning. "I've just never made enough money to pay taxes of my own."

Bill turned to Jennifer. "He was always so good with numbers," he said proudly. "Even when he was a little boy."

Craig smiled at his father. "Maybe now I'll put that talent to some good use."

"I'm sure you will, son." That was Teddy, who until then had been standing a bit apart from the others, as if not to intrude upon the family. "And now that everything's all sorted out, I'll take my leave."

Bill and Teddy shook hands and then the lawyer was gone.

"Well," Ruth said, "it seems to be a perfect time for big announcements and I've got one of my own."

Hannah managed a feeble smile. "Oh, boy, I'm not sure I can handle another revelation! I'm feeling a little weak in the knees."

"Oh, it's nothing traumatic. I've decided to go back to school for a master's in fine arts, just for the hell of it. I've enrolled at New York University. I've got the money and I'm eager to spend it. Can't take it with you and all that. You're welcome to visit me but with classes and papers and all, I might not be such a fantastic host. You'll probably have to take yourselves to the Statue of Liberty."

"That's great, Ruth," Tilda said. "But what about Bobby? He hates New York. He refuses to go there ever since that time he went down for—well, he never did say why he went to New York."

"Oh, I'll be back to Ogunquit whenever I can. This beautiful place by the sea has grown on me. Besides, Percy won't be thrilled with life in a tiny apartment."

"I think this calls for champagne!" That was Susan. "We'll toast to the future and to a very, very long life for Bill. And for Larchmere!"

The others agreed.

It was late, almost eleven o'clock, and though everyone gathered in the sunroom had professed to being beastly tired, no one was inclined to go to bed. Craig occupied a chair to the left of the couch; his legs were draped over one of its arms. On the couch Hannah and Susan sat side by side, both slumped comfortably against the cushions. Tilda, in a chair facing them, had curled her long legs up under her.

"It's been quite a few days, hasn't it?" Craig said, stifling a yawn. "That was meant to be a rhetorical question."

There were nods and murmurs of assent.

Around her neck Hannah wore her grandmother's gold locket. As soon as she got home she would find a picture of Susan and put it inside.

"Tilda," she said now, "will you be honest with me about something?"

Tilda, who was wearing her grandmother's diamond solitaire necklace and feeling rather grand, said, "I'll try to be. I mean, I won't lie but if you're going to ask me to break a confidence or—"

"No, no, nothing like that. I just want to know if you're in any way upset that Dad . . . Well, that Larchmere was left to me."

"No," she said promptly, "I'm not upset. Really. I would have been upset if the house was left to Adam. At least now I know Larchmere is in good hands. And that it will always be part of the McQueen legacy."

"And your home," Hannah added. "Our home, all of us."

There was a comfortable silence for a moment and then

Craig said, "I'm sorry that some of my worst suspicions about Mom were proven true. If we can believe Adam, and in this case, I think that we can."

Hannah nodded at Susan, who said, "I know that we can."

Tilda shook her head. "I'm not sure that I can believe him. What I mean is, I'm not sure I'm able to believe him, yet. What he said about Mom and how she felt about Hannah . . . It's going to take some time for that to become bearable. So many things I thought I knew have turned out to be wrong or partially wrong. . . . I feel as if I need to reassess my thoughts about a lot of things."

"Yes," Hannah said. "I think I need to reassess some things as well."

"Where is Adam, anyway?" Craig asked. "Does anyone know?"

"I heard him drive off hours ago," Tilda said. "I hope he doesn't do something stupid like get drunk and crash his car."

Hannah laughed. "God, Tilda, your mind always leaps to the most awful ideas!"

"I know. Sometimes it would drive Frank crazy, my habit of gloom and doom."

"Don't you think Dad will miss Ruth?" Hannah asked after a moment. "Even though he's got Jennifer?"

"Yes, to some extent," Tilda said. "But Ruth is right to give them some space, at least part of the time. Though I'm not sure giving Dad and Jennifer space had anything to do with her decision to get a master's degree."

"Anyway," Susan pointed out, "Jennifer's got the condo in Portland. That can be their getaway, I suppose. Now that he wants us to take possession of Larchmere as soon as possible . . ."

There was another lull in the conversation, this one longer than the last. Tilda was thinking of Dennis, who would be going back to Florida very soon. She so wanted to avoid an awkward parting. She had no idea what was on his mind concerning their relationship. She dreaded a big declaration of feeling from him at the same time she chided herself for thinking she was special enough to deserve one from a man she had known only a short time. She would miss him, a little. She wanted him to miss her but not to pine for her. She wanted to try kissing another man.

Hannah, though happy and excited about the inheritance, was at the same time nervous and afraid and, against her will, entertaining disaster scenarios. What if she started a bed-and-breakfast only to find out that she had no head for business? What if she neglected to pay the insurance bill and then the house burned to the ground? She was also worrying if she was becoming too much like her doom and gloom sister.

Susan was mentally going through her business contacts, considering which one might best help her find a therapist to deal with Hannah's fears of starting a family.

Craig was thinking about Charlotte. "You know," he said suddenly, "Mom wasn't all bad."

"Of course she wasn't," Tilda said automatically, though she wondered again what her mother had done with all of the knitted gifts she had given her through the years. Some of those sweaters had been very difficult, and not inexpensive, to make.

Susan, who had never met her mother-in-law, was, as always, torn between loyalty to her wife and a more general fairness. "Few people," she said, though without conviction, "are entirely bad or heartless or mean-spirited. Or, whatever."

Hannah shifted against the pillows. "Maybe she really did the best she could do," she said, though it sounded to Tilda a little begrudging.

"Maybe she really wasn't meant to be a parent but just sort of went along with it because all her friends were having kids or it was the thing for women of her generation to do or . . ." Susan trailed off.

"Whatever the truth about Charlotte McQueen," Craig said now, almost as if trying to further convince himself, "she's gone. She has no power over us anymore. We're free to be who we need to be."

Hannah was not quite ready to agree. "I know she gave money to charity," she blurted. "There was some arts organization or something."

"Yes," Tilda said. "Back in Boston. She chaired a fundraiser, I think. I remember her buying a new gown for the event. It was black velvet. I thought she looked like a queen that night. I so worshipped her."

No one had anything to say to that.

"Well," Craig said, hoisting himself from his chair, "I'm off to bed."

The others trailed off after him. Tilda was the last to leave the sunroom. "Goodnight, Mom," she whispered, as she turned off the light.

42

Tuesday, July 31

It was about eight-thirty in the morning. Tilda had just come back from town where she had picked up several daily papers and, in Bread and Roses, had bought an assortment of pastries for breakfast. In the bakery she had run into Pat Riley, who owned a pizza joint in Wells, and Anne Bauer, his wife. Both had been at the party after the memorial. Both were effusive with good wishes for Bill's total recovery and for his upcoming nuptials. (Not surprisingly, word had gotten around!) Love and respect for her father seemed to be universal. It made Tilda feel proud to be his daughter.

Tilda got out of her car and saw that Adam was at his own car. The rear hatch of the Range Rover was open and she watched him reach inside and pull out several pieces of paper on which one of the kids had colored, an empty PowerBar wrapper, and a still dripping juice box. He crumpled these and shoved them in a plastic bag that sat on the ground by the right back tire.

Tilda was appalled by her brother's behavior and by the

things he had said about Hannah and Susan, and her native cowardice argued strongly for her to walk on into the house, to ignore him. But at that moment the desire for family peace was stronger than her disgust, disapproval, or fear. She decided to seize that moment. She walked over to him.

"Adam," she said, "I was thinking that maybe we could talk."

He walked round to the back left door of the car, opened it, and began to rummage inside. "I'm really not in the mood, Tilda."

Tilda followed him. "Adam, please. I know the last few days have been hard on you and maybe if you just talk it all through it would help."

Suddenly, Adam backed out of the car and slammed the door. Tilda flinched. His face was contorted with emotion. "You want me to talk? Fine. I'll talk. I think this entire family is crazy. Dad's a doddering old man with no more sense than his sister, who doesn't have a normal bone in her body. My ex-wife is interfering with my custodial rights. I've lost my rightful inheritance. And this whole thing with Kat is all your fault. Yours and Hannah's and Ruth's. I know you all talked to her. I know you put ideas into her head. Everything was perfectly fine between us when we came to Larchmere. And now, my life is a train wreck."

Tilda squirmed. She could not change Adam's mind about Bill or Ruth or Sarah. But her own sense of guilt forced her to attempt a defense of herself, even if she was, indeed, the cause, or part of the cause, of Adam's current romantic distress. "Don't be silly, Adam," she said. "Hannah and Ruth and I had nothing to do with Kat's breaking the engagement." That was a lie. "She probably just changed her mind. It happens all the time. She's young. Maybe she didn't think she would be a good stepparent. Not everyone can be, you know."

"Yeah, well, all I know is that I'm out fifteen thousand bucks for the ring."

"I'm sure you can sell it," she said, hiding her shock at the cost.

"That's not the point. I don't have time for this crap. I'm a very busy man."

And that was the moment when Tilda realized that her brother was exhibiting no emotion other than anger. The embarrassment had been momentary. But had there never been a sense of loss or grief? He couldn't have loved Kat at all! It was appalling. He didn't seem at all sad that she was gone. Maybe he was hiding a more tender emotion but Tilda doubted it.

She thought about Sarah. She and Adam had dated for four years before getting married. She remembered how happy he had been at the wedding. She believed that he had been in love then. What had gone so terribly wrong for him?

"You know," he said then, as if spitting out the words, "the only person of any use in this family was Mom. Why she had to die like that . . . It makes no sense!"

Tilda could think of absolutely nothing to say.

Adam stalked into the house. She followed him. As Adam passed through the front hall, Percy, who seemed to come out of thin air in the way that cats do, took a swipe at his ankle. If cats could smile, Tilda thought, noting the force of the swipe, Percy would be smiling. Percy disappeared as mysteriously as he had appeared.

Adam leaned over and grabbed his ankle. "Damn that cat! He ripped a hole in my sock!"

Yes, Tilda could feel sorry for her older brother, but she didn't have to like him.

"I'm going right back to Boston and getting in touch with my lawyer. We're going to contest this ridiculous will." Adam headed for the stairs.

Tilda found her father and Teddy in the library. "Adam is leaving," she said. "He's going back to Boston. He told me he's going to contest Dad's will. Can he do that?"

Teddy nodded. "Of course. But he hasn't got a leg to stand on. Don't worry one bit, Tilda. Larchmere isn't going anywhere."

Preparation for the wedding proceeded at a necessary breakneck pace. Hannah made arrangements with the minister, who expressed his joy at the occasion, especially, he said, coming on the heels of Bill's trip to the hospital. God, he said, worked in mysterious ways. Hannah wasn't sure it had been God who brought her father to the altar this time but she just smiled and shook the man's hand.

Tilda—she wasn't quite sure why as a professional cleaning service handled the heavy household chores—scrubbed the walls and floors and windows of her father's bedroom, laundered the curtains, and bought beautiful little bunches of lavender, tied with silk cords, for the dresser drawers in which Jennifer kept her clothing.

Susan spoke to a local florist about a bouquet for Jennifer, who said that she would be wearing an A-line ivory silk dress and that she liked peach and yellow roses best. If they weren't available on such short notice, any color rose would do. For her father-in-law, who was to wear a navy suit with a white shirt and a yellow silk tie, Susan ordered a yellow (or white) rose boutonniere.

At Bill's request, Craig made reservations for lunch upstairs at MC Perkins Cove. There would be a champagne toast and a special cake that Bobby, a smart, thrifty man in a dangerous business, had already ordered and paid for.

Ruth spoke to Lex and Joe, who knew her as a longtime fan and supporter, and arranged for them to play back at

the house that evening, after the ceremony and the luncheon.

Everything that could be done had been done. Ruth,
Tilda, Hannah, Susan, and Craig were now lounging around
the kitchen. Ruth was half thinking about what to make for
dinner—maybe she would make a run to the fish market
and see what had just come in—and half thinking about
what she would wear to the wedding. There was a pale gray
dress she had not worn in an age. With her lilac slingbacks
and a darker gray clutch, she might be set.

Tilda, seated at the table with a glass of iced tea, shook
her head. "I still can't believe that Dad is getting married,
and so soon!"

"Believe it," Craig said. "He got the license and he and
Jennifer bought wedding bands in Swamp John's."

"I wonder what Dad did with his first wedding band?"
Hannah asked. "When did he stop wearing it? I don't remember."

Craig shrugged. "Me, neither. But I don't notice girly
things like jewelry and hairstyles."

Hannah stuck out her tongue at him.

"I have Mom's rings," Tilda said. "Actually, it's not her
original set. She told me not long before she died that as
soon as Dad had been promoted to some high level or another in his company, she traded in her first rings for the
platinum and diamond set she was wearing when . . . Well,
I have the rings in my safety deposit box at the bank. I can't
bring myself to wear them or to have the diamonds reset. It
seems sort of a waste but . . ."

"Maybe you could offer the rings to Jane someday,"
Susan suggested.

Or maybe, Tilda thought, *I will offer my own wedding
ring to her. Maybe someday I will be able to let it go.
Maybe.* Naturally she then thought of Adam and his fifteen

thousand-dollar ring and she voiced a concern that had been at the back of her head all day.

"Should someone call Adam and see if he's okay? I mean, Kat's defection did seem to upset him." Rather, she thought, the loss of time and money and social standing had upset him. But upset was upset. The results could be the same. "We don't even know if he got back to Boston in one piece! What if he has a panic attack, like Dad did? Or a heart attack? I know he was absolutely horrible to Hannah, to everyone, but—"

"No!" That was Ruth. "Adam's not the type to let emotions bring him down. Not like your father. Adam is completely insensitive. He's too self-interested to be overly emotional. It's beneath his sense of dignity to drive off the road in a fit of misery."

"Do you think he'll show up at the wedding?" Hannah asked. Her tone was casual but her face betrayed her concern. "I mean, to make trouble?"

"Don't get me started on the subject of Adam and weddings. If he ever shows his face at Larchmere again I'll—"

"Susan, please," Hannah begged. "There's been enough bad feeling already."

"He won't show up," Ruth said. "I'm sure of it. The next we hear from him will be through his lawyer."

Tilda said, "Teddy says he hasn't got a chance at getting Larchmere. He'll be wasting his time and his money trying."

"Well, that's his decision. Meanwhile, I suggest we put Adam and his evil schemes out of our minds and concentrate on the upcoming happy occasion."

"Hear, hear! Is there another bottle of Prosecco around?" Craig asked. "If not I'll run to the store and get one. Or two."

A bottle was found, as was a bag of almond biscotti

Ruth had bought earlier that day while on her errands. "To the happy couple!" she said, raising her glass.

"To Jennifer, the newest addition to the McQueen family!" That was Tilda.

Around a mouthful of cookie, Hannah said, "To us!"

43

Wednesday, August 1

The beach was almost her own that morning. Except for Wade, down by the shoreline with his fishing gear and folding chair, and a shirtless jogger Tilda had never seen before (a summer visitor, she supposed), she was alone. The sea was calm. The sand felt silky and cool on her feet. Frank would have enjoyed such a morning, though he would have brought a big cup of coffee down to the beach with him. Tilda smiled remembering how, for Frank, waking up was a slow and sometimes painful process.

She tried then to imagine how different her life would have been had she never met Frank. And what she saw, very suddenly and very clearly, was a life so very empty, so very unfulfilled, so very opposite of the life she had now. The vision made her stop in her tracks. And then, toes digging into the cool sand, she felt a surge of pure joy such as she had never felt in her life. Yes, she had met him and she had loved him and she had married him and they had had two wonderful children together. How beautiful her life had been and how beautiful it would always be because she had known and loved Frank and he had known and loved her. No one or nothing could take away the fact of the having. Oh, it was so much better to focus on the having rather than on the loss!

Tilda put her hands to her face in astonishment. Was transformation just this simple? Was it only a matter of shifting your focus from the empty to the full, from the absence to the presence? Was it only a matter of realizing all that you had to be thankful for? Was thankfulness the key?

Almost automatically, Tilda looked up at the sky. And there it was, soaring effortlessly, high above, a magnificent eagle. It was the sign she had been waiting for. Tears came to her eyes and she let them flow. They were tears of joy and of sorrow. She watched the eagle dip and swoop, marveling, as always, at the enormous bird's grace and power. After a few minutes he flew off farther down the beach to astonish someone else in need of his presence, perhaps Wade, who might be thinking of his ailing mother-in-law and his sorrowful wife.

Tilda took off her wedding ring. She put it in the pocket of her windbreaker and zipped the pocket safely. She would always keep it, always; she would not offer it to Jane or to anyone else. But she no longer needed to wear it.

"Thank you, Frank," she whispered, sure now that he could hear her. "Thank you."

The prayer Bobby had taught her came to her, the words of the thirteenth-century Dame Julian of Norwich. In a soft voice she repeated:

> "All shall be well,
> And all shall be well,
> And all manner of things shall be well."

The wedding of William McQueen and Jennifer Fournier would take place in the gazebo on the lawn of the Larchmere estate. Present were Ruth, Tilda, Hannah and Susan, Craig, Bobby, and Teddy and Tessa Vickes. Jon and Jane had driven down for the ceremony, but they wouldn't be able to stay long. Each had to be at work later that afternoon. Jane couldn't stop smiling at the happy turn of events, and exclaimed over Jennifer's ring. Jon slapped his grandfather's back a lot. Craig, much to his surprise, was to be best man. Jennifer's sister, Gwen, who lived in Scarborough, was to be maid of honor.

Tilda had brought only the one suit, the one she had worn to her mother's memorial. It would have to do for her father's impromptu wedding. But this time she wore the floaty silk scarf her children had given her. It took four or five attempts before she found a way to wear it comfortably and, she hoped, stylishly. And then Ruth and Susan had complimented her, so she knew she had gotten it right.

As she stood behind her father and his fiancée, Tilda felt Frank right there with her. He had given her his blessing, he had told her that it was okay to move on, and yet she felt closer to him now than she had since his death. Closer, but also, free. She had not imagined she could feel so well.

The vows were read, the blessing was given, and the pair was married. The groom kissed the bride, most of the witnesses cried, and Susan pulled out her camera. After the photos were taken the group drove down to the Cove for lunch, which, of course, was accompanied by several bottles of champagne. Bobby surprised them all with the special wedding cake, as well as with a beautiful book, a collection of photographs of and poems about the sea. Sarah sent a happy, brilliantly colored arrangement of flowers to the house. Everyone was looking forward to an evening of music and just maybe of dancing back at Larchmere. Craig and Jennifer's sister, Gwen, the owner of an independent bookstore, found much to talk about. There was no word from Adam.

Life, thought Tilda, as the McQueen family headed
back to Larchmere, could be so amazingly good. That was
worth remembering.

The celebrations were over. The Vickes and Bobby had
gone home, as had Gwen. Bill and Jennifer had retired
first, followed soon after by Ruth and the others. Only Hannah and Susan were awake, sitting on the front porch, holding hands, quiet in the late night. The air was cool and
sweet. It was the proverbial calm after the storm and everything felt clean and new and refreshed.

Hannah's mind had been racing since the shocking announcement of her inheritance. And this was the goal it had
come to, at that very moment on the front porch, hours
after her father's wedding.

Life was too short and too precious to waste in hesitation and fear. She had free will. She could choose to
change and to grow. No one had to be a slave to the past. At
least, she, Hannah McQueen, did not have to be a slave to
her mother's child-rearing legacy. She would reject that
legacy! Craig had said that she could, that they all could!

"Oh, what the hell," she blurted. "Let's start that family."

Susan twitched in surprise. "Do you mean it?" she
asked after a moment. "Are you totally, absolutely, one
hundred percent sure? This isn't just the champagne talking?"

"Yes, yes, and yes. And yes. And no, it's not the champagne talking. It's me."

Susan turned to more fully face Hannah. She grabbed
her other hand. "I'm stunned. I'm so happy. But what about
therapy? We talked about seeing a therapist to help you get
past your reservations. What happened?"

"Pooh to the therapist. I'm past my reservations. I'm

tired of them. I am not my mother. I will not become my mother with our children. I promise you and I promise me and I promise those children we're going to have."

"Was that it?" Susan asked. She truly thought that she had misunderstood Hannah's words. "You were afraid of repeating your mother's mistakes? That's all?"

"That was enough."

Susan shook her head. "I'm so sorry, Hannah. I wish you had been able to tell me. I could have assured you. Your father could have told you how different you are from Charlotte!"

"He did. But that wasn't all that freed me from that fear. Now, no more about the past. It's time to concentrate on the future. Okay?"

"We are going to be such great parents, do you know that?" Susan didn't bother to check the tears streaming down her face. "Do you know how lucky our children are going to be? Do you?"

Hannah laughed. "I'm not quite as sure as you are about the great part, but I don't think we're going to suck."

"None of that language once the baby is born."

"'Suck' isn't a bad word. Sucking is a baby's main activity, next to sleeping."

"Don't be bad. 'Suck' isn't the nicest word when you use it like you did."

"Oh, all right. If you say so, Mom."

"Mom. Doesn't that sound amazing?"

"It does." Hannah touched her forehead to Susan's. "It really does."

44

Thursday, August 2

Tilda met Dennis for breakfast at Bessie's diner in town. He had a flight home to Florida that afternoon, leaving from Portland. Tilda, who was nervous about this leave-taking, didn't have much of an appetite but she ordered a cup of coffee and a blueberry muffin. Dennis ordered a full, heart attack special. After all, he said, tomorrow it was back to the real world. He might as well indulge while he could.

The real world, Tilda thought. *Yes. And now, my real world is going to be different. It's going to be new. It has to be. Frank said it was all right and Frank has never lied to me.*

She looked at this man sitting across from her at the Formica-topped table. She was thankful for his having come into her life at a crucial moment and literally waking her up to life's further possibilities. He had been a catalyst for change, not the only one she had encountered in the past two weeks, but an important one. And for that she would always be grateful. But her feelings for him simply weren't deep enough—or passionate enough—to justify sustaining a long-distance relationship. It would be unfair to Dennis. If, indeed, he even wanted such a thing.

It seemed that he did want such a thing. "Tilda," he said, when they had been served, "I thought that maybe we could stay in touch. Call each other, e-mail. Maybe we could even visit each other, not right away but around the holidays. What do you think?"

"I think," she said finally, and carefully, "that it might be best if we didn't. We've had a wonderful time together, here in Ogunquit. I don't think . . ." Tilda struggled to find the right words. "I like you an awful lot, Dennis," she went on. "I'm glad, very glad, I bumped into you in the ice cream shop. But I think that now I need to go home and . . . I'm sorry. I don't seem to be doing a very good job of explaining myself."

Dennis stirred his tea for a moment before answering. "I can't say I'm not disappointed, Tilda, but I do think I understand."

"Thank you," she said.

"So much has happened for you in just two weeks. It would be unfair of me to press for any sort of commitment at all, given the circumstances."

Tilda sipped her coffee and Dennis ate his breakfast in a silence that was only partly uncomfortable. Dennis insisted on paying for their meals, as always. Outside the diner, at his rental car, they parted.

"Have a safe flight," Tilda said. She reached up and kissed his cheek.

"And you have a happy life, Tilda McQueen O'Connell."

Dennis got in his car and Tilda watched him drive off in the direction of Route 1.

When he was out of sight she walked to her own car. Her appetite had returned and now she regretted not having eaten that muffin. Well, she would be home before long and there was always something to eat at Larchmere. That was one thing she could count on—that, and her family's love.

She got behind the wheel and pulled into the street. She felt a little bit sad but also liberated. She felt eager. She thought about a man she knew back in South Portland, someone she had been friendly with since a year or so before Frank's death. His name was Jacob, he was divorced, and they had met at a gathering of the neighborhood watch. About six months after Frank had passed, Jacob had asked her out to dinner. "Just as friends," he had assured her, but Tilda had said no, thank you, and they had gone on as before, chatting after meetings, exchanging e-mails about local issues and sometimes even those unfunny e-mails that were always circulating the Web. Jacob had a good sense of humor (he always apologized for those e-mails) and there was no denying that he was attractive. Maybe, she thought, she should ask him out for coffee after the next meeting of the neighborhood watch. Start small but make the effort. What was that saying, most of success is about showing up?

Well, Tilda thought, as she pulled into the drive at Larchmere, *it's time for me to start showing up.*

It was mid-afternoon. Tilda was just back from the beach, where it had been too crowded for a long walk, but she had wanted to say a farewell for the moment. She would miss Ogunquit Beach—she always did—but she would be back in a week or so. She knew she would always come home. She had not been born in Maine, nor had her parents or their parents, so she would always be considered "from away." But that was all right. She loved Maine and she loved its people. She would not want to live anywhere else.

But on her next visit to Larchmere, she just might stay in another room, try another view, maybe the room Craig often passed up for the library couch. He could move into her old room now, if he wanted to. It was big and pleasant and they were each ready for a change.

She had already said good-bye to her father and his bride. Bill and Jennifer were on their way to Bar Harbor, where they would spend a few days at an inn owned by an old friend of Jennifer's. Tilda was sure they would appreciate some time alone, without the McQueen clan around them, and away from the curious, though kind, eyes of their neighbors in Ogunquit.

Hannah and Susan had already left for home. Just before getting into the car, Hannah had blurted their big news, that they were starting steps to have a family, and then burst out crying. Of course, that had made Tilda cry and then Susan was bawling and even Ruth's eyes had looked a little misty as she waved them off.

Just before heading back to South Portland, Tilda did a final check of her room to be sure she was leaving nothing important behind. She opened the drawer in which she kept her nightclothes and rummaged around for the button of Frank's sweater. She thought she would bring it back to South Portland as a sort of memento of these two important weeks at Larchmere. She moved the clean nightgowns aside. She pulled the drawer out as far as it would go. She bent down and peered inside.

The button was gone. As mysteriously as it had appeared it had disappeared. Tilda smiled. "Okay, Frank," she said.

She went downstairs, hugged her aunt, and gave Percy one stroke on his back, which was all he permitted before stalking off. She hugged Craig, too, who had already begun working on a long list of home improvement projects.

"Take care," he said. "You know where to find me."

Tilda smiled at her younger brother. "Yes," she said. "I finally know where to find you."

Epilogue

The Present

Craig pulled into the driveway at Larchmere. The old red van had long ago been replaced by an old but eminently serviceable Volvo wagon, perfect for transporting everything from groceries to lumber to the family. He climbed the stairs to the front porch, then made his way inside to the kitchen.

"There you are!" Hannah called. "We're thinking of making grilled cheese sandwiches for lunch. You in?"

Craig briefly thought about his creeping waistline and said, "Of course. I think we have Swiss cheese in the fridge. And American." Nigel bounded up from where he had been dozing by the window and Craig rubbed his massive head in greeting. It was always nice to be greeted with enthusiasm. Adopting Nigel was one of the best things he had ever done.

Hannah and Susan and their two children were visiting Larchmere for the weekend. Katherine, called Kate, was nine and James was eight. Susan had borne them both and liked to boast about how easy the deliveries had been. Behind her back, Hannah would shake her head. She had been there with Susan and had heard the screams and seen the ick factor. But hey, if all Susan remembered was the good parts, so be it.

"I'll have pickle relish on mine, please," Susan said now. It was a Sirico family tradition to add pickle relish to grilled cheese sandwiches.

Craig smiled when he saw his sister's look of distaste. "Me, too," he said. "Lots of it." Craig was still single at fifty, though for the past two years he had kept regular company (he liked that old-fashioned term) with a local artist, a painter he had met at a Barn Gallery opening. He was not opposed to the idea of their marrying at some point. In fact, he and Anna had talked about the possibility on several occasions. He just might surprise everyone in his family—again.

Like when he had promised, all those years ago, to settle down at the family beach house, at Larchmere. And he had made good on that promise. He lived there year round and managed the summer bed and breakfast he and Hannah and Susan had established. Craig's dog, Nigel, an American Staffordshire terrier, kept him good company. Nigel was his first animal companion and, while he was trained, he was also spoiled. Percy, now thirteen and more imperious than ever, was surprisingly in love with Nigel and complained angrily for days when he and Ruth went off to New York. No one had expected a love affair between the two animals but it did make life at Larchmere much more pleasant than it might have been. And, Guy Cokal had made good on his promise to mentor Craig. In addition to running the bed and breakfast, Craig was now also a CPA with his own small and respected business. Craig was busy and happy and productive. He felt needed. He felt he was making a difference. His life was good.

"I got a postcard from Tilda," he told his sisters. "I forgot to mention it earlier."

"So did we," Susan said. "Sounds like she's having fun."

Tilda was vacationing in France with her second husband. Joe Harvey was a professor of European history at Southern Maine University. She had met him while auditing a class on the ancien régime. Tilda and Joe, who had no children of his own, lived in Portland's West End, not far from Hannah and Susan and their children, all of whom they saw frequently.

For the past eight years Tilda—who had taken to wearing skirts again—had been volunteering as a grief counselor. Once a week she met with men and women who had lost a loved one and with the knowledge she had gained from her own experience, she tried to help them recover. She planned to retire from teaching high school English at sixty and spend as much time as possible in Ogunquit. And when Joe finally retired—he loved his job and planned to work until the bitter end of his energies—they would move there year round.

Unbeknownst to the others in her family, Tilda had run into Kat Daly a few years after her breakup with Adam. Kat had greeted her warmly and after a bit of a chat Tilda had taken a chance and asked Kat about the night she had begged off going to dinner at The Front Porch. She told her that she had seen Kat having drinks with another man. Kat blushed and laughed. Yes, she had met a good friend that evening. Already she had been having reservations about marrying Adam, and when she had received a text message from Paul saying that he would be in town that night, she had planned to meet him and talk through some of her anxiety. Was he helpful, Tilda wanted to know. Kat laughed again. "Yes," she told Tilda. "Very." She then held up her left hand for Tilda to see. "We've been married for two years and have an adorable little boy!"

Tilda's own children were doing fine. Jane, now twenty-eight, was married and had a four-month-old little girl named Gillian. She and her family lived in her mother's South Portland house, paid rent and maintained it. Someday, they hoped to buy the house straight out. Jane comanaged a small day care center, and her husband, George, was a talented finish carpenter.

Jon, now thirty, lived in Boston. Single and showing no signs of wanting to be otherwise, he was a lawyer at a big firm and hardly ever came to visit his mother or other relatives. This, Tilda knew, bothered Jane terribly as she and her brother had been so close for so long. Though he looked more like his father than ever, in attitude he was becoming more like his uncle Adam. It worried Tilda—Adam was an unhappy man—but Jon was an adult and there wasn't much she could do about his choice of lifestyle. Interestingly, as far as she knew, Jon had nothing to do with his uncle, though they worked and lived in the same city.

"And," Hannah said, "I got a call from Ruth last night. She should be here some time tomorrow afternoon, depending on traffic."

Ruth had long since completed her master's degree in fine arts. She spent half of her time in New York City and half at Larchmere, where she continued to have a special relationship with the now retired Bobby. Tilda, ever the romantic, hoped her aunt would marry Bobby, but she was not holding her breath.

"How long will she stay?" Craig asked. He liked it when his aunt was around. He appreciated her perspective. And she was a far better cook than he was.

Susan laughed. "Like she ever tells us her plans? Other than her showing up, we don't count on anything."

"Like it used to be with me," Craig said wryly.

"Way back in the dim and misty past. Will you get me the butter?"

Craig brought his sister a stick of butter from the fridge—there would, after all, be several sandwiches—and watched as she buttered the bread. His mind leapt to Adam, who, as far as anyone knew, was still probably a health nut. Adam probably had not touched butter since college. More was the pity.

Adam, after going through a very messy divorce, was single once again. Only months after Kat's defection he had married a waitress/model in her late twenties. When the marriage, which was childless, fell apart less than two years later, no one was surprised. No one felt very sorry for him, either. Communication between Adam and his aunt and siblings was almost entirely dead and when it was alive, it was incidental. Interestingly, this state of affairs bothered Craig more than it did the others. He couldn't help but recall a conversation he had had with Sarah the week of his mother's ten-year memorial. They had been sitting side by side on the front porch. Sarah had talked about everyone having a lovable self, even if that self was difficult to see. In the back of Craig's mind was the notion of someday attempting to draw Adam back into the fold, at least, of extending a friendly hand. But that would be someday.

Sarah was happily remarried and continued to keep in touch with her former in-laws. Cordelia, who was twenty, was studying business at Northeastern University and planned to go on for an MBA. Cody, eighteen, went to Clark University and wanted to be a doctor. During summers they split their time between Adam's South End condo and Sarah's house in the suburbs.

Teddy and Tessa Vickes were gone. They had passed within six months of each other about five years back, Tessa dying peacefully in her sleep and Teddy of a heart attack. They were still missed by everyone who had known them.

Bill McQueen had died at the age of eighty-two. He had suffered a massive stroke and was dead within days, unaware of what had happened to him. His family felt that it was a mercy. Still, they mourned his loss. According to the wishes expressed in his living will, he had not been buried alongside his first wife, but in a new plot he and Jennifer had purchased together. Tilda, being Tilda, sometimes wondered if her mother's spirit—assuming there was one—visited her husband's unexpectedly distant grave to give him a piece of her mind. She hoped not. Hannah thought that Adam should be buried alongside his mother, when his time came. Like should be with like. They could criticize together through the ages. Susan scolded her when she said such things but in truth, she agreed with her wife.

Jennifer continued to live in her condo in Portland where she and Bill had spent most of their nine married years together. When she visited Larchmere, which she did when business allowed, she stayed in the guest cottage, as her old room, the one she had shared for a while with Bill, was generally in use for paying guests. When in Portland she met Tilda and Hannah about once a month for lunch. She had recently taken up knitting and her enthusiasm had, unexpectedly, stirred Tilda's old love of the craft. Now, Tilda was taking advanced knitting classes at a yarn shop on Congress Street. Craig had commissioned a sweater for Anna for Christmas and Tilda was hard at work.

"Kids!" Hannah shouted. "Lunch is ready!"

Kate and James charged into the kitchen as if they had been waiting just outside the door for their mother's call. Which, Craig thought with a smile, they probably had been. They were great kids with seemingly boundless energy. And he was proud to say that they loved their uncle.

It was quickly decided that they would take their lunch out to the front porch. Susan carried a pitcher of homemade lemonade and Craig took the tray of hot, gooey sandwiches. The kids ran ahead and Hannah followed with a handful of napkins. Nigel was there before them all.

Once gathered around the lovely old wrought iron table that Craig had bought and restored, the family began the struggle to keep Nigel from snatching the sandwiches out of anyone's hand. Craig settled into his special chair, the big, ornate wicker rocker that had once been his mother's and that he had rescued from the basement, and began to eat his own sandwich—which he shared with Nigel.

Craig smiled. It was a pretty great thing, he thought, eating lunch on the porch on a warm, sunny summer day, surrounded by members of your family, the latest generation of McQueens giggling, and your faithful, furry companion nuzzling at your lap.

So much had changed, Craig thought. So much had not. Ogunquit was still and would always be a beautiful place by the sea. And it would always be his family's home.

**Please turn the page
for a very special Q & A with
Holly Chamberlin.**

**Please turn the page
to enjoy a special Q & A with
Meg Maxwell.**

You have lived in Maine now for ten years, and in Portland for six. Before that, you lived in downtown Boston and grew up in New York City. How has life in a smallish city changed you—if it has?

I'm not sure that life in a smallish city has changed me as much as life itself has taken a toll! I'm fifty now and am more and more content to stay home with my books, cats, and husband (not necessarily in that order!) than go out even for dinner at a local joint. Not that I've become a recluse, but I do think that getting older involves being more selective with how you spend your time. Portland is actually a pretty vibrant city. If I choose to watch my favorite shows on television rather than go to the theater or a concert, well, that says nothing about Portland and everything about me.

You mentioned your cats, and cats appear in many of your books. Would it be safe to say that you are a "cat lady"?

Ha! It would be very safe to say that! Currently, we have fifteen-year-old Cyrus and fourteen-year-old Betty. (We lost our beloved Jackie in 2011.) I don't think Stephen would mind my saying that we are both pretty obsessed with our kitties and happily cater to every whim and need. Stephen grew up with dogs, so the fact that he's come over to the feline tribe is major!

About your work. Do you ever find yourself moved by a character and the situation she is struggling with, or are you always able to keep an artistic or editorial distance?

I am most definitely moved by my characters, particularly by the teenaged girls. While keeping my author head in place is super important for the overall effect of the story, sometimes I find tears filling my eyes when I "see" a character alone and confused or in despair. Characters really do take on a life of their own at some point and can be very powerful! It's a strange thing to be affected by your own storytelling. You can't let sentiment interfere with good plotting.

Do you do a lot of research for your books?

For the books that are built around characters experiencing some sort of trauma, yes. That said, I'm writing fiction, not how-to manuals or informational pamphlets, so I try to absorb what I read about domestic violence or teen pregnancy or bullying and let it influence the storytelling rather than dictate it. For *The Family Beach House* I did a fair amount of reading about becoming a widow, especially at a young age, and it really did help me tell Tilda's story. I can say this because several readers who had lost their husbands contacted me to say they identified closely with Tilda's thoughts and feelings. In the end, more important than reading articles about typical behaviors after an unhappy event, is the ability to see the world around you with clear eyes and an empathetic mind. Or would that be heart?

What is the first thing you do when you've finished writing a book and send it on to your editor?

The first thing I do is collapse. The next thing I do is erase all memory of the book from my mind until I have to deal with it again for revisions or in response to a copy editor's queries. I also try like mad to catch up on reading "for fun." And then, I start to sketch out the next book!

Do you ever see yourself not writing novels? Meaning, do you think about moving on to another career someday?

No, not at all. Pretty much all I'm decent at is writing, so hopefully I'll have the opportunity to keep at it for many years to come. When and if I ever retire, I suspect much of my time will be spent sleeping, reading, and playing with my cats—the same life I lead now!

Bestselling author Holly Chamberlin's heartfelt novel, set in a beautiful Maine beach town, tells of three sisters— and one summer filled with revelations . . .

When Poppy Higgins left Yorktide, Maine, for Boston, she pictured future visits home as brief diversions from her real life in the big city. Fate had different ideas, and at twenty-five, Poppy has been called back to care for her two younger sisters following their father's death.

Sixteen-year-old Daisy resents Poppy's long absence and chafes under her sometimes fumbling efforts to be a parent. Violet, now thirteen, is a virtual stranger to her oldest sister. Once a happy, united family, the Higginses seem adrift, and Poppy longs to escape her responsibilities. But when Daisy befriends Evie, an enigmatic newcomer to Yorktide, the young woman will be an unlikely catalyst in the sisters' journey back to each other. For as Poppy discovers the deep loss in Evie's life, she awakens to the truth about her own, and about the town, and the people, she's tried to leave behind.

Filled with the candid warmth of real sisterhood, *Summer with My Sisters* explores the many forms a family can take, and the unspoken ties that endure, season after season . . .

Please turn the page for an exciting sneak peek of Holly Chamberlin's SUMMER WITH MY SISTERS coming in July 2015!

Chapter 1

Poppy Higgins hung the last of her tops and blouses in the large chestnut armoire that had once contained her mother's clothes and firmly closed the door of the beautiful old piece of furniture. She wasn't at all sure she belonged in this room, what had once been her parents' master suite, but here she was, stowing away her clothes in the armoire and laying out her make-up and moisturizers in their bathroom.

This was the thing. Poppy had decided that there was probably no way she could pull off a role of authority in the house on Willow Way if she continued to sleep in her girlhood bedroom, the place where she had mooned over airbrushed boy bands and cried in frustration when her parents wouldn't let her see a movie all of her friends were allowed to see and dreamed childish dreams of a secret benefactor suddenly leaving her billions of dollars to spend in any way she liked. No, if she was going to succeed (or, at least make a stab) at being her sisters' guardian now that both of her parents were gone, she would need all the psychological props she could find, and installing herself in the master suite seemed like as good a prop as any.

Not everyone agreed with her. Sixteen-year-old Daisy wasn't happy about it; then again, she hadn't been happy about anything lately and Poppy really couldn't blame her. Violet had said nothing about the move but anyone who knew Violet at all knew that she probably had a strong opinion about the matter. Violet was preternaturally mature, almost oddly so. Maybe mature wasn't the right word; maybe simply odd would do. She was as far from the average thirteen-year-old girl (if such a thing existed) as you could imagine, more interested in esoteric subjects like astrology than in pop culture; often shockingly blunt and straightforward in her speech; and possessing a highly developed and always on target intuition about people and their motives.

Now, looking at the king-sized bed in which Annabelle and Oliver Higgins had spent so many nights of their married lives, Poppy wondered. Could you invade a person's private space even when they were dead? Was she indeed trespassing or being disrespectful? Maybe, but she was determined to stick it out in the suite, at least for a week or two. After all, she was supposed to be the adult in the house now, the one who acted with firmness and a sense of being in the right. A person who made a considered decision and stuck to it. The thought was terrifying.

Twenty-five-year-old Poppy had been back home—or, what had once been home—in Yorktide since the sudden death of her father in February and the completely shocking discovery, when his old friend and solicitor Frederica Ross, aka Freddie, had read his will to the family, that he had named Poppy legal guardian of her two younger sisters. He had requested she not move them to Boston, where she had been living for the past several years, but that she return to the house on Willow Way so that Daisy and Violet could finish high school and middle school without being wrenched from the community in which they had been a part for all of their lives.

It made sense, of course. Her father had known that Poppy had no deep roots in Boston. She had moved to the city after graduation from college more in the hopes of stumbling across something 'interesting' than because she had a definite plan for her future. Still, not long before Annabelle Higgins died of lung cancer three years earlier, she had strongly encouraged her oldest daughter to return to Boston when she, Annabelle, was gone; she had urged her not to give up her quest for a meaningful life, not to feel that she need move back to Maine to be with her father and younger sisters. So Poppy *had* gone back to Boston shortly after her mother's funeral but three years later she still had not found anything 'interesting' to do with her life. Her job as a freelance writer for a few online 'cultural' magazines was unfulfilling in the extreme; how often could you write interestingly about a new beer and bacon joint or a pop up dance club or discuss whether socks worn with sandals was actually 'a thing'? The only reason she kept at it was to pay the bills. Unlike her highly motivated and focused parents, Poppy feared she was sadly directionless and quite possibly lazy.

Well, you could be directionless and lazy anywhere, so why not in Yorktide? Leaving her on again, currently off again boyfriend Ian had caused Poppy no regret. Ian could be a lot of fun but not much more than that. The only thing—the only person—that she would miss—that she did miss—was Allie Swift, the woman who owned the beautiful old mansion in which Poppy rented a spacious and sunny top-floor apartment. Though Allie was forty and had seen an awful lot more of life than Poppy had, they had formed a true friendship and Allie had promised Poppy a place to stay when—if—she returned to Boston when her sisters were finally on their own.

Poppy placed the palm of her hand against the smooth, polished wood of the armoire and fought a fresh wave of sorrow. Soon after Annabelle's passing her clothes had been given to charity; Freddie, the aforementioned Higgins' family lawyer, and her partner, Sheila Simon, had orchestrated that for the sisters. First, though, each girl had chosen one or two of their mother's items as keepsakes. For Poppy, this was the slim gold bangle she wore on her right wrist and a black velvet shawl, fringed with jet beads. She remembered her mother wearing the shawl to formal occasions at Adams College, where she was a professor of American History, and to the ceremonial dinners her husband, Oliver, was compelled to attend, many of them in his honor. "You look like a princess," Poppy remembered telling her mother once. "Thank you," Annabelle had replied. "But remember, it's better to be queen."

Now, her father's clothing had to be dealt with, and Poppy had decided she would see to the task herself. She was afraid she had already relied too heavily on Freddie and Sheila, who, as friends first of Oliver's father, Henry, and then of Oliver himself, were the obvious choice of shoulders upon which to lean. Still, she had been back at the Higgins' house for almost four months now and had still failed to take the first step in sorting her father's beautifully tailored shirts and suits. Oliver Higgins had been a brilliant intellectual on the international stage of political theory and practice, but he had also been a bit of a dandy. Alongside his beautiful wife, they had made a stunning couple, the kind of pair that turned heads and effortlessly drew people into the circle of their formidable personalities.

Annabelle Higgins' clothing might have gone to the local charity shop but her jewelry (except for the bangle Poppy wore) was locked in a safe in the master bathroom.

Along with the pearls Annabelle had inherited from her grandmother, her diamond and platinum wedding set, and a hefty collection of Bakelite pieces from the nineteen thirties and forties, was Oliver Higgins' wedding ring. His watch, a Breitling, had been there, too, until a few days earlier when Poppy had decided that she would wear it in much the same spirit she wore her mother's bracelet, as a physical reminder of the two most important people in her life. A local jeweler had removed a few of the links from the watch for a better fit and though Poppy felt a bit conspicuous wearing such an expensive piece, she was glad to have this bit of her father so close.

Poppy turned from the armoire and her eye caught her parents' official wedding portrait next to a spray of dried hydrangea, her mother's favorite flower, on the dresser against the wall opposite the bed. Annabelle and Oliver had been anything but run of the mill types and had eschewed the popular bride and groom styles of the mid-eighties. (Hideous, in Poppy's opinion. Puffy sleeves? Really?) Her mother had worn a tailored white pantsuit; her father, a simple, navy suit with a white shirt and no tie. His wildly wavy hair had already started to whiten though he was only in his early thirties at the time. It gave him a look of distinction and elegance.

Poppy looked more closely at the photograph. There really was a striking resemblance between Annabelle and her oldest daughter; everyone had remarked on it. Like her mother, Poppy was tall and slim, and her features were near perfectly symmetrical. Her eyes were as vividly green as Annabelle's and her hair as glossy a chestnut brown. Her complexion, like her mother's, was clear and pale. Daisy, on the other hand, took after Oliver Higgins, although not in the elegance department, as she would be the first to admit. But she had his darker skin tone, his infectious, lopsided smile, and his medium, slightly stocky build. Violet, Poppy thought, was a charming combination of both parents.

What would her own wedding day be like, Poppy wondered now, looking away from the photograph. No father to walk her down the aisle. No mother to help her plan the festivities. Maybe she would elope. It might be unbearably depressing to get through the occasion without her parents. Assuming she ever decided to get married, which meant falling in love with someone and so far, *that* hadn't happened. Sometimes it bothered her that in her twenty-five years no one had ever captured her heart or inspired her devotion. Sure, she had dated and had even been with one guy for about six months before things just fizzled. Maybe the fault was hers. She knew that she wasn't cold or unsentimental. She cried at the drop of a hat and all it took was a chubby cheeked baby or a fuzzy kitten to cause her to 'ooh' and 'aah.' But for some reason when it came to romance, her heart, her inmost and truest self, just hadn't been brought to life.

How had Annabelle and Oliver done it, she wondered. They had been so deeply in love with each other. How had they found that sort of bliss? Sometimes Poppy wondered if her parents' perfect romantic union had tainted her own romantic career; maybe somehow it had caused her to despair of ever finding her own soul mate. But maybe that was just silly.

Bellisima. That was one of the affectionate names her father had called her mother and his favorite poem was Edgar Allan Poe's "Annabelle Lee." In fact, he had had a few lines of the poem inscribed on his wife's headstone.

And neither the angels in Heaven above
Nor the demons down under the sea,

Can ever dissever my soul from the soul
Of the beautiful Annabelle Lee.

A grand gesture if ever there was one, though the lines had always disturbed Poppy. Maybe it was the word 'dissever'. It gave her the creeps, and that was probably what the poet had intended. Doomed love. Love cut short.

Or, love eternal, Poppy thought now as she left the master suite and went downstairs to start dinner. And this was also something new. For the past few years she had been catching meals when she could, hardly ever cooking (boiling water for pasta didn't really count), and rarely spending more than twenty dollars at a time in the grocery store. Now, she was responsible for putting at least two meals on the table each day for three people and that took planning and time and energy. And money. Who knew the basics like milk and butter and eggs cost so much! Luckily, Annabelle and Oliver Higgins had left their children well provided for, with a mortgage fully paid and a portfolio of sound investments.

Things, Poppy thought as she entered the spacious, thoroughly modernized kitchen, could be much worse. She hoped that being back home with her sisters might help assuage some of the guilt she felt for having left them after Mom's death; that would be a very good thing. Though how she was going to form a definite plan for a productive and meaningful life in the future by playing parent to two strong-willed teenaged girls was anyone's guess!